ARKHAM HORROR

It is the height of the Roaring Twenties – a fresh enthusiasm for the arts, science, and exploration of the past have opened doors to a wider world, and beyond...

And yet, a dark shadow grows over the town of Arkham. Alien entities known as Ancient Ones lurk in the emptiness beyond space and time, writhing at the thresholds between worlds.

Occult rituals must be stopped and alien creatures destroyed before the Ancient Ones make our world their ruined dominion.

Only a handful of brave souls with inquisitive minds and the will to act stand against the horrors threatening to tear this world apart.

Will they prevail?

BY THE SAME AUTHOR

ARKHAM HORROR™

LITANY
of DREAMS

ARI MARMELL

ACONYTE

First published by Aconyte Books in 2021

ISBN 978 1 83908 027 2

Ebook ISBN 978 1 83908 028 9

Distributed in North America by Simon & Schuster Inc, New York, USA

Printed in the United States of America

9 8 7 6 5 4 3 2 1

ACONYTE BOOKS

An imprint of Asmodee Entertainment Ltd

Mercury House, Shipstones Business Centre

North Gate, Nottingham NG7 7FN, UK

aconytebooks.com // twitter.com/aconytebooks

With gratitude to Kirstine, who made this book far better, and made me look like far less of an ignorant, insensitive jackass than I otherwise might.

PROLOGUE

The aromas of life, rich and cloying and congealing in the back of his throat, danced arm in arm with the stink of putrefaction and death.

Wilmott Polaski, a pale and scrawny figure whose element included musty books and dusty shelves, jabbering students and bickering academics – and most assuredly did *not* include copses of thick boughs, glittering eyes peering from the shadows, swarms of insects and waterlogged socks – found himself uncertain as to which collection of scents was worse.

The boots he had hurriedly purchased for this sojourn fit poorly, and his coat was woefully inadequate. Mosquitoes, for which he would have thought the lingering winter chill would be too cold, hovered in thick clouds over the languid waters. Strange birds, or what he assumed to be birds, called in the distance. Ragged moss sagged from tired branches that always seemed to be reaching his way, perhaps attracted to his warmth in lieu of a spring thaw that refused to come.

Did Hockomock have alligators? He didn't think so, couldn't recall ever hearing of such creatures here. With every glance toward the dark and rippling surface, always lapping uncomfortably close to the roadway, however, he grew less and less confident.

In short, the good professor deeply did not wish to be here. With any luck, he wouldn't have to be for long.

Another twenty minutes' walk produced nothing akin to an alligator, nor anything more hostile than those mosquitoes, but it did – finally! – bring into view the community he'd caught the train down from Arkham to find.

If, he observed with some disdain, one could even dignify it with the term.

It had no name, so far as he knew. No fixed borders, no shops, no municipal center or identity. Just a collection of scattered homes and tiny farms huddled on the edge of the Hockomock Swamp, a "community" only in the sense that the several dozen families who lived in these ramshackle domiciles interacted with one another on a somewhat regular basis, and seldomly with anyone else.

The houses were old, rickety, shingles and walls beginning to rot, the supports that held them above the muddy flats and potential floods bowing like the legs of a tired grandfather. While Wilmott heard sporadic sounds of labor in the distance, the striking of tools on wood or wet soil, he saw no one.

Nervously, he dug into his coat pocket, once more checking a bundle of handwritten notes and a hastily sketched diagram. He'd anticipated an unfriendly reception – from Henry Armitage and other fellow academics, he'd heard many a report of just how mistrustful some of these insular Massachusetts communities could be – but somehow the total absence of reception was more disturbing still.

According to his haphazard little map, however, he was still on course. With a sigh he returned the papers to his pocket and continued.

The water of the swamp puddled before him, occupying a shallow dip in the roadway. Mud squelched under his steps, threatening to yank the ill-fitting boots from his blistering feet. Wilmott swallowed a stream of profanity. Damn the useless Arkham police, damn Chester and damn himself for getting caught up in the young fool's endeavors!

He glanced skyward, hoping to estimate the time of day, how long he had to accomplish his self-assigned mission before he had to turn back if he wanted to beat the sunset. The sun, however, skulking behind layers of white cedar branches and fat, ponderous clouds, told him nothing. With more silent cursing, he turned his gaze once again to the path ahead…

Was that it? That house there, hunkered at the very edges of the deeper waters? Its wood sagging, windows sloping like sleep-heavy eyelids?

It could be. To judge by his last look at the map, it should be. Defying the nervous agitation in his gut and drawing himself up to his full, impressive – if woefully spindly – height, Wilmott marched forward and pounded his knuckles on the door.

It shuddered. Paint flecks snowed down to his feet. Nothing more.

Wilmott waited what he judged a polite interval, then knocked again, harder still.

And again.

What to do if nobody was home? Somehow, in all his deliberations about whether to even come, all the time it took him to pinpoint and then reach his destination, he'd failed to consider so basic a hurdle. Perhaps this sort of thing was more complicated than he'd given–

The door finally swung open, with less a creaking than an angry and fiercely startling *crack*, as he raised his fist to try once more. Wilmott found himself staring at a yellowed shirt under frayed denim overalls.

He craned his head upward. An angry, reddened face, covered in the thick stubble of untended weeks, glared down at him.

"What?" The man's voice was as coarse as his chin and cheeks.

Wilmott removed his hat – as much to give himself a second to recover as out of courtesy. "Afternoon. Are you Woodrow Hennessy?"

"Who's askin'?" He spoke with a near-impenetrable drawl; Wilmott, for all his efforts to be kind, couldn't come up with a better term than *backwoods*.

"My name is Professor Wilmott Polaski, from Miskatonic University. I–"

"Got no use for university folk. If you're lookin' for a guide, go back'n ask over in Taunton." The door began to shut.

"No, you don't understand. I'm searching for a missing student. Chester Hennessy."

The door halted.

Taking that as an invitation to continue, Wilmott bulled on. "Chester's been gone for several weeks now, and I'm afraid the authorities have been stymied. I recalled that he'd mentioned you on occasion, and I thought perhaps–"

"Ain't talked to Chester in years. He an' his don't have truck with our side of the family."

Well, *that* wasn't right, not based on what Chester had said. "Mr Hennessy, perhaps if I might come in, we could discuss–"

"I said I don't know. Leave."

And now Wilmott was growing irate, not merely at the constant interruptions but the man's entire attitude. Did he not recognize the seriousness of the circumstances? Was he not concerned for his kin?

Perhaps the man somehow failed to understand. He was, after all, but an uneducated yokel.

"Mr Hennessy, I think perhaps I've failed to make myself clear. Chester is–"

The door opened all the way once more, and while Wilmott might not have been clear, the message conveyed by the pair of steel barrels that now hovered mere inches from his suddenly pallid face was unmistakable.

"Leave!"

Hands rising in sudden terror, one of them still clutching his hat, Wilmott backed away from the shotgun. Sheer luck prevented him from tripping over his own heels, or the rickety steps, as he retreated from the porch. He'd barely reached the roadway when the door slammed, hiding Hennessy – and his weapon – from view. The professor barely even heard it over his pounding heart.

He released a long, shaking breath.

"Well," he muttered. "That could certainly have gone better."

Instinct and rationality both urged him to turn around and leave, to head back to Taunton, check into a hotel for the night and hop aboard the first train back to Arkham in the morning. He'd already gone above and beyond the call of any duty owed a student by his professor.

But the project…

Nor was it merely his own ambitions that made Wilmott

hesitate. He knew, absolutely knew as surely as if he'd read it in one of his own textbooks, that Woodrow Hennessy was lying to him.

It wasn't merely the man's behavior, though that, even for so isolated and unfriendly a community as this one, was certainly suspicious enough. It was Chester himself. On one of the rare occasions his relations had come up in conversation at all, Chester had specifically told him that he got on much better with the low side of the family than his parents did.

While "better" didn't necessarily mean "close," it certainly implied a stronger relationship than Woodrow claimed.

Although he turned and walked away from the Hennessy house, although it ran counter to his better judgment, Wilmott Polaski had already made a decision.

He didn't go far. Perhaps a mile at most, distant enough that Hennessy should think him gone, that no random member of the community – not that he'd seen any – would connect the stranger with that particular house.

And there, sitting upon a log at least marginally free of mildews or fungi or other swamp substances, he waited.

He knew the delay would mean stumbling his way back to civilization in the dark of night, at best; and at worst, genuine bodily harm. He deliberately shunted those thoughts aside. He felt himself on the verge of answers, possibly of saving not only his prize student but the project that would cement his own name in the textbooks he so valued.

Night fell, the avian and insectile songs of the Hockomock changed from one chorus to another and Wilmott Polaski shuffled his way back toward the crooked house.

He approached at an angle, wincing as he deliberately set

his path through the cold waters, soaked almost to his knees. Should Hennessy open the front door and gaze out through the curtained, drooping windows, he ought to notice nothing amiss. And thankfully the sodden earth rose again around the house proper, if only just, so Wilmott shouldn't have to remain long within the muck.

The back of the place was, if anything, even more dilapidated than the front, whole sections softened with moisture and inner rot. The good professor had to remind himself more than once that such disrepair didn't necessarily reflect a slovenly nature on the part of the inhabitants, that the environment might well seep into the wood, strip the paint, bestow a patina of filth, regardless of all efforts to hold it at bay.

Not that he was *too* terribly inclined to give Hennessy the benefit of any doubt.

Lamplight leaking out from the ill-fitting shutters, and a bright moon glowing through the clouds that had grown thinner as dusk fell, provided just enough illumination for him to get by. Enough to note details of the house that he'd failed to observe earlier, when his focus has been entirely on the front door and the man within.

The most salient of those details was the lower level, beneath the house proper.

It had, perhaps, been constructed at a time when the surrounding waters were a bit lower than today. Standing mostly above ground, it couldn't rightly be called a basement, yet it was too large and structurally sound to be simply an under-floor hollow someone had bricked up. Whether it had existed since the structure was built, or whether someone had added it later, Wilmott wasn't architect enough to say.

Neither could he say with certainty why that lowest level didn't fully match the width of the rest of the house, creating a peculiar combination of partial cellar, partial crawlspace. It wasn't unique to the Hennessy place, either, as he'd seen similar construction on some other homes he'd passed. Perhaps it was to do with the inconsistent earth here at the swamp's edges, with portions solid enough to support construction standing adjacent to others that were far too soft? He didn't know.

He knew only that, beneath the sagging floor and between the wooden supports, stood walls of uneven stones and thick mortar.

A half-sunken cellar certainly felt like a good place for Hennessy to hide his secrets, and, if nothing else, one of its own narrow windows might provide ingress. Crouching low, shuddering at the slick mud beneath his fingers as he scrabbled for balance, Wilmott slid beneath the house's outer edges.

Picking his way between puddles and discarded, rusted tools, biting his lip to keep from exclaiming his revulsion at the cobwebs and skittering bugs, he neared the first of those windows...

"Isslaach thkulkris, isslaach cheoshash... Vnoktu vshuru shelosht escruatha..."

It might have been five voices or fifty; he knew only it was more than one. Resonating off one another, echoing in brick-walled rooms, filtered through cracked wood and the natural songs of the swamp, it seemed somehow more than the foreign tongue – or perhaps simple gibberish – that reached his ears.

"Svist ch'shultva ulveshtha ikravis... Isslaach ikravis vuloshku dlachvuul loshaa... Ulveshtha schlachtli vrulosht chevkuthaansa..."

On it went, intertwining until he couldn't tell one phrase from the next, and then repeating once more from the beginning.

Over and over as he sat and listened, trying and failing to make the slightest sense of it, growing somehow *heavier* with each repetition even though it never varied in volume. Something about the litany was… off. Unclean. He felt violated, as though something slick had wiggled on the back of his tongue as he swallowed a bite of what should have been a mundane meal. He found himself lightheaded and nauseated, staggering back a few steps from the window as he struggled to restrain his rising gorge.

The handle of the old shovel on which he stepped was rotten most of the way through, but with enough of a solid center to resound like a gunshot when it snapped beneath his foot. Disoriented and now terrified of being discovered, the professor turned and fled, splashing through the swampy waters and into the night, leaving the Hennessy house behind.

The house, but not the ghastly phrases, which now seemed determined to dog his every step.

"Isslaach thkulkris, isslaach cheoshash… Vnoktu vshuru shelosht escruatha…"

Two nights later, he returned yet again.

As before, he'd initially intended to flee, and found himself unable. Thoughts of Chester Hennessy and their shared endeavors occupied his waking hours, most of which he spent staring at the walls of his rented room or aimlessly wandering about town. When sleep had finally claimed him, he'd tossed in the grip of horrific nightmares, shivering so violently he'd bolted awake from vistas of frigid ice… howling winds… endless shadow… *something* reaching out for him, stretching, grasping…

And always, asleep or awake, nesting at the back of his mind, winding and twisting and coiling around itself over and over, that abhorrent, damnable verse. Had he been honest with himself, Wilmott would have admitted there was something to the mantra itself, far more than his concern for his missing student or even their endeavors, that kept him here.

Even when preparing his return to the house, however, he never allowed himself to consider it.

This time, thanks to a quick trip to Taunton's shops, he came prepared. A set of screwdrivers and miniature blades sat tucked in a bag at his belt, and he clutched a small lantern in one fist, an iron prybar in the other. Flimsy as the wood was, the last was almost overkill. The window frame scooped away like oatmeal; he could practically have made entry with his bare hands.

Wiggling, grunting, he wormed his way through the window and flopped to the mildewed stone floor, flinching from both the impact and the choking scent.

Only as he picked himself up did he realize that the odd recitation continued, that the people down here, whoever they were, were still repeating their mindless refrain. Up to that point he'd thought the words were merely in his head, as they had been for the past days.

That realization brought with it another wave of disorientation, as if the thought itself made him more susceptible. The hallway tilted around him, splintered in a kaleidoscope of fragments, before pulling itself back together and leaving only dizziness in its wake.

Wilmott staggered forward, one hand on the wall while the other clutched the lantern that now seemed a woefully insufficient source of light. The uneven floor made the vertigo harder to deal with, as broken stones reached up to trip him or sudden dips threatened to topple him. More than once the swamp crept in between the stones at the lowest points, resulting in puddles to splash or, on one or two occasions, even wade through.

Surely the passageway couldn't be this long? It must be his own confusion that had him nigh convinced he'd taken scores of steps already, rather than a mere handful.

When he stumbled yet again, glancing down angrily at his traitorous feet, he discovered it hadn't been the floor that tripped him this time.

The blue-gray of a Postal Service uniform, now tattered, hid most, but unfortunately not all, of the half-stripped skeleton beneath. Nor had it been time, the waters, nor even vermin that had torn away the flesh and tissue. Even through his disorientation, his horror, Wilmott clearly saw the jagged indentations on the bone that could only have been left by human jaws.

He found himself continuing, with only the faintest memory of clambering back to his feet. He couldn't remember at precisely what point he'd collapsed, nor did he recall vomiting, though the acrid taste on his tongue suggested he had.

He thought, too, that he might have seen the remains of other savaged corpses beyond that of the unfortunate postman, had flashing, sporadic images of additional limbs, additional skulls, but once more his memory refused to cling to them well enough to be sure it was anything more than overwrought imagination.

His head ached, the skin uncomfortably tight around his skull. By the time the obvious notion of "Turn back! Get out!"

penetrated his feverish mind, he'd already reached the end of the hall.

A cage of some sort, or a makeshift cell. He couldn't seem to focus on it clearly, or at least only bits and pieces stuck in his memory. He recalled stone walls and haphazard iron bars.

He recalled the stench of old sweat, of human filth.

Recalled not the one young man he sought but a small collection of faces, caked in mud and spit and blood and worse, some merely soiled but others subtly misshapen. If Chester had been among them, Wilmott never saw him.

It was from them, from chapped lips and ragged throats, that the alien chorus emerged. Over and over, almost but not entirely in unison so that the words seemed to vibrate in the ear.

"Svist ch'shultva ulveshtha ikravis…"

And Wilmott stepped toward them, his empty hand outstretched to tug at the chain and padlock that sealed them in, his own mouth beginning to move, no thought or instinct in his head save to *join them.*

The vicious report of a shotgun, and the patter of stone fragments falling from the buckshot-marred ceiling, shook him from his trance.

In the entryway to a perpendicular hallway Wilmott had previously overlooked in his distraction, stood Woodrow Hennessy. He gripped his weapon in corpse-knuckled fists, and twisted fabric of makeshift plugs protruded from his ears.

"I told you to leave, God damn you!"

Had Wilmott been more together, more himself, he might have heard not only the fury but the horror and grief burdening the man's outburst.

But he was not, and did not. Howling in confusion and in fear, the professor spun and raced back the way he'd come.

He sloshed through pools, stumbled over corpses, scraped his hands as he scrabbled back through the open window. Even in the pitch dark, he only barely remembered to keep hold of his lantern. His thoughts – all those not wrapped up in the litany, endless, pounding – were of escape only. In his panic, then, it seemed to make sense that the monstrous rustic with madmen locked in his cellar would be far less keen to pursue him into the wild than back along the road.

By the time his pounding heart had slowed and his head ceased spinning long enough for him to recognize the downsides of such a plan, he was already hopelessly lost.

Hours passed. Wilmott shivered violently, soaked to the waist. Beneath the dark waters, the mud had finally sucked the oversized boot from his left foot, forcing him to limp with fear that he would step on something piercing, slicing… or biting.

Unnamed creatures shrieked in the distant dark. The swamp rippled in the wake of swimming things.

From the muck below and the cedars all around, limbs snagged at his clothes, at his skin, making him start with frightened cries no matter how tightly he tried to keep his lips shut. Surely they were only branches, roots, vines. Yet in the flickering light of his lantern and in his thoughts – which felt ever warped, ever more sluggish, compressed in some mental vise – he could have sworn he saw them moving, flexing as they reached for him.

And that light itself had begun to fade, its dancing growing ever more frantic, as the flame licked thirstily at the last few traces of oil.

They both flared, then, the firelight and the panic together, in a final burst.

Before him, half-sunk in the swamp, vine-wrapped and coated in slime, was a black stone. He peered at writings carved in an alphabet unlike any he had ever seen before and could not possibly read – and yet which seemed, at some level below the conscious, perhaps even beyond the sapient, familiar. It tugged at him, a sensation that felt as physical as it did emotional. A shiver began at the back of his neck but died before it traveled far, as though his body no longer remembered how to move.

His lantern died, to reveal another source of illumination, coming up through the swamp behind him.

"Professor!" Woodrow Hennessy's voice was hoarse. He must have been calling out for some time. "Professor, can you hear me?"

He stepped into view, water sloshing around his calves. Wilmott Polaski tore his gaze from the stone, advanced toward the newcomer, and responded in the only way he could, with the only words he knew.

"*Isslaach thkulkris, isslaach cheoshash…*"

Hennessy might not have heard him – he still wore the plugs of fabric in his ears, seemed more frightened of what he might hear than of braving the swamp while deafened – but he clearly recognized the recitation all the same.

With a scream of fury, of guilt, of denial, but above all else of fear, he raised the shotgun toward the oncoming professor and fired.

CHAPTER ONE

It was a soft song, its notes made up of the shuffling of papers; the thump of leather-bound covers; the rolling of ladders and the scuffing of chairs; the swish of trousers, of skirts; and the dull hum of quiet conversations that were never *as* quiet as the students believed they were.

A soft song, filtering from dozens of rooms and arched halls, from every floor of Miskatonic University's famed Orne Library – and one that, on the average day, Daisy Walker found empowering, energizing for all its subtleties.

Today was not an average day. She had not, in fact, had many average days at all for the past few months.

At first, part of her unease might have been anxiety over her new responsibilities. This new term, spring '23, was only the second since Dr Armitage had put her in charge of the Special Collections, the restricted tomes and writings for which the Orne Library was most well known. The least precious of the books therein was worth more than her yearly salary, the value of the entire lot immeasurable, not just in money but in irreplaceable lore.

Daisy knew herself well enough, though, to realize that while nerves might have overcome her poise at first, she'd more than adapted to her new duties in the intervening months.

And some of that unease might be down to the contents of those tomes, which she'd made a point of studying once the position had opened and Armitage had first hinted he might consider her to fill it. While most of the Special Collection was merely old, some of its contents were... peculiar.

She'd perused a few of them, when she had the opportunity: *De Vermis Mysteriis*, John Dee's partial *Necronomicon*, the del Arrio translation of the *Cabala of Saboth*. They spoke, those books, of ancient things, of sorceries long forgotten and of names that should have been. As windows into ancient cultures and beliefs, they fascinated her, but their actual content? She didn't believe a word of it, of course; it was no more real than the imaginings of Gogol or Stoker. Still, that hadn't prevented her from turning on a few extra lights during the later hours of her shifts, double-checking the locks before turning in for the night, or – now and again – waking in a panicked sweat from nightmares she could never clearly recall.

But again, Daisy knew herself well enough to know that no musty old myths or fairy tales would disturb her so thoroughly, or for so long.

No, it was–

"Miss Walker?"

"Oh!" The young librarian jolted in her chair, hands gripping the edge of her desk. It was, to the best of her memory, the first time anyone had opened the door to her office without her noticing.

That idea still took some getting used to: her office.

"Oh!" The echo came from the even younger woman, wide-eyed and round-faced, standing in the doorway. "I'm so sorry! I didn't mean to startle you."

Daisy brushed back a long curl of blonde hair. "That's quite all right, Abigail. I was just… lost in thought, I suppose." Not that she had any intention of revealing said thoughts, either regarding her books or… other concerns.

"I did knock," Abigail offered shyly. "But you didn't answer, and I *knew* you were in here, and I wanted to make sure you were all right." Then, perhaps noting a lingering vacancy in Daisy's expression, "*Are* you all right?"

"I'm fine. I suppose I was even more lost than I realized. You, ah, you needed something?"

Those wide eyes flickered aside, down, back to meet her own. "I just… That is, I thought I should ask if you needed anything done in the, um, the Special Collections?"

"I see." With an iron will, Daisy kept her lips from quirking in a knowing grin. "No, dear, nothing just now."

"Oh." Again the brief gaze off in the direction of the restricted chambers. "Are you, um, are you sure?"

The grin fought even harder to slip onto her face – but at the same time, she had to fight the urge to shake her head. Abigail Foreman was an industrious student worker, and Daisy would be happy to have her stay on once she'd graduated, should her interest in library economics lead her in that direction.

She was, however, a bit too readily diverted by particularly boy-shaped distractions.

"Your duties, Abigail, include providing assistance to students and patrons when they solicit it – not to go foisting it upon those who have made no such requests."

Abigail flushed until her skin practically glowed.

"Yes, miss. Sorry, miss."

Now Daisy did allow herself to smile, hoping to take some of the sting from the rebuke. "Now, I believe someone told me South American Studies needed re-shelving?"

Abigail took the offered escape, fleeing from the office, and Daisy released the sigh that had been building for the past few moments. She liked the girl, would normally have made far more allowances for her latest infatuation, might even have encouraged it.

Raslo. Why, of all the fine young lads Miskatonic's campus could offer, did the poor girl's attentions have to fall on Elliot Raslo? Even if he hadn't been mired in uncertainty and grief, even if everything in his life, everything at Miskatonic University, been fine and dandy, even then...

But that wasn't her secret to tell. The boy would have been mortified even to know that she knew.

Daisy stood – chair scraping across the floor – carefully smoothed her blouse and skirt, and left her office, turning in the opposite direction from Abigail's flight.

The outermost chamber of the Special Collection was a reading room, consisting only of a table, a handful of comfortably upholstered chairs, and a lamp. Students and visitors were permitted to make use of the collection only individually or in small groups, and only on limited occasions depending on seniority, the nature of their research and in exchange for volunteered labor. Over the past weeks, assuming nobody else had reserved time, it was a coin toss whether or not Elliot would be here. Thus, Daisy wouldn't have been surprised to see him even if she hadn't already known, thanks to

Abigail's blatant interest, that he was there.

The young man sat, elbows on the table, head in his hands, so that Daisy wasn't certain he was awake. His brown coat and his black hair were both rumpled. Time was, not so long ago, he'd have been chagrined even to be seen outside in such a state.

"Elliot?"

He was, indeed, awake. He looked up at her, bleary with exhaustion and churning emotion. His face – a bit darker complexioned than her own due to a Mediterranean grandparent – sported several days' worth of stubble.

"Is there news?"

It was his first question almost every time she saw him, no matter that she'd told him over and over that she would let him know the instant she heard anything.

"No." She pulled up a chair and sat across from him. "Nothing."

"Damn!" Then, quieting himself before she had to remind him to do so, "Useless, the lot of them."

She knew he meant the Arkham police. This, too, was part of the ritual, a conversation they'd had so often she had to assume he took some meager comfort in its repetition.

"They've precious little to go on," she told him. Indeed, they had almost nothing. Chester Hennessy, Elliot's best friend and roommate, had vanished without trace – a feat duplicated some weeks later by Professor Polaski, Chester's mentor and advisor in ongoing research.

"They're ignoring what little they have," Elliot insisted, rubbing a knuckle into his eye. "They're still treating them as separate incidents when any idiot can see they're not. Still insisting that Chester ran off because of that bitch–"

"Language, Mr Raslo!"

He recoiled as if she'd slapped him. "I– Of course. I'm so sorry, Miss Walker."

Daisy knew he meant it. Elliot was, if nothing else, a gentle, courteous soul. At least when he wasn't exhausted and frustrated and scared.

She laid her hand atop his, and managed not to wince as he clutched it like a life preserver. Normally she'd have moved the book that sat before him on the table, would have refused to let them rest their hands on its cover this way for fear the oils of their skin might damage the old material, but a brief moment or two wouldn't hurt it.

It wasn't the first time he'd asked for this one, either. He'd been weeks trying to retrace Chester's research, hoping that something in the missing student's recent endeavors – the project that had absorbed him, body and soul, for months – might shed some light, however feeble, on the mystery of his disappearance.

So far, unless he was keeping secrets from her, he'd had precisely the same amount of success as the police he cursed for idiots and fools: none whatsoever.

She didn't mind his presence, and certainly appreciated his help. Like Chester before him, in order to earn himself more time in the Special Collections, Elliot had volunteered to help sort unimportant documents for the Orne Library and the university as a whole: letters and personal papers willed them by alumni; old newspaper clippings; reports of historical artifacts stolen from museums and other universities for which they should be alert; and so forth. He claimed it was solely due to his efforts to find his missing roommate, but Daisy believed it was a way to feel closer to the friend he'd lost. Elliot was, on those days he could focus, even better at such mundane but essential tasks than Chester had been. Still, she'd grown worried at his mounting obsession, to say nothing of the damage to his academic standing. Daisy knew he must be missing classes in order to be here at all hours.

Had her leniency with the Special Collections and his research somehow led Chester Hennessy into harm's way? Unlikely as it seemed, it was that fear more than anything else that kept her awake nights, ate at her composure during the day. It was not a mistake she cared to repeat with his friend, however much he felt the need to follow.

"Elliot," she began finally, "you need to–"

It was only because Daisy hadn't shut the door to the reading room that the commotion reached them at all, that she heard the sudden cacophony intruding on the library's song. Not shouting, not yet, but voices raised in disagreement that could readily *become* shouting.

Or worse?

She rose, her back as stiff as her expression. Even at the best of times, Daisy had no patience for those who would disrupt the peace of her library. Whoever had foolishly elected to do so today, in the midst of all her other concerns, was liable to get an unfriendly piece of her mind. "I'm so sorry. Excuse me."

A swish of woolen skirts, and she was gone.

Elliot watched her go, his weary mind not immediately registering the significance of what they'd heard.

Miss Walker, his instructors, his fellow students. They all attributed his constant distraction to grief and to worry, even if they couldn't possibly understand just how strongly he…

Well, they were partly right. But only partly.

And they attributed his research, his burning compulsion to retrace Chester's research, to an obsessive and almost certainly futile hope of locating him when the police and the man's own family could not.

They were partly right. But only partly.

The other part, he'd mentioned to no one.

That Chester had told him excitedly, on one particular evening, that the clue to finally break his mystery project – the one he claimed would exceed all his ambitions, would cement his name in the annals of archeological studies before he even completed his education – had been found. Though he had then balked at explaining precisely what he had found, or how it could help.

That in the final days before his disappearance, Chester had become distant, listless, constantly preoccupied. He'd slept poorly, barely spoken. Had taken to muttering to himself, sometimes in French, or in languages Elliot couldn't identify, let alone interpret.

Elliot's own studies, focusing as they did on the psychology of the human mind, led him to believe that his friend's efforts had transformed into a dangerous, perhaps even pathological obsession. He had finally committed himself to confronting Chester, though his heart pounded and his stomach coiled in on itself like a dying worm at the thought of what such an intervention might do to their relationship – but Chester had disappeared before he'd gathered the courage to speak up.

And ever since…

Ever since, Elliot himself had awakened from jagged, half-remembered nightmares on more nights than not, shivering from a deep chill unrelated to the temperature of the room in which he slept. Nightmares not only of ice, but of things that moved in shadow, things that dwelt behind endless sheets of hail and sleet.

The dreams alone, he could have managed. It was the constant repetition that threatened to drive him mad.

Just a few words, a partial phrase. Something in that unknown language, something Chester had murmured only the once where Elliot could hear it. It lodged in the back of his mind, a constant itch he couldn't scratch, couldn't stop *trying* to scratch, echoing over and over, winding through every conversation, bubbling beneath every lecture, until he wanted to scream.

To scream those words.

It was that phrase, that fragment, that distracted him more than any search, more than any grief. And he knew, without knowing entirely how he knew, that it would have been far worse, might truly have stripped away all sanity and self-control, if it hadn't been for his *other* discovery in following Chester's research. That *other* mantra.

It *was* just a mantra, was it not? It couldn't really be–

Another burst of raised voices, not quite shouting, from whatever commotion was occurring out in the library, snapped him from rumination. Elliot forced himself from his chair. He doubted Miss Walker or the library staff would require any help to deal with whatever problem had arisen, and on the off-chance they did, he couldn't imagine what help he might be able to offer. So it was with more of a desperate need for diversion than any sense of duty that he proceeded down the hallway in her distant wake.

All normal activity within the library's main hall had come

to a halt as students peered over their books and their papers at the confrontation brewing by the massive entryway. Several of the Orne staffers, and two of Miskatonic's uniformed security guards, were gathered in a clump around a stranger who'd apparently attempted to access the library.

The man didn't look remotely like student, staff, or alumni, and while the Orne Library was open to others, they either had to be invited researchers or to have made a formal appointment well in advance. To judge by the raised voices, some of which were clearly tired of repeating themselves, the stranger met neither qualification.

Elliot hadn't the faintest idea what to make of the man. He wasn't particularly tall, but his broad shoulders and proud bearing made him seem so. He wore a long, heavy coat that would have blended in well enough on the streets of Arkham, but the boots visible below his trouser cuffs, made of some supple leather, were of no style or fashion the young man had ever seen. Nor, for that matter, were the fellow's features, which were flatter and darker than Elliot's own. The young student was not especially well traveled, much as he wished otherwise, and unable to place the stranger's land of origin. He put Elliot in mind a bit of a Mongolian researcher he'd met once, and a bit of American Indian, but not precisely either.

"It's only a few questions!" The stranger's voice was deep, resonant; his accent, like everything else about him, far enough beyond Elliot's experience that he couldn't place it. "Surely one of your librarians can spare me five minutes!"

One of the security guards began again to deny him, taking a menacing step nearer. It was, perhaps, the threat of the confrontation turning into a genuine brawl that inspired Daisy

Walker, hovering at the edges of the commotion, to finally intervene.

"And what questions are those, Mr...?"

"Miss Walker," the security guard protested, "I don't think you oughta–"

"It's all right, Floyd."

The stranger turned her way, his coat drifting open to reveal an array of charms and amulets that hung from his neck by a veritable thicket of leather thongs and animal gut. From where he stood, Elliot thought, but couldn't be certain, he saw old bone, wood, stone, and thick leather trinkets, all of which were carved or stitched with small designs he couldn't, from this distance, make out.

"Shiwak," the man replied to Daisy's implied question. "Billy Shiwak."

"All right, Mr Shiwak. What's so urgent that you had to raise such a fuss in my library?"

No, not bone, Elliot decided, idly wondering why he was so focused on this man's – Shiwak's – accoutrements. *Ivory.*

After the past few moments of tension, Shiwak seemed almost confused now that he had the opportunity to pose his questions. He cast about for a few seconds, as though seeking his words.

"To begin with," he began, "I'm hoping you can tell me where to find a man by the name of Jebediah Pembroke. I've been told–"

Elliot never found out *what* he'd been told, because Daisy Walker went deathly still at the mention of the name, though it meant nothing to Elliot himself. In his three and a half years at Miskatonic, Elliot had never seen her react that way to anything.

"How dare you?!"

Everyone, including the security guards and the newcomer himself, took a step back in shock.

Daisy continued, her voice nearly vibrating. "I don't know what sort of rumormongers and gossip you've been listening to, but I will not subject myself or these halls to your... your *slander*."

"Miss Walker, I'm certain I intended no insult. I simply–"

"I'll thank you to leave my library now, Mr Shiwak."

"Please, I–"

"I will thank you. To leave."

The ice enveloping her every word, and a glance at the stern expressions on the two security guards, apparently convinced the man that further argument would do nobody any good. With a stiff nod, he made for the doors, the guards falling into step behind him.

Daisy spun, her heel digging a divot into the thin foyer carpet. "This is still a library," she announced firmly to staff and student alike, "not a theatre."

Faces swiftly turned back to books or notes or regular tasks. Head high, the librarian swept through the main room, making her way back toward her office.

Elliot alone continued to stare at the doors, contemplating the fellow who'd disappeared beyond. For it was only now that the damnable phrase returned to its accustomed volume in the back of his mind, that he realized it had briefly quieted, if only slightly.

Quieted in the presence of the peculiar Billy Shiwak.

CHAPTER TWO

William "Billy" Shiwak stormed from the Orne Library, jaw clenched, swearing violently – though only in his thoughts, not aloud. The journey had turned poor enough already; to risk attracting the attentions of a hostile toornaq with an ill-phrased curse would be the height of foolishness.

And you've already acted the fool enough for one day, haven't you, Billy?

Over a year spent among them, longer than that studying them, most of his life spent speaking their tongue as well as his own – and for all that, Billy still couldn't even pretend to understand Americans. No doubt the woman had good reason to find his mention of Pembroke offensive, but for the life of him he couldn't imagine what. Personal history, perhaps? A familial feud? Something else entirely?

The Ujaraanni. I should have led with questions about the Ujaraanni.

After all his efforts, after coming this far, he'd rushed where he should have been patient. Made for the campus straight from

33

the train station, given no careful thought how to best approach the people here. Foolishness!

No help for it now. Miskatonic University had been his best lead, but not the only one. He would have to pursue the others, and hope that either they proved fruitful, or at least took long enough that he might find a more effective way to approach the school.

A school which, apparently, the two guards intended to make certain he left. He realized now, as his anger at Daisy Walker and, even more so, himself, began to fade, that the men were still with him, several steps behind. He remained on the clearly delineated pathways, between massive stone structures – any one of which would dwarf every home in Itilleq combined – and alongside grassy lawns so neatly tended that they'd maintained their greenery even through a winter that the folks of Massachusetts doubtless considered harsh.

What did *they* know of harsh winters?

As they neared the edge of the sprawling campus, Billy halted and turned. "Could either of you gentlemen recommend inexpensive lodgings?"

The thinner and older of the two – had the librarian called him Floyd? – scoffed and turned away, but the other nodded. "There's a couple flophouses up in the Merchant District. Ain't fancy, most maybe ain't even too clean, but if you're not picky about where you bunk, they'll do you fine."

Billy tried to map in his head what he'd seen of Arkham thus far. "Up near the train station?"

"Yeah, more or less."

"I would prefer somewhere else." If he was picturing the right place, he'd seen several blocks cordoned off by the local police on his walk from the train. "There's some sort of disturbance…?"

"Oh, right. There's a flu spreading out that way." The guard pondered a moment, then, "Ma's."

"I'm sorry?"

"Ma's Boarding House. Southside. She's usually got a few rooms to let, if you ain't dippy enough to break her rules."

"I see. And how would I–?"

But either because Floyd was sighing theatrically and tapping his foot, or because his own patience had run dry, the security guard was done answering questions. "Just head down Garrison," he said, already walking away. "I'm sure you'll find someone who can direct you from there."

Billy didn't bother calling a thank you. He wasn't sure the man would either have heard or cared.

"Father," he muttered, "whatever anersaat or toornat caused your misfortune, I hope your pain sated them. I've got enough difficulty with *human* impediments, thanks very much."

Still grumbling, he hunted for a street sign to confirm that he was indeed on Garrison, then turned southward.

Asking for directions proved more difficult than the Miskatonic security man had implied.

Not due to any dearth of people to ask. Even in the drifting fog and the abnormally chill early spring breeze of the evening, citizens wandered on business of their own. Motor cars and horse-drawn carriages passed him by on the streets, and the walkways bustled with pedestrians.

No, the problem was finding someone willing to speak to *him*.

Other than his seal-skin boots – he'd just never been able to find any comfort in American footwear – and the amulets he tried to keep largely concealed beneath his coat, Billy had dressed to blend in. And if he'd been trying to vanish into a crowd, or to remain anonymous and keep his head down, that would have been enough.

Coming anywhere near enough a stranger to speak to them, however, was another matter. His features were more than enough to mark him as an outsider, and while he'd visited cities where foreigners – or anyone with a skin tone much darker than a corpse – were treated far worse, that didn't mean the average Arkhamite welcomed him with open arms.

It was, in fact, a young black man, the fifth person he'd stopped, who'd finally (and even cheerfully) given him directions, as well as warning him three separate times not to miss out on either Ma Mathison's Sunday night soup or her apple pie.

"Better'n Velma's cherry pie, even! And you *know* nobody'd make *that* claim lightly!"

"I'm… sure they wouldn't."

Then, later, a second set of directions, when the first proved somewhat insufficient for a man who knew nothing about Arkham's byways, this time offered by a kindly old white couple – a fact that made Billy feel a bit better about the town in general – tooling around in a spotlessly clean Ford Model-T.

And finally, tired and hungry, he found himself on the front steps of Ma's Boarding House, a surprisingly large structure whose severe peaks and almost ominously sharp lines were oddly offset by the bright lights, both inside and out, and the sounds of cheer from beyond the door.

His entrance drew any number of stares, but only a handful appeared suspicious or hostile; most expressed mere curiosity, and all swiftly returned to their own business. People sat about a large common room, in a wide variety of chairs that, though mismatched, had been chosen and placed with care toward which colors and patterns complimented one another.

The room's far end opened into a smaller chamber containing what appeared to be a communal dining table. Although currently empty, to judge by the lingering, mouthwatering aromas, it played regular host to expertly prepared meals.

A large, dark-haired woman in pearls and a floral dress bustled over to meet him. In an accent he'd never encountered, and so thick he nearly had to wade through it, she introduced herself as Ma Mathison, welcoming him to her house, to Arkham, etc.

"Jus' two dollars a night, or twelve for the week, and you won't find yourself any better in Arkham for twice that! And that includes dinner, too, long as you're at the table to say grace with us at six. Six sharp, you hear me? Else you're on your own, 'cuz I don't fill no bellies that miss grace!"

"Uh, I hear you. Yes, ma'am."

Ma ran down the rest of her rules as she guided him to a desk across the room where she happily took both his name and his money. They were numerous, those rules.

"No guests downstairs past nine, no guests in the rooms past eight, no guests of the opposite sex ever. I won't be having scandalous doin's in my house!

"Luncheon costs sixty cents and is served from eleven to whenever the food runs out. You can bring a guest, but it's sixty-five cents for anyone not payin' for a room.

"You can come'n go as you like, but I won't be having my other guests disturbed, so if I hear complaints about noise in the wee hours, out you go!"

Then finally, after catching a glimpse of his amulets, "And you practice whatever you want at home, but there'll be no prayers to anyone but Our Lord an' his son Jesus Christ in this house, you hear?"

"I still hear you, yes." Billy stared briefly at the key in his hand, unable to remember when during the torrent of words she'd stuck it there, and felt vaguely dizzy. *I may need a translator.*

Or earplugs.

"You got any questions," she finally concluded, "you just let me know."

She was already stepping away as she spoke, clearly anticipating none. Most of her guests were probably either regulars, or too overwhelmed by the verbal barrage they'd just endured, to come up with any.

"Actually, yes." Billy waited until she'd halted, processed the unexpected reply, and turned back his way. "I'm wondering if you can tell me where I might find..." He paused, dredging the unusual names back to mind. He had them written down, but he'd rather not have to dig.

"Either the Curiositie Shoppe or a place called Ye Olde Magick Shoppe." *Whatever in the world "Ye" means...*

He watched the narrowing of Ma's eyes, the scrunching of the skin around her lips and chin, and only then realized – given some of what she'd said to him already – why she might take the question amiss.

Doing a marvelous job on the diplomacy so far today, Billy.

"I'm not a, uh, practitioner," he told her, and it was at least partly true. He was certainly no angakkoq, though she would doubtless consider the beliefs he held, the gods he venerated and the spirits he feared pagan enough. "I'm only trying to track down some... cultural relics."

Which was also partly true.

Though the suspicion never left her face entirely, she relented enough to offer general directions to both establishments, and Billy wanted to curse again. He'd been within a couple of blocks of the Curiositie Shoppe, had practically passed it on his walk from the train to Miskatonic. And Ye Olde Magick Shoppe, while more out of the way, had been closer to the university than it was to him now.

"But if you're really lookin' for historical pieces," she continued, "you oughtta start at the Historical Society. They can probably set your feet on the right path, an' they got no truck with the sorts of people who frequent dens of witchcraft and iniquity."

"Historical Society?"

"Yep. Keep all sorts of writings an' pictures an' art an' old gewgaws. Biggest collection in Arkham outside of Miskatonic. Maybe bigger, if you're lookin' for local history in particular."

He wasn't, not at all. Still, this sounded like the sort of place that might, at least, have an ear to the trade in stolen historical objects, or be able to point him toward those who did, if he asked carefully enough. A frisson of excitement ran through him – to say nothing of relief that he might yet recover from the earlier mistakes of the day.

"Would they still be open at this hour?" he asked, shoving his room key in a pocket.

Ma Mathison shrugged. "Couldn't say." She did, however, glance somewhat obviously at the clock across the way.

Billy followed her gaze, saw it was little more than an hour until "grace," then shrugged in turn. "I guess I'm on my own for dinner tonight, then. Thank you, Mrs Mathison."

Though his stomach and his feet both rebelled, he turned from the soft chairs and the scents of dinner to come and headed out once more into Arkham's streets.

The Arkham Historical Society was a massive three-story Georgian manor towering over the surrounding houses, doubtless the home of some obscenely wealthy family before it was willed to the organization. The wrought iron fence coiled around it was not a welcoming sign – but the *literal* sign, a bronze plaque on the gate identifying the society for what it was, proved more enticing.

While several lights shone through various curtained windows, however, nothing about the edifice indicated whether it was currently open to visitors. The evening was still young, but the heavy clouds, lingering since winter had technically ended, made it feel later.

Should he treat it as a private residence, knock and wait to see if it were answered? Or as a shop or public facility, assuming that if the door was unlocked it meant he was welcome to enter?

When a twist of the handle proved that it was not, in fact, locked, Billy chose the second option and stepped inside.

He found himself in a long, carpeted hall, lit from above by fancy electrical chandeliers. Along both walls were portraits of men and women, doubtless important folks in Arkham's history, looking over glass display cases of documents, journals and the like. Beyond, the hall led into further rooms, this size or larger, with their own displays. He couldn't see from here what might be in them, but they were far more numerous, and in many cases larger, than those beside him.

Beyond a sense of vague amusement at what these white

folks considered "old," Billy found himself largely uninterested in their history, built as it was on the bones of those who had come before. Perhaps he'd have been a little more curious under other circumstances, if he hadn't been so driven by concerns of his own – but *only* a little.

Doorways led to other rooms, off to either side, but as he had no notion of what might lie behind them, he chose instead to wander along the main way.

He'd not yet reached the end of this first room, however, when one of those side doors opened, startling him, if only mildly.

"While I'm always delighted to welcome a newcomer to the Historical Society, young man, I'm afraid that I'll be locking up soon, as we're members only after hours. You've scarcely the time to see anything. Perhaps if you'd like to return tomorrow?"

The speaker was an older fellow, spindly almost to the point of frailty, with vaguely colorless hair sprouting from atop a vaguely colorless head. The only real spots of color anywhere about him were the dull plaid elbow patches on his otherwise gray suit coat.

That and a blueish amulet hanging from his neck. It boasted a peculiar design, an uneven star with a circle – perhaps an eye – in its center.

Different from his own amulets as it was, coming from a culture he could not even guess at, Billy knew a protective talisman when he saw one.

From what, he wondered, could this old man need to protect himself?

"I'm not actually here for a tour," Billy told him, "but on behalf of my people." He wasn't sure why, but he felt that this stranger, obviously a man who valued his history, might be sympathetic to such a claim. "If you could spare just a few minutes before, ah, locking up, you would be doing us a great service."

The old man cocked his head, examining Billy as he might one of his displays, and then his face suddenly split in a grin. "You're Eskimo, aren't you? I haven't met one of your people in decades!"

As often as he'd heard that term in his travels, Billy still felt himself stiffen. "Yes, I am. Though we call ourselves Kalaallit. Or Inuit, if you prefer."

"Right, right. I've heard that about many Eskimos."

Billy forced his teeth not to grind.

"Well," the other said, "my name is Peabody. Reginald Peabody. I'm the curator of this hallowed establishment."

"William Shiwak."

"Very well, William. You've got your few minutes. What can I do for you?"

They'd drifted, as they spoke, to the doorway from which Peabody had appeared. Beyond it lay a small office, cluttered with unfiled papers, unshelved books, and some old broken tools that Billy assumed were being cataloged for storage or display.

Peabody did not, however, return to his desk and sit, nor offer one of the chairs – which would have required some excavation to unearth anyway – to his guest. Clearly, when he offered a "few minutes," he meant it.

Billy almost asked about Jebediah Pembroke, but thought better of it. He still had no idea what about that name had set off the librarian, so he couldn't be certain it wouldn't have the same result here.

Instead, for the first time in weeks, he told an outsider the truth, albeit far from the *whole* truth, about his travels.

"I'm looking, Mr Peabody, for something that was stolen from Itilleq. That is, my nunaqarfik, my… village." Not an exact translation, but it would do. "I have reason to think it might have made its way here to Arkham, and while I do not believe for one moment that you or your Society would have anything to do with stolen goods…" A bit of buttering up, as well as heading off any possible offense, couldn't hurt. "… I have to believe that a man in your position, working to acquire artifacts of your own people's history, must hear things. Or at least know someone who could direct me further."

"I see. I'm afraid I don't recall seeing or hearing of anything lately that struck me as Eskimo. But perhaps if you were to describe it to me?"

"It's a stone." He shivered even as he spoke of it, such was the power it held in his mind, in the traditions and taboos of his family. "Blacker than ink, worked smooth on some sides, broken and rough on others. And on it are carved an array of symbols. They might be letters, but not of any alphabet I or my people have ever–"

"Oh! As a matter of fact, I *have* seen something like that."

"I… You *have*?" Billy almost staggered, so unexpected was the response.

"Indeed, yes. It's in the Miskatonic University antiquities collection. I'm afraid I don't remember what it was called, or what might have been written about it – my own focus has always been on Arkham's history, specifically – but I'm sure it…"

Billy was no longer listening. He'd been there. He'd been *right there!* So close, if only he hadn't led with the absolute wrong question.

Well, no sense fretting over it now. He would just have to–

"I'm sorry, what?" Something Peabody said had finally snagged his attention once more.

"I said, young man, that you might have some difficulty finding anyone who knows much about it, even on campus, as it's been there gathering dust for decades. Perhaps generations."

But that wasn't possible. The Forsythe Expedition had come to Itilleq, had betrayed their hospitality and stolen the *Ujaraanni*, less than ten years ago. He'd been in his adolescence, not yet privy to many of the conversations, but still he remembered the commotion, the exchange of stories, the sharing of meals.

The fury of his people and of nature when it was taken.

The grief of saying farewell to his father.

He found himself outside, having made thanks and polite farewells to Peabody that he couldn't recall. Something bizarre was happening here, was waiting for him at Miskatonic University. Even if it wasn't what he sought, the similarities couldn't be pure coincidence, could they? He must, at least, find some sort of clue as to where to go from here.

So yes, he would return to the school this very night.

Only this time, he wouldn't waste his time asking questions – or permission.

CHAPTER THREE

Sleet, falling in thick curtains, glittering blades that sliced skin and muscle and sinew; gaping red wounds that steamed in the cold. Rock blacker than the night sky; treacherous, slick and precarious on its own even before the layers of ice that froze atop it in invisible sheets.

Screams, distant, muffled by the blizzard yet echoing from the stone. Screams of agony. Screams of terror.

Screams of friends, he somehow knew, though he did not know their names, could not bring their faces to mind.

And shrieks of something else, something far less merciful than the indifferent winter. Something that slipped between the falling shards, skittered across the stone, slid into the mind and sluiced beneath every conscious thought…

It would be inaccurate to say Elliot awoke with a scream, for he was screaming long before the pounding of irritated students in the next room over finally roused him.

Nor was that scream a simple, wordless cry of fear. Better, by far, if it had been.

"Isslaach thkulkris, isslaach cheoshash…"

The same four words – and they were words, he recognized

them as words, though he hadn't the faintest idea of what they meant – that Chester had muttered to him, just the once, the day before he'd vanished. The same four words that had resounded in his mind ever since, over and over, murdering focus and devouring thought, every hour, every minute, until he'd been certain they must drive him mad.

Until he'd found…

He staggered from the bed, tripped over his feet, bruised an arm catching himself on a chair. With the wobble of a drunk he crossed the room, hands pressed futilely to his ears – as if he might somehow block out sounds coming from within – until, after what felt like a thousand uphill miles, he reached the squat desk jammed in the corner.

A framed photo of his parents and sister crashed to the floor as he fell against that desk, hauling open a drawer and grabbing for a particular half-crumpled sheet of paper covered in carefully copied French.

Shaking, he read it aloud.

Then a second time. And a third.

With each recitation, the maddening litany faded, though it never fell entirely silent, never faded completely from his consciousness.

In fact, it lingered more today than it had yesterday, nagging at him, making him fret. He'd have to go back to the source soon…

Elliot dropped into his chair, shivering with a chill born of both the icy dream and the sweat coating his brow. He stared, unseeing, at the dormitory room around him: several banners for Miskatonic's football and baseball teams, photos framed and unframed, a poster advertisement for Coca-Cola.

And, across the room, Chester's own bed and desk, neither of which had been used in weeks – unless one counted Elliot's worried snooping through his roommate's papers as "use."

He felt a bit guilty about that violation of his friend's privacy, but Elliot didn't truly regret it. He'd done it in hopes of finding the missing student – and if he hadn't, if he'd not located a few copies of French text, he might not have wound up looking through the same tomes in the Orne Library that Chester had.

Might not have found the mantra.

Although he was having more and more trouble convincing himself that "mantra" was the proper word for it. Elliot looked back at the paper in his hands.

He'd found it in the *Livre d'Ivon*. One of many ancient treatises Chester had said he'd perused in the Special Collection, it was a French translation of what purported to be a far older tome originally scribed in a language predating even Ancient Greek. The Special Collection was home to quite a few such works, though as they focused largely on obscure legend and superstition, or forgotten forms of the occult, he couldn't imagine what Chester might have been looking for.

The passage he himself had found – the mantra – was, based on Elliot's limited fluency in French, some sort of protective incantation. A ... spell.

Nonsense, of course. When reading it had first quieted the refrain in his mind that he'd somehow picked up from Chester's troubled mutterings, Elliot had, as a student of psychology, leapt to the more sensible conclusion that it had served him as a distraction, a mental exercise or meditation. Certainly that, and not some ancient sorcery, was why it had helped him focus and temporarily shut those other, more alien words away.

And yet… And yet…

If that were so, why did his handwritten replica only work for several days before its efficacy began to fade? Why did going back to read the original text in the *Livre d'Ivon* seem to "recharge" its ability to help him, as if it contained some genuine power that his poor copy couldn't completely capture?

And why did the period in which his copy was useful, the interval before he had to go back and re-peruse the original, seem to be gradually growing shorter?

Elliot had a potential answer to that last one: he was slowly losing his mind, developing some sort of genuine psychological condition of which his mental repetition of Chester's nonsense phrase was only the first symptom. It wasn't an answer he much cared for, but if he was genuinely considering magic to be the other alternative, surely that was further evidence.

It was only then, as his mind calmed, as the litany faded as much as he could hope it would, that Elliot realized something else. Something new.

There was another word in his head now, one he had never heard before and assumed must have come to him in some noxious dream. Not part of that terrible repetition. It made him queasy to think it, repulsed him on some reptilian level; but it didn't fit with the phrase, didn't threaten to drive him once more into paroxysms of confusion, didn't make him feel almost compelled to repeat it until his jaw was sore from clenching.

But he also couldn't forget it. It refused to fade with the rest of the dream from which it must certainly have come. It was, perhaps, another symptom of the lunacy he was now half-convinced he suffered, just a random collection of sounds coughed up by a diseased brain.

That didn't feel right either, though. Elliot realized he firmly believed, though he had no basis for such a belief, that it meant something, that word. That *sound*.

Tsocathra.

Elliot rose from the chair and began digging through his clothes. He wasn't getting back to sleep any time soon, that much was certain. He hadn't the focus to read, and he had no interest whatsoever in sitting in this room, staring at the walls or at the reminders of his missing friend. A walk in the cool night air carried risk of a reprimand, but the notion was too enticing to pass up. He threw on a pair of slacks, pulled on a shirt and sweater and made for the door.

For over an hour he simply wandered the Miskatonic campus, illuminated by fog-dampened lampposts and cloud-veiled moon. The cold breeze rustled his hair, forced his hands into pockets, but he wasn't nearly so uncomfortable that he would consider turning back. This, at least, felt natural; the occasional shiver a healthy response to the chill, not the feverish or claustrophobic remnant of nightmare.

He tried to keep quiet, his pace slow. The campus had only a handful of security men, so the odds of running into one were low, but not so slim that he could afford carelessness. Nor was the penalty for violating the nighttime curfew particularly severe, but Elliot was well aware his academic standing had suffered of late, due to his inability to concentrate, his frequent absenteeism, and the fact that, with Chester missing, he couldn't bring himself to care much about his studies. No sense adding more weight to what was an already troubled semester.

It gave him something else to worry over as he walked, in those few moments he wasn't preoccupied brooding over Chester.

Only once did he come vaguely close to being caught, but he heard the clunk of footsteps and saw the glow of lantern or flashlight in the fog with more than enough time to change direction. He cut swiftly across one of the lawns, skirted the edge of a fountain, and then realized precisely where he was.

Had he meant to come here, if only unconsciously, or was it pure coincidence? In either case, he knew the Orne Library now stood ahead of him and to the left, which meant off to the right...

The museum.

It hadn't been intended as such, initially. Rather, this was originally a private archive of the various historical and cultural relics acquired by the university over its many years. At some point, one of the deans had decided that it would be educational – as well as good publicity for fundraising efforts – to make those exhibits open to not just the faculty and select students, but to the public.

The building, which was not the first in which the collection had been housed, was large and imposing, with a great stone facade and ornate windows. Inside, Elliot knew, it more closely resembled a standard campus structure, with broad open halls surrounded by smaller side chambers and offices, as well as a massive semi-basement in which artifacts were examined and sometimes stored when they were deemed either too valuable, too fragile, or too uninteresting to warrant public display. As with the library's Special Collection, students normally required staff approval and supervision in order to study the basement's contents.

Of course, none of the museum was open to the public or the student body at this time of night, but that hadn't stopped either Chester or, on occasion, Elliot in the past. Elliot had been horrified, at first, when his roommate told him of his illicit visits, but Chester had only laughed at his concerns. When his project was complete, he'd insisted, nobody would care that he'd sneaked in to study one particular artifact after hours.

The caretaker and chief curator was the only man technically permitted within during off hours, but one particular security guard each night walked a beat that put him within sight of the entrance every few minutes. As was so often the case, tonight that duty fell to a young man named Jeremy Casterline, who had made quite a tidy sum over the past months – first by allowing Chester to conduct some of his research after hours, and then by allowing Elliot to follow up on what Chester had been doing.

Or, on occasion, to simply stand before one exhibit in particular and wonder what about it had so fascinated his friend. What Chester had seen in it that nobody else had.

Whether it was somehow related to whatever had become of him since.

A few dollars changed hands. A key rattled in a lock. Elliot darted through shadowed halls and darkened alcoves, ducking once into a closet when he mistook the creak of settling foundations for the footfalls of Mr Combs, the caretaker.

It was dim, but not dark. Occasional lights left on for Combs' convenience were more than sufficient for Elliot, who'd walked this path more than once. To the far end of the main hall, through one specific storage room with a door in the back, down the stairs to the half-underground lower level.

And from there, through smaller rooms, around tables, between dusty crates, to the enigmatic monument Chester had spoken of, on which most researchers had given up literal generations back, tucked away unseen because nobody much cared about it any longer.

The Lindegaard Stele.

Except tonight, when he'd casually walked most of that route and was but two rooms shy of his objective, a faint breeze where there ought not be one halted him in his tracks.

By now his sight had adjusted well to the gloom, and it took little effort to pinpoint the problem. There, above a stack of crates and a set of metal-frame shelves, one of the semi-basement's ground-level windows had been left ajar.

No, not "left." Forced. It hung loose from its frame, some of the braces snapped, open wider than it had been built to allow.

Wide enough to permit someone to sneak inside, perhaps.

Elliot froze, sweating despite the chill, struggling to think. He ought to go. Fetch help; Jeremy, or even the police. If not, then simply return to bed, let whatever was happening go on without him, as it would have on any other night.

Whatever he did, no matter what choices, he absolutely must *not* proceed on his own. God only knew what a thief or intruder, caught in the act, might do to a witness.

Yet that was precisely what Elliot Raslo did. This had been his way of connecting with the missing Chester, his own private ritual. That someone had the audacity to sully that, however unknowingly, made his blood pump fiercely with a rage he'd rarely felt.

Besides, might this not be related to Chester's disappearance, or that of Professor Polaski? So far as Elliot knew, nobody had broken into Miskatonic's antiquities collection in living memory. For it to happen now, with everything else going on, would certainly be a remarkable coincidence.

Casting about, Elliot spotted a collection of tools on one of the shelves. After wiping his palm dry on his trousers, he selected a small mallet, swung it a few times to get a feel for the heft, then crept onward.

Peeking around a doorframe two rooms further, he spotted the stele: an obelisk of glossy black stone, taller than any man. It had once been taller still, but the top portion – probably only a small bit, though nobody could say precisely how small – had broken away long before the thing came into the university's possession.

A piece that Chester had said was a major part of his ongoing project – and that he'd claimed to have located. He'd sworn his friend to secrecy on that score and, thus far, Elliot had kept his word. He worried about keeping information, any information, from the authorities, but he couldn't imagine how learning of that broken stone, however ancient and mysterious, could aid in their search.

One smooth side of the stele was covered almost entirely in what looked to be writing, but not in any alphabet Elliot – or any of the many scholars who had studied the thing in decades gone by – could identify, let alone pronounce or hope to translate. It was ancient, that much had been determined with certainty, but the carving of those symbols, letters, sigils, whatever they were, had been achieved with a degree of finesse even modern tools had difficulty matching.

A fascinating mystery indeed, when it had first been uncovered, but one that, after countless years of no progress whatsoever, had been pushed aside and forgotten.

Of more immediate concern was the mystery of who had broken into the basement and now stood, back to Elliot, staring up at the obelisk and muttering under his breath.

As stealthy as he could manage, Elliot crept closer, struggling to keep his breath even, steady, when every nerve prodded at him to gasp. Something about the man seemed familiar, and once the young student was near enough to better hear him, he knew why.

While the language wasn't one Elliot spoke, the voice was unmistakably the same he'd heard earlier that day in the library, raised in aggravation.

Except the muttering abruptly stopped and the intruder whirled, hands rising to defend himself. Elliot, despite all his efforts, must have made some sound that gave him away.

For several long breaths they sized each other up.

"What are you doing here, Mr Shiwak?" Elliot finally demanded, his own tension compelling him to break the silence.

Shiwak's attentions flickered briefly to the bludgeon in Elliot's hand, then settled on his face. "This doesn't concern you. You shouldn't be here."

"And you should? Has the university hired a new caretaker? They should have said."

The intruder's scowl deepened.

"This being your first day on the job," Elliot continued, bravado forcing him on lest he lose his nerve entirely, "I suppose we can forgive you forgetting your keys, but that window'll be costly to fix."

Shiwak, however, had sussed him out. "You're no caretaker, either, boy. Seems neither of us are supposed to be here. So why are you…?" He drew himself up stiff, a thought seeming to occur to him, and he gestured vaguely back at the stele. "This? You study this?"

"I–"

"The *Ujaraanni*! Have *you* got it?"

"The what?"

"The other piece!"

Elliot's gut clenched and drums pounded behind his eyes. The other piece? The man was after what Chester had found.

"You! You did something to him, didn't you? Where is he?!"

Shiwak blinked and took a step back, clearly unprepared for that reaction. "I don't know who–"

"Where is he, you son of a–?"

Elliot didn't even realize he'd charged the stranger, raised the mallet over his head to strike. He knew only that this man *must* be responsible for what had happened, that all his frustration, all his fear, finally had an outlet.

Except Shiwak was no longer there to be struck.

The stranger slipped aside like an eel and lashed out with the edge of his closed fist. The impact caught Elliot in the chest, driving the breath from his lungs, bruising flesh and slamming him painfully to the floor on his back. Shiwak leaned down, startlingly fast, smacking the hammer from Elliot's slackening grip even before he landed and sending it spinning across the darkened room.

"I'm unsure what you think I've done," Shiwak said, backing off rather than pressing his advantage. "But I *am* sure that this… Is not a good idea."

Elliot scrambled to his feet, slightly dazed, still driven by anger. No, it probably wasn't – especially as, from the floor, he'd seen something, a sheath or the like, hanging at the stranger's back, beneath his coat. If it was a weapon, however, the man hadn't gone for it yet, and Elliot wasn't planning to give him the chance, or to let him get away.

He'd been caught by surprise, that was all. While hardly an experienced brawler, Elliot practiced with Arkham's boxing club. He knew how to handle himself. Grimly, he advanced, fists raised.

"Don't do it, boy."

He did it.

With a cry, Elliot lunged, leading with a swift jab.

Shiwak caught his arm, twisted inside his reach, hammered the younger man's throat – not nearly at his full strength, which might well have killed, but enough to make Elliot gasp and gag. Still maintaining his grip, he dropped himself to the floor and rolled, slamming Elliot once again to his back and then winding up atop him, Elliot's arm bent painfully between them. Shiwak scissored his legs, immobilizing Elliot's own between his knees.

Agony coursed through him, but Elliot forced himself not to thrash. He wasn't sure how he'd wound up pinned this way, but he realized that if Shiwak so much as rolled, his trapped arm might well break.

"Are we done?" Shiwak asked him.

"Oh, you're quite done," someone else answered on Elliot's behalf.

CHAPTER FOUR

Daisy Walker, the librarian, stood shaded in the doorway, scarcely more than a silhouette. "Get off him, please."

Then, when Shiwak hesitated, "Miskatonic is currently missing both a student and a well-respected professor, and we've no idea what happened to them. In light of that, many of the staff who have reason to be on campus after nightfall have taken to arming ourselves. A derringer may not be the most fearsome weapon, Mr Shiwak, but I daresay you still shouldn't like to be shot by one."

With a faint grunt, he released Elliot from his grip and rose to his feet. Elliot scampered away, wincing, and then pulled himself upright as well.

"Miss Walker–" he began, worry and relief vying for space in his throat.

"Later, Mr Raslo, you will have ample opportunity to explain to me why you're here, and why I shouldn't report Mr Casterline for allowing you entry. In the meantime, kindly go find either him or Mr Combs and have him summon the police."

"Do you think it's safe to leave you alone with him, Miss

Walker?" Elliot asked, though in truth, the alternative – for him to stay while she went to fetch help – wasn't any more appealing.

"I'm sure I can manage," she said from her darkened doorway. "Now hurry along. The faster you call the police, the sooner they'll–"

"Wait!" Shiwak took a single step forward, not enough to be threatening but definitely attention-getting. Then, far more softly, "Please."

Even in the dark, Elliot sensed Daisy's scowl. "Mr Shiwak, you've broken into the university's archive, you're assaulted one of our students–"

"It was he who attacked me, actually." Then, before she could continue, "You're correct, though, I broke in. And if that means I must go with your police and face the consequences, so be it. But please, I ask you – I beg of you ..." Those last words sounded as if they twisted in his mouth, pridefully fighting to remain behind his lips, yet he forced them out. "Tell me something first. Tell me of this." He turned to gesture at the Lindegaard Stele. "Tell me where it comes from, how it came to be here, all you know of it. Do that, and I give you my word I'll wait for your police, and go peacefully when they arrive."

Daisy and Elliot both stared, bewildered by the bizarre request. The young student wondered if he might not be stalling for time, but it seemed an odd tactic, and he sounded so very sincere. Almost plaintive.

"You first," Daisy decided. She still hadn't come any nearer than the doorway. "Convince me of your intentions. Tell me why this matters to you."

Now it was Shiwak's turn to stare, but he took even less time to make up his mind than she had. "Very well." He sat in place, cross-legged, visibly calming himself. "It's been some time since I told the whole tale to anyone."

One final breath, almost a sigh.

"Itilleq, my home, consists of a very large extended family. My immediate kin, those related to us by marriage, those related to *them* by marriage, and so on. You might call it a 'clan,' though that word has no precise equivalent for us.

"And for so long as we have been a community – longer – it has been the task of one of our angakkut to stand guard over the *Ujaraanni*."

"Um?" Elliot asked in what was, perhaps, not his most eloquent or insightful question.

"The angakkut are wise men and women," Daisy said, her tone suggesting she was casting back to information read long ago. "Shamans. I've no idea whatsoever what the other word means."

Shiwak nodded. "Nor should you. The *Ujaraanni* is a wicked thing. A magnet for malevolent anersaapiluit – ah, 'evil spirits' would be a near enough translation, I suppose."

Elliot scoffed silently. More superstition.

And yet, thinking of the litany he had "caught" from Chester, and the incantation in the *Livre d'Ivon*, he couldn't quite dismiss the notion as readily as he once might.

A thought that, in turn, made him realize that the refrain in his head had grown even quieter in the past few moments than it earlier had been. That, once again, it appeared to be proximity to this peculiar newcomer that helped suppress it.

"It is a stone," Shiwak continued. "A large black stone, smooth on most sides but broken and jagged along the bottom." He nodded again as both members of his audience glanced openly at the stele behind him.

"Yes. The same stone. The same writing, that even the eldest and wisest angakkut could never read. They knew nothing of what it meant, only that it was dangerous.

"For generations, they kept it in a cave some distance from our homes. One angakkoq was chosen to watch over it, and he or she would do so for many years, even decades. Until exposure to the *Ujaraanni* became too much. It slowly drives those near it mad, you see. Perhaps something in the stone itself, perhaps the spirits it draws. Eventually, even the most powerful angakkoq would slip into dotage, unable to function. Then we would care for them, as long as they lived, and the next would take their place."

Elliot found himself drawn into the tale despite himself, his mistrust. "Why not get rid of it?"

"What would we do? Shatter it? Even if our tools proved up to the task, the angakkut worried that doing so might anger the spirits drawn to it, or that its own magics would lash out. Abandon it? Someone else might find it and be threatened. No, it was our sacred duty to ensure the *Ujaraanni* harmed none."

"But something happened," Daisy guessed. Like Elliot, she must have been fascinated, as she'd taken several steps further into the room.

Shiwak gave her a peculiar look, but continued. "Yes. Perhaps nine years ago, a number of travelers came to Itilleq. White men, Americans, and several Kalaallit guides from elsewhere in Greenland. The Forsythe Expedition."

"I've heard of them," Daisy told them. "They were said to have brought back several artifacts of great historical and anthropological... Oh."

"Yes," the Kalaaleq growled. "We didn't learn of their betrayal immediately. They spent several days with us, exchanging stories, trading supplies, learning some of our customs and beliefs. When they departed, we wished them well, told them we hoped the kindly toornat and anersaat would protect them from the hateful. And they repaid us by..."

He paused, choking down the fury and the hurt. "It was only when my cousin made a journey to bring food to the angakkoq guarding the *Ujaraanni*, something we did about twice a week, that we learned how greatly they'd deceived us.

"I don't believe they meant to kill old Palleq. But he was growing older, his health poor due to his isolation, and his mind beginning to go. Even the stress of being restrained might have proved too much. In either case, we found the angakkoq dead in the snow, and the *Ujaraanni* gone."

Daisy visibly flinched, and Elliot could guess why. The Forsythe Expedition had nothing to do with Miskatonic University, but it had likely been funded, at least in part, by a similar institution of academia – and Miskatonic, in its day, had sponsored similar expeditions. The librarian probably felt pangs of guilt, by association if nothing more, and perhaps wondered if any of those efforts had employed equally disturbing methods.

The rest of Shiwak's tale passed swiftly, in that darkened room, with the stele looming behind. His father, one of the community's traders, highly fluent in English and familiar with some of America's ways, had been chosen to go forth and seek out the *Ujaraanni*, to return it if he could, at the very least to learn where it had ended up. Shiwak spoke only briefly of the day his father left, but he remembered it well. The tightness in his voice was proof enough of that.

"For a time," he told them, "we would receive occasional messages detailing my father's progress. Or rather, his lack thereof. Then, about three years after he left, those messages stopped."

"Why?" Elliot asked.

It was Daisy, who had done the math in her head, who answered. "Because that would've been in 1917."

"Indeed," Shiwak said. "When your nation joined the 'Great War.'"

Silence, for a bit.

"I still don't know precisely what my father did for all that time. But it was a couple of years after the war ended that we received a traveler. A Canadian Inuk. He told us that my father had come to them, planning to sail eastward, but was badly injured and could travel no further. I set out immediately, to be by his side and to take up his quest if need be, but by the time I arrived, he had already died."

He spoke it so plainly, without inflection, that Elliot's own heart seized up. Such intense control could only mask an equally intense pain.

His father, Shiwak explained, had given his hosts information to pass along. He had learned, in his travels, that the Forsythe Expedition had been sponsored by the University of Virginia.

"It may not have been the institution itself," Daisy pointed out. "Such things are often financed by alumni, on their own or as part of one of the silly secret societies all these prestigious universities seem to sprout."

Shiwak waved a hand; the difference was irrelevant to him. In either case, the stone was no longer there when he traveled to Charlotte, but in asking around it didn't take him long to determine what had happened.

"The university suffered a theft from its collection. In May of last year, an object was brought to them for study. The 'Blackstone Meteor.'"

"I read about that," Elliot chimed in.

"Yes, much fuss was made over it. A fuss that also allowed one of their security guards, a Mr Addison, to conspire with several outsiders to steal and sell a number of goods. The *Ujaraanni* was among them."

"How did you find that out," Daisy asked him, "when apparently the university and the police couldn't?"

"Oh, they suspected Addison, even terminated his employment, but the authorities had no proof. To me, he confessed."

"Why would … ?"

Carefully, moving slowly to make it clear his movement was by no means a threat, Shiwak pulled back his coat and patted the sheathed blade.

"You didn't!"

"I didn't have to. Merely holding it to his face and making clear how strongly I felt about the matter proved sufficient. I did find it fascinating that he couldn't say precisely *why* he chose the *Ujaraanni* as one of his targets, when other possibilities would have been easier to move and just as valuable, if not more so. He said it 'just spoke to me.'

"In any event, he gave me the names of several men, who gave me the names of several more. And so, after a great deal of work, I found myself here with a handful of clues – only to discover this Lindegaard Stele, and a host of new questions."

What in God's name had Chester gotten himself caught up in? Elliot's thoughts whirled with questions of his own, but even had he been willing to interrupt, he couldn't decide where to start.

Daisy's brow furrowed – Elliot could see it, even in the gloom, and knew she wondered at many of the same things he did – but Shiwak spoke again before she could speak.

"On that topic, Miss Walker, I would like to apologize."

"Oh?"

"It only occurred to me tonight, as I was thinking over all of this, precisely why it might be so offensive – even, perhaps, damaging to one in your position – for me to have asked you publicly about a man like Pembroke. It was ill-considered and rude, and I'm sorry."

"Oh." She seemed uncertain what to do with such a statement from someone she'd clearly viewed as quite a rough man. "Well... Thank you."

Elliot, with the instincts of a student, actually half-raised a hand before remembering these were rather different than classroom circumstances. "I'm afraid I don't understand."

"Jebediah Pembroke," Daisy told him stiffly, "is one of Arkham's dealers in stolen goods. Antiquities in particular. Miskatonic has nothing to do with him or his kind, obviously, but tongues will wag. And as the new overseer of Special Collections..."

"Ah. Right."

"Now, please, Miss Walker," Shiwak said. "I've answered your question, and in rather great detail. It's your turn."

CHAPTER FIVE

It was, indeed, her turn. Daisy didn't ever seriously consider going back on her word. It would serve no purpose – nothing she could reveal was sensitive in any way – and while she wasn't opposed to a bit of falsehood where necessary, lying without need rubbed her, as a lover of knowledge, the wrong way.

"I'll tell you all I can," she said, "though I'm afraid you may find it largely unsatisfying."

Some of it, she remembered. The rest she found in the small bound stack of notes tucked away on a shelf near the Lindegaard Stele.

It had been found on the property of Helfred Lindegaard, a Danish magnate digging for cryolite in Greenland. "It was unearthed from deep within one of the mines," Daisy read, "near Ivigtût." She paused. "Is that anywhere at all near your home?"

"No. Itilleq is many hundreds of miles north of there."

"Hmm. Well, in any event, there are few specifics to speak of. None of the local Inuit made any claim to the stele…" She paused again, then added somewhat apologetically, "Or at least, so it was reported. Your own story makes me wonder, but I'm afraid there's nothing to indicate otherwise.

"Lindegaard had anthropologists study it, but none were able to translate it, nor connect it to any known historical cultures. He then sold it to an American collector of historical oddities, who also had it studied, with the same lack of success. He, in turn, willed it to Miskatonic University, where…" She trailed off with a shrug.

"Where it was studied," Shiwak guessed, "with no success."

"Just so. They finally gave up. Without being able to say much about it, and given how much space it would occupy, they decided it wasn't worth making a display. So they stuck it down here where it's essentially been gathering dust for a few generations. Every now and again, someone takes a stab at translation, or further study. All futile.

"Or," she added with a pointed look at Elliot, "perhaps all futile until now."

He turned his gaze toward his feet and remained silent.

"Elliot," she pushed, not unkindly, "I respect your desire to keep your friend's confidences, but the time for that is past. I made a point to never press him for information on his project, even though I can't remember the last time a student spent so much time studying books in the Special Collections. Most students wouldn't even have been *allowed* to, but he had several professors vouching for his efforts, and of course he volunteered a great deal of time toward helping around the library.

"I didn't press even when it became clear he was deliberately obscuring his tracks, asking for more books than he needed, so even though he was always accompanied by another librarian or myself, we couldn't guess at his goals."

Despite himself, Elliot nodded.

"But I do know, thanks to Mr Combs, that he spent much time here as well – and, given your own presence here tonight, I'm guessing that his studies weren't limited to the museum's proper hours."

"A… Are you going to report him for that?"

Daisy didn't know whether to smile or to sigh. Everything going on, the boy missing for so many weeks, and Elliot was still worried about Chester getting in trouble…

She settled for telling him, "I think we have larger concerns right now."

That, however, seemed to spark another question in Elliot's mind. He gingerly sat on a wooden crate, checking to ensure it would take his weight, and then asked, "How did you know to find *me* here tonight?"

Oh, because Abigail Foreman is obsessed with you, has been watching you, worried sick, since Chester vanished. Because she followed you tonight, saw you bribe the guard, and then – sneaking around the building to try to see what you were doing – spotted the broken window. And because she was also worried about getting someone in trouble when she should have been focused on his safety, and so came to get me from the library instead of running straight to security. God only knows what would have happened if I'd not been working late tonight!

But of course, she wasn't about to tell him a word of that. She *would* have a long and pointed talk with Abigail about proper behavior – for a young lady in general, and an infatuated one in particular – but that wasn't Elliot's business.

"Larger concerns," she said again. "Elliot, it's time to come clean – for Chester's own sake. He *was* studying the Lindegaard Stele, wasn't he?"

The boy's face twisted in a riot of conflicting emotions, but, finally, he nodded. Daisy, for all her talk of "larger concerns," felt a tingle of excitement. Mysterious secrets, hidden studies into ancient lore… This was like something out of her favorite novels!

Of course, many of those hadn't turned out so well for the characters involved, had they? Her excitement faded, replaced by the first stirrings of fear.

"Yes," Elliot admitted. "He swore he'd found a means of translating the stele. He never told me how, only that he'd made some connections nobody ever had before. He was certain this would cement his position in the archeological world, before he'd even graduated. And…" His eyes twitched in Shiwak's direction. "He said he'd located the missing part of it, too. But he never said where," he added quickly.

Shiwak growled something under his breath in what Daisy assumed was Kalaallisut. Switching back to English, he asked, "Who else knew of this?"

"A few of his professors knew part of it," Elliot answered slowly, almost unwillingly. "But I think only his chief advisor on the project had any real detail."

"Professor Polaski," Daisy guessed, irate. She understood why Elliot had kept silent, she truly did, but that knowledge might have helped convince the police that the two disappearances were connected.

"Yes."

She also, Daisy realized, felt more than a touch of annoyance at Chester and Polaski themselves. Damn them and their academic paranoia. Nobody else had access to the missing bit of the stele, nobody else was even *trying* to translate it any more. If they'd been less secretive about their whole endeavor from the start, if they'd let anyone know what they were working on, this might all have been avoided – or at least given the police more to go on.

"Who is this Polaski?" Shiwak asked.

But Elliot's suspicions had clearly resurfaced. "Why should I tell you? Why are we telling you *anything*?"

Daisy understood his reluctance, but she was growing impatient. "Elliot, I don't believe Mr Shiwak is our enemy here. I don't think he did anything to Chester."

"Why not?!"

"Because he probably wouldn't need to ask you about the *Ujaraanni* if he had. More to the point, because he had every opportunity to hurt you, and he chose not to."

Elliot's face flushed. "I didn't do *that* badly."

Shiwak's answering grin was perhaps meant to be kind, but he couldn't quite hide the amused pity beneath it.

"Yes, dear," Daisy said. "I'm afraid you did. And he was holding back." Then, when Elliot's expression turned stubborn, "Mr Shiwak, would you show him, please? Slowly," she added.

Using only three fingers, the Kalaaleq reached under his coat and drew his knife. It seemed to take forever.

The blade itself was well over a foot long, straight-backed, curved and thick along the edge. The handle appeared to be made of old ivory or bone, and was carved with an array of animalistic figures.

"My pana," he said. "Snow knife. Made to carve packed snow and ice for constructing igluvijait. So you can imagine what it does to flesh and bone."

The red in Elliot's face drained away as swiftly as it had gathered, leaving his cheeks pallid, as it finally dawned on him just how their scuffle could have gone if Shiwak had indeed wished to hurt him.

"You should also consider the fact," Shiwak continued, "that I have kept my promise to sit here peacefully, and wait for your police, despite the fact that Miss Walker is not, in fact, in any way armed."

Elliot stared at her, and now it was her turn to blush, if only lightly. *I thought I was doing so well.*

"What gave me away?"

"You gesture a great deal with your hands while you speak. Even in this light, I've had plenty of opportunity to see that you're holding only your purse, not a gun. But also your posture. I've had weapons held on me before by those not accustomed to their use. As best I can put it into words, you are… not relaxed, no, but the wrong sort of tense."

"Well. I appreciate the consideration, then."

Elliot seemed rather more bothered by the revelation – and by Shiwak's awareness of it – than Daisy was. "Do… Do we still run for the police?"

"I don't think fetching the police is in anyone's best interests here," Daisy said thoughtfully. Then, before Elliot could protest, "As I said, Mr Shiwak hasn't hurt anyone. His search is clearly connected to Chester's disappearance."

"Then the police should know about it!" Elliot protested.

Shiwak shook his head. "And they, of course, will listen to, and believe, my story. They will believe I had nothing to do with the missing men. They will ignore the convenient foreign suspect, on whom they can blame the whole thing, and continue to devote manpower to a search that has so far proved fruitless. No, boy, Miskatonic has been more welcoming to me than many American cities, but I'm not foolish enough to believe that would last one minute if I drew police attention."

Daisy wished it wasn't so, but he was right. Furthermore…

"It might not be in Chester's best interests, either," she pointed out. "You said he'd located the *Ujaraanni*. And Mr Shiwak traced it to Arkham through connections to men like Pembroke."

She saw the question in Elliot's countenance. He wasn't following, or perhaps didn't wish to follow.

"How do you suppose," she asked gently, "Chester got hold of such a thing? From what sort of people?"

Again Elliot looked away, fists clenching angrily. He doubtless wanted to protest, to defend his friend – and doubtless knew he could not.

"What will you do now, Mr Shiwak?" she asked.

The Kalaaleq sheathed his blade and rose to his feet, legs seeming simply to unfold beneath him. "Assuming you're not calling the police? Continue my search." He turned to gaze at the Lindegaard Stele. "Although I admit, if you can tell me nothing else about, ah… Chester?"

"Chester Hennessy, yes."

"About Chester's research, I'm not hopeful about my other options. There are others I can ask about Pembroke, but I don't imagine most will be any more willing to speak to me about him than you were, even if they do know something. And while I've no compunction about threatening thieves, I'm less eager to treat honest folk that way."

"To say nothing of less likely to get away with it," Elliot said.

"That, too, yes."

Daisy found herself chewing her lower lip in thought. She could tell him that it might just be possible for her to learn more of Jebediah Pembroke. Her declaration that nobody at Miskatonic would deal with such a man was based as much on hope as on fact, and she'd long suspected that several of the university's less scrupulous faculty members took the occasional legal shortcut with their acquisitions. She could ask. As both a historian and, she hoped, a good person, she felt for Shiwak, and he deserved the best chance of recovering his people's stolen relic.

But her first loyalty had to be to Miskatonic. If she *were* to learn something, and it ever got out why she had access to such information…

No. No, she couldn't risk it. Not just for the university, but also for Elliot. She couldn't expose him to the dangers and temptations of that world. Maybe, maybe if she could be *sure* it would help them find Chester Hennessy and Wilmott Polaski, she would feel differently. But not as things stood now.

"The Hennessys are in town," she said instead.

Shiwak turned. "Pardon?"

Damn. She shouldn't have said that. She'd just been so anxious to find *some* way to help, some lead to offer, other than Pembroke…

Too late now. He'd simply press the issue – either with her, or worse, out on his own – if she clammed up.

"Chester's parents. They live in Boston, but they're staying at the Excelsior Hotel while the Arkham police search for their son. I'm certain," she added swiftly, as Shiwak drew breath to speak, "that the police have already spoken to them, though.

And I can't imagine it's a topic they much care to discuss, let alone with a stranger. I was just thinking aloud." Maybe that would deter him from pursuing the matter.

"The police might not have known what to ask," Elliot said. "Whether he'd said anything to them about his research, about Mr Shiwak's stone. The Hennessys might know something important and not realize it."

"I still doubt they would speak to him," Daisy protested. *I really should not have said anything!*

"Probably not. But what if it's not just him?"

Daisy stared, horrified. Shiwak didn't appear much happier, though for very different reasons.

"My hunt is my own," he said. "And if I *were* to work with someone–"

Elliot didn't let him finish. "–It wouldn't be me. I know I made a… less than flattering first impression. But Chester is my best friend. If there's even a chance someone might find him where the police can't, I refuse to sit by and not at least try to help. And I know Arkham. I won't just be able to get you into places you couldn't go on your own, I can take you to ones you'd never even find."

Daisy's hands very nearly flailed in protest. "Elliot, this is a bad idea. It's dangerous. And you've already been ignoring your studies, missing classes…"

Shiwak, however, had grown thoughtful. "You might be of some help, at that. And I certainly cannot fault your loyalty to your friend."

Elliot smiled his way, then turned toward the fuming librarian. "I know all of that, Miss Walker. But I have to do this."

Shouting at him would do very little good, Daisy knew, but

she very much wanted to anyway. She understood his need to do something in the search for Chester – understood his feelings better than he would have wanted her to – but this was foolish. Dangerous. Now that she knew Shiwak wouldn't have hurt him, she wished she'd never interfered at all.

"Even if I accept that, what makes you think the Hennessys would speak to you either? So far as they're concerned, you're just another student. Even as their son's friend, you've nothing to offer them and no authority."

"No, I don't. But you would."

"I… what?"

"As a representative of Miskatonic, concerned that the police haven't found Chester yet – or Professor Polaski – you and some of the other faculty have taken it upon yourself to see what you can find, and you'd like to ask them a few–"

"No. Absolutely not."

Elliot's face fell, and it was probably only his pride – bolstered by Shiwak's presence – that kept him from crying. "Miss Walker, please. *Please.* What would this take, maybe a few days? No great loss, if it's a waste of time, but what if it's not? What if we find something?"

He stepped forward, hands out, beseeching. "Daisy…" His choice to use her given name was deliberate, she knew. He was too courteous to do it by accident. "They're out there somewhere. Chester, Professor Polaski. In God knows what sort of trouble."

Oh, don't do this to me…

"I… I'm no investigator, Elliot!"

"You're a researcher. Is that really any different? It's certainly closer than Mr Shiwak or I."

Daisy's shoulders slumped. This was wrong in a dozen different ways – but she could not deny to herself that, despite all her objections and all the logical arguments against it, it *felt* like the right thing to do. They just might be able to find something the police could not, they'd convinced her of that, and if she didn't try...

"All right," she sighed. "Meet me outside the library, tomorrow evening at five, and we'll see if we can do this without causing anyone – including ourselves – *too* much trouble."

"Mr Shiwak, have you found a place to stay? I can make some recommendations."

"Thank you, no, I have a place," Shiwak replied. "And if we'll be working together... call me Billy."

CHAPTER SIX

The faint drizzle soaking Arkham the following day might have dampened the Miskatonic campus, but it had no such effect on the gossip among its students – and, though they were perhaps more discreet about it, the faculty and staff.

The broken window at the museum had, of course, been discovered, leading a horrified Mr Combs to call in everyone who worked with the collection, and every professor who knew it well, for a frantic cataloging of relics and displays. As efforts proceeded throughout the day, everyone wondered if this was some isolated incident, or if indeed it was somehow linked to the missing professor and student.

When the caretaker announced, somewhat disbelievingly, that not one item was missing, nor even out of place, the peculiarity only served to exacerbate the spread of rumor, rather than to mitigate it.

Daisy Walker and Elliot Raslo spent the bulk of the day fiercely biting their tongues and, at least in the librarian's case, having more than a few second thoughts. *What are we doing?* Even if they learned something, and Daisy felt less confident about that possibility today than she had in the heat of the moment last night, she wasn't sure what they might do about it.

It didn't stop them, however, from meeting up with Billy Shiwak at the appointed time, to begin their unofficial, unauthorized and quite possibly unwise investigation.

Walking halfway across town would have been an unpleasant proposition even without the chill of the rain, so – given there were three of them to split the fare – Daisy suggested hailing a taxi, to which the others readily agreed. It didn't take long for one of the black-and-yellow Fords to come thumping and puffing their way; a great many drivers made a habit of lingering around the edges of campus toward the end of classroom hours.

How much of Elliot's and Billy's unspoken agreement to pile into the back seat, leaving the front for Daisy, was due to courtesy, and how much to both of them trying to avoid conversation with a stranger, she couldn't say. She wasn't especially inclined to thank them in either case.

"Where to, doll?" asked the slouch cap and thick mustache that seemed to make up the entirety of the cab driver.

"Excelsior Hotel, please."

An eyebrow rose at that, proving the man was not, in fact, all mustache and cap. "You sure?" His gaze flickered toward the back seat.

It might have been a comment on the fact that, while hardly dressed shabbily, neither of the men – nor Daisy herself, for that matter – wore clothes of quite the quality one might expect for guests of that establishment. It might have been doubt that Billy, in particular, would be entirely welcome there.

Or it just might have been coarse commentary on the notion of a young woman visiting a hotel accompanied by two men.

"Quite sure." She kept her smile, though it felt fragile as cheap peanut brittle. "We're visiting a guest." *Not that it's any of your business.*

"Hey, it's your dime." He arm-wrestled the car into gear, and they were off.

The rattle of the engine was sadly insufficient to keep the driver from beating his gums the entire drive, going on about how he rarely got to head out this way, making unwarranted comments about anyone they passed who looked the slightest bit out of the ordinary and sneaking (poorly and blatantly) constant glances at his blonde passenger. Throughout it all, Daisy maintained her Librarian Voice, answering all questions with a formal courtesy, while inwardly she allowed herself many a vision of throttling the man – possibly followed by Elliot and Billy, each of whom gazed out his respective window and seemed utterly unaware of the cloud of discontent filling the vehicle.

The combination of unwanted conversation and the constant bumping of narrow tires over Arkham's roads – only some of which had been paved with automobiles in mind, the rest consisting of old cobbles – had Daisy's head aching by the time they finally arrived. With rather less poise than was her wont, she gathered coins from the others, practically dropped them in the driver's lap and slammed the car door behind her.

Then, standing on the sidewalk, light rain falling on their faces and pedestrians irritably shuffling around them, the trio looked up at the massive edifice that was the Excelsior.

One of Arkham's tallest structures, it boasted a stone facade intended to make it appear far older and more historic than its relatively recent construction. Ionic pillars, glass-and-brass revolving door, a doorman in formal coat and cap, all shouted lustily to all and sundry that this was a place of class, refinement and, of course, no small expense.

Yet the Excelsior boasted that it made the amenities of wealth available to the middle class as well, making some of its rooms and services more affordable than its appearance might suggest. The result was a place considered unnecessarily hoity-toity by some, while far too welcoming to those of "lower status" by others.

Still it remained popular, as it was one of the best Arkham had to offer.

Daisy politely declined assistance from the doorman, hoped Billy either wouldn't notice or wouldn't react to the man's disdainful sneer and pushed her way through the revolving door.

The lobby of the Excelsior was a veritable cavern, boasting broadly spaced columns, as well as lush pathways of carpet across an expanse of marble floor. People clad in their "Sunday best," or outfits more formal still, wandered this way and that, sat about the various tables in elegant leather chairs or spoke with the staff at the counter. Rich cigar smoke filled the air, and what had once been a bar along one wall now, in these days of Prohibition, served coffees and, oddly enough, deli sandwiches.

And every last patron, or so it felt, stopped to glower at the new arrivals.

A few of the guests were not white, though they were a minority. A few of the guests were underdressed, though they, too, were a minority.

None were both.

Billy's expression hadn't changed, but Daisy, for all that she'd known him less than a day, could sense his hackles rising. Uncomfortable as the unwanted attention made her, she couldn't imagine what he must feel like, regularly drawing that sort of scrutiny.

Worse, their reaction had apparently reminded Elliot of something he previously hadn't thought of. Discomfort splashed across his face, as though it had fallen on him along with the drizzle outside, he said, "It's, uh, it's just occurred to me…"

"Yes?" Daisy prompted.

"Chester's told me a bit about his parents. They're, um, old-fashioned. In their attitudes."

He directed that last remark pointedly at Billy, flushing as he spoke.

"I'm sorry," he added. He looked like he wanted to fold in on himself.

"This is my search," Billy began, voice low but hot. "If you think I'm going to sit any of it out–"

Daisy wanted to agree with him. It was unfair, unjust. Instead, she forced her anger down and laid a hand on his arm. "What good will it do if they won't speak to us? We're in this together. Elliot and I will tell you anything and everything we learn. I give you my word."

"And mine," Elliot added, drawing himself up to his full height.

Billy glared, turned away and paced several steps, then back, fists clenched.

"All right." It clearly took everything he had to keep from erupting, but he was no fool. "I'll trust you. I'll wait."

Daisy squeezed his arm, then she and Elliot moved to the desk to ask after the Hennessys' room number.

Billy watched, first as they spoke to the concierge, and then made for the elevator. The mechanical contraption swallowed them up, and only then did he turn, casting about for a place to sit.

He met a veritable sea of hostile, or at least suspicious, expressions. Without his local companions, loitering here alone, he stood out more than ever. Scowling, he crossed his arms, stubbornly planting himself, silently daring anyone to say anything.

It was a pose he retained until people began literally drifting away from him, to sit at a greater remove. Until two of the staff began whispering to one another behind the welcome desk, one of them allowing his hand to drift ever nearer the phone hanging on the wall behind them.

It might not be related to him. And if it was, it might not be the police the man intended to call. Still, that wasn't a risk Billy was prepared to take, not a hassle he remotely needed.

Muttering under his breath in Kalaallisut, he made for the revolving door to continue his wait outside.

The drizzle hadn't stopped, but thankfully the Excelsior boasted multiple canvas awnings. Even distancing himself from the front door, he could at the very least keep himself relatively dry. And while he drew occasional sidelong glances here as well, they were less frequent – not everyone walking by was nearly so parochial as the bulk of the hotel's clientele – and, as he was no longer "invading" an exclusive space, less openly hostile.

He wanted to go home.

Hands in his coat pockets, he leaned back against the stone wall, watching the sopping city moving around him, snickering occasionally at peoples' shivers or expressions of discomfort – nobody here had the *slightest* notion of what "cold" truly meant – until …

Billy Shiwak had grown up a hunter, first and foremost, and he had learned to keep alert, to heed the world and its creatures and its spirits, to *notice*. This time he wasn't certain, at first, what had drawn that notice, but he knew far better than to ignore it.

A car sat parked down the street, one of many. He knew almost nothing of automobiles, their makes or models. He could only say this one was of a different sort than the taxi that had brought them here; longer where the taxi had been squat, green instead of black and yellow.

Nothing about it should have drawn his attention.

The same held true for the driver. A white man in a tan suit and hat. He seemed to be watching Billy, true, but so were many others. So what...?

Wait. Had he seen them before?

He had spent the ride here from Miskatonic staring out the window. Ignoring the blather from up front with which the driver pestered Daisy Walker; ignoring, too, the rattle of the engine and the shake of the vehicle, sensations which discomfited him more than he'd care to admit. Billy wasn't afraid of technologies unknown to Itilleq, but he didn't entirely trust them, didn't care to be cooped up inside them. Give him a sled and a team of dogs over any clattering contraption.

But in his glancing about, his casual perusal of Arkham as it flowed past, had he seen this precise green car, with this man behind the wheel? Was this stranger following him, or one of his new companions?

He couldn't say for certain – most of these white folks looked alike – but that the thought had even occurred to him made him think he was onto something.

It might have been wiser to ignore the man, pretend he hadn't noticed him. To wait until Elliot and Daisy returned, and see if the green car continued to show up wherever they went next. Billy was irate, however, frustrated, and patience was not currently an enticing option.

Instead, he moved down the street, not straight toward the potential watcher but in that general direction.

At first, the stranger didn't react. He continued watching, but his attention appeared casual, just a local curiously observing an obvious foreigner wandering by. When Billy finally drew near, however, and abruptly turned to make his way directly toward him, the man immediately fired up the ignition and pulled into traffic.

Coughing and growling, the car took long enough getting up to speed that Billy could have caught it in a sudden sprint, but then what? Throw open the door and climb inside? Scare the wits out of someone who, probably as not, had done nothing wrong, had merely panicked at a stranger's sudden approach?

He watched the car merge into traffic and fade away into the rainy twilight.

Probably nothing, anyway, he told himself as he wandered back toward the hotel, and his comfortable waiting spot beneath the awning. *You're letting this unpleasant city get to you.*

Even as he leaned back against the stone facade of the Excelsior, however, he wasn't certain he believed it.

In the years they'd known one another, Elliot had seen Chester truly angry on only a handful of occasions. While he wasn't quite so courteous as Elliot himself strived to be, and was quite a bit more garrulous, his jests a bit rougher and his observations more pointed, Chester remained, for the most part, reasonably polite. Rarely crude, rarely boorish.

In those rare circumstances when he had become truly heated, however, he'd shown a tendency toward not merely disrespectfulness but genuine cruelty. It was a side of him Elliot strenuously disliked, and had hoped, with some effort, to coax him away from.

Tonight, after meeting Chester's parents, Elliot at least had a much better notion of where that side of his friend came from.

In the long walk from the elevator, down hallways adorned with thick carpeting and gold-patterned wallpaper, he and Daisy had decided that she, as the proper representative of the university, would do most of the talking. He, they would explain, had come along as Chester's best friend, just in case a line of discussion sparked additional questions in him that Daisy wouldn't think to ask.

When he answered their knock, however, the look of angry disdain Mr Hennessy had greeted them with had driven most potential questions from Elliot's mind.

The man had Chester's deep brown hair, and a shaggy, old-fashioned mustache to Chester's neat, pencil-thin one, but otherwise they didn't look terribly much alike beyond basic build. It was clearly Mrs Hennessy after whom Chester had taken, with her angular features. She reclined in one of the sitting room's brightly upholstered chairs, a cup of tea upon the table at her side, and the glare she cast him, framed within red hair tied severely back behind her head, was even less friendly than her husband's.

"Good evening," Daisy began. "My name is Miss Walker, from Miskatonic University. This is Mr Raslo, one of our students. We–"

"You told us all this when you called up from the lobby," Mr Hennessy barked, lowering himself into a chair across the room from his wife – and not, Elliot noted sourly, asking his guests to do the same. "What news?"

"Ah…" Elliot swore he could see Daisy pulling her "cloak of librarian" around herself, shifting into formal and proper mode. While neither of them had expected the Hennessys to be in a jolly mood, given the circumstances, this was not the welcome Elliot had anticipated. "We've no new information to speak of, I'm afraid. We–"

"Then what the hell are you here for?!" Mr Hennessy exploded right back out of his chair, finger aimed like a weapon. "Why are you wasting our time?"

Daisy drew breath to answer, but now that he'd begun, Chester's father wasn't about to wind down again so readily. "This *town*." He practically spat. "The Arkham police. Useless fools, every last one of them. 'No news.' It's the same every time we speak to them, when we can speak to them at all, when they aren't more concerned in avoiding our questions than in *finding our son*. He's only been missing for coming up on two months now."

"They don't care," his wife snapped in turn. "Nobody cares. Nobody who *matters*."

Elliot recoiled at the implied insult, very nearly snapped something impolite, but thankfully, Daisy answered faster than he could.

"We agree," she told them. "The Arkham police are overworked and overwhelmed, particularly now." She didn't specify what she meant; it wasn't necessary. The memories of the worldwide Spanish Flu epidemic were less than half a decade old. So far, the fever near the Merchant District hadn't spread, and the Arkham municipal government was spending most of their resources, the police included, on keeping it that way. "They can't focus on finding your son, not to the degree he deserves. That's why we're here. The university is concerned–"

"The university." Mr Hennessy stalked across the room to stand by the window. His furious expression, softened only marginally by fear and sorrow, glared back at them from his reflection in the darkening, rain-spattered glass. "For all the good you've done him. We already *had* someone from Miskatonic asking after him, weeks ago. One of your professors. And what did that accomplish? What answers has *he* come up with?"

Elliot felt a small charge run through him. If nothing else, that was confirmation of what everyone on campus had already figured: Wilmott Polaski's disappearance was, indeed, connected to Chester's own.

"We don't know what Professor Polaski might have found," Daisy told them with a growing frown. "He's disappeared, too. I would have thought the police had told you that."

Their host waved a dismissive hand. "They might have mentioned it." He turned back their way, shaking his head. "I should have sent Chester to Harvard, but no. Miskatonic had the better ancient languages program." He scoffed. "Where's the prestige in that?"

"It's what he loved," Chester's mother protested from her chair. "What made him happy."

"It was stupid. Childish. He should have devoted himself to something that *matters*."

This was threatening to blossom into what was clearly an old argument – but at least the topic had come up. "Did Chester ever talk to you about his work?" Elliot asked. "Particularly his current project? Did he mention his research or... or a... black stone...?"

He wanted to duck back behind Daisy, to get away from the twin murderous expressions now turned his way. Oh, he'd headed off their argument, all right – by giving them both something new on which to focus their frustrations.

"Chester didn't tell us much about his studies," Mrs Hennessy told him, her words nearly leaving a wake of frost between them on the carpet. Her glare darted briefly back toward her husband, blaming him for their son's reticence, but when it settled back on Elliot it was more hostile still. "I expect you enticed him to talk to *you* about such things far more than anyone else, Mr Raslo."

Her obvious hatred nearly sent him reeling, and he didn't for the life of him understand why, where it came from. Daisy took a step nearer to him, and he found himself grateful for even that gesture.

Possibly as much to draw their attention from Elliot as anything else, she took it upon herself to ask the next question. "I'm certain the police must have asked this already, but is there any other family Chester might have gone to? Any relatives you might–?"

"No." If anything, the missing young man's father grew even angrier at the change in topic. "No, there's nobody. We have no other family. It's just the three..." He stumbled on that, as if struck again by the very real possibility that he might have to revise his count. "...just the three of us."

His wife opened her mouth as if to speak, then decided

against it, pressing her lips firmly together. To comfort him in his obvious distress, despite the sharp mood and harsh words of a moment before? Elliot wasn't sure. He almost had the sense there had been something else she'd wanted to add…

It was, instead, Mr Hennessy who spoke again, after taking a few heartbeats to recover himself. "I think you had better leave now."

Daisy clearly agreed. "Yes, we've taken up enough of your time. Thank you for seeing us. We'll let you know if we learn anything." She started toward the door.

For his own part, Elliot wasn't certain they'd learned everything they could from Chester's parents – they'd not really learned anything at all! – but hadn't the slightest notion how to ask any further questions in the face of such obvious unexplained hostility. No, Daisy had the right idea. It was time to go.

Still, his own sense of decorum, his deep concern for Chester and his sympathy for what his parents must be going through, wouldn't permit him to simply depart without another word.

Would that he had.

"Mr and Mrs Hennessy, I… I know how worried you must be. I'm worried too. We care about Chester, and I promise you I don't intend to stop until–"

"Don't you dare." Mrs Hennessy spat her words, her hatred, as if they were venom. Even in rising finally from her chair, she seemed almost, snake-like, to uncoil. "He told us all about you, Mr Raslo. You were supposed to be his friend. I know he told you what he was doing. You could have stopped him at any time. Whatever trouble he's in is because of you!"

The blood drained from Elliot's face so swiftly he felt on the verge of passing out. His feet took root in the carpet of the fancy suite. "Wh– What…? It was a *research project*! I didn't know he was in any danger. I–"

"You should have! I know he was sneaking around behind his professors' backs, getting up to all sorts of things, and you let it go on. And if… *when* he returns home, I promise you I intend to make certain he has nothing more to do with Miskatonic University, or any of his so-called *friends*. This is your fault. *Yours!*"

The room blurred. The world tilted. It took an iron grip, absolutely everything Elliot had, not to fall to his knees and empty his stomach. He didn't recall moving, only knew that he was passing through the door when he slammed a shoulder into the frame.

Later, it might bruise. In the moment, it only barely registered.

Mrs Hennessy was angry.

Is she right?

Grieving. Lashing out. It didn't mean anything.

Is she right?

Whatever had happened to Chester, it wasn't his fault. It *wasn't*.

Oh, God, is she right?

Behind him, he heard Daisy bidding the Hennessys good day in a tone icier than any Chester's mother had managed, than he had known she was capable of. And then he heard her in the hall behind him, calling out his name.

He didn't halt. If he did, he wouldn't start again.

Step by step, the hall swaying like a rope bridge beneath him, he staggered on. He should have reached the elevator by now, shouldn't he? He should…

He'd turned the wrong way upon leaving the room, gone right instead of left. He realized it now only because the door to the stairs appeared before him. It took him four tries to read the sign through welling eyes.

He pushed through it, stumbled down two steps, three, and finally stopped, clinging to the bannister.

He couldn't go any further. However embarrassing, however unmanly, the tears began to fall.

Then Daisy was behind him, folding him in her arms. "That witch! Elliot, I'm sorry. I'm so sorry."

He turned, face pressed to her shoulder, and she held him while he sobbed as though his world had ended.

CHAPTER SEVEN

Not even two full days ago, it had taken every argument young Elliot Raslo could muster to convince her to take any part whatsoever in the investigation on which he and Billy Shiwak intended to embark.

So how is it, Daisy wondered irritably as she maneuvered through the early bustling traffic that marked the start of Arkham's business day, *that I'm the only one doing any investigating this morning?*

It wasn't a fair question, seeing as how it had been her own suggestion that she make these first excursions alone. Still, even if she'd have admitted it to nobody else, she was feeling out of her depth and not a little bit put upon to be the one running all over town while the others waited. At least Dr Armitage had been happy to approve her sudden request for time off, and the rain had briefly ceased, even if the weather remained unseasonably chilly, the sky streaked with gray as if by a frustrated painter.

Today, she intended to ask questions of any number of strangers, questions that – even if they accepted her implication that she spoke on behalf of the university – many might feel disinclined to answer. It was why she'd recommended, however reluctantly, that Billy allow her to handle these errands, and why he, with equal reluctance, had agreed. These folks were going to be hesitant enough as it was; they might react poorly indeed to an obvious outsider.

As for Elliot, well… He seemed barely there at all this morning. Last night's emotional wound had sent him spiraling back into the exhaustion and preoccupation he'd suffered since Chester's disappearance. Daisy was sure there was more to it than worry, that something was genuinely wrong with the young man, but he hadn't confided any such thing, and she wasn't ready to press.

All of which left her, but just because it was logical for her to lead the investigation didn't mean she had to like it. Holmes or Dupin she was not.

The bulk of the day was spent in near-constant motion. Occasionally by taxi, when crossing much of the city was necessary, but mostly on foot, wandering from this place to that, one interview to another.

She decided to get Saint Mary's out of the way first. Not only did she anticipate learning nothing of use, but she thought this, of all their ideas, was the one where she was most probably retracing steps the police had already taken.

The hospital seemed a drab, depressing place, though how much was the building and how much her own dislike of such places she couldn't say. She spent almost an hour sitting in the lobby, staring at the slightly yellowing walls, watching white-coated doctors and white-uniformed nurses escorting patients, talking to relatives, wheeling gurneys, and so forth. Every now and again an ambulance crew delivered emergency cases, and then the relative quiet was broken by a mad bustle of activity.

Given their own uniforms, she couldn't help but picture those ambulance attendants, disrespectful as it might be, as milkmen delivering particularly large and uncooperative bottles.

It was, finally, Dr Regensteiner, Saint Mary's old and perennially exhausted chief physician, who finally deigned to take a few moments out of his busy schedule to address her queries.

"As I told the police some time ago, Miss Walker," he scolded from behind a white beard held to his face entirely by the folds of his wrinkles, "no, Chester Hennessy is not currently a patient at Saint Mary's. And if you'd checked with them before coming here, you could have avoided wasting both your time and mine."

Daisy kept her professional smile plastered to her face. "Has he, perhaps, been a patient here in the recent past, then? Or has he sought treatment for any particular malady? You must understand, any information at all could lead us to–"

"Any such information at all," Regensteiner interrupted, "would certainly be inappropriate to share without his consent, or at least that of his family. Whatever interest Miskatonic may have in his whereabouts, or whatever your reasons for not leaving this to the authorities, doesn't change that."

"But, Doctor–"

"Now, unless you *have* written consent from the family, or you're suddenly empowered to make a legally binding police request, I will bid you good day. I have a hospital full of patients, to say nothing of influenza raging through the Merchant District slums, thank you very much."

He swept away, coat billowing like a melodramatic stage cape, before he'd even finished speaking, leaving Daisy inwardly seething in his wake.

Daisy's visit to the offices of Joe Diamond, Arkham's most famous private detective, was equally fruitless if, at least, less unpleasant. Frustrated as they were, she'd thought that Chester's parents – and she still almost shook with fury when she thought of them and their treatment of Elliot – might have hired the man to hunt for their son. If so, Daisy hoped she might be able to wheedle a bit of information out of him. But ...

"I'm afraid Mr Diamond ain't here." Daisy stood before the desk in a cramped but surprisingly personable outer office, speaking to a brunette in a dress surprisingly fashionable for a receptionist. "I can take down a message, or if you want to share some details, I can pass it along when he gets back, see if it's a job he's interested in."

"I, ah, didn't want to hire him, actually. I wanted to find out if he's already *on* a case."

The secretary's nose did a bit of a twitch, almost retracting into her face. "I don't share the boss's beeswax, lady."

"No, I know." She sighed, perhaps a tad theatrically. "Someone very important to me is missing. I just figured, if he was on the job, maybe he'd found something out he could tell me."

Nothing for a moment, then the other woman's expression loosened ever so slightly. "Look, I can spill this much. Mr Diamond's over in Salem, has been for a few weeks. And yeah, it's a missin' person, but it's a guy from out that way. So unless your friend lives in Salem ... ?"

Daisy shook her head. "Arkhamite. A student at Miskatonic."

"Then no. Got no cases like that. Sorry."

Daisy thanked her, left her a card in case Diamond somehow found himself on the case once he returned and cared to share notes, and then once more went on her way.

Those two stops might have been useless, but they were also the easy ones. The next? Daisy was going to have to ask, or at least dance around the edges of, precisely the same sorts of questions that had gotten her hackles up when Billy first approached her. And while these were no proud, centuries-old institutions to be threatened by ill rumor, nobody wanted to be caught up in possible scandal.

Especially not where their livelihoods were involved.

Uptown, not terribly far from Saint Mary's hospital, sat Ye Olde Magick Shoppe, a cramped establishment spilling over with purported eldritch writings, mystical reagents, and the occasional relic or talisman. Clear across Arkham, in the Northside district, was the Curiositie Shoppe, a larger storefront specializing in the unusual, the intriguing and the historical; odds and ends from all corners and all times.

Polar opposites in terms of owners and their attitudes. Miriam Beecher, a venerable and gray-haired woman wearing fashionable blouse and slacks, but enough antique jewelry to supply an entire stage production, was notorious for taking her "magic" seriously indeed. Walk into her store with the intent of purchasing "tricks" or mastering illusions, or offer up the slightest hint that her grimoires were anything but genuine, and one could expect only disdain in return.

Oliver Thomas, however, a British expatriate, saw his curiosities solely as product. So long as they looked interesting enough to sell, the man couldn't appear to care less what one thought of them, and the only "magic" that mattered to him took the form of hard currency.

Both shops, however, marked two of the most likely locations – alongside the Historical Society and Miskatonic's own collections – where the general public might cross over into the world of historical or anthropological oddities, to say nothing of the obscure religious sects that cropped up now and then, that always seemed to ebb and flow beneath the civilized skin of Arkham.

Surrounded by the scents of dried herbs and musty old books that permeated Ye Olde Magick Shoppe, and then the aged dusty atmosphere of the Curiositie Shoppe, Daisy asked her questions. And in both locations, with both proprietors of such wildly differing attitudes and beliefs, the conversation ran much the same way.

"Yes, indeed," Beecher told her, earrings and bracelets jingling like distant church bells. "Mr Hennessy was here, and more than once."

Thomas, too, admitted as much. "Don't normally talk about my customers, you understand. Keeping their business private's part of mine, right? But what with him gone missing and all… Yeah, Mr Hennessy was here, quite regularly."

"I'm afraid I couldn't begin to tell you what he might have been seeking," the old woman continued. "He looked through several of my books, even bought a few. Nothing of any note or significance, mostly general overviews. Initiate material. The bulk of his interest lay in my selection of talismans and objects of power, though. He was looking for something specific, but he never saw fit to tell me what it might be."

"Nah, love, couldn't say what he was after. Every few weeks, he'd come in, spend time looking over the shelves, as if he was waiting for something specific to turn up. Never did, though. Even let him look in the back room once, where I keep the *really* good stuff. Don't usually do that for blokes his age, but he'd been in enough... Still didn't have whatever he wanted, though, and he never told me what that was."

Both shopkeepers agreed that Chester had finally stopped coming in a few weeks before they'd heard about his disappearance, and both suspected that was because he'd finally found whatever he was hunting.

No real surprises, then. Given his efforts, Daisy would have been rather shocked had Chester *not* paid visits to either establishment. Hoping to learn more, she'd then asked both Beecher and Thomas about the *Ujaraanni*, since Billy wasn't here to ask himself. Unfortunately, both denied having ever come across such a thing.

And, as both had grown stiffly reticent when Daisy asked if they knew of anyone who might trade in such materials under the table, insisting that their establishments were entirely proper and above board, she'd chosen not to pursue any further questioning about Jebediah Pembroke or his ilk.

Finally, she asked both proprietors if they knew of any other dealers or private collectors – legitimate, of course – who might trade in such artifacts, and thus might have received a visit from Chester, or have heard of something like the black stone she sought. Both of them had provided her with a list.

"This doesn't represent all my clientele, of course," Beecher clarified. "That wouldn't be proper."

"This is just the ones who've given permission," Thomas told her. "Y'know, said I should feel free to pass their names along to anyone looking to buy or sell the sort of goods they're interested in."

It was, at least, a start, and Daisy thanked each of them, hopeful and heartened to have acquired *something,* no matter how she might have preferred a more comprehensive listing. She found herself an open table at a small café; no Velma's Diner, this little place, but she couldn't face any unnecessary walking after all the travel she'd done today. There she spread out the handwritten notes while waiting on the coffee and pie she'd ordered in lieu of a proper luncheon.

Most of the names on each list were, as best she could determine, just random citizens of Arkham with a bit more money and a bit more historical, or perhaps religious, interest than most. A few were on both lists, and it was those she found most interesting:

Dr Armitage and Mr Combs, as well as several others from the staff and faculty at Miskatonic. No surprise there.

Mr Peabody and a few other members of the Historical Society. Again, no surprise.

A handful of Arkham's wealthy, whom she knew – particularly as some were frequent visitors to the Orne Library or the museum – as either students of history or dabblers in the esoteric and the occult. One name, a Victoria McCutcheon, drew a moue of personal distaste.

Carl Sanford, leader of the local Twilight Lodge, New England's very own Freemasons-esque elite club and fraternal order. She'd have been surprised *not* to see his name on both lists.

And at the bottom of each, where one might anticipate finding the newest clients, one Hyrum Lafayette-Moses.

Daisy frowned over her newly delivered rhubarb pie. It would be the height of arrogance to assume she ought to know of every collector or student in Arkham, but this one not only rang no bells whatsoever, it didn't even strike her as local. "Lafayette-Moses" sounded, to her ear, far more like a Southern family name than one likely to be found in Massachusetts.

Perhaps not much of a lead by itself, but combined with the fact that he appeared to be a new customer to both locations... Well, Daisy was coming to distrust coincidence.

A quick visit to the rear of the café, and the payphones located there, and she had her answer, straight from Dr Armitage himself – who was also good enough not to inquire as to why she was asking such questions, particularly on a day off.

Lafayette-Moses, he'd explained, was an old-money gentleman from Louisiana with a fascination for all materials both historical and purportedly mystical. Armitage knew who the man was because he'd visited the Orne Library on several previous visits to Arkham. Apparently he'd even attempted to buy a few of the university's rarest books. Unsuccessfully, of course.

Armitage didn't know for sure if Lafayette-Moses was back in Arkham now, but Daisy found herself assuming he was, or at least had been not long ago. That his name appeared on the lists meant he'd been in contact with both shops, and, again, its place at the bottom suggested said contact had been recent.

Which meant his visit might well have overlapped with Chester's efforts on his project. Perhaps even his disappearance.

Another "coincidence." Nothing she'd found was remotely sufficient to assume Mr Lafayette-Moses was guilty of any wrongdoing, but she definitely wanted to learn more of him.

Daisy considered the matter as she left the café to rejoin the constant pedestrian traffic, pleased to have made some progress, fretting that it might be insufficient or leading her in the wrong direction. She had no idea how to find or to contact the man, nor did she know for certain that he'd done anything other than patronize the same establishments as the missing student. Nothing she and the others could take to the police, but she would certainly mention it to Billy and Elliot as a name they ought to keep in mind.

And speaking of Billy and Elliot...

CHAPTER EIGHT

Afternoon now, moving rapidly toward evening. As the more sensitive of the day's tasks were complete, Daisy had returned to campus to fetch her companions.

Billy, who'd spent his day waiting around Ma's Boarding House, was raring to go. They'd all agreed the town's train station was a potential source of clues, and that was a part of the investigation in which he could actually participate. Though his life as a hunter had taught him patience, Daisy was sure anyone else would be all but vibrating in their shoes.

Elliot was another matter.

His shirt was wrinkled beneath his coat, his hair a tangle, and the bags under his eyes deep and dark as the inside of a pocket. How much of his condition was due to yesterday's unpleasantness and how much his ongoing issues, she couldn't say. When she'd proposed that she and Billy go off on their own, however, and leave him to get more rest, he'd all but barked at the suggestion.

All three of them headed out, then, though more than once she questioned that decision. On occasion, throughout the remainder of the day, she heard Elliot muttering under his breath in what sounded like French, a strange mantra against some nameless evil, the precise details of which she could never fully make out.

It made her worry for him, but, more than that, it made her afraid for reasons she could not begin to name.

As Daisy didn't want the taxi driver to overhear, she'd filled them in on all she'd learned, or failed to learn, before and after the ride across town. When she finally finished, evening had well and truly arrived, and they stood in a small cluster before their destination.

The train station resembled nothing so much as a fortress, looming over the winding currents of the Miskatonic River and the iron pathways that were Arkham's greatest connection to the world beyond. The stone was old, worn, particularly on the two great towers that flanked the rails, almost as if the place had actually weathered a siege or two.

Those gates, however, were always open, and the constant flow of humanity nearly matched the aquatic flow of the Miskatonic. The trio of would-be investigators were hardly the only clump of people standing about and talking. The throng simply parted almost mindlessly around them.

Although he'd been here once before, upon his arrival in Arkham, Billy's expression as he took in the size of the constantly shifting crowd was dismayed. "This is ridiculous. No chance some overworked porter or ticket vendor will remember one particular passenger who might or might not have come through more than a month ago!"

Daisy had to admit she wasn't feeling much more optimistic, especially as this was almost certainly another avenue the police would have followed up themselves. She was running short of ideas, however – or at least of ideas she was willing to pursue. "We won't know until we try," she said. The bright lilt to her voice sounded forced and false even to her own ears.

They split up, then, Billy toward the nearest porter, Elliot the ticket counter. Daisy went looking specifically for Bill Washington.

The chief porter was an Arkham staple, a mainstay of the station for nigh on twenty years, not counting his brief service in the Great War. He was friendly, honest, a man who enjoyed the chance to welcome newcomers and wish his fellow Arkhamites safe travels, and if anyone *would* remember a single face amidst the protean mass of humanity, it'd be him.

Tonight, as business – despite the Kalaaleq's chagrin – was actually relatively slow, Washington had hauled his guitar out from where he kept it behind the counter, and casually strummed to entertain the passersby. Nobody would mistake him for a professional musician, but he was talented enough that his efforts were generally appreciated.

"Good evening, Mr Washington."

"Well, good evening, ma'am!" The porter rose with a touch of awkwardness, thanks to an old war injury.

She identified the expression he wore immediately: he recognized her, but couldn't entirely place who she was. Well, that was fair. They'd only interacted a handful of times. She wasn't a frequent traveler, and Bill Washington wasn't precisely a regular on campus.

"Daisy Walker. I work at Miskatonic."

"Of course, Miss Walker! What can I do for you?"

Unfortunately, the answer turned out to be "nothing." Recognizing Chester Hennessy from an old photograph Elliot had provided, and then recalling if he'd been one of the hundreds to pass through the station at any point in the past few months, proved beyond Washington's abilities.

When Daisy reconvened with the others, just beyond the station's entrance, their looks of frustration mirrored her own feelings perfectly.

"We're wasting our time," Billy insisted. "We should be asking after Pembroke."

Daisy shook her head, blonde curls bouncing. "And how would you go about that, exactly? You're talking about a man who deals in stolen goods. Most people have no idea how to find someone like that, and those who do? Aren't likely to admit to it."

"I know how to make people talk," he grumbled. Then, before she could object, "But you're right. I've no idea where to start."

A surge of guilt made Daisy's stomach clench, and she could only hope the others saw nothing in her expression. *I can't*, she reminded herself. *I can't risk it.*

"What about Hennessy's friends?" Billy asked. "One of them might have an idea where he's off to. Or perhaps a sense of where he might hide something valuable to him."

It was Elliot's turn to shake his head. "I'm Chester's best friend." Was it Daisy's imagination, or was there a touch of bitterness in his voice? "I can't think of anyone he'd tell such things, if not me."

"Besides," Daisy added, "the police would surely have followed that line of investigation as well."

Billy growled something unintelligible, then asked, "What about a lover, a girlfriend?"

This time Daisy knew she hadn't hidden her reaction well enough, felt her jaw twitch before she could stop it, and Elliot looked suddenly sick. Billy's eyes flickered between them, then narrowed.

"What aren't you telling me?"

Elliot answered first, almost spitting. "Nothing!" Even his obvious anger, however, couldn't keep him from slowly wilting beneath Billy's disbelieving glower.

"Miss Walker?"

"I…" *Damn it, why did he have to ask this?* "I really don't feel this is a proper topic of discussion…"

The man standing before her went as cold as his homeland. He wasn't "Billy" any more, but once again the stranger who'd first set foot in her library. "I thought we were working together. That you wanted to find your friend as much as I want to find the *Ujaraanni.* That I could trust you."

Daisy felt herself floundering. She *did* want to find Chester, they *did* need his help. "It doesn't matter. I can't imagine she'd be willing to speak to us, anyway."

"She *who?*"

Then, when Daisy and Elliot both hesitated, Billy shrugged. "Fine. I'll start asking around campus about who Chester Hennessy was seeing. I'm sure someone will prove willing to tell me about whatever it is you won't say. Gossip's always best when it's 'inappropriate' anyway, isn't it?" With that, he started away.

"No!" Elliot called after him, a cry less of defiance than of pain.

Damn, damn, damn. "Mr Shiwak. Billy. Wait." Daisy jogged a few steps to catch up with him, put a hand on his shoulder. "Wait, please. Let's talk."

They shuffled down the block, away from jarring shoulders and curious ears, settling in the mouth of a narrow alley where only the rats might overhear.

"Chester *was* seeing someone," Daisy admitted. "Not many people spoke of it openly, but it was all over Arkham high society – and campus. A woman by the name of Victoria McCutcheon."

Elliot's gaze dropped to his shoes and his fists clenched, but as much as Daisy knew he didn't care to discuss this, didn't even want to hear that woman's name spoken aloud, he held his place.

Billy appeared no happier, though for very different reasons. "And you felt the need to keep this secret… why?"

How to make him understand? If what she'd read of his people was accurate, his own cultural understanding of taboo was primarily religious, not social.

"Chester's family have done very well for themselves," she told him, "becoming quite wealthy. But McCutcheon comes from old money, one of Massachusetts' elder families. Even more to the point, she is only recently widowed, after a marriage one might most courteously describe as 'turbulent,' and more than twice Chester's age."

Then, as Billy continued simply to stare, "Am I not being clear at just how inappropriate this was? The scandal, where both parties are concerned is… not insignificant. Chester might well have found his attendance at Miskatonic called into question if–"

"For this, you jeopardized my search?" Billy exploded. "For *this*?"

Daisy felt the last of her patience evaporate in the heat of his anger. "Because of precisely this reaction." Then, when he appeared sufficiently taken aback by her reply that he might listen despite himself, she continued, "Because I knew you wouldn't understand the significance. That you'd want to run off and find Mrs McCutcheon, demand answers of her. Which would, at best, offend her to the point that she would refuse to help and might spread word of your actions throughout Arkham's elite. And at worst, would be another means of drawing the police down on you."

"You believe she would call the police simply because I approached her with this?"

"Very possibly. But she might not even have to. Do you suppose they're ignorant of the gossip about her and Chester? They would have been careful with her when he disappeared, questioning her lightly, if at all, but they would have watched her for a while, in case she's involved. And as I've no idea how long 'a while' might be, I can't say they aren't still doing so."

Billy slowly nodded, his anger receding. "You've given this a lot of thought."

"Her name was among the list of customers at the shops I visited," Daisy acknowledged. "Not surprising, really. A lot of Arkham's wealthy are dabblers in history. Or," she added, lips quirking in distaste, "the occult. So it's been on my mind."

"All right." Billy took a final, steadying breath. "I would have preferred that you had simply told me and explained all this up front. But I understand why you didn't."

"I'm glad. Thank you."

"Damn it!"

The both of them jumped, turning at Elliot's sudden curse, having all but forgotten his presence. The student had wandered paces from them, punctuating his exclamation with a kick aimed at a loose length of broken wood. It skittered across the alley to rebound from the far wall.

"What's wrong?" Daisy asked, moving to his side.

"Listening to you talk about that… about McCutcheon. We missed something."

"How do you mean?"

"I mean, we've been asking the porters at the station about Chester. One young man in a crowd, with no reason to stand out. But…"

It appeared he couldn't bring himself to utter the words, but he'd said enough. And he was right.

If Chester and Victoria McCutcheon had done any traveling *together*, a wealthy and well known older woman with a younger man might well stick in the mind where a lone traveler would not – particularly if the observer had heard the gossip of her scandalous affair.

"I'll go back," Daisy offered. "You can wait here."

And indeed, salaciousness and scandal proved the key, as it so often did. When she spoke to Bill Washington once more, this time with her new approach, his memory proved far better than it had.

"Not only did he remember seeing them together more than once," she told Elliot and Billy upon her return, "but now that he had context, he remembered seeing Chester come through the station on his own. He bought a ticket – at right around the time he disappeared."

Oh, but she had both their attentions now. "He said Chester looked… rough," Daisy continued, with an apologetic glance to Elliot. "Unkempt, exhausted. Talking to himself. Washington doesn't recall his destination – he helps so very many travelers – but he remembers Chester muttered something about going to see family."

Elliot frowned. "Was he sure?"

"He was." Daisy had asked him the same, and for the same reason she knew Elliot brought it up.

Chester's parents had told them he *had* no other family.

Someone was lying to them – and they'd no reason to suspect it was Bill Washington.

Furious as she was that Mr Hennessy had lied to her face, confusion won out. What was he so determined to hide? Or was he truly so enraged at anyone to do with Miskatonic that deceiving them was an end unto itself, even with so much on the line?

To a mind that clung to order as hers did, that cared for others as hers did, it was truly unfathomable.

"What now?" Billy asked. "Do we go back and demand the truth from his father?"

"I doubt that would accomplish much," Daisy said, pulling herself from her contemplations. "He wasn't precisely cooperative the first time."

Elliot cocked his head, brow furrowed, as though struggling to think. Then, "Christmas lights."

Daisy and Billy both stared. "Pardon?" she asked.

"Chester told me that when he was a boy, he and his parents would go to visit family for a Christmas light display. I guess, when his father said he had no other relatives, I assumed whoever they used to visit was gone, but if they're not... If he lied to us..."

"And where was this display?" Billy asked.

"Taunton." This much, at least, Elliot had no difficulty remembering, and no wonder. That town put on the most famous Christmas display in the state of Massachusetts. "They went to see the lights on Taunton Green."

CHAPTER NINE

The sleet no longer bit, no longer sliced. Instead it had somehow thickened, until it was no precipitation but a chilling weight, a constant pressure that impeded every movement, rendered the entire world a gelid slurry.

He staggered onward, fighting that pressure; fighting the snow that slurped at his ankles, his calves; fighting the slope of the earth itself, the base of a mountainside whose contours he couldn't see beneath thick banks of devious white. He never so much stepped as staggered, falling with each pace and catching himself with a jolt of effort, praying every time that he'd moved forward more than he'd listed to one side or the other.

Every inch of him burned with the cold. His breath warmed his teeth only just enough that they throbbed anew with every inhalation of the frigid air.

In the distance, blunted by the sleet and snow, the screams of allies, friends, family. He wished, more than anything else, those screams would stop, though that would almost certainly mean they were, to the last of them, dead.

At least they would only be dead.

For those shrieks never ceased, never paused even to draw breath. They were continual, constant as the roar of winter wind. No human lungs could have sustained them, no human throat endured them, yet they continued. They were needles in his ears, fire in his mind.

And they would. Not. Stop.

He couldn't tell from where they might be coming, had long since forgotten if he struggled to reach them or to get away. He knew only that, at some point back before the furthest reaches of his memory, he'd chosen a direction, and he dared not deviate now.

Dared not… until a new sound echoed above the wind, above the screams. A constant, dreadful pounding, paired percussions like the beating of some dreadful heart.

Dared not, until the mountain before him shifted. Visible only as a darkened shape beyond the sleet, something impossibly huge, thicker around by far than any boulder or any tree, winding and writhing in twitching segments unlike any serpent, stretched his way. Seeking, reaching.

Maintaining his course no longer felt quite so vital.

He retreated before it, or tried, but the deep snow that had impeded him before redoubled its efforts. It clung to his legs, tighter with every step, as though a co-conspirator with whatever it was that came now to claim him. For half a dozen paces he fought it, wresting a foot free every time, though each was slower, more difficult than the last.

Until finally he could not free himself at all.

The snow held fast. The thing in the sleet, sliding this side to that like a questing tongue, drew near. The terrible heartbeat grew louder, louder, until he scarcely heard the distant screams, until the mountains shook.

Desperately he twisted, pulled, striving to free himself.

His leg separated just below the knee, leaving his foot and the better part of his calf behind.

There was no blood, no bone. No pain. Only a dull tugging sensation and peculiar fibers, dangling, stretching long and thin before finally splitting, like ropes of drool or tufts of cotton candy.

The formerly clinging snow now felt solid as stone beneath his back as he toppled. With both hands and his one good leg he scrabbled back, desperate to escape, a single nerve-thin strand still linking him with the bit of himself he'd left behind.

Already dimmed nearly to midnight by the clouds and the sleet and the shadow of the mountain, the day grew darker still as the unseen thing loomed high. The far-off screams grew suddenly louder, blending into a single shriek that rose even above the pounding heartbeat, and his own cry of despair rose high to meet it…

Billy nudged him hard by the shoulder, rocking him in his seat. "Elliot. We're here."

Elliot clawed toward consciousness, toward understanding, his gaze bleary and blinking, his pulse pounding until the back of his skull ached. The shrieks lingering in his head transformed into the squeal of wheels braking on iron tracks; the heartbeat into the oh-so-familiar *clack-clack, clack-clack* of the train.

He started to speak, to answer his companion, until he felt the words forming in his throat, lurking on the back of his tongue in wait to spring forth.

Isslaach thkulkris, isslaach cheoshash…

Instead he clasped his teeth shut and began digging in his coat pocket for a familiar piece of folded paper.

"You all right?" Billy asked.

"I… Yes. Just… a bad dream." With an addict's shaky desperation, he opened the paper and read through the French printed there, vocalizing under his breath. He almost sobbed in relief as the *other* words, the beginning of the litany, once more faded to the recesses of his mind.

He'd returned to the library mere hours before departing Arkham, reread the *Livre d'Ivon's* original copy of the protective spell. It should be some few days before he needed to again; his handwritten version should be sufficient for the duration of their journey.

Should.

What might happen to him if it weren't, or to others if he found himself unable to prevent himself from repeating the phrase that seemed to have spread to him, as a virus, when he heard it from Chester, didn't bear thinking about.

Elliot wished Daisy might have come with them. Yes, he'd grown more comfortable in the company of Billy Shiwak – especially since, for reasons he still couldn't begin to understand, the litany seemed less intrusive, to hold less power in his mind, in the Kalaaleq's presence – but he didn't really *know* the man. He certainly couldn't consider him a confidante, couldn't openly express himself, or his fears, as he could with the librarian, whom he viewed more as a colleague than as a member of the Miskatonic staff.

As much as she wanted to help, however, Daisy couldn't abandon her job duties for multiple days on end to go chasing down an amateur investigation. She'd been fortunate indeed to have had even the time she'd already devoted to it, to have a supervisor as understanding as Dr Armitage. Disappointed as he might be, Elliot could hardly blame her. She might poke around a bit more in the probably vain hope of tracking down Lafayette-Moses or other leads, but otherwise would be returning to her professional duties while he and Billy were away.

As it was, Elliot himself was missing yet more class time for this. Had he room in his thoughts for any more worry, on top of his concern for Chester, his nervous fascination with the mystery Billy had brought them, and his fear of his own deteriorating mental state, he would have been deeply troubled over the possible consequences for his academic future. As it was, however, he could scarcely find it in himself even to care.

Both of them rose, along with most of the other passengers, and began shuffling out onto the platform of Taunton Central. The traffic in the station was enough to shame Arkham's own. In addition to being slightly larger than that more infamous city, Taunton also served as a nexus for train travel across much of the state. A great many passengers wandering the platform, the station and the surrounding block were simply killing time between one train and the next.

That the station itself was larger, more open and certainly more welcoming than the one with which Elliot was familiar helped alleviate some of that sense of crowding. Where Arkham's station resembled a hunched fortress, this was almost more akin to a church, with a more cheerily hued brick facade, broadly arched windows and a single steeple.

The difference in architectural attitude carried over into the city itself. If Arkham seemed determined to stew bitterly in its history, Taunton had elected to age more gracefully. Its structures were less tightly packed, their style not so Old World, not so overwhelming. The streets and sidewalks looked wider, though that might have been an illusion evoked by the larger property lots and the multiple open parks, of which Taunton Green was only the most renowned.

Even the weather seemed to embrace a more open feel. While it was no less abnormally chilly for being this far into spring, the clouds weren't quite so gray, nor did they crouch so low to the earth.

Under other circumstances, Elliot might have enjoyed this brief sojourn. As it was, that he was even aware of these differences was due mostly to a deliberate effort to distract himself from tumultuous thoughts.

A few quick questions of one of the porters, and they were off. The walk was relatively pleasant as they fell in with the rest of the pedestrian traffic. Conversation and the chug of automobiles embraced them, making it difficult for the two of them to speak much to one another. Elliot welcomed that fact, as his lingering nightmare and other preoccupations disinclined him to friendly chat.

It was only after several moments of travel that he noted Billy's stiff expression, and then the occasional glances thrown his companion's way by a few of the more uncouth locals. Perhaps, given how unsociable Billy appeared to be feeling, Elliot hadn't needed any excuse to remain silent.

Their path carried them through Taunton Green, and even in his dour mood Elliot could understand why so many might travel to see it. The green was a massive open space of walkways drifting between verdant lawns, punctuated by a handful of trees here, a rippling fountain or polished statue there. It wasn't the largest urban park he'd ever seen – though it certainly dwarfed any Arkham had to offer – but it was somehow the most dignified, for lack of a better word. Clearly Taunton's citizens took great pride in their parks. When decorated with light displays and other adornments for the holiday season, it must be quite the sight indeed.

Not far beyond was Church Green, a much smaller park, and it was at the edge of that one where they finally reached their destination.

Taunton City Hall.

It seemed, at least for a municipal office, a welcoming place, designed in the Renaissance Revival style, its facade adorned with attractive but unnecessary arches and columns. Perhaps it was that same sour mood, but Elliot couldn't help but feel almost patronized, even deceived, by its demeanor.

Which is why he wasn't surprised when they walked inside, toward a secretary's desk, and the bespectacled woman behind it – who had just been all smiles, waving and nodding a few of the locals past her – turned suddenly stone-faced.

"Is there something you need?" she asked, the blatantly deliberate lack of discourtesy in her tone somehow, in and of itself, discourteous.

She had, Elliot observed, scarcely noticed him at all. The bulk of her attention, and doubtless her ill-concealed hostility, was reserved for the obvious foreigner beside him.

With a smile that might have appeared genuine to this stranger, but which Elliot already recognized as the unhappy baring of teeth, Billy replied, "We're here to consult your public records."

"And your business?" she demanded.

Time to step in. "I'm trying to track down the family of a close friend," Elliot said, casually sliding himself somewhat between the two of them. "I understand they're from here."

Which wasn't necessarily true, of course. He knew only they'd *come* here at some point. As Elliot and his friends had decided even before leaving Arkham, however, it was the only place they had to start.

For a long moment the secretary looked at him, attention darting between Elliot and Billy. If he had to guess, she was trying to come up with a valid reason for denying the request.

"They are," Elliot asked in what was clearly not a question at all, "*public* records, aren't they?"

With a final, put-upon sigh, she pointed down a hallway and rattled off a brief set of directions.

"Thank you," Billy told her, before Elliot could. Her lips twitched.

They turned and entered the hall, footsteps echoing on the stone-tiled floor. "I'm sorry about that," Elliot said finally, ashamed at how his companion had been treated.

Billy shrugged. "Not your fault. You can't choose what people you're born into."

Not entirely sure how to take that, let alone address it, Elliot kept quiet.

The public records, occupying several large rooms, were overseen by a stuffy little man in a slightly threadbare suit and a substantially more threadbare head. He was quite proud of his little fiefdom, however, and more than happy to order one of his minions to assist Elliot and Billy in their search. It took almost no time at all before they had the addresses of all properties owned by a Hennessy within the limits of Taunton.

Of which there were, surprisingly, five.

The two seekers exchanged exasperated sighs, then Billy began scribbling down the addresses while Elliot went in search of a city map.

The first home they visited was a tiny house on a tiny lot,

one Elliot might have called a "hovel," if it hadn't been so neatly painted and well kept. The young couple who lived there glowered at the interruption once Elliot knocked on their door, and insisted they'd never met anyone named Chester, before firmly closing said door in his face. Not that he'd really required an answer; it was pretty clear just to look at their facial features that neither could be related to Chester in any way.

The second was a butcher shop, its proprietor living in the apartment above. The establishment had already closed for the evening, however, and either the owner wasn't home or was ignoring the pounding, however fierce, upon his door.

Dark had fully fallen by the time they reached the third, a house larger, but older and more decrepit, than the first, on the edge of one of the town's business districts. Elliot's feet ached at the unaccustomed walking, his jaw hurt from constant clenching in frustration at their failures so far, and while the refrain hadn't returned to the forefront of his mind, it tickled at his thoughts, twisting them just enough that he felt a constant mild dizziness.

"We should have found a room for the night already," he complained to his fellow traveler. "Saved this one for tomorrow."

Billy, who didn't appear remotely tired, merely cast him a look and went to knock.

Nothing. A second knock...

"Just a moment!" The voice floated to them, soft and fragile as cobweb, scarcely audible through the wood. It was well over a minute before they heard the sound of the latch, and the door creaked open to reveal a hunched old woman leaning on a cane. She barely came up to Elliot's shoulders, though she was sufficiently wrinkled that, if fully stretched out, he could imagine her as ten feet tall.

"So sorry," she told them. Even without the intervening door, hearing her was something of an effort. "Not as quick on my feet as I once was. Something I can do for you?"

"Mrs Hennessy?" Elliot hazarded.

"I am."

"I'm terribly sorry to disturb you," he said, "and I'll try not to take much of your time."

She smiled at that, revealing a marked insufficiency of teeth. "I don't get many visitors, my boy. You take as much time as you like. In fact, would you care to come in? I've just made some tea…"

She was already shuffling back from the door, clearly anticipating no refusal. As he didn't want to be rude, Elliot followed, Billy a moment later.

The place could have used a good scrubbing, but it was the simple patina of age rather than a sign of sloppy housekeeping. The walls boasted several photographs, black-and-white images of a woman Elliot took to be their host when she was younger, and a bearded man of the same age.

He squinted at the photos as he passed. The man *could* have been a relative of Chester's – but none of the pictures were clear enough to be sure.

Other than those, the house was decorated with crocheted and needlepoint designs, mostly of the floral or snowflake variety.

She sat them down at a rickety table with a worn tablecloth, and poured them each a cup of tea in yellowing china. Only when they'd both taken a few sips, and she'd asked them a few polite questions about how they were liking Taunton so far, did she cease bustling about and seat herself across from them.

"Now, what was it you wanted to talk to me about?"

"Ah." Elliot swirled his half-empty cup, realized he was fidgeting, and put it down in its matching saucer with a rough *clink*. "The truth is, Mrs Hennessy, I don't even know for certain if you can help us or not. You see, I'm looking for a friend of mine. He's gone missing."

"Oh, dear. How awful." While she sounded genuine, however, there was something else to her tone, a hesitation so tiny Elliot wasn't even positive he'd heard it.

"Thank you. I… don't really have a strong reason to suspect he's here in Taunton, but I know he's visited in the past, and he has – or at least had – family somewhere nearby. And as his family name is Hennessy…"

The old woman was already nodding, to herself it seemed more than to them. "Tell me, is your friend named Chester, by any chance?"

For a heartbeat or two, Elliot couldn't move, could barely even draw breath. He felt as though he'd been struck by lightning.

Perhaps sensing the younger man's reaction, Billy spoke in his stead. "So you *are* related!"

"Oh, my, no. I'm afraid I don't even know the poor young man."

And now Elliot felt only confusion. "I'm sorry, I don't understand. If you don't even know him…"

Their host took a sip from her teacup. "Then how do I come to know his name? He must be quite popular, your friend. Or important. You aren't the first to come looking for him, and to find me instead."

"Professor Polaski," Elliot whispered.

"Yes. Yes, that was his name. I couldn't call it to mind. More tea?"

"Uh... No, no thank you."

Billy shook his head.

"Suit yourself." She shifted in her chair, wincing at some unspecified pain in her tired bones. "Yes, your professor came to my door, with many of the same questions you have, and I'm happy to tell you what I told him."

Elliot leaned forward, fingers clasped tight on the table.

"I've been in Taunton more than half my life. Can't say I know everyone who lives in town, of course, or even swear I've met everyone who shares my family name. Far as I can remember, though, there's never been a Chester Hennessy lived here, nor even made any sort of regular visits I ever heard of."

Now it was a good thing the young student had a solid grip on the table's edge. The world tilted beneath him, and without it, he might have slid from his chair. All his effort, all his *hope*, for nothing. He'd continue going through the motions, visit the last few Hennessys on the list, but he couldn't pretend it would matter. This whole thing had been a waste of–

"But..." the woman across from him continued, arresting his spiral into despair. "That was before Professor Polaski mentioned the swamp."

Elliot stared at her. Blinked in confusion. Stared at Billy, who could only blink in return.

"Swamp?" he finally asked.

"Indeed. He said he remembered something Chester had mentioned in passing, about his kin holding property near a swamp." Again she smiled that broken-window smile. "I guess you didn't know that?"

"I didn't, no." Elliot choked back an irrational surge of jealousy. Chester had worked with Polaski for months. It was to be expected they might have exchanged occasional conversation about their histories or personal matters. And Chester had always been reticent where his own family was concerned. That he'd told Polaski something about them which he'd never mentioned to Elliot was hardly any sign of mistrust or deliberate slight.

He couldn't help feeling, however, as if it were. Just a bit.

"Well, of course he meant Hockomock." She said it as though it were the most obvious conclusion in the world. "Only swamp around here. Goes on for miles and miles, big as you like. And I told him, like I'm telling you, there's a whole lot of folks who live out there, more than you'd ever think. Bunches of little towns, 'cept you can't really even call them towns. Just handfuls of people living as neighbors, here and there."

Elliot felt sick from the constant emotional up and down, the hurdles that seemed to rise up every time hope was nearly within his grasp. He took another sip of his tea, now unpleasantly cool, so that he might have a moment to think.

It was another lead, another possibility. That was good news.

But Hockomock… He didn't know all that much about it, but as an educated citizen of Massachusetts, he possessed a passing familiarity. The old woman hadn't exaggerated the enormity of the freshwater swamp. Surveys and estimates placed it at over *fifteen thousand* acres. He wasn't giving up, would *never* give up, but…

"'How are we supposed to find his family in all of *that*?" Elliot didn't realize he'd uttered the words aloud until he felt the weight of both his companion's and his host's attentions.

The woman *tsked* at them over her cup. "You boys didn't do your research before coming all this way, did you?"

Billy offered a shallow grin. "He's the local. I'm not *supposed* to know these things."

"I…" Elliot flushed. "I've been a bit preoccupied." In truth, he wasn't even certain what he'd missed, what she intimated he ought to have known, but embarrassment washed over him all the same.

"Even folks living out by the swamp," she explained kindly, "have got to buy their land, don't they? All neat and legal, if they want the government men to leave them alone. And nobody lives out there doesn't want to be left alone. Told your Professor Polaski that, too. No reason you can't find those Hennessys same way I assume you found me."

Deeds and property records. Of course. But, "Those wouldn't be in Taunton, would they?" Elliot mused.

"Not in City Hall. But Taunton's also the seat of Bristol County, with its own offices. Hockomock Swamp's not entirely in Bristol," she acknowledged, "but most of it is. And if your Hennessys aren't in that part, well, there's other county seats you can go to."

She was right. They still had a chance. "Is that what Professor Polaski did? Did he find anything?"

"I couldn't rightly say for sure. It was the last thing we talked about, though, and if he had any troubles after that, he certainly never came back to talk to me about them."

Which meant whatever had happened to Polaski might well have happened out there. In the swamp.

Might be waiting to happen to them, as well.

Elliot shivered once, then shrugged it off as best he could. It was all they had, and Chester – and possibly the professor, too – might need them, danger or not.

He saw little point in lingering much after that, though he remained long enough to assist their host with cleaning the cups and the kettle. The night was dark and cold by the time they bid their farewells, but he scarcely noticed, nor did he say much to Billy beyond a brief discussion of where they might find a couple of rooms for the night. Tomorrow, first thing, he intended to be waiting at the Bristol County Hall of Deeds.

And after that? If luck was with them, by midday they'd find themselves within the Hockomock Swamp – and perhaps finally within reach of some answers.

CHAPTER TEN

Except where Chester's attentions were concerned, Elliot had never been one for envy, or for the resentments it caused. His family had always been comfortable enough that, when he saw the luxuries available to his wealthier compatriots – travel, finer clothes, fashionable trinkets – he'd shrugged them off as unimportant. When a fellow student had a greater facility with a classroom topic, and thus an easier time keeping their grades up, it had only inspired Elliot to work harder. Even as he'd suffered the hideous affliction he battled constantly, the repetition in his mind he'd somehow "caught" from his friend, he'd never once wished it had struck someone else instead of him.

Right now, however, as he struggled – his breathing grown labored and his calves protesting in agony – to keep up with Billy's constant, tireless pace, he felt himself harboring the first glowing embers of a desire to kill his traveling companion.

Finding county property deeds in the Hennessy name had been the work of mere minutes, narrowing those down to a single property at the Hockomock's edge a few minutes more. They'd retreated to the cheap flophouse on the edge of town where they'd spent the night to discuss the matter, and both agreed that, while they had no guarantee this Hennessy property was the right one, it fit their parameters better than any other. They had little choice but to try.

Which had left only the question of how to make the trek. All eleven and a half miles of it.

The business of car rentals hadn't yet come to Taunton. No trains ran out that way. Even if they'd found someone willing to rent them horses, neither man had any experience in the saddle.

Eventually, though it proved pricier than Elliot would have liked, they'd hired a taxi – but the man was willing to take them only a bit more than halfway.

"Roads out that away ain't any good," he'd explained at their protest. "Muddy and uneven, barely fit for horses'n wagons, let alone automobiles. It's more'n my hide's worth to return my taxi to the company damaged, savvy?"

So they had disembarked on one of said muddy roadways, with a hike of over four miles to their destination. Hardly an insurmountable distance, but on the unfamiliar surface, after days of wandering and toil far in excess of his custom, Elliot was ready to have his legs surgically removed.

Or he was until that thought reminded him of the previous day's dream, and he firmly yanked his thoughts off in a different direction.

Cedars began to line the roadsides, sprouting from shallow waters, fresh but murky. Moss dangled, waved in the breeze, shedding moisture gathered from the thick humidity. *Beards*, Elliot mused. *The tangled, unkempt beards of old winos.*

The mud grew thicker, until every step was accompanied by a moist *squelch*. Between the added exertion and the midday sun – even shaded, as it was, behind what had become a ubiquitous layer of cloud – Elliot found himself perspiring despite the cold. He removed his coat, slinging it over his shoulder, and rolled up his shirt sleeves. The newly exposed skin instantly formed goosebumps, but the extra chill was welcome, for a few moments at least.

The mosquitoes were not. One alighted on Elliot's wrist, fat and black and buzzing. He stared at it, more fascinated than disgusted.

"I'm hardly an expert," Billy observed when Elliot lifted his arm for a closer look, "but I'd have thought it too cold for them."

"So would I." Elliot's response was distant, almost hypnotized. Then, sharply awakening to the real world, he grunted and smashed it flat with his other hand. It burst, already ripe with someone else's blood.

As if in response, the buzz of other insects grew louder from far over the placid waters, along with the cries of frogs, the calls of birds, and other voices less readily named.

"Elliot," Billy rumbled, a warning in his tone.

"It's just a mosquito. I don't think–"

"Elliot!"

He looked up from the crimson and black mess on his wrist.

Ahead of them, the trees grew thicker, looming over the roadway – but it was what stood *in* the roadway that had Billy concerned.

Several automobiles – open-bedded pickups, mostly, all covered in layers of dried muck suggesting they belonged to folks who lived and worked out here – had been parked in a cluster, blocking the path. A wooden horse-cart and an array of logs and branches, dragged from the surrounding swamp, lay alongside them. Together, they formed a barricade, one clearly intended to bar passage.

A few other trucks had apparently attempted to skirt around them. They sat, now, halfsunken into the mud and the swamp water. They had failed in their efforts, and were never likely to move again, at least not under their own power.

Not a soul stirred. Whoever had been here, either blocking the road or attempting to traverse it, was long gone. The outermost layer of mud, only partly dry and adorned with fallen leaves, implied perhaps a day or two, no more than four or five at most.

Elliot and Billy took in the tableau, breathing the flowering and rotting aromas of the swamp. Neither of them spoke, but a shared glance indicated they'd both noticed one last, troubling detail.

This was no defensive construction, the effort of a community of country locals who, for whatever reason, had believed some terrible threat bore down on them from outside.

The cars that had gotten themselves mired, half-swallowed by the swamp in a failed effort to go around the barricade, were all pointed *out*, back the way Elliot and Billy had come. The townsfolk who'd arranged the makeshift barricade had meant to keep their own neighbors and kin from departing.

"What does this mean?" Elliot asked when he finally unearthed his voice from the nervous fear that suddenly weighed it down.

"I have no idea." Billy opened his coat and rested a hand on the hilt of his pana. Freed abruptly of their confinement, the collection of talismans, leather and ivory and stone, clattered where they hung about his neck. "But unless there's some truly bizarre local custom you've not told me about, I'm confident in saying it's probably bad."

Carefully they approached the collection of metal and glass, rubber and wood. While no other vehicle could travel this road, as pedestrians they ought to have little difficulty working their way through. Either the townsfolk had had no concerns that anyone might depart on foot, or the barricade had at some point been manned.

That last thought gave Elliot some hope he might find a weapon with which to defend himself in one of the cars, and he paused to check. If anyone had stood sentry here, with gun or blade, they'd taken their arms when they'd departed. He did, however, locate an old axe handle in the bed of a truck, and while a makeshift bludgeon might not have been his first choice, he felt better for the solid weight in his fist.

Billy offered an approving nod, and they continued – more slowly, more warily – on their way.

The calls of the wildlife grew softer; still present, but at what felt a far greater distance. It didn't make sense, and Elliot was about to ask his companion if he'd noticed it too, when he realized another sound had begun to take their place.

A sound not from without, but within.

Isslaach thkulkris, isslaach cheoshash... Isslaach thkulkris, isslaach cheoshash...

Elliot staggered, nearly falling. Several paces ahead of him, Billy failed to notice.

No! Please, God, not now!

He whispered his French mantra, which he knew now by heart. It calmed the other, more alien words, but not so well as it normally did. The incomprehensible phrases seemed not louder, precisely, but more insistent.

As though something new somehow reinforced them. As

though they were, nonsensical as the idea might be, fighting back against his efforts to subdue them.

Still, he wasn't so disoriented, not yet at least, that he missed the grim concern – in tone, if not in vocabulary – when Billy murmured something in his native tongue.

"What?"

Billy pointed.

At first Elliot saw only a small farmhouse, old and rickety, listing drunkenly where its soft foundations had shifted. Not an enticing place to live, but otherwise nothing worth remarking on.

"It's not the Hennessy place," he began. "They're supposed to be at the far side of–"

Then, finally, he noticed the door. It hung wide open, idly drifting in the sporadic breeze.

"Maybe they just didn't bother shutting it." His protest sounded weak even to himself. "If they're just coming right back, or… I mean, everybody knows everybody in a community like this. I'm sure they all trust each–"

"Do you see anyone running errands? Do you hear sounds of work? Any at all?"

Elliot hadn't paid much attention to any such things, thanks to the warring phrases in his head, but an instant's deliberate effort proved Billy correct. There was nothing. No nearby movement, no sound of tools on wood or vegetation, no grunts of exertion or time-passing conversation, no motors.

He heard the remote animals and insects, the uneven wind, the slow lapping of the waters on the muddy banks. No more.

Not good. Really, really not good.

"Should… Should we go inside? Take a look?"

"We should find who we came to find and finish our business here. Quickly."

With that, Elliot couldn't begin to argue. They moved on.

More houses, shacks really, and occasional barns, on either side of the roadway. All were more or less as decrepit as the first. Many also had doors or windows gaping wide, and none produced a single human soul.

Elliot's heart pounded until he could feel his pulse in his limbs, his neck. Sweat beaded on newly raised hackles.

Isslaach thkulkris, isslaach cheoshash…

Over and over he forced the French mantra through his throat in a counter-rhythm, punctuated ever more often by a plaintive "Shut up, *shut up!*" that he never once realized he'd spoken aloud.

"Look out!"

He failed to register his companion's shout, finally snapping back to awareness and retreating only when the flapping, thrashing brown mass appeared in his face.

It squawked and screamed, some sort of swamp-dwelling bird he'd never seen before. A bit smaller than a crow, it was all coffee-hued feathers and long yellow legs and beak – a beak that drove at Elliot's flesh, a living piston, over and over as he fell back before it.

He'd encroached on the territory of an avian nest before, been swooped at a time or two by an irritated songbird, but he'd never suffered this sort of aggression. He flailed his coat and his makeshift bludgeon wildly, face turned away from the living dagger stabbing at him. Something in his path, or perhaps the muck of the roadway itself, snagged at his heel and he tumbled, landing on his back with a wet smack.

Still it came. He felt a sharp, ragged agony across his cheek as the tip of the beak ripped at him.

Then Billy stood over him. A single swipe of an arm and the bird hurtled aside, struck by an impossibly swift backhanded blow. It fluttered about, half-stunned, before finally hauling itself, soggy and dripping, from the water and flying on its wobbly way.

"The anersaat of this place are angry," he said, reaching down to offer a hand. Elliot took it almost mindlessly, not even looking at it. "Perhaps they've even been sickened somehow." He hauled the student to his feet. "Unless you want to tell me that sort of behavior is normal here?"

No response. Elliot continued staring straight ahead, jaw clenched but eyes glazed, oblivious to his companion, to the blood running down his cheek, to the mud coating his back, soaking into his trousers, matting his hair.

"Elliot? *Elliot!*"

He finally turned, offered a single slow blink. "Yes." It came out in a rasp, as though he'd gone for days without a drink.

"We need to keep moving."

"Yes."

Billy cast him a long look, then started walking. Elliot followed.

He'd had to strain to hear Billy at all, even to see him behind a haze of... Of what? Nothing stood between them, nothing obscured his view, yet he felt as though the other man was unclear, obfuscated as if by a thick vapor or mirage.

Isslaach thkulkris, isslaach cheoshash... Isslaach thkulkris, isslaach cheoshash...

Ever nearer, in all directions, louder, louder... Not as though any one speaker had raised their volume but as if the chorus itself had grown, as if what had been a single voice, or perhaps a handful, was now a choir, its numbers expanding until it blotted out the world, blotted out the mind, leaving no room in his brain for his own thoughts or notions or dreams...

The sucking patches of mud became open mouths, tongues slurping out for him, wetly wriggling throats contracting in the wake of his footsteps. The puddles in his path transformed into misshapen pupils that tracked his progress. To either side, stretching as far as he could see, the ripples in the swamp became the wake of hidden things, slipping ever closer beneath their aquatic veils, and the great trees loomed ever more inward, stretching over the road as grasping tendrils so they might reach down upon passersby. Massive heaps of wood and stone pretended feebly at being simple structures, but they knew not how to rest at angles recognizable by human senses, and he saw an inkling of the alien truths and unnatural passages beneath their careless facade.

Elliot began to shake, to whimper. He turned as he walked, struggling to look every which way, lest something unspeakable creep up on him. A voice called to him, emerging from a looming shape some paces ahead, but he could make out none of the words, nor the ever-shifting features of the speaker, melting like spent candle wax before reforming to melt once again.

A limb stretched toward him, impossibly long, grasping with countless talons. He screamed his terror, his defiance, hefted his axe handle and swung it hard.

A second limb appeared and yanked the weapon from his grip. He was helpless.

And now it came closer, that waxen figure, and he saw

not merely the two great limbs to either side but an array of smaller ones, dangling and thrashing from its chest. He wailed, retreated until he felt it latch onto his shoulder, then beat his fists upon it. All to no avail. It drew him closer, closer, and now he couldn't help but sob in the face of the unclean thing, roaring its nonsensical syllables at him, syllables he barely even heard for the litany.

The litany.

Isslaach thkulkris, isslaach cheoshash…

He fell, and it leaned over him, holding him so he didn't strike the earth. Dangling, one of those smaller tendrils drifted over him, brushed his face…

Elliot gasped, a drowning man finally surfacing for air. The swamp around him, though unpleasant, was merely the Hockomock once again. The road was mud, the trees simple plants, the waters rippling slow and lazy, with nothing of sinister intent below. The houses of the village were, again, just that.

The words in his head, though not silent, once more occupied only a single dark corner of his consciousness.

It was, of course, Billy who had caught him, who stared down at him in deep concern. Billy whom he had instead imagined as some shifting, waxen thing.

And it was one of his many talismans, an ivory amulet carved with sharp angles that resembled, in the proper lighting, some manner of caribou or other antlered beast, that hung loose enough to drift against his bloodied cheek.

That amulet – Inuit protections, Inuit magic – had saved him. Had brought him back. He realized, too, that it must have been the presence of those talismans that had quieted the litany previously, had made him more comfortable in Billy's presence.

Tears welled at the corners of Elliot's eyes. Tears of relief, yes, that the madness had passed – but tears, as well, for a life, for a *world*, he had lost. For he could no longer cling to even a thread of pretense that what afflicted him was mere mental illness, that the spell he recited from the *Livre d'Ivon* served as nothing more than a mantra to focus his thoughts.

Curses. Sorcery. Magic. All real.

"I'm sorry." He allowed Billy to help him stand, then flushed and looked away as he realized he had attacked his companion in his madness. He didn't immediately recognize the terrain or the specific houses nearby; they must have walked farther than he'd realized during his delirium. "I... I don't know what to say."

"The truth would be a good place to start." Billy took a step back once Elliot proved able to stand on his own and made no further violent move. He still hadn't returned the axe handle. "Something's troubled you. Even for as scant a time as I've known you, I could see that much. I ignored it as no business of mine, but if it's going to drive you to fits of madness–"

"Not... madness. Not exactly." Elliot pointed to the talisman that had brought him back to himself. "That saved me."

Billy glanced downward, inhaled deeply. "You're beset?"

"Beset?" Even having acknowledged the truth to himself, it took Elliot a moment to admit it to another. "You mean by... spirits. I suppose I am."

The Kalaaleq fingered his collection of talismans, then removed the one in question and handed it over. "For the moment only," he warned.

Elliot almost burst into tears again – particularly when he placed the cord over his head, and instantly felt the pressure of the refrain lessen further. Not since he'd first heard it, since the words had initially taken root in his soul, had they felt so distant.

"Thank you." It felt woefully insufficient.

"Now, the truth. All of it."

He would have told it, right there, in the middle of the swamp-kissed road. Even as he opened his mouth to speak, however, the alien phrases grew loud once more. Indeed, he could make out nearly a dozen separate voices, coming from multiple directions. He trembled, nearly fell to his knees in the mud, despair washing over him in a suffocating wave.

Until he saw Billy turn, hand reaching for his blade, seeking the source of the sudden chant, and realized what was happening.

The litany wasn't coming from inside his head, not this time. It came instead from all around them.

CHAPTER ELEVEN

From behind several houses, from inside one of the barns, emerging from copses of white cedar and tussocks of underbrush to wade through the murky waters, nearly a score of the locals at last revealed themselves.

They might, at a casual glance, be taken for average rustics, the sort of folks who carved out a laborious life here at the outskirts of the Hockomock. Most wore thick trousers or overalls, heavy boots, hats or caps to keep their hair from their faces and the sun from their eyes.

Most, but not all. Several were half dressed, shirtless or barefoot, and a couple dressed only in filthy underclothes. Their skin was mud-slicked, covered in abrasions, and they seemed utterly oblivious to the pain of those minor wounds and the bite of the unseasonable cold.

Many were empty-handed, but others carried rakes, shovels, saws or knives, tools of gardening or farming or butchering far too easily wielded as weapons for Elliot and Billy's comfort.

It was none of that, however, that sent the first frisson of terror dancing spider-like down Elliot's back, set his brow to sweating and his limbs to shaking.

"*Isslaach thkulkris, isslaach cheoshash... Vnoktu vshuru shelosht escruatha...*"

The litany, more of it than he'd heard from Chester, more than had ever infected his thoughts, drifted over the swamp in an unending chorus. It pounded over him, a heavy rain, a noxious fume.

"*Svist ch'shultva ulveshtha ikravis... Isslaach ikravis vuloshku dlachvuul loshaa...*"

The chanters drew breath at awkward moments, between words, in the midst of words – but unlike the syllables, all uttered in unison, they sucked the humid air at different intervals. The result was an incantation that never broke, continued even when a voice or two dropped briefly away.

Within Elliot's own mind, the single phrase he knew, that had troubled him for so long, swelled in joyful echo of the recitation without, until it felt like a physical pressure, and he feared his head might burst.

Yet it also remained clear, as if the sounds could not quite gain purchase. Perhaps it was his recent recitation of the protective spell – and he knew now, beyond any doubt he ought to feel as a modern student of science, that it *was* a spell – from the *Livre d'Ivon*. Perhaps it was the talisman Billy had offered him, or some combination of the two.

Oh, God. Billy.

He turned, seeking any sign of incipient madness on his friend's visage, but that concern, at least, seemed unfounded. Although clearly troubled by the approach of the entranced villagers, and disturbed by the alien sound of their refrain,

Billy showed no signs of an ill mind. Elliot remembered how he'd faltered when he'd first heard the words, as though struck a physical blow, and saw no such reaction here. He could only assume that Billy, too, benefited from the warding magics of the remaining amulets he wore.

Which hardly, he realized as the first trio closed to within reach, made them safe.

Billy passed the confiscated club back to Elliot, then took a single step toward the advancing mob. He raised his hands defensively before him, empty left fist further forward than the knife in his right. "I don't want to hurt you…" he began.

A heavyset man, who looked, between his beard and his build, more lumberjack than farmer, raised a heavy spade like an axe over his head.

He never brought it down. Billy stepped in, staggered his attacker with a fist to the side of the head, then slashed upward. His snow knife drew twin lines of blood across both the local's forearms, lines that swiftly opened into deep smiling maws of red flesh and a glimpse of bone. The spade dropped wetly to the mud.

The agony should have been crippling. The arms should have been useless. Instead, without so much as a gasp of pain to break the cadence of his mantra, the bearded man swung his arm from the side, twisting at the waist. Not the strongest blow, or the swiftest, but its sheer impossibility caught even the hunter by surprise. Billy grunted, staggering several steps.

And cried out in pain as a young woman, barely more than a girl, opened the meat of his own arm with a wild swing of a rake.

Not a severe wound – Billy's coat and his own reflexes

absorbed the worst of the blow – but it bled freely through the rent sleeve, and his face twisted briefly before he resumed his mask of stoicism. The woman raised the rake again...

Elliot's club cracked viciously into her right knee, sending her tumbling to the roadside. Even in the face of the obvious threat, it had taken all his will to strike her that way, and he felt a surge of nausea that had nothing to do with the constant litany or his mounting fear.

When she began to stand back up, though, oblivious to the unnatural sideways angle at which that knee now bent, it absolutely *was* fear that spurred Elliot to retreat to Billy's side. The third of the initial trio of attackers lay bleeding at Billy's feet; Elliot hadn't the slightest idea how he'd gotten there.

"We have to get out of here!" He sounded hysterical, knew it, and couldn't bring himself to care.

"Yes."

Elliot tore his attention from the approaching throng, only steps away. Billy's reply... Had he hesitated, for just a heartbeat? Had Elliot heard just the smallest hint of distraction in his tone?

It might well have been his imagination – but just maybe, perhaps due to their proximity, the litany was beginning to penetrate his ward. Elliot himself felt no different, but already tainted by his earlier exposure, he wasn't sure he'd notice.

"Run, then!" Elliot screamed at him.

Whether the hesitancy had indeed been in his imagination or whether that shout snapped Billy out of it, the hunter obeyed, Elliot following close behind. Billy made his break along the very edge of the road, ankle-deep in the swamp. Tricky footing, but not impossible, and the route took them between two of the larger oncoming groups.

One man moving ahead of both clusters, wearing only long underwear and a single tattered shoe, put himself in Elliot's path. A desperate swing of the axe handle swept him aside, and Elliot forced himself not to look back and see what damage he'd inflicted.

Another, armed with a hatchet, leapt from a grassy tussock toward Billy. Elliot couldn't entirely track what happened next, saw only a blur of hands and blades. Crimson fountained halfway across the roadway. Billy kept running, shaking his knife clean. The other man dropped, twitched twice and lay still.

It happened so fast, Elliot was already past when it finally registered on his beleaguered mind that he'd just watched a man die. Now he did turn, twisting as he ran to stare behind him in horrified fascination at the unmoving corpse. He found himself strangely furious with Billy, not because he'd killed his attacker – he'd had, Elliot knew, little option – but because it didn't appear to bother him much.

A ludicrous objection, particularly when they were fleeing for their lives, but one he couldn't shake.

Not, at least, until his backward gaze rose from the dead body to the living ones still in pursuit.

The locals ran after them, but it was no sort of gait Elliot could fully comprehend, let alone accept as normal. With each pace they nearly toppled forward, rear leg unnaturally stiff, only just catching themselves on the front before straightening up and repeating the process. They didn't appear injured or pained so much as somehow unfamiliar with their own bodies. The result was a peculiar lurch, unnatural yet somehow rapid enough to keep them from falling too far behind. Through it all their arms remained straight – ahead of them, carrying weapons, or rigid by their sides – and their breath barely seemed to quicken or deepen despite their exertions.

And still the chant, never ending, a profane liturgy beyond religion, beyond fanaticism. "*Vnoktu vshuru shelosht escruatha…*"

Gradually, Elliot and Billy indeed increased the gap between them and their pursuers, but the cost was high. Elliot gasped for breath, shook with the sharp pain digging into his left side, and even the seemingly indefatigable Kalaaleq was panting lightly. If they failed to change their circumstances soon…

Billy broke right, the move so sudden Elliot almost failed to follow. He ducked past a pile of old straw, through a small copse of trees and pointed.

Ahead was a small shack, far more decrepit even than the rest of this ill-kept, swamp-battered community. It leaned so precariously to the side that Elliot worried even Billy's gesture, meant to draw his attention to it, might be enough to topple it.

It was, however, the only shelter in sight that, thanks to the trees, they just might reach unseen by those who followed.

Elliot burst in and fell to his knees, started to gulp for air – and then froze, nearly choking, as Billy clasped a gloved hand over his mouth.

"Dust," Billy hissed in his ear, before turning back to quietly latch the door behind them.

Indeed, Elliot realized their entry, to say nothing of his near collapse, had kicked up huge amounts of dust, dirt, mildew, and God knew what else. Gasping that in, as he'd begun to do, would have sent him into a coughing fit that nobody outside could have failed to hear.

Pulling his shirt over his mouth, Elliot battled with his lungs, his instincts, forcing himself to take slow, controlled breaths.

Billy did the same, for only a moment. Then he examined the blood and worse still clinging to his pana, and casually wiped it clean on his sleeve.

"What?" he whispered in response to Elliot's clear disgust. He moved his arm, so the rips from his earlier wound flared. "Going to have to either throw it away or get it cleaned and mended anyway."

Elliot looked away. A minute later, having finally gotten himself somewhat under control, he studied their feeble shelter.

No interior walls, no furniture. Only the dusty floorboards and the structure itself, slumped enough to be almost dizzying, the wood sporting a roadmap of cracks and faults. The door was a thin bit of lumber with a simple latch, a pitiful barricade against any determined assault. What had once been an open window was now roughly boarded up, rusty nails jutting awkwardly every which way.

The coughing fit Elliot had barely avoided wouldn't have had time to draw their attackers, he figured, before it brought the whole rickety heap down on their heads.

"This place looked better from the outside," he grumbled, wandering over to the thick boards covering the window.

"Mm. I'd hoped for a little more," Billy admitted.

Elliot placed his hands on the wood, careful not to lean too heavily – and only then realized both his hands were empty. He'd lost both coat and bludgeon somewhere in his mad scramble.

Nervously fingering the talisman now hanging from his neck, he turned to ask Billy what their next step might be. Instead, he caught the briefest glimpse of a shadow, faint in the light of the overcast day, beneath the ill-fitting door.

He hissed, pointing. Billy glanced downward, nodded, pressed his ear to the wood, softly lifted the latch…

Then, in a wild flurry of motion, he swung the door open, lunged out and hauled one of the townsfolk inside. Billy swung a swift blow to the side of the man's head, grabbed his shoulders and hurled him to the ground, then slammed and latched the door once more.

By the time the villager began to rise, garden trowel clutched like a dagger in his fist, Billy had his own knife drawn and buried in the man's throat.

Elliot swallowed his gorge and averted his gaze until the thrashing and gurgling stopped.

"Was that…" He gagged, tried again to maneuver the words around a suddenly dry tongue. "Was that necessary?"

Billy kicked the trowel his way. "What do you think?" Then, without waiting for an answer, "Whatever's come over them, they can still think. Still plan."

"How do you mean?" Elliot reluctantly picked up the makeshift weapon, wishing desperately for his lost axe handle. A club was one thing, but the idea of striking someone with this dull blade, trying to drive it into moving, resisting flesh…

"I mean one of them came close, alone. A scout. And he was quiet. No chanting."

Or maybe he was quiet and alone because you just slaughtered an innocent man who hadn't yet succumbed to the litany! Elliot wanted to shout. It wouldn't do any good, though – and he recognized, even as he struggled not to voice the protest, how improbable it was.

More improbable still when, not seconds later, the mantra began once more from outside the shack.

"Isslaach ikravis vuloshku dlachvuul loshaa…"

Billy had been right; the dead man had been a threat. Under other circumstances, Elliot would have been relieved to know that.

"Get away from the window!" Billy growled, before shoving the fresh corpse up against the door and retreating toward the center of the room.

Elliot took a moment to obey, struggling to listen. "I don't think they're on that side," he said, pointing at one of the walls. "Maybe if we can break through…"

"Isslaach thkulkris, isslaach cheoshash…"

He started forward, but Billy halted him with an outstretched hand. "Why? Why not surround us?" He paused. "Why aren't they already inside? That door should barely slow them–"

A roar from outside, distant but swiftly growing closer, drowned out the chanting. The dust near the floor began to dance.

And the wall – on the "clear" side, where Elliot had meant to stand – disintegrated as the pair hurled themselves aside, one to each corner.

Rust-splotched red metal and water-stained wood paneling tore through the shack. Driven by a slack-faced, chanting young man probably no older than eighteen or nineteen, the light truck – a Chevrolet model 490, Elliot would later recall, though of course he had no thought for such details at the time – seemed utterly unimpeded by the flimsy walls. Whether he even tried to hit the brakes or not, it ripped apart the flooring beneath its spinning tires and punched through the back as easily as it had the front.

Boards and old lumber screamed as they leaned, twisted,

snapped. Scrambling to their feet, Elliot and Billy dashed for the newly made gap, stumbling and scrambling over broken floor. Mere paces behind them, the structure that had threatened to come down from the moment they'd seen it finally made good on its promise in a cacophony of shrieking and shattering.

Wood settled. Dust cleared.

On the other side of the debris and all around the idling truck, as though coalescing out of the waters and the drifting mists of the swamp, the throng appeared once more. Still. Unblinking.

Chanting.

Billy winced, shaking his head as through trying to clear it. This time, even Elliot felt the pull. Their defenses against the litany wore thin.

They turned to run once more, only to discover a second group – far smaller than the first, but plenty large enough to slow their flight until they were overwhelmed – approaching from behind.

Billy's face once more settled into its grim mask, but he couldn't entirely hide a faint quiver in his jaw. He raised his pana, prepared to fight until the option was lost to him. Seeing no other choice, Elliot did the same, trowel trembling in his sweat-slick palm.

A fearsome crack rang out across the scattered community, echoing through the hollows and branches and waterways of the Hockomock.

Elliot yelped despite himself, and even Billy started. He wasn't certain, initially, what the sound had been; wasn't certain until he saw one of the smaller group of locals tumble to the mud, bleeding from a wound in his thigh that hadn't existed an instant before.

A second shot. Then a third, a fourth. With each, another person fell to a bullet placed with expert precision, an injury that was not – or at least, with proper treatment, might not be – lethal.

Nor did Elliot require anything rivaling Billy's keen eye to note that the unseen gunman had selected targets to clear the two of them a path through their attackers.

Again they required no words between them. They just ran.

A short way down the road, they spotted a figure atop what might have been a barn built, in part, to resemble a church, or might have been an actual church, constructed with unusual simplicity. A squat steeple protruded from the roof, the only bit of construction that marked the building as different. From that, in turn, jutted a thin rod of metal, almost invisible against the low clouds, that might once have been the base for either a cross or a weathervane.

The gunman crouched beside that steeple, braced against the brick, rifle aimed downward. The weapon barked, and another of the distant figures fell.

"Keep goin'!" Now, having heard the heavily accented voice, Elliot recognized their mysterious savior as a woman, despise his inability to make out much detail from this distance. "You'll want the house with the red door, white trim. Get upstairs." She slammed a hand against the bolt, fired yet again.

Billy and Elliot resumed their sprint, electing to trust her advice. Whoever the stranger was, she'd rescued them, drawing attention to herself in the process. More significantly, she hadn't succumbed to the litany.

Two more shots, but no more. Elliot glanced back and saw her scrambling down the roof, out of sight. At least for the nonce, nobody pursued the two of them any longer. All those who'd been close had fallen to their guardian angel's rifle, and the rest had now turned her way, converging on the barn or church or whatever it was.

"Should…" He struggled to breathe, to speak, as he ran. "Should we go back… and help her?"

"We should do exactly what she told us to," Billy insisted. "She's been here longer than we have, and she saved us. Trust that she knows what she's doing."

"And if… we're wrong?"

"Then there's not much we could have done anyway, is there?"

CHAPTER TWELVE

By the time they reached the house she'd described, some three or four lots away, Elliot's run had become a stagger. Again his side felt as if he'd been stabbed, and spots danced in his vision with every labored breath. He stumbled up the steps to the porch, through the door and found himself bent double, leaning against the railing of a staircase.

Billy slammed the door, far heavier than that of the shack, behind him and twisted the bolt. It fell into place with a reassuringly weighty *clunk*. He then left Elliot to recover while he made a quick circuit of the first floor.

"House has been abandoned for a few days," he reported upon his return. "Most of the food's gone, and what's left is rotten. Whatever reason they had for leaving, they had time to prepare. Furniture's been moved to block the back door and the windows, so we should be secure for a while. She said to go upstairs."

Elliot nodded, waved off Billy's offered hand and clumsily followed him up the steps. The whole house, now that he had the presence of mind to notice, smelled foully of mold. He suspected it had little to do with being abandoned; it was hard to imagine anyplace built in the swamp *not* harboring such an odor.

On the second floor, too, the windows had been blocked and many of the doorknobs were dusty, but the bed looked as though it had seen recent use. Next to it was an American infantryman's footlocker from the Great War. Elliot opened it while Billy expanded his search to the neighboring rooms. Inside he found a canteen of lukewarm water, some smoked meat and half a chocolate bar, a roll of gauze, a broken bit of soap and a pile of bullets. A quick examination showed him ".30-06" stamped into the rim.

Elliot wasn't certain why it was here, but gift horses, mouths and all that.

When Billy returned, he carried a stack of clothes and towels scavenged from the other rooms. The folks who'd lived here might have packed to leave, but they hadn't taken everything.

When Elliot showed him the stash in the footlocker, Billy only nodded. "Our friend, or someone, left emergency supplies here." He poked at the rumpled bed. "Probably in a few houses around the community, I'd imagine. Wise."

Helping one another where necessary, they peeled off the filthiest bits of their clothes – Billy's coat, Elliot's shirt – to get at the bloody contusions beneath them. "Maybe she's just staying here," the younger man suggested. As he spoke, he moistened a towel with the canteen, scraping it with soap before using it to scrub at a nasty cut.

"I don't think so." Billy stoically poked at the gashes in his arm, nodded in contentment at the scabbing they'd already done. "This bed's been slept in recently, but not *too* recently. Not last night. I guess someone's using it as an emergency shelter. And I guess anyone who'd think to do that probably has more than one."

Elliot considered asking him precisely how he could figure when the bed was last used, then thought better of it.

"That's a good sign," he said instead. Then, at Billy's quizzical look, "It means they've been active for a while, right? If they've had the time to set up emergency shelters since this… this nightmare started? Whatever means they have of avoiding or resisting the litany, it works long-term."

"Hmm."

After slaking their thirst and cleaning the worst of their wounds, the canteen was nigh on empty, and while the property doubtless had a well, neither man felt particularly inclined to step outside to find it. Elliot's skin crawled with the feel of the mud drying across his back, where it had sluiced in under his shirt, and in his hair.

As best they could, then, working with dry towels, they worked at scrubbing away the worst of the filth.

They were still at it when…

"See you two've made yourselves nice and cozy."

Elliot jumped, but more startling even than the woman's sudden appearance in the bedroom doorway was the soft but unmistakable gasp of shock from behind him.

"How… ?" Billy gathered himself. "How did you get inside? If you'd unlocked the front door, I'd have heard the latch!"

"Nuh-uh." Rifle aimed their way, she braced herself on the doorframe, then carefully took her left hand from the barrel. With two quick tugs, she removed twisted wads of fabric from both ears, then resumed her grip on the weapon.

Protection against overhearing the litany, Elliot realized. He found himself almost disappointed that the solution was so mundane, even if it proved him correct that she – and probably others – were aware of what was happening and had found ways around it.

"You're the ones owe me for savin' you," she continued. "And you're the two strangers come to my home after the devil himself reached up outta hell to damn us, so *you're* the ones gonna be answerin' *my* questions, unless you wanna get up off that bed and march right the hell back outside!"

She didn't actually shout that last, clearly too smart to risk attracting attention, but from the way she snarled each individual syllable through a cage of clenched teeth, Elliot hadn't a doubt in his head that she meant every bit of it.

Under other circumstances, he wouldn't have found her remotely intimidating. She was quite slight; the top of her head barely reached his chin, and she couldn't be much more than half his weight. Furthermore, the smattering of freckles, and the fact she wore a coat and trousers clearly intended for someone taller and broader, gave her an almost childlike mien, even if she was probably, in truth, a few years older than him.

Today, though, between the fury in her tone and the rock-steady steel barrel gaping at them – a weapon she'd already proved herself quite willing and able to use – Elliot found her more than sufficiently frightening.

He raised his hands, though it felt a foolish gesture given that they were full of nothing more deadly than a filthy towel.

"First off," he began, "we're not your enemies."

"Oh, yeah? I just shot down folks I know – my neighbors, my friends, my *kin* – to save you, so you best be *real* convincing."

"I assume there's no coming back, then?" Billy asked softly. "From whatever's come over them?"

The young woman flinched, though still the rifle never wavered. "Why... Why'd you think that?"

Elliot wasn't certain he'd ever heard the Kalaaleq speak so softly, so gently. "Because I know what family means to people like us. People who live away from the large cities, off what the land chooses to provide. And while I am deeply grateful for your rescue, I don't believe you *would* have shot at kin to save us, even if only to wound, if you still had hope they'd return to you."

Tears rolled down her face, cutting furrows into the dirt she'd picked up running through the swamp.

"My name is Billy. Billy Shiwak. This is Elliot Raslo. And what he told you is true. We're not the enemy. We didn't do this."

"No. No, I know you didn't." She sighed, wiping her face with the back of her hand – and, in the process, finally lowering her weapon. "Wouldn't have needed savin' if you did, I suppose."

Then, "Ida Glick. And I guess I'm pleased to meet you, considerin'."

Elliot let his hands fall. "So, uh, Ida. Would you mind terribly...?" He poked at his mud-caked shirt.

He took her wan smile as permission, started to dig through the pile of garments Billy had found, and then stopped. "Uh... Your family's?"

"Naw. This house belongs – belonged – to a friend of my daddy's. Go ahead an' take what you need. They... won't be comin' back for any of it."

Most of the men's clothes were a touch big on Elliot, but not too badly. Billy's broad-shouldered build proved more of a hindrance, but eventually he found a long canvas coat, almost a duster, bulky enough that it wasn't too restrictive.

"We're searching," Elliot explained as they changed what clothes they could while remaining decent in front of Ida. "A friend of mine's gone missing. So has a carved stone – a religious relic, basically – from Billy's people."

Ida looked Billy's way at that. "You Injun?" At least the question sounded merely curious, not hostile.

"Inuit," he replied. Then, at her obvious confusion, he sighed. "Eskimo."

"Wow. Long way from home."

"I am."

Ida leaned the rifle against the wall – still within easy reach – and sat on the floor. "What kinda stone?"

Billy described the *Ujaraanni* as he struggled into the coat, but all Ida could do was shake her head. "Can't say as I seen anythin' like that. Why'd you figure it was here?"

"Mostly because we traced my friend Chester here," Elliot explained. "He was researching the stone – or one much like it – when he disappeared, and we think he's got family in your community."

The young woman frowned, tapping a finger to roughly chapped lips. "Can't say as I know anyone by the name of Chester, either."

Elliot's stomach dropped. They couldn't have found *another* family of the same name but no relation, could they? But no. Whatever was happening here, the litany – the same one he'd "caught" from Chester – was involved. That *proved* a connection.

"Are you sure?" he pressed. "Chester Hennessy. He's about–"

He never finished the description. Ida was back on her feet with a feral growl, the rifle once more in her hands and pointed with terrifying stability at Elliot's skull. "Hennessy? You're with the Hennessys?!"

He retreated to the wall, hands again held high. "Whoa, whoa! We're not *with* anyone! I just want to find my friend. That's all."

Billy tensed beside him, ready to spring if he had to, though the odds of him reaching Ida before she could fire were poor at best.

Thankfully, it proved unnecessary. With a foul curse Elliot had never heard from a woman before, she lowered the weapon once more. "I dunno about your friend, but you'll want to take care who you tell about him. None of us left got any love for the Hennessys, may they rot in hell!" Then, at the puzzled looks from across the room, "Was the Hennessys brought this curse down on us in the first place."

True or not, Elliot couldn't even find it in himself to be surprised she thought so. That sort of luck just seemed par for the course at this point.

He and Billy glanced at one another, peeled themselves off the wall, and settled on the edge of the mattress. "Maybe you'd better tell us exactly what's happened here," Billy said.

Ida turned away, paced as far as the room allowed, then faced them again.

"It was more than a week ago. I... Maybe two?" Her expression shifted, anger draining away to reveal the sorrow and the lightest touch of the fear it had masked. "I've lost track. It's hard to...

"Anyway, more than a week. We already knew somethin'

wasn't right, 'cuz a few folks round here'd already disappeared. Bobbie Marsh went out fishin', never came home. Sarah Loomis, she… Well, a few of us, just gone.

"'Cept we found out they *weren't* gone. That day, somethin' happened at Woodrow Hennessy's place. Dunno what. We heard gunshots inside the house, a lotta yellin'. Then, for a few minutes, nothin'. Bunch of the men got together, went over to see what was goin' on. My daddy and… others…"

Ida held herself together, for the most part. She cried for only a short while, all but silently.

"They got to the house," she resumed, sniffling, "just when the door opened and the missin' folks all come pourin' out. Them, and most of Hennessy's family. And every last one of them was like the people you've seen for yourselves. Violent. *Empty*. And all of them chantin' that horrible chant."

"Your father was killed?" Billy asked, his obvious sympathy doubtless stemming from the loss of his own father. But Elliot knew better, knew the answer to that question was no even before Ida shook her head.

Knew what was coming, knew the fate of her father, of the others who'd dared approach the Hennessy place, was worse than mere murder.

"He ain't dead. None of them are. That *chant*. Those unholy words, whatever they mean… They *infected* everyone! They're *part* of it now!"

Elliot dropped his head into his hands, groaning softly. He'd known this was coming for a while, or part of him had. He'd refused it, buried it, unwilling to face what it could mean for Chester.

For himself.

Billy stood and wandered to the far side of the bedroom, arms crossed, expression unreadable.

"I know how it sounds!" Ida protested. "But it's true. You gotta believe me!"

"I believe you," Elliot reassured her. "Go on, please."

"Not sure there's much more to tell. More of us went to see what was happenin'. By the time we figured it out – by the time any of us believed it – more than half of us were already... gone. Taken or mad or whatever it is.

"Some tried to escape, but the... the mad ones, they got there first. Blocked the roads, waited for anyone to try to run."

"We saw. On our way in."

From the corner, Billy said, "Some of you might still have gotten out on foot."

Again Ida shook her head. "There's some of them still waitin' in the swamp. You never know where they'll come from, or when. Tryin' to get out on foot, it's suicide. And even if we did, where would we go? We don't have much money, don't have much use for it here. Nobody in Taunton's gonna believe us. They'd turn us out or lock us up – or worse, send someone back here to see for themselves."

"How long does it take?" Elliot asked, hoping he didn't sound too panicked. "From the moment someone hears the litany, I mean? Is it instant? Minutes? Hours?"

Ida could only shrug. "Ain't always the same. I've seen people turn in mid-step and start repeatin' those words, and I seen people take *days*. Got no idea what makes them different."

Elliot's head spun. He'd hoped for a pattern, a solid answer. He'd hoped to learn whether he'd simply gotten lucky, how much time he might have if he couldn't get back to the *Livre d'Ivon*, whether he'd done better because he'd heard less of the alien speech. If what Ida said was true, however, if there was no pattern to it, no sense...

He had to learn more. He had to find Chester.

A single footstep and the rustling of clothing snagged his attention. He turned to find Billy facing them again, arms still crossed, looking even more inscrutable than normal.

"I'm sorry. I'm having difficulty believing this."

Him? Of the two of them, *he* was proving the skeptic? "Billy," Elliot protested, "everything we've seen..."

"I don't doubt that some great wickedness has beset this place. But while I am no angakkoq, I grew up with their tales and their warnings. All the children of Itilleq did, more so even than most of our brethren. You know why."

"Uh, I don't," Ida reminded him, but he ignored her.

"And I spoke to the angakkoq for many days before I set out to take up my father's burden, before he gave me these." Billy brushed a hand over the cluster of talismans about his neck. "I know much of the anersaat of beasts and men, how they can grow hateful or corrupt after death if mistreated or sickened in life, and of the toornat, who never wore flesh or bone, or ever lived as we understand life. I know the many ways the evil among them can harm us, punishing us for violating taboo or tormenting us simply because they can. If you wish me to believe this misfortune was drawn down on Ida's people because the stolen *Ujaraanni* was brought here, or because Chester Hennessy had contact with it and then came here, I accept that as an unfortunate possibility."

His knuckles tightened until they turned white, and he couldn't entirely hide a scowl. "But a toornat or anersaapiluk that possesses people, one after the next, through the speech between them? Or passes on a curse through echoed phrases implanted in living minds? Not the wisest of my people have ever heard of such a thing, and you'll find it difficult to convince me that, as long as we've watched over the *Ujaraanni*, we've remained ignorant of–"

"But you never transliterated it."

Elliot hadn't meant to interrupt; it just came out. Now that he'd done it, however, now that he had Billy's attention – not to mention his ire – he knew he couldn't let the man's pride in his people, his steadfast faith in their spiritual awareness, get in the way of his seeing the truth.

Even if it was a truth against which part of Elliot himself still howled in protest.

"You said so yourself. Your people could never read the carvings on the *Ujaraanni*. But we know Chester had made some new discovery – of the *Ujaraanni* or the Lindegaard Stele. And you told us that your shamans, your…"

"Angakkut." Yes, Billy sounded angry, but he was also listening.

"Yes. Your angakkut went mad, if only slightly, after spending years watching over the stone.

"So what if Chester *did* transliterate it somehow? What if the litany is the pronunciation of the carving on the stones? Who's to say they *couldn't* transmit that madness, far stronger than mere exposure? Your people would never have known."

Silence for a moment. Ida gawped at them, and Elliot wondered how much of this she truly followed. Enough, at least, to remain quiet, to listen and learn.

"Even if your friend could have done this," Billy replied, his tone making it quite clear how he felt about that particular possibility, "you're only guessing that it's those words, and not some other unseen force, causing the—"

"They infected me."

Billy's jaw snapped shut like a bear trap. Then, "You said my talisman protected you."

"It did. I don't mean today. I mean weeks ago. Before Chester disappeared."

Ida could no longer remain a bystander. "Not possible! It takes days, at most!"

"I got less of it. Just one phrase. And I've been… taking precautions." Then, at Billy's glare, "I told you I was 'beset.'"

He revealed it all then. Chester's growing peculiarity, his utterance of the single phrase shortly before vanishing. Elliot's own distraction, his nightmares, his efforts to hold the litany at bay with the protective spell from the *Livre d'Ivon*. How he'd nearly succumbed when they arrived, when he drew nearer the other "infected," until the Inuit talisman brought him back.

For the first time, he spoke it all aloud. With it came the trembling, the fearful tears at the thought that he must eventually succumb, and his horror now that he'd seen what he might become once he did. But with that also came relief, the lifting of a weight he'd forgotten he carried. At least the burden was no longer his to shoulder alone.

Billy remained silent through the entire tale, for several long breaths after it was complete. Then he burst into a long diatribe in his own language, spitting words so harshly and savagely that Elliot knew, without translation, they could only be the vilest profanities.

"What is it with you?!" he finally demanded in English, his breath ragged with fury. "Is it an American thing, or are all white people liars?"

"Hey," Ida protested.

Elliot said, "I'm not sure what–"

"You and Daisy Walker. First Victoria McCutcheon, and now this. We are supposed to be partners. Working together. I should be able to trust you!"

Something coiled, worm-like, in Elliot's gut. The man wasn't entirely wrong, he knew that, and some small bit of guilt gnawed at him. At the same time…

"This isn't easy for me to tell, Billy. I spent weeks believing I was going mad. I still may be, only now I know there's some… some curse or black magic or evil spirit behind it. Things I didn't for one instant lend the slightest credence to before all of this began!"

"You still–"

"And besides, you doubted Ida's claim that the litany caused the madness, and that was after you'd seen the results for yourself. Would you have thought me anything but a lunatic if I *had* told you?"

Billy's gaze narrowed. "You owed me the opportunity to decide for myself what I believed." Some of the rage seemed to have faded from him, however, his face and posture relaxing, if only just. "It's obviously far too late for me to decide not to work with you," he said, "even if I wanted to. You are going to tell me *everything*, though. No more secrets."

"There are no more. You know it all now."

Elliot lied without hesitation, without flinching. Because the final secret was one he'd kept for years, one that was nobody's business but his own. It had nothing to do with Billy, nothing to do with the *Ujaraanni* or curses or Chester's disappearance.

One that he'd no intention of sharing with anyone until and unless the day came where he told Chester himself.

After a moment, perhaps deciding whether he believed Elliot or not, Billy nodded. "So. Your spell protects you in part from this… litany. My talismans are effective as well. But neither is inviolate. Exposure to enough of these… corrupted souls, or for too long, and the wards fail. We'll need to be careful."

Elliot nodded. "Ida, I saw that you'd fashioned earplugs of a sort…"

"I did, but they don't work real well. Okay from a distance, but you wouldn't ever wanna count on them."

"No, I'd imagine not, but every little bit helps."

"Won't be enough. I don't know about your, uh, spells and charms." Her mouth twisted around the words. Elliot wasn't sure if she still, despite all she'd seen, had difficulty believing, or if perhaps she felt some religious objection. "But even together, those ain't gonna get you outta here. They'll grab you in the swamp, drag you down and drown you or hold you until you can't help but hear 'em."

The two men again exchanged glances, each confirming with the other what they already knew.

"We're not trying to leave," Billy told her.

"Not without Chester or the *Ujaraanni*, if they're here," Elliot added. "We're going to the Hennessy place."

CHAPTER THIRTEEN

That declaration had gone over about as well as Elliot expected it would.

Ida spent some time informing the two of them, in no uncertain terms, that they didn't *need* the effects of the litany as they were clearly quite out of their minds to begin with. She'd grown even more emphatic when Billy asked if there was any way she might assist them. She literally laughed at the suggestion before declaring that, if she'd any intention of either committing suicide or succumbing to the spreading madness, she'd already had far easier opportunities to do so. She'd even gone so far as to retrieve her rifle in preparation for leaving the pair of them to whatever idiocy they were determined to undertake – with the stern warning that she'd not go out of her way to rescue them a second time – when Elliot had stopped her cold.

"You said there only a handful of you left?" he'd asked.

"Yeah," she said, shouldering her weapon. "Me and a few others."

"And how long do you expect you'll survive, or be able to protect them, if nothing around here changes?"

She'd frozen in the hallway, almost twitching.

"You said it wasn't worth the risk of trying to escape," he'd pressed, "because you have nowhere to go. But I can fix that."

His family had never been wealthy, not compared to Chester's parents or their peers, but the Raslos were well-off enough. Elliot could certainly afford train fare for a "handful" back to Arkham, and to put them up in cheap lodgings for a time. Months, even, long enough for Ida or some of the others to find employment. Even a flophouse, he reckoned, would be more comfortable, and certainly far safer, than their constant fearful sheltering here.

"But only if I help with your lunatic plans, right?" she'd demanded, her shoulders slumping.

"No." That had earned him two shocked stares, one Ida's, one from Billy. "Assuming I survive ..." He had to rush through those words. He'd never counted himself courageous, and wouldn't have been today, either, if it hadn't been Chester who needed him. "... I'm not going to leave you or the others to suffer or die, whether you help us or not. But I'd also be lying if I said the likelihood that I *will* survive wouldn't be greatly improved by your help. It's up to you."

And so she'd led them from the house, through a hatch beneath a throw rug in the downstairs hall to the muddy crawlspace beneath the floor. After listening for long moments, to be sure none of the "corrupted" were near, she'd pushed aside a cluster of loose brush concealing the entrance to that crawlspace, and they'd found themselves outside.

Billy had expressed a quiet delight at the whole affair, as he finally had his answer as to how she'd gotten inside without him hearing the door.

From there they'd crept through shallow swamp waters and scattered cedar copses, quietly working their way around the edges of the community. Quietly and *slowly*, as Elliot – and even the others, to a lesser extent – flailed and stumbled in the dark of night. Inwardly he cursed the gloom, for all that he understood why a flashlight or a lantern were utterly out of the question. Ida had insisted the darkness would help conceal them, but Elliot still wished they'd waited for dawn.

"The mad ones don't use fire," Ida had whispered at one point while they crouched behind a thick tussock. "Least not that I ever seen. So you gotta keep your ears open, 'cuz you won't see them comin.'"

Nerve-racking as the journey was, they reached their destination without incident. It was another house, little different than the one they'd just left.

"My aunt and uncle's place. Or it was." She led through a similar brush-hidden entry, a similar crawlspace, and up through a similar hatch.

"Wait here while I tell the others I ain't alone. Don't want one of you gettin' shot."

"That would be inconvenient," Billy agreed blandly.

Elliot sat on the floor, back to the staircase, while Ida proceeded upward. This place smelled subtly different than the previous house. It had the same atmosphere of mold; inescapable, as he'd expected, given the environs. It held other scents as well, however, odors he couldn't identify but that might well have told him, even if he hadn't already known, that this place was occupied where the other had not been.

Maybe this is the sort of thing Billy's learned to pick up on, he mused, entertaining himself by trying to focus in on the smells.

A faint odor of cooking, perhaps? Nothing strong, maybe just a simple soup or the like. Sweat? Could be old sweat. And…

His nose wrinkled. He wasn't sure he wanted to know why, but he'd have sworn he'd caught just the faintest hint of feces.

Ida's call, barely more than a whisper, drifted down from above. "All right. Come on up."

Elliot and Billy obeyed, the stairs creaking beneath their feet. Ida stood in a narrow hall, its carpeting so old and cheap and worn it appeared the floor just hadn't shaved lately, outside an open doorway. She fidgeted as they drew near.

"Listen, before you go in…"

But they both had already looked over her shoulder, drawn perhaps by the sound of muttering.

There were several people in the room, some furniture, another door, but they scarcely noticed any of that.

In the room's center, a man wearing a filthy shirt and trousers was tied to a chair with heavy rope. His hair and beard were wild, tangled, partly hiding his face, but not so thoroughly that Elliot failed to spot a family resemblance to Ida.

His head rocked limply side to side, and with every breath, every move, he murmured those dreadfully familiar words.

"Isslaach thkulkris, isslaach cheoshash…"

Elliot cried out, wrapping his fingers instinctively around the amulet Billy had given him. His friend hissed something unintelligible, his own hand dropping to the pana at his waist.

"No!" Ida stepped in front of them, hands raised. "He's harmless!"

"How can you say that?" Elliot demanded, even as Billy reached out to shove her aside.

"*Listen*! What do you feel?"

"I…" Elliot stopped, jaw dropping. Nothing. Even with the protection of the talisman, of the spell, he'd felt the litany's pressure on his mind every time he'd heard it spoken. But now, other than the familiar pull that had been his constant companion for weeks, he felt almost nothing. After the first shock of it, a peculiar sense of initial impact, they were just normal – if disturbing – sounds.

Billy, too, froze, frowning. "I don't understand."

"I told you before," Ida said. "I told you folks don't all respond the same to hearin' the chant. Well, some of the infected don't seem the same *sayin'* it as others, either. A few of them, it's like they can't spread it. You hear them, and it feels like you got punched in the head, but nothin' else happens. You don't go crazy, don't start repeatin' it. It's the only reason I'm still me," she admitted. "One of them caught me by surprise."

Then, possibly anticipating the questions and concerns that might follow, "It was only a day or two after this all started. If I was gonna… gonna change, I would've by now."

Elliot struggled to think. *God, every time I'm starting to get a handle on this…* "There's no commonality? Nothing about them to suggest why they may not be able to pass it on?"

"If there is, I don't know it." She was about to say more, stopped and quailed beneath Billy's glower. "I wasn't keepin' secrets from you!" she insisted, doubtless remembering his angry rant from before. "I just got distracted by everythin' else we was talkin' about and didn't think to mention it. I swear."

His only response, after a long pause, was "Hmm." Without another word, he walked into the room. Ida and Elliot, each hesitant for their own reasons, trailed in behind him.

Now that he had the attention to spare, Elliot took in the somewhat dim surroundings and the other survivors. In addition to the bound man, the room held a rickety table and several mismatched chairs, probably dragged in from elsewhere in the house. An oil lamp glowed from atop that table, a risk they could afford because the only window was both boarded over and heavily curtained. The other door was only slightly ajar, and Elliot couldn't begin to make out what might be in the next room.

Two figures waited beside that table, a young woman and another man, both clad in heavy cottons and denims, and both as pale as most of the community's inhabitants. She was dark-haired, her eyes surrounded by deep hollows of exhaustion so she appeared almost skull-like, making it difficult to guess her age. She stared absently into the burning lamp.

Her companion was lightly bearded, perhaps in his early thirties, his hair the color of summer hay.

"This is Virgil," Ida said, pointing first to the man, then the woman, "and Lucy." Then, indicating with the other hand, "Billy and, uh, Elliot."

Virgil advanced, warily, and extended a stiff hand for the newcomers to shake. "Don't really trust outsiders right now," he told them pointedly. "But Ida says you're okay, so you're okay. Until you're not, hear me?"

"Uh, yes," Elliot agreed. Billy nodded.

Lucy glanced vaguely up from the lamp, then went right back to her staring.

Ida's voice dropped to a near-whisper. "Forgive her. We ain't seen her husband Abraham in almost a week now. She don't say or do much, except when she's helpin' me care for–"

A faint, ragged groan floated in through the second door. Ida sighed.

"And that'd be him." She headed that way, and the two newcomers followed.

In that next room, she struck a match and lit a second, smaller lantern. Here, too, the windows were boarded and curtained. The room held another table, a rocking chair, an open chest full of linens, topped by ratty cards, discolored dominoes and the like ...

And a narrow bed, on which a young man tossed and turned beneath rancid, sweat-stained sheets.

"This is Alfred. Alfie. My fiancé." She reached down with a sad smile and brushed a lock of blond hair from a forehead sticky with perspiration.

Alfie was probably about the same age as Ida, though furrowed brow and clenched jaw made him appear somewhat older. He gazed up at her touch, eyes fluttering open, but they were glassy, unfocused.

"Oo's 'at?" he mumbled at her.

"Just some travelers, hon. Go on back to sleep."

"'Llrght." He was out once more almost instantly, and swiftly resumed his tossing and turning. Mechanically, Ida began carefully stripping the filthy sheet and blanket from atop him.

"There're clean ones over in the chest, if you don't mind?"

Elliot stepped over, cleared away the bits of games and other entertainment, and returned to Ida's side with an armful of blankets. This close, he could smell the alcohol on Alfred's breath, even in his sweat.

She must have seen something in the flicker of his expression. "He ain't a drunk, you know." As she changed the blankets, his legs were revealed. The left was swathed in thick bandages, with two wooden planks set to hold the limb immobile. "He broke it real bad, gettin' away from the crowd that came pourin' outta the Hennessy place that night. We set it best we could, but all we can do for the pain is keep him in moonshine."

Not wishing her to feel she had to defend herself, Elliot said, "It looks to me like you're doing everything you can for him."

"Yeah. I… I'm tryin', but it's hard. Lucy watches him when I'm out huntin' supplies or just need a break, but she's got her own loss…"

"And you're still caring for him, in the midst of everything," Billy added. "That speaks well for you, and your feelings for him."

Ida turned away so they couldn't see her face at that. When she spoke, her voice was thick.

"Virgil'll find you some more blankets, show you where to bunk, where we keep our food and water. Get some sleep. Tomorrow we'll start figurin' on how to pull off your suicide mission without the actual suicide."

Elliot welcomed the meal, even if it was only beans and dried meats, washed down with well-water.

Sleep he welcomed even more, as the exhaustion of the day overwhelmed him. He tossed and turned at first, trying to absorb all he'd learned and seen, to say nothing of his fear that they might be attacked in the night. Ida assured him, however, that the corrupted, though occasionally cunning, were not especially smart, had so far failed to realize there were survivors holed up in this house. Further, she and the others took turns standing watch at night, just in case. They were safe here, or at least as safe as might be managed.

None of those precautions protected Elliot from more of the snow-swept, flesh-rending nightmares, but one could hardly expect miracles.

He awoke several times – sometimes from those awful dreams, once because he could have sworn he heard what sounded very much like a slamming door. No other noises followed, however, neither movement from within the house nor chanting from without, and he eventually drifted off again, convinced it had been a remnant of a dream, or perhaps the shaky old structure doing a bit of settling.

The following day had brought countless aches and pains, to say nothing of a fatigue against which a single night's sleep was woefully insufficient. For that, and because Ida was in no rush to engage in what she still considered a fool's errand, Elliot and Billy did little more than catalog their supplies and discuss various possibilities – What if Chester wasn't here? What if the *Ujaraanni* wasn't here? – over which they had little power anyway.

It wasn't until the following day, then, that their planning began in earnest. Lucy and Virgil faded in and out of their conversations, which ranged throughout the house but always returned to the small room upstairs so Ida might spend time with Alfie, or so one of the three could try – usually with little success – to force Richard, the man in the chair, to eat or drink something.

Five final, untainted survivors, so far as any of them knew, of what had been a thriving community.

A rough map of the community – which Ida had sketched in chalk on old paper – and several guns lay on the table. She had insisted that Billy and Elliot help themselves to the small arsenal she'd collected from the many abandoned homes. "If you think I'm goin' anywhere near the Hennessy place with an unarmed man," she'd told them, "you're madder than they are."

The Springfield rifle, which she'd carried the day she met them, and the Colt pistol, however, were off limits. "Daddy brought them back from the war, and ain't nobody usin' 'em now but me."

Billy had selected the next largest rifle, a lever-action Winchester. Elliot had no idea if his people used guns, but the ease with which the man worked the breach and loaded the weapon proved he had some experience with them.

It was experience Elliot himself lacked. Eventually he'd chosen a simple revolver, similar to the sidearms he'd seen the Arkham police carrying, under the assumption – the hope, really – that it would be the easiest to manage. Ida gave him a few pointers, showing him how best to use the sights, correcting his stance, and eventually told him, "Look, just try not to use it till you're close enough you can't miss."

Perhaps not the most inspiring words he might have hoped for.

Evening had fallen once again, and the three of them sat about the table, twisting torn bits of cotton into makeshift earplugs. Alfred snored loudly from the next room, and even Richard seemed to have dozed off, though he mumbled occasional bits of the litany even in his sleep. They'd given him one of his regular cleanings earlier in the day, so the room smelled a bit less foul than it had.

"… ran just fine the day before all this started," Ida was telling them as they worked out the kinks in their plan. "I figure it still ought to. We do this right, it should draw any of them away from outside the house."

"From inside, too, if we're lucky," Billy said.

"Maybe, but we still don't know how many're even in there. I don't like–"

"Ida…"

The trio rose from the table, turning toward the door at the weak, shaking call. Virgil stood in the adjoining room, hunched, hands clutching his head as if to keep it from bursting. He staggered toward them, his steps less steady than any drunkard's, only to collapse halfway. He struck the table on the way down, making no effort to catch himself, and landed with a dreadfully hollow sound. Knocked askew by the impact, the lamp on that table – currently and thankfully unlit – dribbled a stream of oil, glistening as it crossed the wood.

Billy acted first, reaching the man's side almost before he hit the floor. Seeing no obvious injuries, he carefully lifted Virgil in his arms and carried him back toward his companions, rather than leaving him to lie near the spilled fuel. There he and Ida carefully looked the stricken man over while Elliot grabbed the nearest fabric, an old tablecloth, to mop up the all too flammable mess.

"What happened to him?" he asked, upon returning from his task.

"Don't know," Billy said, not glancing away from Virgil's supine form. "We haven't found any wounds."

Ida, however, did look up abruptly from her friend. "Lucy! Where's Lucy?"

"I'll go–" Elliot began, but a groaned word from the floor stopped him.

"No…" Virgil opened his eyes, jaw taut with even that much effort. "She's gone. Left."

"Left?" Ida grasped his shoulders as if to shake him, visibly restrained herself at the last second. "What do you mean left? What *happened*?"

"Left after… after she told me…"

"Told you *what*?"

But Elliot knew what the answer would be even before Virgil confirmed his fears. "Told me *them*. The words."

"No. No!" Now Ida did shake him. "It ain't possible. She couldn't have been exposed!"

"She's been… sneaking out at night. To look for Abraham."

Ida cursed, shoulders slumping and head hanging. "Of course she did. I shoulda known. And *you* shoulda told me!"

"I know." Virgil managed a faint smile. "But she knew you'd try to stop her. She begged me, and I thought… I thought she was OK."

"Virgil," Ida said then, the words cracking, "there's no way…"

"I know," he repeated. "No way back. No way to know how long I got. No way to know if I can spread it. Just… make it quick."

Billy stood and stepped aside, thinking. "No need for that yet. We know my amulets offer some protection. We can wait until you succumb, let me feel it when you begin to chant. I should be able to tell if you're dangerous. If not, we can–"

"Can what? Tie me to a chair for the rest of my days, like Richard? That ain't any kinda life. I told you before, Ida, you ain't doin' your brother any favors – and I'm tellin' you now, I don't want that for myself."

Elliot turned away, brushing past Billy to reach the far side of the room, standing near the sealed window beyond the table and the chest. This wasn't an argument he wanted to hear.

He didn't want to be reminded of the choice he himself might have to make.

They'd actually gotten lucky, he realized, in a twisted sort of way. Lucy could well have exposed more of them than just Virgil, with only the tiniest twist of fortune. Particularly if – like Chester before he'd disappeared – she'd only slipped into the recitation on occasion, had otherwise kept control of herself, she could, without even meaning to, have worked her way through the entire household, and they would never have known until–

"*Iiiiii…*"

A single, drawn-out sound, high-pitched and trembling, ended the argument across the room, drew Billy's attention, drew Elliot's. He fought a moment to keep himself from turning. Every nerve in his body, every instinct, every thought in his head, shrieked in a single chorus that he did not, oh, God, he *did not want to look.*

He turned. He looked.

They all did.

Alfred stood beside the bed in which he'd lain, swaying with an unsteadiness that didn't look to be caused by either pain or drink. His leg bulged obscenely where it shouldn't, the makeshift splint failing to hold it entirely straight, but he seemed oblivious to the injury. He stared, but now it was not intoxicated bewilderment Elliot read in the man's gaze.

It was nothing. Nothing at all.

"*Iiiiii….*"

Ida was gasping, her body unsteady. Billy, so unshakable, so ready for anything, seemed paralyzed. Elliot wondered, crazily, if he looked as horrified to them.

The sweat beading up across Alfred's face, his neck, his arms, thickened as if purging all the impurities from his body at once. A pungent mélange of sickness and rot and alcohol made eyes water throughout the room.

Finally, after an eternity of seconds, the syllables began to emerge.

"*Isslaach thkul–*"

Ida screamed, a piercing, banshee's wail, swept her rifle up from the table on which it lay, and pulled the trigger.

CHAPTER FOURTEEN

Well into the following evening, frogs, insects and night birds conducted their nightly orchestra, hidden behind curtains of darkness and trees. The slow-moving waters lapped almost silently at the skirts of solid ground. Dozens of near-mindless townsfolk, chanting softly, wandered about the Hennessy property where most of them – save a few scattered stragglers and lurkers in the swamp, waiting to waylay would-be escapees – gathered every night as the sun descended.

Elliot and Billy, huddled behind a fallen log across from the discolored old house, worked hard at making no sound at all.

It hadn't been long enough, not by far, to call the plan a failure. Ida might reasonably need more time, several more minutes at least, to complete the first stage of her task. Intellectually, Elliot fully understood that.

Emotionally he was a disaster, bordering on sheer panic. Bad enough he was already neck deep in circumstances that would petrify or even drive mad braver men than he, with every intent to dive in deeper still. But to be relying so heavily on Ida Glick, after all that had occurred…

She'd sworn, time and again, that no vile chorus resounded in her head, that her fiancé's abortive chant had failed to take hold. Indeed, Elliot had no good cause to doubt it; he saw in her expression and her posture, heard in her voice, none of the vague preoccupation that had fallen over him after he himself had been exposed. She could, of course, just not be showing symptoms *yet*, but it truly seemed – perhaps because she'd heard so little of it, perhaps because her own scream had deafened her to it, perhaps because Alfred had been one of those incapable of spreading the malady – that she'd been spared.

Elliot almost wondered whether she believed that to be a mercy or a curse.

In the twenty-some-odd hours since she'd fired those three shots – the second one to save Virgil from his own oncoming transformation, at his request, and the third to put down her brother Richard – she'd spoken almost not at all. She insisted her mind was whole, insisted the plan would go ahead as discussed, and otherwise retreated to some inner sanctuary where Billy and Elliot could not follow.

If she slept, it was only moments at a stretch. If she ate, the others hadn't seen it. Worst of all, after a single initial outpouring of grief, during which she'd dropped her weapon and fallen to her hands and knees in the blood of those she'd loved, she hadn't shed a tear.

Elliot certainly understood. He couldn't imagine how he'd react if he had to do the same for Chester, and she'd lost a friend and a brother as well as the man she meant to marry. It hardly required Elliot's many courses on the topic of human psychology to suggest that her reactions to what had happened and what she'd felt forced to do, however understandable, were neither healthy nor hopeful. That counting on her playing her part in a plan on which their own minds and lives depended was perhaps ill-advised.

Even as his stomach redoubled its efforts to tie itself in knots, however, and he began to feel that things had fallen apart, a new sound filled the Hockomock night, drowning out all the others. First a series of mechanical sputters, and then a steady chugging roar, announced that Ida remained on task.

As she'd expected and they'd all hoped, the gasoline-powered tractor belonging to the Hennessys' nearest neighbors – one of the most modern pieces of equipment in the entire community, albeit only usable on the highest and driest portions of the property – still ran perfectly well.

Also as they'd hoped, the sound was more than sufficient to attract attention. Almost in perfect unison, the chanters on the Hennessy grounds turned their heads, their stares somehow simultaneously intent yet empty. They raised their voices, until the refrain grew louder than the tractor and Elliot began to flinch from the pressure in his mind. He muttered his own protective spell, time and again, and clutched at his borrowed talisman. Billy, too, clenched his own amulets in his fist. They could remain only a few moments, if the corrupted didn't…

But they did. In some foul midpoint between a marching platoon and an advancing hive, they set off, every one, toward the mechanized siren's song. Their voices faded with distance, if only somewhat, and the young student gasped in genuine relief.

They still had no way to know if any of the locals remained inside the house, but that was what their weapons were for. Elliot prayed it wouldn't come to that.

"Go," Billy breathed at him. Bodies bent low, they dashed

from behind their cover and made for the next nearest hiding spot: the Hennessy barn.

It wasn't large, as barns went, but it looked to be in solid shape; more so, in fact, than many of the nearby houses. The main doors were chained shut, but trying to haul those open without attracting attention would have been a fool's errand anyway. Instead they moved to a smaller side door. It, too, was padlocked, but a blow with the butt of Billy's Winchester fixed that.

The single, sharp sound shouldn't prove sufficient to draw the attention of those who currently pursued the rumbling engine.

They hoped.

They meant to slip inside for only a moment, to wait long enough to be certain the corrupted had all gone, that nobody loitered or had returned to spot them, and then continue on to the main house. They hadn't thought to find anything of import here in the barn itself.

Once they were inside, however, and convinced it was safe to do so, Elliot switched on a small flashlight he'd taken from Ida's store of supplies. He'd intended to take only a swift glance around, to get his bearings and ensure nobody else lurked in here with them, though they would surely have heard chanting already if anyone had.

Instead he found himself staring at a deep red Lexington series T, one headlight shattered, its whitewall tires coated in dried, cracking mud.

It was very much not a practical vehicle, nor an inexpensive one, certainly not the sort any of the locals were likely to own. It would have stood out for that reason alone, even if Elliot hadn't recognized this automobile in particular.

But he did.

"That's Chester's car!" It was the weight of a hundred conflicting emotions, more than deliberate caution, that kept his voice low. Billy whispered something in reply, but Elliot didn't hear it. He'd already sprinted to the vehicle, flashlight thrust out before him, peering intently through the open windows.

It was empty. Of course it was empty. He already felt foolish for thinking it would be anything else.

Billy appeared behind him, placed a hand on his shoulder. "Look at the dust. Thing's been here for weeks, at least."

"Yeah. I know, I…" He stopped, considering. "But Chester took the train to get here."

"Hmm." A moment, then, "Obviously he'd come here more than once recently."

"That makes sense, but why leave the car?"

It was puzzling enough for a second, more meticulous inspection. Unsurprisingly, it was Billy, with his keen hunter's gaze, who spotted it.

A few shallow tears in the upholstery of the back seat showed where something had pressed deeply into the leather. Something that had sat there for some time before finally being moved. Something weighty, for its relatively small size. Something generally rectangular, with one side rough enough to snag.

They absolutely were here, then, or at least lately had been. Chester and the *Ujaraanni* both.

Elliot was too worn down by the past few days, too frightened by what might yet lie ahead, for the elation he might otherwise have felt. Still, it was a hopeful enough sign to draw a ragged grin, one that Billy mirrored with his own.

The flashlights clicked off, and the two men crept back to the side door of the barn, listening for any trace of movement. It was time, and past time, to get to the main house and, God willing, the end of both their quests.

Their ignorance of who or how many might remain within the Hennessy place made entering via the doors, or any of the obvious windows, a foolish endeavor. Ida had assured them, however, that – as with many of the community's dwellings – this house contained both a partial cellar and a crawlspace beneath, the latter occupying what space the unevenly shaped former did not. Through that crawlspace, they ought to be able to locate a viable means of access.

And so they found themselves, after a swift but uninterrupted dash across the open yard, amidst the muck and the cobwebs below the house. From unseen sources, the soft drip of water and the occasional skitter of some small creature provided a constant background noise. Listening past those, they could still hear the chug of the tractor's engine, far down the road.

Once or twice, they heard the report of Ida's rifle. When Elliot had turned to Billy, his worry written clear across his face, the older man had shaken his head. "Nothing we can do for her right now but see the plan through. Remember, long as she's still shooting, she's still alive and still herself."

And was still in enough danger that she needed to keep firing. It wasn't the reassurance Elliot imagined Billy thought it was.

They searched about them, covering themselves in mud and worse. They kept their hands hovering over the bulbs of their flashlights. This ensured they wouldn't be spotted by anyone on the property, but in exchange they had only a weak, diffuse illumination to work with.

Still, after long, uncomfortable moments, it proved sufficient. Several windows looked to provide access to the house's cellar. One of them, in fact, appeared very much as if it had been pre-prepared for them: it had been completely removed, the rotten wooden frame all but destroyed, and then haphazardly shoved back into place. A simple nudge should pop it right back out.

"Some sort of lure?" Elliot asked.

"For who? Not us. This happened a while ago."

Cautiously, suspiciously, they worked together to pull the window free without knocking it off to the inside, where it might shatter and alert someone. Once they'd cleared it, Billy slid through first, falling a short way to a broken stone floor, Elliot close on his heels.

Complete silence was not an option, though they did their best. The uneven stone floor occasionally tripped even sure-footed Billy, and puddles of the intruding swamp splashed now and again beneath their feet. Elliot, not generally claustrophobic, felt trapped, suffocated, and the hallway seemed to him the worst combination of sewer and tomb. As though encouraged by his fear, the chant reared up in his head, requiring he split his concentration even further in order to mouth his protective French words against it.

Because of that distraction, it took longer than it should for him to realize that his difficulty breathing wasn't entirely an illusion of his mind. The aroma of mildew sat not only in his lungs but on his tongue, so thick he tasted it – of mildew, and of worse. He gagged suddenly, keeping his most recent meal in his belly only by an act of will.

"God! What *is* that?"

"Rot." Billy's voice was grim as Elliot had ever heard it. "Don't look down."

Elliot, of course, did exactly that – and could no longer stop himself from vomiting.

At least it kept him from an embarrassing, and possibly dangerous, scream.

The swamp water had collected at a low point in the corridor, creating the largest puddle yet. It was larger, in fact, than the hallway was wide, for here a break in the wall created something of a natural niche.

Within that hollow, and spilling out into the corridor, lay a heap of decayed and waterlogged corpses. One wore shreds of a blue uniform, though it was too far gone to identify what it once had been. Police, maybe?

The freshest of them wore a suit coat, perhaps of tweed.

Even had the body been saintly, untouched by a hint of decay, it would have been impossible to name. Whatever had killed the poor soul, probably a small detonation or a shotgun blast, had obliterated his face.

"Get up!" The tone wasn't unsympathetic, but clearly brooked no argument. "We have to keep moving."

Elliot straightened from where he'd hunched against the far wall, having caught himself there when his stomach heaved. "In a hurry?" he asked, wiping his lips.

Either Billy missed the sarcasm or chose to ignore it. "Since some of those bones have been *gnawed on*, yes, I'd prefer to be elsewhere."

Not for half a second did Elliot believe his friend might be joking. He felt his gorge rise again, and he knew his eyes must be wider than the empty sockets of the skulls at his feet, but he nodded and resumed walking.

After a bit of thought, he realized that the walk itself had begun to bother him.

The hallway couldn't be this long, not unless this underground level extended further than the house above. It turned and doubled back a short way ahead; also peculiar, but that, at least, might be due to irregularities in the earth. This was swampland, after all. Perhaps the cellar had to be constructed around patches that were too soft to serve. That didn't explain though, why the cellar would be broader than the stories above.

Once they rounded the "U" in the corridor, they saw a junction coming up. To one side, it led into what appeared to be a storage or utility room, which in turn contained a staircase leading up into the main house. To the other…

They stared, neither entirely sure what they were seeing. Or rather, why they were seeing it *here*.

A long, open chamber, its brick walls covered in stains of mold, mud, and – to judge by the smell – far worse, held a number of cots and several scattered chairs. The bedding on those cots was balled up, torn, tossed aside, stained with urine, sweat and blood. Most of the chairs lay scattered on a floor partly stone, partly mud, and entirely covered in perhaps an inch of sitting water. Other lumps of ripped or discolored fabric appeared to have once been various pieces of clothing.

The entire room was divided from the hall by iron bars, unevenly and inexpertly mortared into place at some point well after the cellar was constructed, possibly quite recently. A gate of those same bars hung open, and a heavy padlock lay on the floor where it had fallen nearby.

What was this place?

When Billy finally spoke, he sounded almost casual. "Were you aware Chester's family had their own dungeon?"

Elliot raised his hands, dropped them again. He found no words with which to answer.

The hall continued beyond the makeshift cell, but a quick look revealed only more storage space, either filled with old detritus that hadn't been touched in years, or entirely empty.

They found themselves left with no other option but the stairs. Billy unslung the Winchester from where it hung at his shoulder, Elliot reluctantly drew his revolver, and they crept nervously up the steps. Elliot flinched with every riser, the creak of old wood, the dull slurp of the wet mud scraping from his shoes.

The trapdoor at the summit stood open, allowing ingress into the darkened house. After a whispered consultation, both men decided reluctantly they'd have to keep their flashlights on, despite the danger of being seen; the other choice was total blindness. Again they kept their palms near the bulbs, hoping at least to minimize their chances of discovery.

They stood in a wide hall that, other than its larger size, would have fit quite well in either of the other houses they'd recently experienced. A throw rug lay in a crumpled wad, up against the wall. Perhaps it normally covered the hatch to the cellar?

Also on the floor were a number of broken frames, torn paintings and photographs lying amidst shards of wood and glass. Between the peculiar passages, the trapdoor and now the signs of rage and ruin, Elliot found himself thinking back on various gothic novels. The association was far from comforting.

At the hall's far end, invisible from where they stood, what sounded like an old grandfather clock hollowly ticked away the passing seconds. Seeing no reason to choose otherwise, they moved toward the sound.

The clock coalesced from the shadows, a genuine antique, but it, too, had suffered from whatever happened within this sulking beast of a house. Though the brass pendulum still swung, the glass casing had been shattered, the intricate hands bent and mangled so they pointed outward instead of at the Roman numerals surrounding them.

The intruders now saw a pair of rooms off the main hall, one to each side. From the right came a constant mumble of those phrases now as familiar and as unwelcome as a recurring nightmare. Elliot felt only a minimal pressure at the base of his skull. Against a single speaker, his protections held. He advanced into the room, Billy at his side.

It was, or had been, a sitting room of some sort, to judge by the various chairs and upturned table, the ash-coated fireplace, the old radio atop a credenza. Another door led back into what Elliot guessed would be a kitchen, and a broad staircase ran up to the second floor, an overhead world currently doused in gloom.

In the center of the chamber, hunched in an upholstered chair, sat the man whose voice they heard. He was older, filthy and unshaven, and he cradled in his lap a double-barreled shotgun.

At the realization that he might actually have to use it, Elliot's own gun suddenly weighed a hundred pounds, his fist growing numb around it.

Even as they entered, he ceased his recitation and looked up. Infected he might be, but he wasn't gone yet, not utterly. His grip shifted on his weapon.

"Who're you? Why're you in my house?"

Elliot advanced a single step, pistol held to the side so the stranger could see it wasn't aimed his way. "We're sorry to intrude."

At this, the old man cackled until he choked. "If you ain't yet, you surely will be," he wheezed.

"Um. Yeah, we've gotten that impression. My name is Elliot Raslo. We're looking for–"

"Chester. You're lookin' for Chester."

"Yes!" God, at last someone here had *heard* of him. Elliot felt a tiny ember of hope. "Do you know him? Is he here?"

"My nephew," the old man said. "Chester's my nephew."

From behind Elliot, Billy cleared his throat, stepped more fully into the room. "Chester's father told us he had no other family."

"Yeah, he would. Bastard. Never had much use for the 'lower' branch of the family, not after he struck it rich." For an instant, the old man – *Woodrow*, Elliot recalled from the property deed; *this would be Woodrow Hennessy* – seemed incensed enough over the old grudge that he forgot to be frightened, forgot his incipient madness. "Wanted nothin' to do with us any more. Chester wasn't that way, though. Chester never forgot where he came from."

Again Woodrow cackled, but this time it ended in a sob and a wet, ugly spit. "Wish he had, now."

He went on, before Elliot could ask. "Raslo, was it? Yeah, he mentioned you, before he… Before. Said he was glad he hadn't dragged you into his 'research.' Guess he shouldn't have been, huh? Huh?"

Elliot knelt beside the chair. Part of him wanted to weep at the revelation that Chester had, at least for a time, remained sane enough – *himself* enough – to care about Elliot's safety. He swallowed the urge, knew this wasn't the time. "Mr Hennessy, what happened here?"

"Chester happened!"

The shout nearly knocked the young student back on his heels.

"Chester and that damned *thing* he found."

Billy's head cocked to the side. "If it's what I believe it to be, that 'thing' is the sacred charge of my people."

If Woodrow heard, he made no acknowledgment. "First he only wanted to hide it here a spell, while he went on researchin'. Said it wasn't safe any more where it'd been, that he'd figured out he couldn't trust somebody. Don't recall if he ever said who. Kept it in his car, in the barn. And that was fine. The animals didn't care for it much, wouldn't settle down around it, but we figured it was just somethin' about the car they misliked.

"But then he came back. He wasn't… wasn't right in the head. Wanted our help to get rid of it. So we took the damn thing, carried it into the swamp. But the swamp…" He grinned, showing browned teeth, but tears flowed down his cheeks. "The swamp refused to take it."

Elliot heard a soft hitch in Billy's breath.

"And then," Woodrow told them, "then Chester started… blithering. I didn't hear it myself, then. Ears ain't what they once was. But my family… It disturbed them, but that was all, at first. Chester tried to leave, but we wasn't sure it was safe, so we locked him in a room. Then my Sally, she started…"

More tears, now. Snot leaked from his nostrils, saliva dribbled from the corner of his lips.

"We needed a place to keep them, see? And we had the cellar my great granddaddy built as a stop on the Underground Railroad. Me and my boys, we mortared in some bars, started keepin' the mad ones there till we could figure out what to do.

"But I never *did* figure out what to do. And the madness kept spreadin', until my whole family... And then some of the neighbors..."

He looked up, and Elliot wondered if the man wasn't seeking some form of absolution. "I couldn't stop it. I couldn't spend much time with 'em; even stoppin' up my bad ears with cotton, I almost heard it. I kept workin', much as I could, but one man can't manage this property alone.

"And we got discovered. A few of the folks from the far end of town. A nosy postman. Some professor from Chester's school."

It was Elliot's turn to choke. Polaski *had* gotten this far! So what had happened to him? Was he one of the corrupted wandering the town? Was it sheer luck Elliot and Billy hadn't run into him?

"I couldn't... I couldn't let them leave, let them bring the authorities. They'da took my family. And I couldn't let them change, spread the madness any further! You see that, right? You see that?"

The temperature of the room seemed to drop by twenty degrees. "Mr Hennessy... What did you do?"

"I couldn't let them. I couldn't." Woodrow began rocking his chair, hunched around the shotgun. "But I didn't let them die for nothin'. The crazy ones, they don't care what they eat, and God knows I couldn't keep them fed on my own..."

Now Elliot *did* fall back, scrabbling away from the old man like a crab until he struck one of the overturned tables. He'd have vomited, then and there, had he not emptied his stomach moments before. For now he realized just who the faceless corpse in the tweed jacket must have been.

"I got careless, finally." Woodrow didn't appear to have noticed Elliot had moved, still gazed down at the spot in which he'd crouched. "Didn't know they was clever enough to play a ruse. Went downstairs, saw my boy Thomas face down in the mud. I ran in to check on him – and he grabbed me, pulled the cotton from my ears. Hissed that damned chant until I couldn't help but hear…" Another sob.

"Been here ever since, just waitin' on my turn to… turn. For a while, the mad ones went out, takin' folks from wherever they could find them and bringin' them back here for Chester to infect. After a while, though, they just started spreadin' out, convertin' more and more on their own. Dunno if there's anybody left, now."

Billy moved to the table, reached down to assist Elliot to his feet. He remained strong and steady as ever, but his face had gone sickly pale. "This is worse than we thought."

He had no idea how true that was. Because, for once, Elliot had caught something his friend had missed, something that turned his stomach to ash, his blood to ice.

"What do you mean," he asked Hennessy, voice quivering, "they brought people 'back here' for Chester to infect?"

"What do you think I mean, boy? Chester ain't never left the house."

CHAPTER FIFTEEN

The sound began in that instant, as if summoned by Woodrow Hennessy's declaration. It came from overhead, somewhere on the darkened second floor: an uneven pattern of thumps, like staggering footsteps, but not quite.

Thump... thump-THUMP. Thump... thump-THUMP.

Slowly growing louder as they neared the broad staircase.

Thump... thump-THUMP.

Billy turned his flashlight on the stairs, but the beam was weak, illuminating only a tiny pocket beyond the topmost step. He swept it, first to one side, then the other, hoping to see whoever – whatever – might be moving along the landing, but between the feeble luminescence and the shadows cast by the wood-barred railing, anything up there remained invisible.

In the far reaches of his mind, nearly as distant as the litany he fought constantly to keep locked away, Elliot wondered if that felt right, if the light hadn't seemed more potent mere moments before.

Then they heard the voice.

It was low, quieter than the shouting of the other corrupted they'd encountered, yet somehow stronger, more zealous.

Thump...

"Isslaach thkulkris, isslaach cheoshash..."

...thump-THUMP.

"Vnoktu vshuru shelosht escruatha..."

Elliot recoiled, crying out, the chant pounding against his skull, against the magics warding him. Billy's flinch and the sudden pallor of his skin made it clear he felt it too.

Thump...

"Svist ch'shultva ulveshtha ikravis..."

...thump-THUMP.

"Isslaach ikravis vuloshku dlachvuul loshaa..."

Though the flashlight now shuddered in his hands, Billy kept it trained above – and finally the figure stepped into the woeful puddle of light.

Elliot's scream was one of a horror confirmed, not a horror discovered, for he'd already known. He'd recognized more than the words; he knew the voice that uttered them.

Thump...

"Ulveshtha schlachtli vrulosht chevkuthaansa..."

Chester Hennessy stood unblinking, hair and skin and tattered clothes stiff with dried mud, blood, and God knew what else. With every second step he seemed to fall forward, barely catching himself with the opposite foot before he completely toppled. The effect was a peculiar, almost alien back-and-forth sway that no thinking man could have maintained for long.

And still the venomous liturgy poured from him, phrase after phrase, verse after verse, at least twice as many as Elliot had heard from any of the corrupted before. They hammered at him, called to the partial echoes already embedded in his soul. He shook, his skin clammy with cold sweat. This was a power he'd never experienced, as far beyond the chanting he'd heard so far as that chant had been beyond ordinary speech, and he knew the protections on which he and Billy were counting could hold for only minutes at best.

"Chester!" His cry was loud, carrying despite the tremor in his throat. "Chester, it's me. It's Elliot."

Chester heard, he must have. Yet he showed no reaction at all, let alone a hint of recognition. He took two steps down the stairs, again catching himself well beyond the point where physics and human anatomy demanded he fall, and the litany continued without interruption. When he finally reached its conclusion, some dozen or more lines beyond those Elliot had heard before, he simply began again from the start.

"*Isslaach thkulkris, isslaach cheoshash…*"

"Damn it, Chester." Elliot felt his voice break, his stomach drop. Had his heart stopped, frozen solid in his chest that instant, he wouldn't have been at all surprised. He felt almost betrayed that it hadn't. Unshed tears turned the room into a cracked kaleidoscope of blurred, partial images. "This is me. Don't do this. Come back to us." And then, far more softly, "Come back to me."

Another two steps. Another near fall. Another line of that cursed refrain.

Billy charged, leaping onto the credenza and from there to the stairs, vaulting the bannister to land on the broad step beside the filth-encrusted Chester. Rifle in his left hand, he struck with his right, and Elliot experienced a split second of gratitude. He knew the hunter's instinct – to say nothing of his fear, the pressure of the alien syllables in his mind – must have driven him to shoot, to end the threat as swiftly and surely as possible. That he made the effort to strike without killing was a gesture Elliot hadn't been sure he could expect.

For all the good it did.

As was his wont, Billy struck with the edge of a closed fist, delivering what should have been a debilitating blow to the madman's temple.

And Chester's head... *bent*.

From the jaw downward, he did not so much as budge. Above, the rest of his skull canted sharply to the right, lips compressed tightly together on one side, stretched far apart on the other, as though the joint itself had dislocated and separated by nearly the thickness of the striking fist.

Arm still half-extended, Billy froze, unable to absorb what he was seeing.

Still chanting, the sounds only marginally garbled by the deformation of his jaw, Chester lashed out casually as though shooing a mosquito. Billy crashed through the bannister, wood shattering and splintering, to land with a painful impact back on the floor.

Elliot couldn't move, wasn't certain he even breathed. Chester once more began his descent down the stairs.

Billy shouted, but Elliot didn't hear the words. Only the litany rang in his ears.

When he realized his companion would not or could not listen, Billy scrabbled for his rifle, lifted it toward Chester...

Now Elliot found the strength and the freedom to scream, trying to stop his companion before he fired.

And Billy *did* stop, but not because of Elliot. Woodrow, his own lips now once again moving in that alien tongue, leapt at Billy from behind, swinging his shotgun as a club. Billy rolled aside at the last second and the pair of them crashed away into the far side of the room, wrestling and striking at one another.

Leaving Elliot to face Chester alone.

He found his revolver in his hand, barrel pointed toward the advancing figure. He couldn't recall drawing it, let alone aiming.

"Oh, God. Chester, *please*! Please stop."

Two steps. Another line. Well more than halfway down the stairs now.

"*Please!*" He couldn't truly see Chester at all through his tears, could only aim at the center of the moving blur. "Please don't make me."

Two more steps. Elliot could barely tell where his mind, his memories, his soul, left off and the litany began.

A new phrase. The beginning of another step.

Elliot opened his mouth. What emerged was so soft, it was scarcely a breath. "I love you."

He tightened his finger. The trigger twitched.

Chester finished his step, another, nearly falling, impossibly catching himself.

The revolver didn't fire.

Elliot couldn't do it. The last fraction of an inch that would drop the hammer might as well have been a thousand yards. Elliot couldn't shoot, only sob, as Chester neared the base of the staircase.

But *someone* fired, twice in rapid succession.

The shots were the trumpet of Gabriel signaling the end of days. Everything in the room – even, for a heartbeat, the litany in Elliot's head – went silent.

Chester's skull rocked back. Thick, black blood ran from a hole in his forehead, slightly right of center, and from a second through his befouled shirt, just above his heart. Slowly he straightened, as if even these were but a mild inconvenience – and then pitched forward, toppling face first to slide and bump to a heap at the bottom of the stairs.

Bits of glass tinkled audibly to the floor, and at that signal the world began to move again. The pained grunts and bruising blows of Billy and Woodrow's struggle again sounded from the chamber's far corner, but Elliot paid them no heed, his shocked gaze drawn inexorably leftward.

One of the room's windows bore a pair of shattered holes, from which cracks still spread and chunks still fell. Beyond, barely visible in the darkened yard, stood the pale shape of Ida Glick, the Springfield in her hands, her eyes wide with shock, presumably at however much of the impossible tableau she'd witnessed before acting.

Something inside Elliot broke.

Where his hand had trembled earlier it now stood steady as a rock, cold steel aimed squarely at Ida's chest. Every other part of his body, however, every molecule, shook and twitched and burned. He screamed, shrieking until the pain in his throat grew near to rivaling that in his heart.

He wished, later, that he could blame his behavior solely on the litany, on some unnatural outside force. But it would have been a lie.

He never could remember, afterward, exactly what he said. What foul epithets he called her, what protestations he made, what threats he uttered. Vaguely he recalled branding her a murderer, wishing her to Satan's deepest pits, swearing that he could have – would have – reached Chester, talked him back from his insanity, reclaimed his soul, if only he'd been given that one final chance, those last few miraculous words.

Utter nonsense, of course. Even in the moment he knew it, but he buried that knowledge deep rather than accept it. He stoked his near-murderous rage, made it his furnace, searing away all other thought, because what it held at bay – the unfathomable grief, the clenching, gut-wrenching loss, the knowledge of what had just happened and the overwhelming guilt despite knowing there was nothing, *nothing* he could have done to change it – would have frozen him as surely as any blizzard.

Through it all, beyond the slightest tilt of her head and the twitching of a cheek, Ida did nothing. Said nothing. Whether the night's events had cast her into her own exhausted state of shock or because, after the fate of her last friends and family, she didn't care if Elliot gunned her down – or some other cause known only to herself – she made neither move nor argument to save herself.

Elliot wondered, afterward, if he would ever have truly fired on her, or if his mad fury would have wound down, run itself out, and it shamed him that he did not know. He was never to find out, though, because finally Ida's expression *did* change, becoming a mask of limp horror as she stared past Elliot's shoulder.

At first he didn't notice, as he failed to notice the faint sounds of something shifting, sliding across the floor. Even in his frenzy, however, what came next he could not help but hear.

"*Svist ch'shultva ulveshtha ikravis ...*"

He didn't deliberately turn around; it simply happened, his body racing ahead of his mind.

On the far side of the room, the struggle between Billy and Woodrow had paused in mid-grapple. Both men stared at a sight so impossible it had reached even the corrupted elder Hennessy, snapping him briefly back to sanity.

Chester, head still contorted partly to one side and his forehead still gaping wide where Ida's bullet had passed through, had clambered back to his feet.

"*Isslaach ikravis vuloshku dlachvuul loshaa…*"

Elliot emitted a primal bark, a sound of tangled, undifferentiated emotion, neither laugh nor sob. Rational thought was a squirming eel in his grasp, and he felt himself tempted to let it go, to sink into either the litany or some more mundane delirium, rather than try to grapple with what could not be, yet undeniably was, the reality before him.

Chester was dead. Surely he *must* be dead, yet he stood, moved, spoke. His chant continued unbroken, no longer even pausing for breath, and Elliot once again nearly let himself submerge in a wave of lunacy when he observed the faint wriggling of the torn threads around the rent in Chester's shirt. Saw that they danced in measure with the recitation.

Somehow Chester drew air into his lungs, into his voice, *through the bullet hole in his chest*.

Yet, for all the horrors tormenting Elliot, pounding in his mind like a wild stampede, he also found one train of thought grown suddenly and absolutely clear. It parted the confusion, the rage, the madness, all of it, his very own cerebral Moses at the Red Sea.

This thing before him, possible or impossible, living or dead, was not Chester. It had been, once, but his friend, the man he loved, was gone.

Again the room grew smeared behind a new font of tears, but this time when Elliot raised his revolver, he felt no hesitation.

Six rounds, rapid; he continued to pull the trigger, producing nothing but metallic clicks, well after the weapon ran dry. How many struck their target he couldn't say, but the being that had once been Chester Hennessy staggered, catching itself on the end of the bannister.

Still it didn't fall, didn't cease its recitation, but Elliot's action freed the others from their own paralysis. With thunderous reports, Ida and Billy both emptied their rifles into the wavering thing.

Ida dropped her empty rifle, drew her Colt and kept firing, even as Billy began feeding bullets into the open breach of the Winchester. When her magazine ran dry, she retrieved the rifle, ejected the spent clip and snapped in a new one.

But the barrage had finally proved too much. Chester fell yet again, the impact heavy and wet, and even had he somehow remained upright, somehow survived, not enough remained of his throat and jaw to make sounds at all, let alone form coherent words.

Woodrow staggered to his knees, reached to tug at Billy's sleeve, not in any attack, but a feeble call for attention. As Billy knelt to hear whatever the old man had to say, Elliot – and, soon after, Ida – carefully advanced on the mauled and mangled corpse.

It's not Chester. It's not Chester. It's not!

Easier to tell himself that earlier, though, when it stood as a man couldn't, survived what a man couldn't. When it spoke horror into the thoughts of all who could hear.

Now, when it was just raw, dead flesh…

Elliot screamed, an anguished howl, and collapsed. The world faded, his memories faded, his own name began to leave him. He grew hollow, empty.

And from within, those Godforsaken words – not the entire litany, though he'd heard it all several times now, but the fragment planted within him so many weeks ago was more than enough – surged up to fill that emptiness.

CHAPTER SIXTEEN

Not, however, for long.

In truth, it was but a scant few minutes – though Elliot didn't know that, having lost all sense of time along with the rest of himself – before his mind, his soul, began to return. It spread from a peculiar warmth in what he slowly recognized as his right hand, a sensation sharp yet somehow comforting. It spread, and carried awareness with it. All he was seeped back through his body as the refrain fled back to the closet in his soul where he locked it away, leaving room for his return, and he was again Elliot Raslo.

He felt unyielding wood beneath him, looked up to see Billy kneeling over him, hands clasped around Elliot's own, muttering in Kalaallisut. The cadence sounded very much like a prayer, or perhaps a protective mantra. The many cords around his neck were gathered into a single thick strand, for the many amulets...

Elliot blinked. The talismans were clutched in his own fist. They had been the source of that strange sensation, were – at least in part – what had driven back the darkness to which he had nearly succumbed.

"Th…" His throat, raw and abused by his earlier screams, produced a sound that couldn't even be called a proper croak. He swallowed, sucked in a deep breath, tried again. "Thank you. I'm… all right."

He wasn't, of course. Might never be again. But he was himself, and in control.

Billy broke off his prayer with a nod and a faint smile. Gently, he released his grip and carefully disentangled his protective amulets from Elliot's fingers. Elliot felt a surge of fear over their absence, but the words did not return. His own protections, and the borrowed talisman around his neck, were once again enough.

Leaning on Billy until his equilibrium returned, he climbed unsteadily to his feet. Ida still stood by the body, from which Elliot swiftly turned his attentions lest grief overpower him again. Woodrow Hennessy remained on the room's far side, watching them all, lips quivering with the battle taking place behind them.

Then, when Billy saw Elliot stand, he nodded once and turned back toward where Woodrow Hennessy had collapsed.

He was gone.

Elliot tried to speak, to wonder…

From the next room came the shotgun's roar. A dull, hollow thud followed. And Elliot didn't wonder any longer.

Neither Billy nor Ida appeared especially surprised, nor inclined to speak, so Elliot didn't either. Not out loud.

Please, God, let that be the last of it. He didn't think he could take any more horrors that night, or for a long time to come.

Instead he shuffled to the young woman's side, approaching at an awkward angle to keep the terrible mess at her feet out of sight.

"Ida, what I said… I'm sorry."

It took a moment for his words even to register. "Hmm?"

"Before? When I was… After you shot… I wasn't myself. I didn't mean those things I said to you."

"OK."

That was it? After his vicious, shrieking tirade? Elliot felt a flash of anger, until he reminded himself of all she'd gone through. That she'd seen the same horrors he had, and lost even more than he had. No wonder she might be distracted, numb, with far more to concern her than the insults of a grieving, selfish boy.

Instead he asked, "Are you all right?" Then, to clarify what would otherwise be a truly foolish question, he managed to gesture down at Chester's ruined body without letting himself think about it. "I mean, his chant…"

"Oh. Yeah, I'm fine. Couldn't hear him, out in the yard."

That made sense. Chester's recitations had been rather quieter than the others. Lucky, damned lucky. They–

A loud scrape scattered his thoughts like a flock of doves. They looked toward the noise to find one of the doors open, and Billy gone. Whatever they'd heard had originated in the next room.

Elliot bent to retrieve his fallen pistol, digging in a pocket with his other hand for the spare rounds. "Billy?"

He was relieved beyond measure when he received an answer. "Yes, be right out."

Indeed, the hunter emerged from the doorway seconds later, carrying a small steamer trunk he'd salvaged. Thick dust covered the old leather and the brass fittings, announcing that it hadn't seen use for quite some time even before everything here had gone to hell.

Billy let it drop to the floor, flipped open both latches, and prodded at the central mechanism. Then, with a shrug, he took his rifle and smashed the lock until it snapped completely off.

As the others watched, he opened the trunk to reveal old bottles, jars and smaller boxes, which he proceeded to dump. Then, finally looking up, "I can carry it by hand if I have to, but if you can help me find some straps, that'd be better."

Understanding finally dawned. "You mean to use that to carry the *Ujaraanni*," Elliot guessed.

"I do."

"But we've no idea where it is. He said they dropped it in the swamp."

Billy rose and began rummaging around the chamber. "No, you see, that's what Woodrow Hennessy told me in his last moments of sanity. He told me how to find it."

They set out not long after morning light, from that house of horrors further into Hockomock Swamp.

Billy wore the trunk strapped to his back with a number of belts he'd found in one of the rooms, an arrangement that couldn't possibly have been comfortable – and that would doubtless be even less so with the weight of the stone added. It failed to slow him down, however, and whatever directions or pointers or landmarks Woodrow had given him were sufficient that he pressed on through the shallow waters and across muddy knolls with little hesitation.

Nobody stood in their way, and no sound of chanting interrupted the natural song of the swamp. They passed several bodies on their way out of the community, bullet wounds serving as mute testament to Ida's struggles of the previous night. Elliot recognized one of them as having been her friend

Lucy, the source of the infection that had driven them from her uncle's home.

Whatever hesitation she'd previously shown to kill, whatever spark of hope or affection had driven Ida to attempt disabling injuries rather than lethal ones, had died with Virgil and Alfred. Most of the bodies displayed wounds to head or heart, and more than a few boasted those in addition to other, less severe damage. The inescapable conclusion, Elliot realized with a shudder, was that she'd made a deliberate point of finishing off the wounded.

The majority of the community's citizens hadn't died by gunfire at all, but by fire of a far more literal sort. One of the largest barns was nothing more than a pile of charred wood, still smoldering, tendrils of black smoke winding upward to merge obscenely with the lowering clouds. The metal skeleton of the tractor stood in the center of the ruin, and Elliot couldn't doubt that, were he to go look, he'd find a sizable collection of bones. Perhaps even evidence that the door had been barred from the outside after the corrupted were lured in by the rumble of the engine.

He did *not* go look.

He also remained unsure just how long their sojourn in the depths of the swamp took them. He retained only broken, sporadic memories of the trek, and he never quite figured out why. It wasn't the litany; though it troubled him – and his protective mantra was growing less effective, suggesting that time ran short before he would need to get his hands once more on the *Livre d'Ivon* – it wasn't strong enough to account for his fractured memories. Even if it were, why only this, their travel through the muck, beneath the shadow of the looming cedars, and not the morning before, or the afternoon after?

No, it was as if the swamp itself had absorbed some measure of the ambient madness that had afflicted the community, a madness through which these foolhardy intruders must pass to reach their goal.

He remembered the water, cold and murky and still, usually shallow enough to ignore, but occasionally so deep as to soak them to the knees or even higher. It felt vaguely gelid, as if the fluid itself strove to impede them.

He remembered the cries of the animals turning discordant, hostile. The swoop of birds, as he'd suffered before; the thrashing of small reptiles, of mink, even of a deer or two splashing through the water or struggling across the clinging mud, not fleeing from the three humans but *advancing* on them, teeth bared. He remembered gunshots, his own and the others', and the hot spray as Billy's pana drank freely.

He remembered the trees, clustered like bitter old men around a cigarette or a bottle, casting baleful glares over their shoulders at those whose lives still lay before them. Occasionally they hunched further still, their branches dangling fingers that brushed the wanderers' heads and shoulders. Elliot was certain they must surely clench into a sudden fist, yanking him from his feet by his skull.

And he remembered the stone.

Although they couldn't possibly have crossed so much of the sprawling Hockomock, it waited within a hollow of ridges and tussocks that felt like the very center of the swamp, perhaps of the world entire. The press of the water grew stronger, and he thought they approached through one of the wetland's random currents, or perhaps the remnants of a feeding stream.

Until they drew nearer, and he watched the ripples, the

tiny waves, and realized the water flowed away from the stone *regardless of angle or direction.*

The glistening black rock protruded only a few inches from the swamp, but even that was far too much. Assuming it was roughly the size Billy had claimed, small enough to fit within the trunk, and particularly given how much it must weigh, it should have been completely submerged, perhaps even having buried itself within the subaquatic muck.

It wasn't, yet neither did it appear to float. It sat absolutely still, without the slightest bob or drift, as if set in a base of hard soil or even cement. And Elliot recalled what Woodrow Hennessy had said in his half-mad rantings.

The swamp refused to take it.

"I heard tales," Billy whispered, though whether he tried to explain what they were seeing to his companions, or to himself, Elliot wouldn't guess. "That at times, when wicked anersaapiluk grew numerous and plotted against the Kalaallit, when the *Ujaraanni* sang to them more loudly than normal, the angakkoq would approach the stone, and say his ceremonies. Call upon friendlier toornat to guard us from the enemy spirits and lull the *Ujaraanni* to sleep again. And sometimes, he found the *Ujaraanni* buried deep within the ice of the cave – but inside a hollow. A bubble, as if even the ice drew away from it."

Carefully he unstrapped the steamer trunk and lay it on a thick tussock beside him, then stepped carefully toward the stone. "Whatever the *Ujaraanni* really is, even nature rejects it. I don't know if I fully believed … before."

Then, with a quick lunge – perhaps so he had no time to think twice – he bent and plucked the stone from its swampy cradle. His muscles bulged with the weight, but otherwise he seemed to meet no resistance. Although it sat in the water as though held in place, it emerged without struggle, slimy and dripping. Billy twisted, dropped it into the waiting container, and slammed the trunk shut.

Just that simple.

Elliot had caught only a glimpse of the symbols etched into the stone. He still couldn't begin to read it. Nevertheless he knew, with absolute certainty, that he'd been right. The litany in his mind, that had driven Ida's entire community to madness, came from that ancient, unknowable writing.

You did it, Chester. I wish you hadn't, but you did. I hope enough of you remained, at least for a while, to be proud of your achievement.

Billy hefted the trunk, straining with the weight until he found the proper balance. Elliot and Ida assisted him with the straps, and they set off once more, back the way they'd come.

"Why?" Ida made the demand, sounding more alive than Elliot had heard her since the death of her nephew. "Why in the name of Christ would you wanna go back there?"

Billy said nothing, but the narrowed glower he wore conveyed the same question.

They stood once more on the border of the now-dead community. Billy and Ida had just begun discussing whether they ought to shelter until tomorrow, rest up or head out for Taunton and then Arkham immediately – and, if the latter, whether they should travel by foot or attempt to make use of one of the remaining vehicles. The conversation hadn't gotten far, however, when Elliot had announced his own intentions.

"Look, nobody here wants to see the inside of that house again…" *And the tattered body of poor Chester.* "… any less than I do. But I've got to find something, come back with *something*. A token, an heirloom. Something for his parents." *And for me.* He sniffed once, otherwise refusing to break down again, to let the emotion take control.

"I don't think–" Ida began, but Billy interrupted.

"No, he's right. Chester's family deserves something of him to hold onto."

Somehow Elliot felt that the "family" he referred to wasn't Chester's mother or father. He smiled his thanks, though he received only the usual stoic facade in return.

Ida looked from one to the other, then shrugged. "Fine. A few minutes."

They entered by the front door this time, and Elliot went nowhere near the sitting room with the stairs. He might need to yet – it was the only way to the second floor, and he'd no idea if he could find what he required elsewhere – but he fully intended to put it off until absolutely necessary.

Instead he slipped down other halls, leaving his companions to their own devices, and back down the hatch to the peculiar cellar. His flashlight occupied one hand, while he kept the other pressed over his mouth and nose in a futile effort to mitigate the terrible scent of the cell where multiple corrupted souls had dwelt in their own filth for days or weeks.

Slipping through the open gate, he found himself again facing the bunks, the scattered bedding, the odd piles of abandoned clothes. Wondering how he could possibly have thought to find anything worthwhile here, he idly prodded at those heaps, first one, a second…

The third partly fell aside, the top part a single chunk glued together by mud and worse, to reveal a familiar coat.

Away from his friends, Elliot allowed the tears to come again, stood over this remnant of Chester as sobs racked his whole body and his gut felt like a pit that would never again be filled, that he could only wish would swallow him whole.

It didn't, and eventually his eyes ran dry, burning and raw. Only then, finally, did he pick up and examine the coat. He couldn't bring the garment itself back; it meant nothing much to him, would mean little to Chester's parents, and was indelibly soiled in any case. But maybe something within?

The outer pockets were empty, nothing but fabric meeting his questing fingers. In the inside left breast pocket, however, Elliot found a fountain pen – which might have been quite nice, before it spent days not merely coated but filled with the muck's seeping fluids – and a thickly folded array of small papers. This, he carefully removed and laid out atop one of the cots.

Most was unsalvageable, the ink having run into meaningless smears, the paper itself soaked through and discolored. A few bits in the very center, however, had been partly protected by their less fortunate brethren. Elliot looked them over in brief perusal.

Before him were, in fact, two very different sorts of document. Most of the collection, and thus most of the survivors, were small sheets of modern paper torn from a pad. These bore notes in a handwriting Elliot immediately recognized as Chester's. Later he might read through them, see what he might learn, but for now it was enough to identify them as his.

The others, of which there were only a very few remaining scraps, were of a far older, thinner, less hardy material. It might even be some manner of parchment, rather than true paper. The few portions that weren't soaked were, instead, so old they had dried, and threatened to crack if not creased *just so* along preexisting folds. Even after lying in the filth, even in the heart of the room's thick miasma, they gave off the slightest whiff of age.

Elliot couldn't guess where Chester might have acquired them, and was even more at sea regarding what they might say. He was learned enough to recognize the writing as Greek, but he had no education in the language.

This was something, at least. He frowned, though, as he carefully refolded the documents and slid them into his own pocket. It was Chester's, yes, but it held no special memory or emotional association. It wasn't anything his parents would appreciate, and to Elliot himself, they were, as far as their value as a memento, worse than useless. They were a symbol of the obsessive project that had taken Chester from him.

He'd have to keep searching, then, and not down here. Hardly a surprise, but he'd hoped–

"Elliot!" Billy's shout echoed from the hatch atop the stairs. "You'd better come up here."

Oh, God, no more. How can there possibly be anything more?

Oddly stiff, as if his body anticipated whatever latest horror his mind could not conceive, he shuffled back to the staircase, hauled himself up, riser by riser, through sheer habituation and muscle memory.

As he crested the hatch, he saw Billy and Ida waiting in the hall, and while both stood still, they somehow conveyed the impression of nervous fidgeting.

"What's happened?"

Both of them glanced away a moment, reluctant to answer or even meet his gaze. Then…

"Chester's gone," Billy told him.

The words literally had no meaning, not any more than the litany had. "I don't understand."

Ida tried now. "Elliot, Chester's body. It's gone."

He waited for understanding to dawn. When it didn't, he simply walked forward, pushing past them both and toward the sitting room.

"Elliot…"

He ignored the call, turned the corner.

The furniture remained overturned, the room crimson-spattered.

Other than a pool of drying blood and scattered bits of unrecognizable carnage, however, nothing remained of Chester. Not where he'd fallen at the base of the stairs, nor anywhere else in the room.

"Animals," Elliot announced, even as he swept the room for paw prints, claw marks, a blood trail, and found none of them. "Animals took him. We should have covered up the broken window."

"No animals of significant size have been here, Elliot," Billy told him, speaking slowly, as to a child.

"One of the corrupted, then. Surely Ida didn't kill *all* of them. One of them crept in, dragged him off."

"To what end?"

"*I* don't know, do I? They're *mad!*"

Ida shook her head. "Ain't any sign of that, either. Besides, why'd you think we left you alone down there long as we did? We looked around first. All down here and upstairs. No trace, no tracks."

"Then you missed something! You saw him! You saw what we…" The room spun. Elliot put a hand on the bannister to steady himself, then recoiled when he discovered it was still tacky with drying gore.

"You saw what was left," he muttered, staring in terrible fascination at the red on his palm. "He sure as God's in his Heaven didn't get up and walk out of here!"

"Probably not," Billy agreed, though his refusal to rule it out wasn't lost on Elliot, even in his dismayed and distracted state. "But then it means someone else was here, strong enough or numerous enough to carry him out, and stealthy enough to do it without leaving a trail. We don't know who, and we don't know why.

"That means we go. Now. Before he, or they, or *it*, comes back."

"We can't leave." Why couldn't he tear his attention from the filth on his hand?

Why did part of him want to let the mantra rise once more from the corner of his thoughts and wash his concerns and his grief away?

"We can't leave until we know what happened to him. We can't. We just can't!"

He was still protesting, screaming even, but still staring intently at his open palm, as Billy took him by the collar and dragged him from what had long been, but would never again be, the Hennessy house.

CHAPTER SEVENTEEN

No matter how Daisy wished the lingering chill would break already, spring refused to commit itself, like a reluctant swimmer dipping a toe now and then into a frigid pond.

It was especially peculiar, as Daisy and her compatriots at Miskatonic frequently discussed because, according to the radio – when it wasn't going on about the Influenza outbreak near the Merchant District, and the economic damage it was causing Arkham – the weather was properly seasonal across the rest of the country. Even other portions of New England had long since warmed and thawed, their grasses green and their flowers blooming. Only over this pocket, from Vermont to Rhode Island, from the coast to the Catskills, did winter's shadow refuse to wane.

If only the weather had remained the most significant of her problems.

Daisy wrapped her arms around her and leaned into the breeze, to keep warm in her heavy overcoat and to keep her cloche from flying off her head – but mostly to protect the parcel, wrapped in multiple layers of waxed paper and thicker packaging paper, clutched to her chest. Although she'd left work a bit early, the heavy cloud cover accelerated the fall of night, so she made her way home illuminated primarily by the glowing streetlamps and the headlights of passing cars.

What she was going to *do* when she got home, she'd no idea.

Elliot and Billy Shiwak had returned to Arkham yesterday, accompanied by a young woman they'd introduced only as Ida – and even that she'd had to coax from them, as none had been in any state to hold intelligible conversation. They'd simply showed up at her door, begging shelter so they might recover in privacy. She'd not yet even discovered how they'd learned her address, as she was fairly certain it didn't appear in Arkham's quite limited telephone directory.

She knew her neighbors would talk if they saw she had two single men staying with her, let alone a university student, and even Ida's presence made it only moderately less scandalous. She'd had to sneak them in past the tenants on the lower floors then, and insisted on silence.

Elliot's condition was threatening to make even that requirement impossible to enforce.

Whatever in God's name that condition might be. Concerned as she was, she also wrestled with more than a little irritation – legitimate, she felt, under the circumstances – that they seemed reluctant to share the whole story.

She'd gotten *some* of it out of them, mostly from Billy. He'd explained that they tracked down the Hennessy family, that they'd discovered not just Chester but the whole community gripped in some sort of mania, that things had gotten… ugly. They found many dead, including Professor Polaski. Blood was spilled, Elliot had been forced into acts for which he was emotionally unequipped and they'd barely escaped with their lives, fighting off multiple ambushes in their flight. That they had retrieved the *Ujaraanni*, but were uncertain as to the fate of Chester himself.

When Daisy told him, with some heat, that he obviously wasn't revealing everything, and that she didn't appreciate being kept in the dark, he'd muttered about evil spirits and ancient curses and strange things she would never believe, and was happier not knowing.

Oddly enough, she didn't *feel* any happier.

Oh, the whole bit about spirits was hogwash, of course. Her study of ancient tomes and the cultures that produced them left her more openminded than many in this modern age of science and industry, but she drew the line at this occult nonsense. She didn't even like to *imagine* how horrible a world it would be if such possibilities, worse by far than the ghosts and revenants and vampires that occupied her leisure reading, could be real. Billy's beliefs might include those sorts of things, and Ida might be a poorly educated yokel, but Daisy knew better – and she was surprised Elliot Raslo, a student of psychology and all-around modern fellow, bought into it.

Then again, right now he was delirious at best. Daisy suspected that Chester, having gone mad with his own obsession, had introduced the community to some sort of intoxicant or hallucinogen, and it was Billy's own beliefs that had encouraged the three of them to see a more uniform pattern in the villagers' behavior. Whether she was correct or not, however, whatever truly had happened there, she certainly couldn't deny its impact on the poor boy. Between that and whatever violence he'd committed to defend himself, whatever crazed behavior he'd witnessed on Chester's part, he'd broken.

For the entire night after their arrival, Elliot had tossed and turned as though stricken with terrible fever, muttering in his sleep, waking frequently with a sudden cry that was, often as not, in French rather than English. His sweat soaked the sheets of Daisy's bed – she'd given it to him, letting Billy sleep on the floor beside him, while she and Ida shared the living room – and his somniloquent murmurs had somehow floated through the closed doors to disturb her own dreams.

Like Jonathan Harker at the convent, she mused despite herself. The recurring notion that this whole situation mirrored her beloved novels was no longer remotely enticing.

When she'd asked about the French, Billy explained that Elliot had found a warding spell in one of the books he'd studied, but that, even though he'd kept a copy, it grew less and less effective if he didn't return on occasion to reread the original.

More mystic absurdity, but if he'd convinced himself the mantra protected him, it might serve as a meditative focus. Again, however, while she might dismiss the Kalaaleq's explanations, she couldn't argue with what she saw occurring with her own eyes: Elliot was, indeed, deteriorating, even over the course of the single night.

But how to help? She could hardly go to the police. Billy – and even Ida, who'd remained sullenly quiet most of the night, doubtless out of grief – made it very clear that the entire town had died in the violence. That, without evidence to support their story of a community gone mad, any claims of self-defense would almost surely be waved away.

Indeed, under other circumstances, it was a tale she herself would almost certainly reject. Yet Daisy had already known Elliot Raslo for a trustworthy and upright soul before he became this muttering shell, and she'd come to feel, in the time she'd known him, that Billy was not one for wild flights of fancy. So even if she doubted some of the specifics, she couldn't dismiss the entirety of their account.

No police. Which also meant, unless they could come up with a convincing and unimpeachable lie, no hospital for Elliot – assuming medical science could even do anything for him.

It also meant, though Daisy did not consider this until later, she could never reveal to his friends and colleagues the fate of poor Willmott Polaski. She couldn't possibly justify her knowledge that he was dead, killed in a tiny unnamed village in the Hockomock Swamp. His was a fate that would have to remain an unsolved enigma for all concerned. It was a guilt she would struggle with for many nights to come.

All of which left her only one way to help, and it terrified her.

At first, she'd dismissed it. It couldn't do much *real* good, anyway, just play into Elliot's delusions. Then again, what if that were enough? What if that gave him the fortitude he needed to gather his wits?

It was foolish, an incalculable risk to maybe, *maybe* help someone to whom she didn't really owe anything. Someone for whom she'd already gone out of her way. Someone who, while she liked him well enough, was just one of her many student patrons at the library, not even a proper friend.

She could lose her new position, her employment, her whole career. She might face charges. Worst of all, she might, if anything untoward happened, be responsible for the damage or loss of precious writings and the knowledge, the history, the culture contained within.

A dozen times throughout the day, she'd talked herself out of even considering it. And a dozen times, after a few moments, she recalled Elliot's clenched features, trembling with an inner suffering.

A face that, in the past, she'd seen slowly lose its accustomed cheer as his friend – someone she knew he loved, though he would never tell a soul – had failed to reappear. Seen the determination in it, how unhesitatingly he'd risked himself when he saw the most minuscule chance to help locate the missing Chester.

And for all those efforts? Nothing in return but violence and guilt, loss and, perhaps, lunacy.

So Daisy Walker had sighed as the workday neared its end. She made excuses for her early departure, claiming headache. She'd gone into the Special Collection, after making sure nobody was there and Dr Armitage was nowhere in the building at all. And she'd broken what she considered her near-sacred charge as a librarian.

Her home, only a few blocks from the Miskatonic campus, came into view, and she clutched the parcel ever more tightly.

Thank God and all his angels it wasn't raining that evening.

The next island of mist-diffused illumination revealed a row of brownstone townhouses, one of several nearly identical blocks. Constructed deliberately close to the university, they had served for many decades as homes for large swathes of the faculty, staff and student bodies, though a smattering of inhabitants without connection to the school dwelt here as well. No formal divisions or bylaws prevented one group from living near the others, but through unspoken agreement, the staff and the students had largely segregated themselves. It made things less potentially awkward for all concerned.

Daisy swept up the steps, grabbing her mail from one of the hanging boxes purely out of habit, and let herself in. Lace curtains and an unfortunate paisley carpet, neither of which she'd have chosen if the whole place belonged to her, welcomed her home. She ignored them, as well as the doors to either side, making directly for the stairs.

Miss Albertson and Miss Lindsworth, who shared the second floor, had a Ted Lewis record on the gramophone, audible as fuzzy, muffled sounds even on the staircase. Louder, really, than it ought to be, but Daisy wasn't the sort to complain even on a normal evening. Tonight in particular, she welcomed it, as it should serve to cover any excess noise from her own chambers.

Finally, she reached the door to the third-floor flat she called her own.

It wasn't large, as such places went. Living room, bedroom, a couple of small closets, a tiny washroom, an only slightly less tiny kitchen. The place felt even smaller than it was, for while her decorative tastes were minimal – a few pictures and a historically old Miskatonic banner hung on the walls, and a couple of potted plants sat here and there – she owned rather more bookshelves than the place was designed to accommodate.

Living alone, the lack of space had never disturbed her. Three guests, however, were more than enough to strain the flat's limits.

Ida looked up from the sofa as Daisy latched the door behind her. The younger woman had a bottle of Coca-Cola on the end table beside her – Daisy had told them to feel free to raid whatever they liked from the refrigerator – and an open copy of *The Mysterious Affair at Styles* on her lap. It didn't appear she'd gotten very far into the text, and Agatha Christie certainly wasn't the most challenging writer on Daisy's shelves. Nevertheless, the librarian found herself taken aback. She realized then that she'd assumed the rustic Ida to be so uneducated as to be an indifferent reader, if not downright illiterate, and felt a flash of shame at her presumption.

Perhaps she'd allowed the swiftness of her rise at the Miskatonic library to go more to her head than she'd thought.

She thought about asking Ida how she was enjoying the mystery – her own way of making up for her ill-considered suppositions, even if the other woman couldn't possibly know about them – but Ida spoke before she had the chance.

"They're still in there," she said, inclining her head toward the bedroom. "Have been most of the day. Billy's real worried."

"I see." Casual chat later, then. Dismissing any last-minute doubts about her course of action, Daisy removed her hat and coat, hung them in the closet, and proceeded to the next room, nervous fingers plucking at the wrapped parcel.

Elliot sat in bed, reclined against a few pillows and the headboard. Although ostensibly awake, he stared at nothing, and his mouth moved in silent shapes.

Beside him, Billy had removed most of the amulets from around his neck and held them like a bizarre bouquet against Elliot's chest. He chanted a ritual or prayer in his native Kalaallisut, the sounds formed in his throat more than by tongue or lips or teeth, and waved his other hand in simple patterns in time with the cadence. He ceased, however, mid-word and mid-gesture, at Daisy's appearance.

"Please, don't let me interrupt," she said.

"You're not. I've been through the song a hundred times, but it doesn't do a lot of good. I'm no angakkoq, and even if I were, I lack the drums, the masks and the other tools to make the spirits obey. Elliot's sickness isn't in his body or even his mind, I think, but his anersaaq. His soul."

She wasn't about to argue it with him, and besides, even if it *was* in his mind, as she believed… "Here." She held out the package, began to unwrap it oh so carefully. "This might help."

Billy raised an eyebrow, and even Elliot turned his head, seeming to pay attention for the very first time, as the scent of old paper filled the room and the light fell upon cracked leather binding. A faint gasp emerged from the feverish young man, and he extended both hands as though beseeching a benediction.

"How did you know which one?" Billy asked. "I couldn't remember a name."

"You said it was a protective incantation in French. Not many books it *could* be, and I've a record of every text Elliot requested." She turned her attention to the student, slowly passing him the *Livre d'Ivon*. "Elliot? Elliot, can you hear me?"

It took him a moment, but he nodded.

"*Please* be careful. If anything happens to this… 'I'll be in trouble' doesn't begin to cover it. I would lose everything. *Everything.*"

Again, he nodded, and though his head literally twitched with whatever insanity or illness he battled, his lips trembled and the veins in his neck stood out, he took the book from her with surprising care, turned the pages with a gentle touch. Daisy released a breath she hadn't meant to hold.

"Come." Billy rose, taking most of the talismans with him, though he left the one Elliot wore about his neck. "We should give him some space."

Daisy frowned, reluctant despite Elliot's surprising caution to leave the book unsupervised.

Billy came around the bed, stopping beside her. "It's better for him."

With many a fretful glance back, she allowed herself to be guided to the living room, and she insisted on leaving the door ajar.

They sat with Ida – Daisy on the sofa, Billy in a small chair – and tried to focus on the other puzzle before them.

The centerpiece of the room was an oak coffee table, its base carved with intricate patterns of ivy and leaves. It was, by far, the fanciest element of Daisy's furniture: a gift to her from her parents when she'd set off on her own, years before. It still carried a sheen, as though freshly polished, even though she'd have been forced to admit that she'd left it untreated far longer than her mother would have approved.

Scattered atop that table were the scraps Elliot had salvaged from Chester's abandoned coat. In all the chaos of the trio's arrival last night, and then her work today, this was her first opportunity to look them over in any depth.

For several moments, then, she did just that, barely touching them – particularly the older, more fragile fragments – prodding lightly with a fingertip, at most, when she needed one moved. Other than the occasional crinkling, and the sounds of whispered French from the bedroom, she worked in silence.

Elliot's hushed voice dissolved into soft snores, and she finally straightened, nodding more to herself than to the others.

"This," she announced, pointing at the writing on the older pieces that resembled parchment as much as paper, "is Ancient Greek. There's not enough of it left, and I'm afraid I'm not near sufficiently fluent, to tell you what it says or what its source might be.

"But I can tell you that Chester was using it as a step in some sort of transliteration. These," and here she pointed to the student's own notes on more modern paper, "is a list of sounds and syllables."

Billy and Ida continued to watch her, clearly awaiting further explanation.

"All right. You have Language A, Language B and Language C. They all use different alphabets. If you can find a guide for pronouncing Language A, written in Language B, and you know Languages B and C, you can use it to spell out an acoustical translation in Language C. It won't tell you what the words *mean*, but you could pronounce them aloud. You… What's wrong?"

Her two guests stared at one another, expressions grim, before focusing on her once more.

"So Mr Hennessy," Billy said, "somehow found a way of transliterating some language to Ancient Greek, and then wrote himself instructions for transliterating from Ancient Greek to the English alphabet?"

"That's what this suggests to me, yes."

"And the original language?" He seemed particularly driven on that point. Recalling their discussion in the university's museum, Daisy understood why.

"If you're asking me if it's the writing on the Lindegaard Stele, I'm afraid I can't say. If he wrote down the original script at all, it's not among the notes that survived."

"I think it a safe assumption, though."

She nodded. "Probably."

"I'll need to destroy those notes, or take them with me. I don't *think* the infection of the litany can be passed from the notes themselves – I guess it only works if the original source is the *Ujaraanni* or the stele – but I'm not willing to take the chance, or risk someone else using them to translate the stele."

All right, enough. Daisy had tried to respect his beliefs, but she wasn't about to let him take the last remnants of Chester's work, to say nothing of the surviving scraps of what was clearly a far older text, because he was afraid of passing along some curse.

"I'm sure we can discuss that," she said delicately, "when the time comes for you to return home. But–"

"The time *has* come. I intend to leave tomorrow."

Daisy gawped, and Ida seemed fully intent on the conversation for perhaps the first time. "But this ain't done!" the younger woman protested.

"It is for me. My task was to retrieve what was stolen from my people. I've done that. I must deliver it to them."

A cold burning, a protective urge mixed with a dull fury, welled up from Daisy's stomach. "You're going to just leave? With Elliot in his condition?"

Billy at least had the grace to look abashed, casting his gaze first at the steamer trunk he'd left in the corner, then down at the table. "I've done all I can do for Elliot. My amulets seem to help, and I will happily leave several with him, but beyond that–"

Biting back an angry retort, Daisy rose and swept into the kitchen, hoping the time it would take to fetch herself a cup of tea might calm her down.

It did no such thing. When she returned, the warm china in her fingers, she still seethed, her fury at the Kalaaleq's stubbornness unabated. Nor was she the only one; Ida and Billy argued still in rasps and whispers, fighting to keep their voices down lest they wake Elliot in the next room.

"… a sacred responsibility." Billy was insisting as she returned to the sofa. "This was my task, and my father's task before me. My duty is clear."

"Aw, bullshit."

Daisy spluttered into her tea, but Billy… Billy went first pale, then flushed. The tendons stood out in his neck, and his breath quickened. "Because we've fought side by side," he growled, "and because you cannot possibly understand the offense you've just given, I will forgive that. But–"

"Bullshit," Ida insisted again. "Ain't me who's offending your people or your father here."

"Um, Ida…" Daisy carefully set her cup down on the table, well away from the paper. "Perhaps you might consider–"

The other woman obviously had no intention of stopping, however. "We got no idea if Chester Hennessy's even alive, or where he might be, or even *what* he might be!"

If he's alive? "What" he might be? How much of the story haven't they told me? Even if Daisy had meant to ask, however, Ida didn't pause long enough for her to get a word in.

"We don't know how many of those twisted madmen might still be alive out there, or if Chester's got any way to start the whole damned mess all over again. Right?"

Stiff-necked with injured pride and boiling rage, still Billy eventually nodded.

"And all because of that damn stone. So you tell me, William Shiwak, how exactly are you honoring your daddy or doin' right by your people if you ignore the harm caused by you losing track of your 'sacred charge'?"

Silence for a time, broken only by the harsh rumble of Billy's angry breathing. Finally, however, his fists unclenched and his stare lost its edge.

"Perhaps I'm not," he conceded, leaning back in his chair. "Maybe… your words have merit."

Daisy's shoulders relaxed like someone had just taken her off a clothes hanger.

"Tell me, then," he continued, in what could have easily been a challenge, a genuine query, or both. "Say I agree. Say I decide to stay until this matter is concluded. What does that mean? When is it over? What exactly must I do that I haven't already done?"

To that, neither Daisy nor Ida had an answer.

CHAPTER EIGHTEEN

All about him, the ravaging ice, the barren snow; the jagged peaks and the hollow, hungering skies.

The howl of distant winds and even more distant voices, and none to say which was in greater pain.

His own horrified shrieks, as he once more saw his leg separate from the rest of him, linked only by thread-like strands without blood or flesh, without even pain.

And the massive scrape of something on frost-covered stone, as the tree-broad tendril crept its way toward him around the slopes – followed, this time, by a second, a third.

Not wood, not stone, not scale, not bone, but something entirely... other. A hide that was not hide, a flesh that was not flesh. A substance that was not, in some indescribable way, even substance. Solid, tangible, real, and yet... not.

Nor was "tendril" even the proper term, he realized with the tiny portion of his mind that wasn't lost to thoughtless gibbering at what drew near. This was not the long, stringy appendage of some floating medusoid, nor the thick, grasping tentacle of a cephalopod, nor even a winding serpent.

No, each seemed more an impossibly long digit of uncountable segments, a giant's finger with not two knuckles, or three, but hundreds upon hundreds of separate phalanges until they formed a grasping chain of skin and bone – or rather, of whatever comparable substances made up this inconceivable monstrosity.

He scrabbled backward, pushing himself along with hands, his remaining foot and the awkward stump of his leg which left almost paintbrush-like strokes in the snow. The flailing limbs followed after, no matter how far from the mountainside he scurried, until at last he reached the end of their length. The source of the first shambled into sight, followed by the other two.

Each was a cluster of people grouped together, their mouths stretched into gaping maws with nothing but hollow darkness beyond. Every person had their arms stretched forward, and it was these that had lengthened, twisted, twining and knotting together to form the base of a questing coil. It should have been too heavy, overbalancing and toppling the throng of people who supported it, but they appeared not to struggle with it at all.

"Isslaach thkulkris, isslaach cheoshash… "

From those cavernous mouths emerged the opening phrases of that familiar damned liturgy, repeated over and over – not by these wretched souls, for their lips and tongues and throats did not move, but through them, as if they were naught but megaphones or radio speakers. From a few score faces, in three separate clusters, emerged the voice of a chorus of hundreds, perhaps thousands.

Yet even this was not the worst of it, not the final horror that dragged a last soul-rending scream from the pit of his stomach, the depths of his soul. No, that was elicited by a few specific faces, faces whose deathly slack and hideous stretching could not prevent a flash of recognition.

Professors. Fellow students. The inhabitants of that poor, nameless hamlet on the edge of the Hockomock.

Polaski. Woodrow. Jeremy, the security guard. Lucy. Virgil. Alfred. Ida. Daisy. Billy.

Chester.

And though he struggled to flee, as fast as his maimed body could go, he found himself sliding toward the nearest tendril, the first of the shambling group, his own limbs betraying him, and he felt in his heart nothing so much as a fearful yearning to join them, to offer up the flesh of his own limbs to become part of that writhing, seeking whole...

Elliot thrashed, flipping himself over on the sweat-soaked mattress, blankets and sheets flailing around him like shed feathers, pillows hurtling across the room to bounce from the walls or tangle in the curtains. He couldn't breathe, gasping, hyperventilating. Resounding in his head, louder even than the partial refrain, was that other word, that strange word he'd awakened to before, laying so heavy on his mind that he couldn't help but whisper it aloud.

"Tsocathra..."

It helped, in a peculiar way. It forced him to break his pattern of gasps, allowing him to draw a slower, more controlled breath. And that, in turn, made him realize something else.

Namely, that he *was* realizing. That he was thinking.

That he *was*.

For the first time since being dragged from the Hennessy household, Elliot – exhausted, terrified, grieving as he might be – was fully himself.

He cast about, taking in the bedroom that was clearly not his own. The quilt he'd sent tumbling was patterned in blue and gold, with a neat frill running along its edges. The sheets and pillows were a light violet, the curtains a darker shade of the same.

Across from him stood a mirrored vanity, with an array of perfumes and toiletries laid neatly atop. Only sheer luck had prevented the cushions he'd hurled from taking any number of them to the floor, or knocking the mirror askew. God knows Daisy wouldn't have been happy with–

Daisy! This was Daisy's bedroom. He must have been in a state indeed, for her to let a young man, even one she trusted, sleep it off in here.

Bits and fragments flooded back to him. He recalled their careful walk to the edge of town, in order to open a gap in the barricade of cars. Ida had trailed behind him and Billy, ready to pick off any lingering corrupted who ambushed them. He couldn't remember if she'd needed to or not.

Once they'd cleared a path, he'd held it together long enough to drive one of the community's abandoned cars to Taunton, but he couldn't possibly manage it any further. He couldn't recall if Ida had driven them back to Arkham – she knew the basics, though she'd never driven more than a few miles combined in her life – or if they'd taken the train.

Then nothing, nothing but the litany and the grief and the dreams, until Daisy had come into the room, and he'd somehow *felt* what she brought with her.

He turned, afraid to look, but the *Livre d'Ivon* sat on a small end table to his left, still pristine. He gasped in relief; if he'd damaged it in his flailing, it would've been the end of him. Even if Daisy hadn't killed him, he was doomed without access to the spell within.

Finally, Elliot looked down at himself. Someone had made a cursory effort to bathe him, freeing him from most of the swamp's mud, from the blood and sour sweat of their ordeal. They'd dressed him, too, and he wondered who he owed for what must be a brand-new suit of men's pajamas, and how much.

He sat up, anticipating that the room would probably spin around him, and clutched a bedpost when his prediction proved accurate. Once the worst of the dizziness passed, he stood, testing his balance. He wouldn't care to attempt the stairs, let alone actually go anywhere, but the next room should be manageable. He needed a glass of water; his throat was parched, painfully so, and he wondered how much screaming he might have done, and whether he'd disturbed Daisy's neighbors.

Staggering steps and one near collapse brought him to the door, which stood open a few inches. He didn't mean to eavesdrop, but the others were deep in conversation, and he found himself pausing to get a sense of it.

"... as though we've covered all this," Daisy was saying.

"I agree." That was Billy. "Which brings me back around, yet again, to the same question. If I stay, it would be to accomplish ... what?"

If I stay? What had Elliot missed?

He continued with, "We have no more of a trail to follow now than we did before Taunton. Less, in fact. Chester might have gone anywhere if he's still alive. Or might have been anywhere even *before* he went to his uncle, and infected any number of people! Even if we find a way to prevent what happened to Ida's home from happening elsewhere, we might well be too late."

The room fell into a helpless silence that Elliot knew all

too well, not only from their previous efforts but his own studies. This was a group that had gone round and round in conversational circles, and come up with nothing new.

They didn't know Chester, though. Not the way he did.

"He won't have gone just anywhere," Elliot rasped, pushing the door open.

Immediately Billy and Daisy were up and at his side.

"Are you all right? How are you feeling?"

"Do you need anything?"

"What do you remember?"

The questions overlapped until he could barely keep them straight, wasn't certain who had asked what. Without requesting it, and almost against his will, he found himself physically helped to the sofa. The glass of water Daisy pressed into his hand was welcome, however, and he allowed himself a moment to gulp it down, nearly choking in the process.

Finally everyone settled. Billy and Daisy watched him intently, he standing, she seated in a chair across the coffee table. Ida, too, waited for him to speak, though he seemed to have only a portion of her attention. He felt a deep pang of sympathy, and hoped the others hadn't been rushing her to recover from her own losses any faster than she was able.

When he spoke again, the water had restored some of his voice, though it still felt, and sounded, rough as tree bark.

"Chester lost himself to his obsession," Elliot said, forcing himself not to flinch when speaking the name. "And to the object of his obsession. The madness, the litany, it came from the *Ujaraanni*. Everything in his life has revolved around that damn... Around that stone." He cast an apologetic glance at Billy, who merely shrugged.

He noticed, though, that Daisy was looking quizzically at him. He wondered how much of the tale his friends had shared with her, and how much of that she'd believed. Indeed, he thought he sensed a tiny flash of disapproval, even disappointment, directed his way.

Well, he understood. He wouldn't believe either, in her position. But she hadn't been there, and he had.

"I don't know how much of Chester is left. I don't know if he's thinking or remembering or… guided by something else entirely. But I'm quite certain that, if he's not… gone… then he'll be looking to retrieve the *Ujaraanni*. Or at least to be near it, or the Lindegaard Stele, again."

Various shifting and sidelong expressions met that assertion. "It's possible," Billy allowed. "But I would hate to rely on it. There's a great deal of supposition involved. And even if you're right," he bulled on, holding up a hand to forestall Elliot's objection, "knowing that he might 'be near,' *if* he's alive, isn't much to work with."

"What about his notes?" Elliot gestured to the paper spread across the table.

Shaking her head, Daisy explained to him what she'd learned going through them, that they were a transliteration from some language – probably but not definitively that of the stone – through Ancient Greek, to English. Nothing that would help them here.

"Perhaps if we had more of his notes…" She trailed off with a meaningful look.

"Not in our room, certainly," Elliot said. "He always kept any notes of significance on him. He took them with him when he left. Although…" His forehead creased in thought. He wished the remnants of the dream and the constant echoes of the alien tongue would let him think!

"He didn't keep his research materials there," he finished. "We didn't have the room."

"Would those offer anything that would be useful to us now?" Billy asked doubtfully.

Daisy frowned. "I don't see that we have anywhere better to look. Elliot, do you know where he might have kept them?"

"He never said, but I assumed…" Again he paused, letting ideas and memories catch up and slowly realizing the implications of what he was about to say. "He was working with Professor Polaski's help. I assumed the materials stayed with him."

The librarian shrank in her chair. She knew the question that was coming before Billy voiced it.

"Do you know where Polaski would have kept such things?"

"I might," she admitted, "have some idea."

For God's sake, was she *trying* to get herself fired?

Elliot, though greatly improved, was not yet in any position to leave the townhome, and he'd begged her to leave the *Livre d'Ivon* with him a bit longer. To let him spend more time with the original copy of what he truly seemed to believe, much to Daisy's dismay, was a genuine protective incantation.

She'd acquiesced, as he certainly seemed enough in his right mind, now, that the book itself should be in no danger. Still, her gut churned at letting it out of her presence, and at missing what might have been a perfect opportunity to return it unnoticed.

What was she up to instead, then, in the deepest hours of this blustery Arkham night? Why, merely leading a pair of relative strangers across the Miskatonic campus, hoping to evade the patrolling security guards, with the full intent of *breaking into a missing professor's office.*

"Fired." She almost laughed aloud at herself. Was she trying to get herself *arrested*?

She couldn't help herself, though. For all that common sense told her to extract herself from this entire affair, both the fascination of a mystery unsolved and a sense of fidelity to Elliot, and even Billy, given all they'd gone through, demanded she continue to assist.

No matter how foolish.

She worked at convincing herself that Willmott Polaski would approve of what they meant to do. He'd gone off on his own to find the missing Chester, even if he was motivated by his own vested interest in their project. She might not be able to tell anyone what had befallen him, let alone do anything about it, but if the materials in his office could help them learn more about what had happened to Chester, or even locate him again, she thought the old man, from wherever he now watched them, would welcome their prying.

Of course, while that might assuage her conscience, it did nothing to mitigate her worries regarding…

"Hey, you three! Hold it right there!"

… possible discovery.

"Don't say a word!" she hissed at the others, then turned to face the oncoming guard, smoothing her coat with hands suddenly sweaty despite the chill.

"Good evening, Floyd," she said with a forced cheeriness.

The old security guard, his face an unfortunate leathery

amalgamation of flat patches and deep wrinkles, drew himself up, blinking in confusion. "Uh... oh. Miss, uh, Miss Walker! What..."

It wouldn't do to laugh at the poor thing, but she'd so thoroughly short-circuited his expectations it was difficult not to. Obviously he'd anticipated corralling a group of youngsters, shooing them back to their dormitories and writing up a disciplinary report.

Unlike the student body, faculty and staff had no curfew, no regulations prohibiting them from wandering the campus at any hour, no matter how ungodly. Technically, Floyd had no authority and Daisy was committing no infraction.

That didn't make seeing her here in the middle of the night any less unusual, though.

"Uh, Miss Walker, if you don't mind me asking..."

"Of course, Floyd. I was up late working, and I'm afraid I only just realized that I needed some particular paperwork to finish up my task."

If one turned it sideways and squinted at it a bit, it wasn't even a lie. A single nervous finger tapped against her palm, a fidget she couldn't quite suppress, but otherwise she forced her posture, her expression, to remain relaxed.

"I see. And, uh..." He glanced at her companions, lingering on Billy as though he recognized the man but couldn't place where from.

She waved dismissively. "Friends from out of town who are staying nearby. It wouldn't do for me to be wandering around this late on my own, of course."

Floyd chewed on that, quite literally. She could see his jaw moving.

Eventually, he conceded, having no other real option. "Well, all right, Miss Walker. Just, uh, you be careful. And I don't know that I'd make a habit of this sort of thing."

"Oh, believe me, Floyd, I've *no* intention of *that.*" It felt like the truest thing she'd said in days.

He wandered away, still glancing back, as Daisy and the others resumed their trek.

The pathway wound about several small lawns, a fountain, a gated garden around the base of a statue, through various patches of Arkham's nearly ubiquitous fog, before finally delivering them to the front of a building a short way from the library itself. Like most of its brethren, it wore a stone facade, stood several stories in height, and somehow conveyed a sense of great, looming weight.

Ignoring a sudden attack of nerves, Daisy removed a heavy keyring from her purse. Getting into the building itself was no trouble; most of the educational halls on campus, including the library, made use of the same key. It was far easier than assigning different ones to the cleaning and security staff, to say nothing of swapping them out any time an individual professor's classes might be shuffled about between terms.

If only finding a means of ingress was their biggest hurdle.

Maneuvering through a gloom broken only sporadically by the cloud-diffused moon and fog-scattered lamplight leaking in through the windows, they proceeded down broad, echoing halls. Polaski hadn't been the Orne Library's most frequent patron on the faculty, not by half, but she'd been to his office often enough before she'd obtained her current position – delivering or, more frequently, retrieving old books – that she remembered well enough where it was. Up those stairs there, down that hall there, fourth door on the left.

Just one amidst a row of offices, distinguished only by the name carefully stenciled onto the frosted glass window in the door.

Daisy tried that door. It was, to nobody's surprise, locked fast.

"I live in hope," she said a bit defensively, able to sense the disbelief from her companions that she could only scarcely see in the dark.

"What's your backup plan," Billy asked, "now that hope hasn't proved sufficient?"

She sighed, and then had to confess, "I'm not entirely sure. None of my keys will work here." The buildings might have a more universal lock, but individual faculty offices most certainly did not.

"Perhaps this is something we ought to have discussed before we got here."

"To what end? My answer would have been the same. 'I've no idea how we're to get in. We'll have to figure something out.'"

"Hmm." He moved past her and rapped a knuckle against the wood. "I could probably break it down, given a few minutes. It wouldn't be easy, and it wouldn't be quiet, but unless someone's in the building, or just outside–"

"I'd *really* rather not. Campus is still buzzing over the break-in at the museum last week, and security's still deeply unhappy about it. Another would almost certainly draw more attention from administration and from the police than we–"

"Oh, for heaven's sake!" Ida pushed between them, literally shouldering Billy away from the door. "Stand back and lemme work." She crouched down on one knee, putting herself at eye-level with the latch. "Either of you think to bring a flashlight?"

Billy dug into his coat and tried to hand it to her, but she shook her head. "Just hold it so I can see what I'm about."

Then, bathed in the yellow illumination, she drew a small pouch from one of her pockets, and a few bits of wire and metal from that.

Apparently she, like Daisy, could feel the weight of the others' stares. "What? How'd you figure I gathered all those supplies for our hideout back home? Not *everyone* went nuts with their doors unlocked, and not every house had a crawlspace I could get into."

"Break a window?" Billy suggested, shrugging.

"Sure, and leave a big sign I was in there in case anyone wandered by. They were nuts, not dumb." Metal scraped and mechanisms clicked as she worked. "I ain't hardly an expert, but I known the basics since I was a girl. I don't guess a teacher's office ought to be too tricky."

Perhaps not, but it was a good three minutes, filled with aggravated grunts and a few curses that made Daisy's hair curl, before a loud click announced that the door was finally unlocked.

At least the diversion might have done Ida some good, Daisy hoped. That effort, and the accompanying conversation, had been the liveliest she'd seen the young woman since they'd first met. Unfortunately, if it *had* helped, it was only in the moment. By the time Daisy stepped past her, felt her way to Polaski's desk, and switched on the lamp, Ida's expression had reverted to the same preoccupied, half-defeated mask she'd shown earlier.

Daisy moved back and carefully shut the door behind them. The office had no window to the outside, and while the glow of the lamp was visible through the frosted glass, there shouldn't be anyone walking the building's halls to see it. Barring the truly unexpected, they had some time.

The office wore a light coating of dust, suggesting that nobody had been in here since Polaski locked up and embarked on his ill-fated journey almost a month past. It didn't bother Daisy much – she was used to handling old tomes that had gone untouched for far longer – but Ida sniffled a few times behind her, and Billy sneezed outright with a blast Daisy imagined was not unlike a small explosive.

He could only offer an apologetic grimace.

Other than that dust, the office was precisely as she remembered, and as she would have expected even if she'd never been here. The desk held a typewriter, several pens, an old mug and a stack of folders. Multiple shelves, and an old sofa, displayed books and yet more documents. A large filing cabinet occupied one corner, and, throughout the entire room, an array of boxes sat stuck into whatever niches they would fit, stacked two and three high.

"Lot to go through," Ida said.

"Yes, well… Professor Polaski spent as much time in his own research as he did teaching. And I doubt Chester's was the only student project he was assisting with, even if it was his priority."

Billy carefully moved a stack of books so he could sit on one arm of the sofa without knocking anything askew. "Why *would* he be so involved in Chester's research?"

"At first, probably just as an advisor and a guide. Students who are assigned such projects, or think they've found something worth pursuing on their own, often ask for that sort of assistance.

"I think it went beyond that, though. Even before either of them disappeared, they both spoke about their endeavor in emphatic terms, and I saw them together in the library on multiple occasions. So many students feel they're on the verge of some great breakthrough that will make their careers, cement their reputations – and, not incidentally, show up all the stodgy old codgers who've come before them and grown too tradition-bound and intransigent to accept anything new."

That drew a soft chuckle. "I take it you've heard a lot of these complaints."

Daisy grinned. "More than a few, especially when I was only a junior librarian, not much older than the students." She sobered swiftly. "A lot of them feel that way," she repeated. "But it seems Chester actually *was*. And Polaski saw it. I think he hoped some of Chester's coming glory would rub off on him, give him one last boost among his peers."

That he might have meant to steal the younger man's discovery, to pin his name on Chester's work, crossed her mind. She dismissed it as best she could – Willmott Polaski had never struck her as any such a fraud – but she wished the suspicion hadn't even occurred to her.

"You're right, though, Ida," she said, putting on her best all-business librarian voice. "There's a lot here to go through. We'd best get started."

CHAPTER NINETEEN

For a discomfortingly long while, the trio dug through the late Willmott Polaski's boxes, crates, folders and files. Daisy swiftly adopted the leadership role, not merely because of her organizational expertise but because she, of them all, had by far the strongest grasp of what they were looking for, what sorts of materials might prove informative.

Still, there was much to sift through, and her frustration mounted in almost perfect sync with the minutes, and then hours, as they passed.

Stacks of material developed, sorted into three broad categories in descending order of size: irrelevant to their purposes; potentially related, pending Daisy's closer examination; and materials unquestionably linked to Chester or his project. As that last pile grew to a volume that, while still dwarfed by the others, at least suggested their cause wasn't hopeless, Daisy found her frustration fading, replaced by equal parts anger and admiration at Chester's cleverness.

"He's not even supposed to have these!" she blurted at one point, startling her companions where they sat, backs hunched, on the office floor. She held a small stack of photos and written reports, information on missing or stolen materials disbursed by other universities. These were some of the materials Chester had sorted during his hours of volunteer work. He'd undertaken those labors to earn himself extra time in the restricted collections, but apparently he'd had other, ulterior motives even then. Whatever track Chester had followed, he'd been on it for many months, perhaps more than a year.

Finally, as the hour grew late and they found themselves nearer to dawn than to midnight, Daisy called for her companions' attention. They huddled together, each nursing stiffened fingers and a collection of jagged, painful papercuts. The librarian had an array of files and photos spread before her like the fan of a peacock's tail, and she felt literally dizzy from piecing together the trail she now believed Chester's search had followed.

He really had been a genius, in his way. A shame his obsession had cost the linguistic and archeological fields a brilliant, possibly even world-changing, mind.

"All right," she began, "I think I've got it. I don't know when Chester decided to focus on translating the Lindegaard Stele as his great triumph, or why. I suppose it was just one of those fascinations people develop sometimes."

Billy seemed less inclined to wave it off. "Perhaps. Or perhaps it called to him, even then."

"Yes, well. At any rate, he surely studied all the existing writings, and ran into the same walls everyone else had. He must have been disheartened, realizing there were good reasons nobody had even taken a crack at it in decades.

"Now look here." She pointed at the photos and reports she'd indicated earlier. "The various universities that keep collections of relics like Miskatonic does … we've something of an unspoken arrangement. If we discover a fraud, or an artifact is stolen or goes missing, we alert the others to be on the lookout for it."

"I see where you're going," Billy said, leaning back against the sofa. "Addison's theft of the *Ujaraanni* from the University of Virginia."

"Right. Of course, it doesn't mention Addison here. As I recall, you said he was never formally charged. And the *Ujaraanni* wasn't the only artifact stolen. But the report includes photographs and sketches, and Chester must have immediately recognized the writing."

"And decided he had to get his hands on a relic stolen from my people, without concern for what was right or just."

"Well … Yes, I suppose, though of course there's nothing in here about *that*. It clearly stoked his ambition, though, because it was after this report that he started digging into other university documents." Her head drooped. "I'm afraid, by accepting him as a volunteer, I gave him the position that offered him access to such things."

"You didn't know."

Daisy cleared her throat, wishing she'd thought to somehow bring a beverage with her. Of course she couldn't have known, but she felt culpable all the same. She was supposed to be the responsible one. The authority. "In any event, his next discovery appears to have been these." Again she reached out and shifted a few documents around, indicating a new bundle.

"These are the personal notes and records of one Lemuel Abernathy, a Miskatonic alumnus and something of an adventurer and explorer. Upon his death, he'd willed his notes and related documentation to the university. We receive a great many such bequests from former students," she explained, "and I'm afraid we're quite behind in having them all sorted, and anything useful cataloged."

Ida chimed in, then, nearly making Daisy jump; she'd all but forgotten the young woman was there. "So Chester found somethin' you all hadn't yet?"

"Um, indeed. From an expedition Abernathy had undertaken in Mongolia before the turn of the century."

She pulled an old ferrotype photograph from the pile and passed it around. It showed a slab, possibly granite, at the base of a rocky slope. The stone itself might or might not have been artificially shaped, but there could be no mistaking the symbols carved upon it as anything natural. It held but a few lines of text, roughly chiseled and partly worn away by the elements, but those sigils that remained were familiar enough.

"Mongolia?" Billy breathed in confused wonder.

"Whoever the language once belonged to," Daisy said with just a tinge of humor, "they were certainly well traveled."

"Clearly."

"Obviously, Chester also noticed the connection," she told them, resuming the narrative. "According to Abernathy's notes, the locals told him this was some sort of protective incantation, meant to ward off evil spirits. I imagine that must have made him wonder if the same was true of the *Ujaraanni* and the stele, because his own scribbled notes here…" A finger indicated yet another document. "… suggest that he started specifically looking for defensive and warding rituals in the restricted books he was researching.

"I'm sure he found quite a few. Such things are quite common in the occult writings of older cultures. He appears to have found a reference in the *Livre d'Ivon* – it contains many such wards, so I suppose it's not surprising Elliot found his own, ah, mantra there – to incantations in Ancient Greek, supposedly copied from an even older tongue."

She was nodding to herself as she spoke, putting the pieces together, remembering when Chester had come in, asking for some especially restricted books, how he'd needed Polaski to sign off on the request before she'd grant it.

"And as there aren't many grimoires older than the original *Book of Eibon*, and even fewer that were originally in Greek, process of elimination led him to the *Pnakotic Manuscripts*." She couldn't help it; her voice hushed as she spoke the name of one of the rarest of the Restricted Collection. "But it says here even that frustrated him. He found a few lines of a spell in Ancient Greek, yes, and even a few of the older symbols that matched those on the stele, enough to convince him he was on the proper track. That's all the English translation had for him, though, and we haven't got any of the others. Certainly it wasn't enough for him to transliterate the *Ujaraanni* or the stele."

She paused, tapping a finger to her lip. "His notes don't indicate where he went next, I'm afraid, and I'm not sure I can think of any options. Obviously, if he had access to the *Pnakotic Fragments* in the original Greek, prior to any of the abbreviated manuscript translations like the ones in our library, that might have offered him some answers, but I can't imagine where–"

Daisy must have shot upright, beginning to stand, as the full implications of what she'd already seen finally dawned. Must have, though she didn't recall it, because the next thing she *did* remember was slumping back down, half-sitting and half-sprawled in the midst of the scattered notes, Billy rushing to her side in a belated attempt to catch her.

"What is it?" he demanded. "What's wrong?"

"The *Fragments*..." She felt herself on the verge of tears, heard the same tremor in her words she felt in her gut, in her hands.

Ida was beside her, too, now. "I don't understand."

"In Chester's coat. Ancient Greek, written on parchment. Those were genuine. From the *Pnakotica*!"

Probably not torn from the true Pnakotic scrolls, no, but even if they had been copied from the original – or even copied from copies – that made them, by far, the oldest documents Daisy had ever handled, some of the earliest mystical and occult writings in the *world*. Irreplaceable, both for what they were and for what they might have contained, if they'd happened to include any of the lost segments never before collected or translated.

Destroyed, save a few incomplete scraps. Lost to the mud and filth beneath the Hennessy house, soaked through, smeared and disintegrated. Gone forever. As a librarian and a historian, her life devoted to preserving such cultural treasures, she found this hit her harder than the deaths of strangers, or even Polaski's, and the guilt over that realization only added to her misery.

"Would that have allowed Chester to complete his transliterations?" Billy asked. Whether the query was meant to distract her, snap her out of her shock, or simply because it was the next logical question, Daisy wasn't sure, but either way it gave her something to cling to.

"It, um..." She coughed and tried to regain some of her earlier poise, though embarrassment over the brief breakdown kept her from meeting his gaze at first. "It might, if it contained a sufficient sample of the original writing along with the matching text in Ancient Greek. Chester was a linguist, and now he would have had at least some idea of the... spell's purpose. It would have taken work, I imagine – being able to read Ancient Greek isn't the same as knowing quite how to properly pronounce it – but yes, that may well have been the last piece he required."

"So," Ida said, "that's that, then?"

Billy stood, stretching. "That is most certainly not that."

No doubt he had the same question Daisy did. "Where in God's name could Chester have gotten hold of these? Leaving aside the exorbitant cost, you can't just walk into a library or somewhere like The Curiositie Shoppe and ask for the *Pnakotic Fragments*! People in our field spend years, sometimes lifetimes, hunting handfuls of scraps."

"Perhaps Chester was less concerned with propriety or..." Billy cast about for the proper term. "... or provenance than your fellow archivists. And maybe he had a more personal connection."

Daisy looked up, the gesture and her expression both sharp. She could think of only one person with whom Chester had a "more personal" connection, and Daisy had hoped never to hear the woman's name again in the context of the investigation. Or at all. "Are you suggesting...?"

"You did tell me, did you not, that she was a customer at several of the shops you visited? That she was a 'dabbler' in history and the occult?"

"Who're we talking about?" Ida asked, but Daisy barely heard.

"*Dabbler* is precisely the word. I sincerely doubt that woman has the connections necessary to come up with anything even close to the age or significance of the *Fragments*. And if she did, you'd be asking me to believe that, in addition to his good fortune in stumbling on these clues here, Chester also had the miraculous stroke of luck to be involved with one of the few people who could... could..."

The spark of suspicion Billy had ignited in her thoughts flared abruptly into a crackling bonfire. She raised a hand toward him, with which he kindly helped her to stand. Then, her steps slowed by stiffness from sitting on the floor – but also by a deep reluctance, an intense desire not to risk discovering her unpleasant notion had any foundation in truth – she hobbled her way around Professor Polaski's desk. A quick shuffle through the documents on top, then a series of rough rumbles and thumps as she scoured drawer after drawer...

There, in the bottom right, a small leather-bound parcel. His address book.

Almost unwillingly, tense enough that she earned herself another papercut for her troubles – drawing from her a sharp hiss but no other response – she flipped the pages toward the center.

When she got there, all she could do was sigh.

McCutcheon, Victoria. Address. Phone number.

Polaski knew her. Had known her for some time, based on the page's general wear and other nearby entries.

Given his parents' wealth, it had never before occurred to Daisy to wonder just how Chester had met the attractive and relatively young widow in the first place. Now that she knew, it left a deeply sour taste in her mouth.

"He sought her out," she told the others, unaware it emerged as a partial growl. "Chester Hennessy involved himself with Mrs McCutcheon because they thought she might be useful." She dropped the address book and its damning entry, now stained ever so faintly with a smear of her own blood, back into the drawer and slammed it shut with a resounding *crack*.

"All of this is important to know," Billy said, "but it doesn't tell us anything about where he might be now, or where he might have been prior to his uncle's home. We're going to have to speak with McCutcheon after all." If he had any thoughts about ending that declaration with *As we should have done before*, he was good enough to keep them to himself.

Daisy shook her head, but it wasn't a refusal so much as a commentary on their situation. "Certainly not tonight. It's nearly morning. We'll take a day, try to figure out some way to approach her that won't get us immediately shown the door, or worse."

And for me to sneak the Livre d'Ivon *back into the collection. I'd rather at least cut down the number of incredibly foolish chances I'm taking at any one time.*

Grudgingly but swiftly, they began shoveling documents back into the boxes whence they'd come, though they didn't bother attempting to sort them into their prior order. It only mattered that nobody who might come into Polaski's office down the road – to clean, or to empty it out once Miskatonic acknowledged he'd never be returning – had any reason to suspect they'd been here.

"Billy, Ida." She closed the box on which she'd been working and turned to face them. "Elliot doesn't need to know this. He's suffering enough with his friend's loss. We don't need to poison that memory with this new insight into Chester's behavior."

Two quick nods, and they were at the boxes once again, racing to be out of here and back home before the dawn.

CHAPTER TWENTY

Keeping the less savory elements of their discoveries from Elliot proved easy enough. While bedrest and access to the *Livre d'Ivon* had greatly improved his mental state, he remained exhausted, worn out by his ordeals and the internal battles that followed. If he wasn't fully satisfied with their abbreviated account of the night's activities, then at least he was too tired to press.

He didn't object even when Daisy informed him, somewhat nervously, that she would be returning the ancient text to the library in the morning. He seemed to feel that he'd spent enough time with the original spell that his scribbled copy, or even his memory, should be enough to sustain him for a few days.

Rather more startling was the fact that finding an opportunity to speak with Victoria McCutcheon also turned out to be easier than anticipated.

It was again the same trio that had broken into Polaski's office. Elliot remained behind once more, at Daisy's insistence. She felt further rest would do him good, but she also didn't fully trust his ability to keep his emotions in check when dealing with Chester's former paramour.

Heading out that evening after her shift at the library, she and the others had concocted a fiction they hoped might at least get her into McCutcheon's lavish apartment building. Approaching alone, she informed the doorman in his starched navy-blue coat and cap that she had come on behalf of "the shop" – she deliberately failed to specify which. She must see Mrs McCutcheon on the matter of a rare book in which she'd expressed interest, and might now be available for purchase.

They'd had some hope that the tale, vague but believable, would satisfy the sentinel's sense of protocol. Once inside, she would then slip around to the servants' and delivery entrance and let the others inside.

Instead, the doorman told her, with a sort of apologetic boredom, that Mrs McCutcheon had only recently left the premises, and he could hardly venture to guess how long she might be out. A bit of dissembling about the need for haste, as other parties were interested in the book – combined with a few dollars discreetly slipped into a white-gloved hand – persuaded him to reveal that, while he couldn't say with certainty where McCutcheon might have gone, she'd recently made a habit of dining at Salton and Lindall's, a newly opened restaurant just a few blocks distant.

"Can we risk talking to her in public?" Billy asked as they made their way along winding streets, through crowds perhaps a bit thinner than normal thanks to growing fears of the Merchant District flu. "When I wanted to question her before, you said the police might still be keeping an eye on her."

"They might, yes, but I shouldn't think they've got officers *inside* an establishment such as Salton and Lindall's. They'll see us enter, but we won't mean anything to them. They won't know we're speaking with her unless she's right by a window or willing to make a public fuss. And if they do, well, I'll tell them my worry over Chester inspired me to confront her." It wouldn't make the Miskatonic administration happy, but it ought to earn her nothing worse than a reprimand. It most certainly wasn't as grave a transgression as many she'd already committed in the name of this investigation.

"You weren't prepared to take that chance last week."

"Our options weren't so limited last week."

"Hmm."

Ornate signage, gold script on green, and a pair of Corinthian columns adorned the restaurant's entrance. Through broad windows, Daisy saw rows of tables, their cloths and the upholstery of the chairs a matching verdant hue to the exterior, and great glass chandeliers hanging above. She also saw that she and her compatriots, garbed in reasonably nice but everyday outfits, were a bit underdressed compared to the more formal – or simply wealthier – patrons within.

Well, nothing to be done for it now. Thankfully, other than an involuntary twitch that might have grown into a grimace had he allowed it, the tuxedo-clad *maître d'* made no objection.

"May I help you?"

"Ah…" Daisy scanned the room and swiftly found what she sought. "Thank you, we're just meeting a friend." She brushed past him, shoulders back and stride purposeful, as if daring him to interfere.

Daisy had never met Victoria McCutcheon, but she'd had no difficulty picking her out. The restaurant was not crowded that evening – perhaps explaining why their outfits hadn't elicited more of a protest – and she'd both heard McCutcheon described by those who knew her, and read similar descriptions in the society pages, which she would, if questioned, have strenuously denied ever perusing.

A physical description might have proved insufficient on its own, but the fact that the woman was dining on her own – not only without companions, but with a barren no-man's land of empty tables surrounding her, as though the other patrons feared social ostracism was contagious – was indication enough.

Chester might have been gone for months, but the stigma she suffered for the relationship would linger quite some while longer.

She sat with her head held high, her red hair hanging freer and longer than the current style. She wore a fringe-layered dress in even brighter crimson, one that seemed almost to challenge anyone who would judge it – or her – and she steadily stared back at anyone who glanced her way until they returned to their meal.

Daisy found herself admiring the woman's courage and, though it neither justified nor excused McCutcheon's own inappropriate choices, the discovery that Chester had deliberately taken advantage made it difficult to maintain the simmering anger she'd nursed.

So it was with genuine feeling, not mere etiquette, that she announced, "Apologies for disturbing you, Mrs McCutcheon." She, and then Billy and Ida, seated themselves at the woman's table, ignoring the shocked gawking of the other patrons. The woman hadn't been here long, apparently, as the table held only a near-empty cup of coffee and a plate of cheese, olives, and crackers. If she'd yet ordered an entrée, it hadn't arrived. "But I'm afraid we require a few moments of your time."

This close, neither McCutcheon's regal bearing nor her expertly applied makeup could quite conceal the line of worry, nor the circles of fatigue, marring a visage that otherwise defined statuesque. The look she turned on the newcomers, however, was full only of suspicion and defiance.

"I don't believe I know you," she said. "And I'm quite sure I didn't invite you."

"No, you don't. And you didn't. I promise, we won't take long."

"No, you won't." McCutcheon twisted in her seat, as though to signal the waiters.

"We're friends of Chester Hennessy."

She stopped, turned back. Her expression was, if anything, even stonier than before. "No, I don't believe so. Colleagues, perhaps, but he told me of all his friends."

"Fine, then. Colleagues. The point is, we're looking–"

"I have spoken to several of his friends. I have spoken to one of his professors. I have spoken to the police. I had nothing helpful to tell them, I have nothing helpful to tell you, and I will thank you to leave me to my supper in peace."

My, this is going well. "Mrs McCutcheon, please. We have information the others didn't, we might–"

"I will ask, politely, only one more time. Please leave me alone." This in the unmistakable tone of a woman out of patience, and unaccustomed to being refused.

Daisy struggled to remain calm. McCutcheon's anger and uncooperativeness were entirely understandable, and they were strangers to her. Nevertheless…

"We have reason to believe that Chester got into trouble, in part, thanks to some of the connections you helped him make. Don't you want to try to set that right?"

McCutcheon tensed so violently that Daisy recoiled, frightened for a moment that the older woman might actually come at her over the table. "Chester was his own man," she snarled. "His studies were everything to him, and I was *delighted* to be able to help him!"

And with that, Daisy had one of her answers. The anger was deep, genuine – but so was the faint tremor beneath it, a frisson of worry and guilt that, just maybe, her "help" *had* contributed to her lover's disappearance.

Which proved, so far as the librarian was concerned, that McCutcheon didn't know. She'd never discovered that, whether the relationship had later become at all real to him or not, Chester had sought her out specifically to advance his cause. If she had, the emotions wound and woven through that response would assuredly have been quite different.

Daisy found herself uncertain how to proceed. The part of her that made her living on research, on fact, insisted she tell McCutcheon the truth, rebelled at leaving the lie in place. The other, the part that remembered past times in which she'd given her own heart away unwisely, ached in sympathy with the other woman; disliked the idea of causing her further pain, of shattering the memories that were all she had left of the lover she'd lost.

And though it shamed her, she also had to contemplate which option was more likely to lead to the information they sought, which would advance their own investigation – but then, would acting based on those considerations make her any better than Chester?

Her hesitation cost her. Before Daisy could choose her next words, McCutcheon had raised a hand and waved, attracting the attention of a young waiter across the dining room. He excused himself from the fellow employee with whom he was speaking and began wending his way through the tables. Daisy, who couldn't come up with a single argument as to why McCutcheon shouldn't have them removed from the restaurant, felt disappointment welling like bile within.

Billy leaned over the table and hissed, "Chester Hennessy has been cursed!"

Well, that tears it. No chance, now, that McCutcheon would waste one more breath on them, save to have them expelled. Anger at the impulsive and frankly outlandish assertion burned in her cheeks as she made ready to rise...

"What?" Every dish and utensil on the table jerked toward McCutcheon, and Daisy realized she must have clenched her fists on the tablecloth. "What are you saying?"

"The *Ujaraanni.*" He lowered his voice further, barely whispering, so that the approaching server couldn't overhear. "When he unlocked the writing on the stone, he unlocked something else, too. It drove him mad, along with dozens of others, and it hasn't finished corrupting him, twisting him. We can't say for certain if he's even alive or dead, but if he lives, he is beset, and it will only get worse – for him and all who come near him – if we don't–"

"You require something, madam?"

Four pairs of eyes turned to the waiter, and then three of them dipped toward Victoria McCutcheon, wary and waiting.

Seconds passed, until the waiter began to shift where he stood, the situation growing awkward.

"More coffee, young man," McCutcheon said almost too softly to hear. "Please."

"I… Of course, madam," he agreed, though clearly confused. "Will your friends be needing anything?"

"No, I… don't believe they'll be here long."

More time to converse was precisely what Daisy and the others needed, but she almost wanted to protest. For Billy's argument to have carried any weight with an educated, modern woman of high society… Even as a dilettante student of the occult, she couldn't possibly believe such things.

Except, based not only on her response but her sudden pallor, she so very obviously did.

Until the waiter returned with her refill, McCutcheon said nothing. Once the hot liquid was poured, she took a large, indelicate gulp. It must have been near to scalding, but she appeared not to notice. Reaching into the purse by her chair, she removed a silver flask and poured a sizable dollop of something clear and acrid-smelling into the cup to make up the difference. Daisy swallowed nervously, glancing around to see if anyone had spotted the lawbreaking that had just blatantly occurred in the middle of the restaurant, but if it had been noticed, it went unremarked.

McCutcheon proceeded to empty well over half the coffee cup in a series of quick swallows, then dabbed at her lips with a napkin.

"Tell me what happened."

Billy did, with occasional commentary from Ida. Much of the story Daisy had already heard, but the Kalaaleq delved into details here he'd never so much as hinted at previously – doubtless because he knew that the librarian would never have accepted them. He spoke not merely of the spreading madness, the power of the litany, to a degree she hadn't yet heard, but also of *physical* alterations Chester had undergone, and his apparent inability to die.

Still she felt he left out a few gruesome specifics, but the tale was complete enough.

And no matter that she knew it was rubbish, that they could not have seen what they claimed to have seen, Daisy couldn't entirely repress a shudder. Billy and Ida were confident they spoke nothing but unvarnished truth, she could see that in their expressions, hear it in their tone. McCutcheon was equally convinced; her hands shook as she clutched the cup, and though her cheeks were no longer pale, the only color they held was the redness caused by the potent spirits in her drink.

It was enough to start just the faintest crack running through Daisy's own bastion of doubt. Not enough to make her believe, but enough that she could not quite dismiss the tiny, burrowing worms of "What if?"

McCutcheon once again raised her napkin, this time to blot away a wayward tear. "I never thought… There's always danger in unearthing forgotten things, learning of the old powers, and I knew something must have gone wrong when he disappeared, but I didn't…" Another dab of the napkin. "If I'd any idea something like this could happen to Chester, I would never have helped him. Never."

She went on, before any of the others could speak. "I spend very little time in that world, you understand? I make a… poor student, and I never meant to be anything more. It was fascinating to get a peek behind the curtain, that's all. But I know people, people part of the Silv… part of brotherhoods and orders who take these things far more seriously. Even some who claim to be part of witch cults older than Arkham!

"I don't know if I ever believed them, but it didn't matter. I didn't want to know more. I was happy where I was. Even happier when I realized my position meant I could help Chester with his work."

She paused long enough to finish the last of her coffee. She half-raised a hand to signal for yet another cup, then seemed to think better and dropped it to her lap.

"I asked them for help," she confessed. "When Chester had been gone a week or so. I thought, if he'd run into trouble delving into… into matters he shouldn't, perhaps those who studied that same lore could tell me something. Or maybe, if even a bit of it was true, *really* true, they might have… other means of finding him. Methods the police would never know existed.

"They agreed to help, at first. But only a few days later, they reneged. Told me they weren't to get involved, that Chester had nothing to do with them. I… said some things that cost me friends I could ill afford to lose, but none of them would budge. One let slip that the decision was made by someone from out of town, though why anyone in the Arkham occult community should care to listen to an outsider is beyond me."

Something about that rang a very faint bell of familiarity, though Daisy couldn't say why and hadn't the spare attention to devote to it just now. She found herself caught up in the implications of the woman's story. She knew Arkham had more than its share of occultists, of secret societies, but that there were apparently so many who were such fervent believers they would accept a tale like McCutcheon's… It made her wonder how much she truly understood about the town she called home.

"I think…" McCutcheon's eyes, which had gone blurry with

unshed tears and the effects of drink, steadied for an instant. "I think they were afraid. I think they were instructed to stay away by someone they didn't dare disobey." She seemed to go fuzzy again. "I realize how paranoid that sounds..."

Did it? Daisy wasn't sure any more.

She *was* sure, however, that the conversation was nearing its end. That the woman had finally shared a guilt, a burden, she'd long carried – her tongue loosened by fear for Chester and by alcohol – but had little more to say.

So she asked the most pressing question, the one for which they'd sought out the twice-bereft widow in the first place.

"How did Chester get his hands on the stone? On the *Pnakotic Fragments*? How did he manage *any* of this?"

"One of my friends knew a man who could help him. She introduced him to Chester – and then later to me, when I was looking for connections to help me *find* Chester."

"Yes? And who was that?"

"His name was Jebediah Pembroke," said McCutcheon.

They'd convinced her to dig into her address book and scribble out the information they needed before retreating from the restaurant and leaving her to her lonely meal. For the journey back across town to her home near the university, other than her instructions to the taxicab driver, Daisy had remained silent. Even after going upstairs, getting settled in, filling Elliot in on the basics of what they'd learned – while still avoiding the less pleasant revelations regarding Chester – she'd allowed Billy to do the talking.

It was only after a good half hour, when everyone had grown weary but remained too energized over the new revelations to take to their beds, that she finally made her decision, and her announcement.

"I'm sorry," Elliot said softly, disbelievingly, sprawled across half the sofa. "You want us to what?"

He'd been half-dozing, while Ida had her face buried in the mystery she'd borrowed off the shelf and Billy played dominoes against himself on the coffee table.

Now he was wide awake, the others paying complete attention as well.

"I said," Daisy repeated, as she stepped to the table, digging in her purse, "I'll need all of you to leave come the morning."

Still Elliot appeared to be the only one willing to speak. "I don't understand. I thought we–"

"You're well enough now, Elliot. It won't hurt you. You have your room, Billy and Ida can easily take lodgings." She gestured toward the steamer trunk they'd taken from the Hennessy household. "You can take that with you, or I can hold it until you're prepared to return home. And, of course, you can still access the library, through Elliot. I'll help you find anything you need there."

"Then why…?"

Daisy carefully lay a scrap of folded paper on the table and slid it across. Billy opened it to reveal the address they'd acquired at Salton and Lindall's.

"I'm through," she told them. "Finished, with all of this. I'm truly sorry, but I have to be. I've already taken risks, not only with my own wellbeing, but others' as well. I *cannot* be seen dealing with a trafficker in black market artifacts. Not in any capacity, not by anyone. If so much as a *rumor* were to spread that we were dealing with Pembroke, the damage to Miskatonic's reputation, its standing in the academic and historical worlds, would be catastrophic.

"It's why I tried to steer us to alternate avenues of investigation, back when we had any. We don't any longer, and I... have no choices left to me."

It was the truth, but not the *entire* truth. The primary reason to extricate herself, but not the only one.

Their tales of what had happened, what they'd seen, were impossible. Utter madness, without even delving into what they *hadn't* told her. And yet...

Yet a part of her, a very tiny part, the part that had insisted she keep the lights on after flipping through those ancient tomes, was starting to wonder. She'd begun to cast Billy and Elliot, in her own thoughts, as akin to Henry James' literary governess: a disturbed woman who imagined she saw ghosts—unless, of course, she wasn't. Unless they weren't.

Daisy, who if nothing else had to keep her head as a librarian and caretaker of the Special Collection at Miskatonic, couldn't afford to let herself slip into the flights of fear and fancy that must surely result if she ever seriously allowed herself to follow them down that path.

So she could do nothing but harden her resolve.

Elliot looked as if he wanted to cry, and she felt as though she'd just kicked a puppy out of her home. A worm of guilt writhed in her gut, trying to gnaw its way out. She desperately didn't want to do this, and would still assist them should they require any further library research, but beyond that, her responsibilities permitted no further option.

Even as she watched, Elliot's expression smoothed out as he thought it all through. "I understand," he finally told her.

"You don't, not entirely, because I haven't finished yet. I don't know everything that's happening, and I'm unsure how much I believe of what I do know." An understatement at best, that last! "But Chester is still missing, and we have a genuine lead that I cannot pursue, but I also cannot ignore. I do not want to get any of you – or anyone I work with – in trouble with the authorities, or do any harm to the university. But I also can't sit on this indefinitely if there's still even a chance of saving Chester or preventing harm to others."

"There's *no* chance of–"

She raised a hand, halting Elliot's protest. "I am giving you until the weekend to find him, or at least to find me additional reason – reason I can *believe* – to continue leaving this in your hands. If you cannot do so by then, I will have no choice but to tell the police what I know of Pembroke's connection to Chester, no matter who – or what – might be damaged."

Silence fell. Nobody cared for the ultimatum, or for the repercussions. Again, Daisy didn't like it any better, but faced with an array of nothing but bad options, she had to choose the one that felt the most right or, failing that, the least wrong. Had to obey the dictates of her conscience. She'd skirted the edges too often lately as it was.

Even when the following day had come, however, when her guests – her companions, people who could have been her friends – had gone their way, when she'd returned to her work at the Orne Library and tried to put all thoughts of mystery and investigation behind her, she still found herself wondering, with every free moment, if she was doing the right thing.

CHAPTER TWENTY-ONE

After something of a scramble the following morning – Billy once more taking a room at Ma's Boarding House, and Ida, with a few dollars of Elliot's money, doing the same – the trio were all but exhausted. Neither of the newcomers to Arkham had slept much the past two nights, and while Elliot had done little *but* rest, he found himself craving a little longer to put himself together. He might understand intellectually why Daisy decided as she had, but that didn't make him any happier about it, and while the abrupt change in accommodations wasn't difficult, it was a hassle he didn't need right now.

Thus, though they begrudged the wasted time, particularly with Daisy's deadline weighing on them, they reluctantly granted themselves the remainder of that day, and the following night, to recuperate.

Shortly before noon on the second day after leaving Daisy's flat, they assembled in Ma Mathison's dining room for an early luncheon. All three looked to be in a healthier state than they had been, though only some of that was due to the extra rest; the remainder from the opportunity to thoroughly clean up and change into freshly laundered clothes.

It was a somber and subdued meal. Planning had neither taken long nor accomplished much. As none of them knew a lot about Pembroke, his organization, or his activities, they seemed to have little choice but to play whatever came by ear. And as none felt any desire to rehash recent events or previous speculation, they found themselves with little to talk about.

A couple of hours later, with luncheon and an equally taciturn cab ride behind them, they found themselves braving the cold drizzle and damp breeze of the Merchant District streets.

It would have been a gross exaggeration to say the neighborhood felt abandoned, and it was entirely possible that neither Ida nor Billy even noticed anything amiss. To Elliot, however, those streets were definitely underpopulated. For a weekday afternoon, foot traffic on the sidewalks was mild, the automobiles in the roadway a sporadic trickle.

Every now and again, a glance down one of the longer cross streets, during a pause in the mild but steady downpour, provided a hint as to why. In the distance, barricades and police vehicles marked the line of demarcation between the district proper and the poor warehouse and residential blocks beyond, where Arkham's authorities still worked to keep the localized outbreak of influenza from becoming an epidemic. According to the radio and the papers, they'd so far been successful, and patronizing the Merchant District posed no risk at all. Elliot could certainly sympathize, however, with any who elected not to take the chance, to put off their shopping or conduct their business elsewhere.

Here, however, was where the address McCutcheon had provided them was located, so here they must be.

Elliot and his companions found themselves before a plain brownstone, a structure that, while of more recent vintage than much of Arkham's Colonial or faux-Old World construction, was hardly new. The paint had begun to peel off the window shutters and doorframes.

He couldn't help frowning at it. "This doesn't look very like the lair of a fence and smuggler, does it?"

Ida snorted, and Billy raised an eyebrow.

Elliot flushed. "Okay, yeah. Dumb thing to say. What room?"

"2C," said Billy, who had memorized the address rather than bring the note along.

The front door led to a dim hallway with numerous smaller doors. None were open, or showed any sign of activity or even illumination through their frosted glass windows. Most didn't even name whatever enterprise they belonged to, displaying only a suite number. Those few that did provide more information had unhelpful names such as "Bellington and Windsor" or "Neidermeyer Inc."

"Business ain't boomin'," Ida observed.

A broad staircase groaned beneath them as they ascended to find a nearly identical hall above.

Billy pointed. "There. 2C."

It was one of the few doors with a business name as well as a number, though that name – West Side Rental and Storage Management, Ltd – was scratched and worn enough that one had to be right next to it to read it.

Elliot shrugged, knocked and opened the door.

There had been a time, he couldn't help but note, when this sort of thing would have had him racked with nervousness. After the past week, it barely made an emotional impact at all.

Within stood a few chairs against one wall, a rust-stained drinking fountain and a desk. Behind that desk was a door leading into another room, and the room's only occupant.

Her complexion was dark, making her bright red lipstick stand out all the more dramatically. She wore a stylish scarlet beret and a navy pantsuit, and – other than being just a few years older – would not have looked remotely out of place among a group of Miskatonic seniors on a Friday night.

And if she was excited to see potential customers, she did a masterful job of hiding it.

"Something I can help you with?" she asked, polite but a touch cold.

"Well, yes," Elliot replied. "We'd like to see Jebediah Pembroke."

Naive he might be, but the young student wasn't a fool. He knew, before he spoke, that one probably didn't just walk in and ask to see a black marketeer by name. On the other hand, he had neither the slightest notion what the proper criminal etiquette might be, nor the patience to try to figure it out.

A sharp blink was the woman's only indication that he'd startled her. "I'm afraid there's nobody in today who can help you. If you'd like to leave a name and an address or phone number–"

Billy, it turned out, had even less patience than Elliot. "We haven't the time for games. Is he back there?" He took two steps toward the door behind her.

Something metallic clattered, the source of the sound hidden by the desk, and the woman finally stood…

An M1921 Thompson submachine gun in her hands, muzzle gaping wide, the heavy ammunition drum dangling like some monstrous growth beneath the barrel.

"He's not, and you're not going there, either."

Ida drew her Colt, dropping into a crouch. The other woman twisted to aim her way; every muscle in Elliot's body clenched as the barrel passed across him on its way toward Ida ...

And Billy, too, drew a pistol. The part of Elliot that wasn't screaming recognized it as the revolver he'd carried during the horrific confrontation with Chester. He hadn't even known Billy had picked it up, let alone brought it back with him.

"Whoa, *whoa!* Everyone just... wait a minute!" Elliot kept his hands raised. "Calm down!"

Then, "Look, Miss... Uh, Miss," he continued when she didn't fill in the blank for him, "we're not here to rob you, or to hurt Mr Pembroke. Or you."

"Damn right you're not."

"Um. But I do think you should talk to us."

"And why's that?"

"Because there are lives at stake. Because something terrible may be happening – maybe even here in Arkham. And because the very best you can hope for, if everyone starts shooting, is a real ugly cleaning job."

The woman finally cracked a faint smile. "You don't scare easy, do you?"

"Are you kidding? I'm terrified. But after what we've seen in the last few days..." He shuddered, despite his best efforts. "You wouldn't believe it."

"You might be surprised what I believe, Mr Raslo."

And here he'd thought he was done being surprised for a while. "How...?"

"Big hulking Eskimo like your friend here comes to Arkham, and suddenly people start asking around the shops about an item we… moved? Of course I've had people shadowing you. Or at least I did until you left town."

"Inuit," Billy corrected. Then, abruptly, "The man outside the hotel *was* watching me, then!"

Elliot tried to ask what in God's name he was talking about, but the woman didn't offer the opportunity.

"Yeah, and he wasn't real happy you spotted him. Neither was I." She paused, mulling something over. "All right, here's the deal. That you're here looking for Mr Pembroke already answers some questions I had, but it opens a whole lot more. So yeah, I'll talk to you – soon as you hand over your bean-shooters."

Ida and Billy both protested, but Elliot shushed them. "We need answers. Miss…"

This time she proved more forthcoming. "Bentley. Alice Bentley."

"Miss Bentley might have those answers for us. And besides, Daisy knows where we are, and she's waiting to hear from us." That last was as much for Bentley's sake as for his friends', and another quick smile suggested she well knew it.

She didn't know, of course, that Daisy didn't expect to hear from them for several days – and Elliot saw no reason to clarify.

Ida grumbling, Billy deathly silent, they handed over their pistols. Bentley put them in a drawer and slung the Tommy back under the desk. "Don't think that means I'm unarmed," she warned.

Elliot and Ida nodded. Billy – who, Elliot knew, still wore his pana beneath his coat – merely smiled in his turn.

Bentley opened the door behind her and led them into the next room. Based on its size, and the additional doors, the bulk of the floor must have actually been devoted to Pembroke's business. The other offices were facades.

Bookshelves covered most of the open walls, containing both rare tomes and modern ledgers. Here and there were a variety of old statues, bits of jewelry, bronze weapons – tiny relics of a dozen cultures that had presumably caught Pembroke's fancy.

Again, Elliot yearned for simpler times when he'd have had the energy to be fascinated. Though he couldn't help but think, with a touch of amusement, at the collective apoplexy the staff at Miskatonic's museum would have over it all.

Their host directed them to a table in front of one of the bookcases, and the chairs surrounding it. Elliot and Ida sat, but Billy crossed his arms and glared.

"Does it bother you even a little that you're dealing in treasures and sacred objects stolen from any number of–"

"No. I've never stolen anything, and if anyone wants to come to me with the proper provenances to prove ownership, I'll be happy to make them a good deal." With that, she joined the others around the table.

Growling softly, Billy finally did the same.

Elliot decided to go first. "Your boss won't mind you talking to us?"

"I don't know. I'll be sure to ask if I ever find him."

His companions were taken aback. Elliot was not. He hadn't quite expected that answer, not consciously, but he realized he wasn't shocked.

"You said 'I,'" he commented. "*I* had someone following you."

Bentley nodded. "Mr Pembroke disappeared a couple weeks ago. And he was acting oddly before that. Preoccupied."

Elliot briefly squeezed his eyes shut. He didn't much approve of Pembroke, but he wouldn't wish what he knew must have happened on anyone. Even worse, that made the missing smuggler another possible point of origin for an outbreak of the maddening refrain.

"A couple weeks ago." Not too long after Chester. It almost had to be connected, didn't it?

"When I caught wind of…" Now it was her turn to pause. "Your name I was able to dig up, Mr Raslo. Your friends' eluded me."

"Mr Shiwak and Miss Glick."

"Well. When I learned Mr Shiwak was in Arkham, looking for the *Ujaraanni*, and the rest of you asking around about the boss's newest client, I thought maybe you'd done something to him. That's why I had you all followed. Once you came in here looking for him, though, I guessed I could rule that out."

Newest client. "You mean Chester," Elliot breathed.

The woman paused, her professional – and doubtless habitual – caution flaring, but nodded. "Chester Hennessy. Yes."

Finally. *Finally* it might all be coming together. Elliot struggled to focus on that, and not on the torment shooting through him at each mention of Chester's name.

"That's why you're helping us. To try to find Pembroke."

"So far, I'm only talking to you. We haven't agreed on 'helping' yet. But yes, that's partly why."

"And the other part?"

She didn't answer, instead saying, "You're a close friend of Hennessy's, I understand."

"I… yeah. I am."

Bentley scowled in what appeared to be disapproval. "Your friend isn't good at this sort of thing, Mr Raslo. May be sharp when it comes to his studies, but a real sap. Maybe if he'd been wiser, none of this would have..." She trailed off, gazing at the table, the first time since they'd walked in the door that Elliot had seen her anything but confident.

A few minutes of conversation confirmed what Elliot and the others had already pieced together: that one of Victoria McCutcheon's high society friends had introduced Chester to Pembroke, and the former had then employed the latter to acquire both the *Ujaraanni* and whatever relevant bits of the *Pnakotic Fragments* he might manage to unearth. Due to the infamy of the theft from the University of Virginia, acquiring the stone proved relatively simple. The *Fragments*, however, were far more challenging, and indeed the acquisition had only been made possible by the sheer quantity of money Chester had been willing to throw at the problem.

Every time Elliot thought he'd finally gotten a handle on Chester's obsession, he somehow managed to discover it had been even more consuming than he'd thought.

"That was his mistake," Alice told them. "You just don't toss around sums like that willy-nilly. Mr Pembroke's never outright cheated a client, least not that I know of, but he knew immediately this was something big. A lot bigger than some rich boy's whim, and a *whole* lot more valuable.

"I'm not sure what his end goal was, if he just wanted to squeeze a little more money from Hennessy. Or maybe he figured, if he could learn the whole picture, he could sell information about the kid's discovery. He started looking into everything Hennessy was doing, coaxing more details out of him. He lent the kid one of his rooms – Mr Pembroke owns several properties, flophouses and warehouses – to keep the stone, to do some of his studies."

Another piece clicked into place in Elliot's head. That must be where Chester had stored the *Ujaraanni* – and hidden himself, as well, after his disappearance – before eventually sheltering at his uncle's home.

"He took every opportunity to sneak looks at Hennessy's notes, to study the *Ujaraanni*. He even snuck into the Miskatonic museum to examine some other related piece."

Elliot was starting to have trouble buying this. "Wait a minute. Chester spent months, maybe years, on this, and he was a linguist. I'm sure your boss was a clever guy, but there's no way–"

For his troubles, he earned a return appearance of Alice's hard, cold visage from earlier. "What do you think we do here, Mr Raslo? You figure we just scoop up a bunch of pretties and try to hock them off like some street-corner pawnbroker?"

"Uh…"

"Jebediah Pembroke knows more about the objects he deals in than most of your professors, and he's taught me… maybe not *everything* he knows, but more than enough that I've had no troubles running the business without him. He's an expert in the historical and the occult. So no, he could never have worked out the specifics or the acoustical translations on his own, but he was more than capable of following Hennessy's work."

"I… Of course. My apologies."

"Yeah." Again Alice bowed her head. "Actually, I wish you were right. I wish he hadn't been able. I don't know if he meant to beat Hennessy to the discovery, or sell what he'd learned, or… what. But he vanished not long after Hennessy did.

"So, your turn. What's *happening* out there? And don't tell me I won't believe it."

They told her, or rather Elliot and Billy told her. Ida, perhaps troubled at the notion of revisiting what had happened to her home and her community, once more retreated into her own thoughts. She seemed not to hear a word that was spoken, let alone contribute one.

By the end, Alice gawped at them in horror – but not, much to Elliot's surprise, disbelief.

"Dear Jesus. Jebediah and I, we've come across a few curses in our time, had to rely on protective charms and such, but I've never heard of *anything* like this. Least not quite…"

"Not quite?" Billy repeated.

Alice dithered a moment, then rose and left the room. When she returned, she carried a small stack of old, musty, leather-bound tomes. Had she been present, Daisy Walker would doubtless have been horrified to find them locked away in a private collection, let alone that of a criminal.

Rather than opening any one of them, however, Alice instead drew a scrap of paper, covered in neat handwriting, from between two of the texts. "There's… a language. One that's referenced in more than a few of these books. A specific sentence, if you'd even care to call it that, appears more often than any other."

She cleared her throat, loudly, something Elliot dismissed as a bit of an affectation – until she began to read. Only then did he realize their host had been preparing herself for what could only be a flawed attempt at an impossible utterance.

"*Ph'nglui mglw'nafh Cthulhu R'lyeh wgah'nagl fhtagn.*"

It was ugly, discordant; a snarly, phlegmy thing, grating on the ears, and assuredly on the throat. Elliot flinched, and saw that his friends had reacted similarly.

"What in God's name is that?" he demanded.

Alice frowned. "So that's not how your litany sounded?"

"No! It's…" He struggled for a description, a task made even more difficult by his refusal to think too heavily on the phrases. "The litany is just as alien, but less inhuman. If that's not a contradiction."

"Huh. I don't know if that's a good thing or not." She laid the paper aside and put a hand on the books. "I've read through many of these in my time working with Mr Pembroke, and I've studied several in more detail in the past weeks."

"Felt in the mood for some light reading?" Billy muttered.

"I'm no fool, Mr Shiwak. The boss told me of Hennessy's odd behavior before he vanished, and then he showed the same before *he* disappeared. I knew something unnatural was happening long before you three showed up at my door. I thought I might try to figure out what, but I never came up with much.

"And the language I just read to you is the only one I can't identify that appears regularly in any of these. If it's not the one you're speaking of, I'm afraid none of this…" She thumped the pile lightly, "…is liable to help."

"We should check the *Pnakotic Fragments*," Billy suggested. Then, after several startled glances cast his way, "What? I may not know these writings, but that was the one Chester consulted to transliterate the *Ujaraanni*, was it not?"

"Unfortunately," Alice said, "I don't have access to anything older than an abbreviated English translation of the *Pnakotic Manuscripts*. It took every connection Pembroke had to locate the *Fragments* he sold to Hennessy."

Elliot scratched nervously at his wrist. "We don't need someone willing to part with them, though. Only someone who could help us learn more about what's in them. Does that change anything?"

"You know, it just might." Again Alice rose from her seat. "I have Mr Pembroke's client list. Some of them have private libraries like you would never believe. I'll make some calls." She cast them a mirthless grin. "I hope you're comfortable. This will probably take some time."

"Some time" had stretched itself to four hours, and still counting. Alice Bentley had completed her phone calls in the next room and then rejoined the others after the first hour, and the rest had been spent waiting for assistance she assured them was on the way. The trio briefly discussed the possibility that they might be wasting their time, and any "help" she conjured might prove useless. In the end, however, they had no other real options.

Elliot napped in his chair, head slumped down and – he would have been mortified to know – drooling lightly on his lapel. Ida had attempted to lose herself in one of the modern, non-artifact books the room provided, in this case a treatise on the Massachusett nation, the indigenous people of the region. For a while now, though, she'd simply sat, scarcely blinking, her reading apparently forgotten. She might as well have been as deeply asleep as Elliot.

Which left Billy, his own thoughts awhirl and still seasoned with resentful anger, alone with his host in hostile silence.

A silence he finally elected to break, though he kept his voice low in order not to awaken his friend.

"Do you ever plan to tell us the truth?"

She looked as if she'd forgotten he was present at all. "I'm sorry?"

"The truth. Of why you're assisting us."

"Mr Pembroke–"

Billy snorted. "Mr Pembroke is almost certainly mad, either infected by Hennessy or from his own unwise reading of the *Ujaraanni*. And that assumes he's even alive. If he confronted the madmen, or tracked the boy to his uncle's home, he very well might not be. In either case, there's no guarantee we'll ever learn what happened to him, and if we *do* run into him, we may well be forced to kill him. And I believe you're smart enough to be aware of all that."

"That doesn't mean I don't have hope," she insisted.

"You also said as much, that it wasn't your only motive. Elliot may have forgotten that. I have not."

"Oh, I don't know. Maybe I'd prefer not to see a plague of unnatural lunacy unleashed on Arkham?" She, too, spoke softly, but a growing exasperation rang clear all the same.

"I see. Out of the kindness of your heart, is it?"

Alice sucked in a breath between her teeth. "Just because you think so poorly of me–"

"With good reason!"

"–does not mean it's so. I've no desire to see anyone hurt who doesn't need to be."

"No, you're content to hurt them in ways you *can't* see!"

She stood, fists clenched, and paced to the door, but turned back rather than reach for the latch. "I've seen the aftermath of curses far less severe than the one you've spoken of, and I've no wish to see anything of the sort again. Believe what you like. If it helps, you can assume I'm simply protecting myself and my business."

Billy's expression was less a smile than a baring of teeth. "Yours, is it? Hoping Pembroke's gone for good?"

"Go to hell, Shiwak."

"Wha's goin' on?" Only half awakened by the exchange, Elliot spoke as through a mouthful of cotton.

"A cultural exchange," their host sneered, "with your Eskimo friend."

"Inuit," Elliot and Billy corrected in unison.

Alice snarled and dropped back into her chair.

Perhaps alert enough to sense the tension, Elliot changed the subject. "Would you be so good as to tell us who we're waiting on?"

"One of Mr Pembroke's most important clients," she answered, sullen at first but swiftly regaining her composure. "One of the most discerning collectors I've ever met, and a man of some renown in occult circles. You're fortunate he's even in Arkham just now."

"Oh? He's not from here?"

"No. Louisiana. A small town outside New Orleans, if I'm not mistaken."

Elliot sat upright, now fully awake, and Billy felt his brow furrow.

"Mean something to you?" she asked.

"The client Daisy mentioned?" Elliot wondered aloud.

Billy nodded. "And McCutcheon said her occultist friends were told to stay out of things by someone from out of town…"

"Well, now." It came over the sound of the door opening, in a rich Southern drawl thicker than Arkham's infamous fogs. "I do believe my ears are burnin'."

Everyone stared, though Alice seemed more surprised than anyone. Billy wondered what safeguards she had in place that were supposed to have alerted her when someone entered the outer office, let alone the inner rooms.

The man in the doorway didn't appear to match the voice at all – and Billy realized swiftly that, in fact, he wasn't the source. The first figure wore the formal suit and cap of a professional chauffeur, and kept his gaze turned to the floor, his face partly obscured. After opening the door he stepped aside, allowing another fellow to enter before returning to the outer chamber.

It was this other man, presumably the employer of the first, who had spoken.

"Good evenin', my friends. Hyrum Lafayette-Moses, at your service."

CHAPTER TWENTY-TWO

Elliot knew he was staring, knew it might come across as rude. He couldn't help himself, and his companions seemed to be waging the same inner struggle. Something about this man *commanded* attention.

Lafayette-Moses was tall, thin without being gaunt; an older man, perhaps a very healthy sixty. The hair on his head was silver, as opposed to the salt-and-pepper mix of his goatee. The charcoal suit he wore cost more than many people's entire wardrobe, and he walked with a cane – probably an affectation, as his steps appeared surefooted enough.

In every way, to Elliot's mind, the very picture of an Old Family southern gentleman.

"Miss Bentley tells me I might be of some small assistance here," he continued, approaching the table. "And I'm quite happy to oblige. Why, I'd feel just awful if somethin' happened to dear Jebediah and I hadn't done everythin' in my power to help."

Elliot found his gaze drawn with an almost magnetic pull to the walking stick. The round head of the cane was made of black glass, perhaps obsidian, but sported an array of white and silver flecks within. It resembled nothing so much as a small piece scooped from the night sky.

And the fingers clasped around it... They were long, thin, swift. The fingers of a pianist, perhaps, or a surgeon.

Or a conjurer.

The nails were perfect, evenly manicured, almost reflective. All save the one on Lafayette-Moses's left ring finger, which was absent entirely. It didn't even appear to have been removed: the finger simply bore a flat and featureless expanse of skin, without even a bed to mark where it should have been.

As the table was a chair short, the newcomer snapped his fingers. His chauffeur appeared almost instantly carrying a chair from the outer office, as though he'd already known what was required. He placed it halfway between the table and the door, then departed once more. Lafayette-Moses seated himself, hands folded atop his cane.

"Tell me, my friends, what it is you require."

And just as before, Elliot, with a bit of assistance from Billy, told their tale. All of it. He hadn't intended to, had meant to gloss over the more personal or uncomfortable details, omit the bits he expected most listeners to discount as sheer nonsense, but somehow it all emerged. It required conscious effort to avoid revealing even the details of his feelings for Chester, something he would never even *consider* sharing under most circumstances.

Only when it was done did Elliot wonder, with a vaguely sick feeling, precisely *why* he'd been so forthcoming.

The peculiar old outsider said nothing at all until the recitation was complete – and when he finally did, it was the last thing Elliot expected to hear.

"You're a student of the mind, Mr Raslo?"

"I... Sorry, what?" Had the man listened to a single word he'd said?

"The human mind. Your field of study?"

Bewildered, Elliot nodded. "I'm a student of psychology, yes."

"Thought so!" Lafayette-Moses rocked back with a smile, almost an aborted cackle. "I could tell that about you. How you speak, how you think. Your thoughts," and here he abruptly grew serious once more, "on the refrain in your head and the dreams you've been having."

His fingers flexed in unison atop his cane, a butterfly slowly fanning its wings.

"You did well to master that protective incantation of the *Livre d'Ivon*. Not an easy thing to do. I'm impressed. Tell me, are you a man of faith as well?"

Elliot was starting to feel dizzy.

And Billy, apparently, impatient. "Mr Lafayette-Moses, time is something of a–"

The old man's head came about faster than a shot, startling even the unflappable hunter, and the jovial charm drained from him equally quickly. "We'll get to you, Mr Shiwak."

Back to Elliot, back to his subtle smile. Somewhat offended on his friend's behalf, the student elected not to answer, not to play along with this any further – except he was already replying before he'd fully made that decision.

"I mean, I was raised a good Christian, and I suppose I believe. It's not much a part of my life, though."

"No, I don't suppose it is. Doesn't mean much to a lot of folks these days. But to others... Oh, to others... Such as your friend here." He waved toward Billy, with no trace of his former hostility. "The Inuit are *fierce* believers, are you not?"

"I wouldn't say we believe," the hunter replied cautiously. "We *know*. We know what shares this world with us, and what dwells in the other, and we fear."

"Oh, but you don't know, my friend. You only think you do. You're right to fear, though."

Lafayette-Moses leaned back in his chair, laying his cane across his lap.

"There are some who still remember gods older than your spirits," he said to Billy, "or your Jehovah in his Heaven," he continued to Elliot, Ida, and Alice. "You have more than a few here in Massachusetts, in Arkham. You call them 'witch cults,' or think them the primitive superstitions of backwoods yokels. And I suppose that's all some of them are. But only some."

He pointed the obsidian head of his cane across the table at their host. "She knows, if she's paid attention to what Mr Pembroke sells, and to whom. If she's read half as much as she claims. Have you, Miss Bentley?"

She took a deep breath – almost reluctantly, Elliot thought – and once more placed a hand on the stack of tomes she'd produced earlier. "Some of these do speak of cults, yes. Many long gone, but others that, from what I've learned, may survive even today. Not simple religious sects, splintered from Christianity or Islam or whatever pagan faiths you like. They venerate… things. Terrible things that make any conception of Satan and his hosts pale."

Elliot felt a chill, as though the unseasonable weather outside had crept through the closed doors. Alice's words weren't especially frightening of themselves – he knew humanity had concocted a great many peculiar and even nightmarish beliefs in its time. Today, though, in light of all he'd experienced, and in the presence of the ever-more-disturbing Mr Hyrum Lafayette-Moses, the notion felt far more plausible.

More real.

"What things, Miss Bentley?" the old man pressed, somewhere between a demanding professor and a zealous inquisitor. "Whom do they serve?"

Her posture screamed that she'd no desire to answer, but just as Elliot had felt before, she seemed compelled to respond. "They… appear to have different forms. So many titles. Imprisoned in the far reaches of our world, or our universe, or even 'Outside,' but always lurking at the threshold, ready to cross over at the proper call.

"Some I've only found obliquely described so far. I'm sure their names can be found somewhere in these books, but I've not had access to full translations. The Black Goat of the Woods. The Crawling Chaos. The Dreaming Priest." She swallowed, as though merely speaking of them had parched her tongue. "But I don't know if any of those mean anything to most of you, or if what Hennessy dug up is related to any of these sects…"

"Stop it!" Elliot didn't remember standing, and now that he had, he couldn't say why he'd had so vehement a reaction. It just all felt… dangerous.

The old man raised an eyebrow. "Stop what, Mr Raslo? We're simply havin' a conversation, establishin' some basic facts. You did ask for my help, after all."

Slowly, Elliot sat. Beside him, Alice nervously scraped a fingernail over the spine of one of the books, tracing the title etched into the leather.

"That why you asked about these cults?" Ida asked. Elliot jumped, having once again all but forgotten her presence thanks to her prolonged silence. *She must be having a harder time dealing with her grief than I'd realized.* "You figure the litany's related to one of 'em somehow?"

"It's not impossible. More than a few worshipers of the Ancient Ones are driven mad by the secrets they learn, or the horrors they witness."

All right, Elliot thought, that made some sense. It wasn't identical to the effect they'd seen, but similar enough.

"So," Lafayette-Moses continued, "let us see what answers we can unearth together."

Again he snapped his fingers, and again his servant appeared in the doorway. This time he carried a small wooden box, polished smooth, without adornment or decoration but for a single iron latch. He carefully handed it to his master, then stood at his shoulder rather than retreating.

"The *Pnakotic Fragments.*" Lafayette-Moses sounded near rapturous. "Not complete, of course. So many remain undiscovered, perhaps long destroyed, or survive as but a single copy in the hands of others. Still, I think you'll find few collections in the world, if any, as comprehensive as my own."

He leaned his cane against the chair, straightened the box in his lap and flipped the latch with a dramatic flourish.

The scent of old parchment wafted across the room, but what first emerged were several papers of far more modern vintage. These Lafayette-Moses handed to his driver to hold, save for a single sheet, which he kept.

"Now, Mr Raslo, I realize this is likely to make you uncomfortable, and I do apologize, but I'm afraid I'll need to hear a bit of your litany."

"You can't! The infection–"

"Now, son, I was hardly born yesterday. As I said, you did well to make use of even a simple incantation, but let me show you a little of what a true adept can do."

He began to read, then, from the paper he'd retained – or rather, to recite, referencing the writing only occasionally, perhaps to jog a memory. The words were Latin, and carried the cadence of ritual, but this was nothing ever heard within the walls of any proper church. Elliot's education had afforded him only a passing familiarity with the ancient tongue; Chester would doubtless have known what it all meant, but Elliot could interpret only a word here and there.

Yet even without understanding, he sensed its effects. He felt as if he'd been wrapped in something… not constraining but comforting, like a swaddling blanket. The constant infernal echo at the back of his skull grew as quiet as it had ever been since the moment he'd been exposed.

Having reached the end, Lafayette-Moses reverted to English. "Every one of us in this room is protected," he declared. "Not for very long, but most assuredly long enough for you to tell me what I need to hear."

Apprehensive still, Elliot looked to his friends. Ida offered him a shrug, as if she could only just be bothered to care, and Billy a slow nod. Taking a deep, steadying breath, he began.

"*Isslaach thkulkris, isslaach cheoshash…* Uh…"

How peculiar. He'd heard the rest of it, numerous times, while under other protections. Now that he tried to bring it to mind, however, he found he could recall only that first phrase, the part that had genuinely infected him. As if the words, unable to take root as they intended, had instead slipped away entirely.

"*Vn… Vnosh?* No, that's not right…"

The old man waved a dismissal. "Not to worry, Mr Raslo. That's enough."

"It is?" Alice dubiously asked the question they were all thinking.

"Oh, yes." His pupils unfocused, delving deep into remembered lore. "That tongue… It's the language of one of the last of the antehuman races."

Alice's jaw dropped, but the others expressed only bewilderment.

"Peoples," Lafayette-Moses explained, "or somethin' like peoples, who walked the Earth before man. This one, in particular… Not reptilian, precisely, but more akin to reptiles than to us. Some few survived long enough to live alongside our first ancestors, and they taught us things. Secrets. Writin's. Magics. Tells me where to start lookin', at least." His fingers darted once more to the box.

Stunned silence wafted through the room like a cold breeze. Elliot looked to each of the others in turn, as if desperately seeking one expression of disbelief, some measure of doubt he could cling to.

He found none. Alice and Billy stared back at him, while Ida gazed at nothing at all. Outlandish as it was, they believed every word. So did he.

He wished he didn't.

"Do you, um, need the table?" their host asked. She sounded hesitant, a reticence Elliot shared. He didn't want the strange visitor any nearer than he already was.

Lafayette-Moses, however, shook his head, then reached out a hand and retrieved the other papers from his chauffeur. Finally, he pointed down at his feet. Without hesitation, the servant dropped to all fours, back held straight. His master placed the box on him as if he were nothing more than a piece of furniture, and began to shuffle through it.

Elliot swallowed a surge of revulsion.

The occultist sorted thick sheets of yellowed parchment almost like a deck of cards, scanning and dismissing. Despite his alacrity, the care he took with the old, crackling material was clear.

"Yes, here we are. Most of the rites and invocations in that tongue are wards and bindin's, shared to protect us and them from forces fearful to both races. They formed some of the very first foundations of humanity's sorceries. Tell me, Mr Raslo, did you see anythin' in these dreams of yours that might help us narrow it down?"

So Elliot once more began revealing to this disturbing stranger intimate details he'd prefer to have held close to his chest. The ice. The screams. The terrible, impossible limbs formed of the mad, and the partial disintegration of his own form.

To each element the other nodded, then asked Billy more of the history and myth behind the *Ujaraanni*, absorbing those answers as well. Until, with a final burst of sorting through the scraps and fragments before him...

"Yes. It's here. A power, a monstrosity, a spirit, a god. An entity formed in part of unearthly matter, but also, in part, a being of *notion*. Of idea. It awoke from within the fears of a people already beset by nature and by angry spirits, and it stretched forth its grasping tendrils from horizon to horizon, through the clouds of storm above and the clouds of nightmare within.

"They called it the Fetid Thought. The Weaver of Flesh. The Thousandfold Dream. But even the *Pnakotic Fragments* don't give its name…"

"Tsocathra." Elliot hadn't meant to speak; it just came out. Yet now that it had, he knew, though he'd never heard it as part of the litany or from any living mouth, though it had come to him only as he emerged from his own terrible dreams. "Its name is Tsocathra."

If anyone wondered how he knew, they chose not to ask. Perhaps they had reached the point, as he had, of taking much of what they learned on faith.

"Well. Tsocathra, then."

"Was this vile toornaq imprisoned in the *Ujaraanni*?" Billy demanded. He leaned sharply forward in his chair, as though straining toward the answers he sought. "Or in the Lindegaard Stele? These ancient, 'antehuman' magics were meant to bind it somehow?"

The occultist glanced again at the parchment, frowning at ragged holes in the material where whole sections were missing.

"To bind it, yes," he answered eventually. "But not in the stone, not precisely. Oh, perhaps that was their intention, but the ancients failed to comprehend Tsocathra's nature. Part physical, remember, and part thought.

"The Old One was not bound in your *Ujaraanni*, Mr Shiwak. He was not bound *by* the spell, but *in* the spell. In the writin's etched into the rock. In the symbols. In the *sounds*."

Elliot choked, which turned into a full-on coughing fit that took minutes of reddened cheeks and streaming eyes to overcome. The words in his head… Shards, seeds, of Tsocathra itself! He felt nauseous, even violated, and had to repress an urge to slam his skull into the wall in a desperate hope to purge the intrusion.

Only after he'd recovered, and Alice had produced a glass of water for him, did he nod weakly for Lafayette-Moses to resume.

"Some of this they learned when those who were meant to guard the great stone fell victim to the madness you've seen for yourselves – to the madness, and worse. The rest, speculation of their greatest wise men and sorcerers.

"Those who read the carved words became obsessed with them, repeatin' them, and that repetition tainted others. Their thoughts, their very dreams, slowly replaced by the essence of somethin' they could never hope to comprehend. If the source lived long enough, infected enough, he'd start to… change, his body growin' as corrupted as his mind. And if ever *enough* minds were tainted, and if even one among them had the *whole* litany in his head…"

"Tsocathra," Elliot whispered helplessly. "Reborn."

"Just so, I'm afraid. Only in a physical body, at first, sculpted and molded of the madmen who'd fallen to the litany, absorbed and remade. But eventually, given the time, and the minds, and the flesh… A *full* awakenin'. A complete transformation. And the Old One would walk the Earth again, in all his unnatural glory."

Elliot found his head between his knees as he struggled not to vomit. Ida, who seemed fully engaged for the first time in a while, leaned over to place a hand on his shoulder.

"How…" Alice struggled with the words. "You said some of the guardians were corrupted. How could they have stopped this? How did they contain…?" She seemed unwilling to utter the name.

"If I'm understandin' this correctly, Miss Bentley, the litany can only spread so far from the source. A can infect B, can infect C... But once you get to, I don't know, E or F or thereabouts, it cannot continue. The words lose their power."

The young student straightened, casting a meaningful glance at Billy and Ida. That, at least, explained why her brother, and some of the others, had proved harmless.

But Lafayette-Moses wasn't finished. "Accordin' to this, anyone infected by the source, by the writin' on the stone, was lost. Anyone else, though, if they could be isolated from anyone else tainted for long enough – months, maybe more – might recover. Without reinforcement, or the chance to spread, it just might fade away on its own."

"Wh- What?" Everything else in the world, everything fell away from Elliot then. Everything but a single thought. *This might end!* He might, one day, be himself once more.

"Says so right here. I won't lie to you, Mr Raslo, the odds are grim indeed. Maybe one out of five, one out of six, ever convalesced. But I do believe that's better than nothin.'"

It was, indeed. A slim chance, but it was hope.

A sudden clatter, a chair falling to the floor as its occupant retreated from the table, and then the room filled with a piercing scream, a wail of purest agony and despair.

Ida writhed in the corner, fingers clenched in her hair, yanking several tufts out by bloody roots. Still shrieking, she fell with bruising force to her knees, and finally the throat-rending howl devolved into a series of body-racking sobs.

Oh, merciful God. Elliot was at her side in an instant, trying to hold her, but she shoved him away in a mindless flail. He could do nothing but stand over her, helplessly staring, crying in sympathy.

"Oh, dear," Lafayette-Moses sighed from his seat, shaking his head. "How many of her people did you say she shot? How many of her kin?"

Billy crouched before her. "You couldn't have known, Ida." Elliot wouldn't have believed the implacable hunter could sound so gentle. "And even if you had, you had no choice. We would all of us be dead or insane if you'd not done what you did."

Her weeping didn't stop, but it grew softer, her breathing less ragged, more controlled. This time, when Elliot gingerly reached out, she let herself be held, then guided tenderly back to the table. He placed his own glass of water, only half-emptied, before her. It seemed to be all he could do.

"This must be why the *Ujaraanni* wound up with my people," Billy said after a brief lull. "And no doubt the rest of the stone with others of a similar bent. People who would honor the power within, guard against it – but lacked the knowledge to read it. So the Thousandfold Dream could never come again."

The old man began carefully laying the sheets back in the box. "Indeed so. And it does appear to have been effective. Until now."

"Yes, but 'now' is what we're dealing with," Alice pointed out. "So what do we do? Destroy the stones? Scratch out the writing?"

"I can't say that *that's* a wise idea. It might work, or it might undo the bindin' completely. There's no way to know. Whatever split the *Ujaraanni* and the stele in two, it cracked between the lines, didn't disturb any of them, so we've got nothin' to go on. We've gotta figure there's a reason nobody tried that way back when, and I don't think I'd care to gamble somethin' of this severity on a coin toss."

Elliot actually chuckled. "Yeah, that would've been way

too easy." He paused, worrying at his lower lip. "Magic?" he ventured. Even after everything, he sounded silly saying it out loud. "My invocation and Billy's talismans held the litany at bay, for a while, anyway. And you seem to have access to much more powerful, um, spells."

"Oh, son, you flatter me. I can access some potent rituals, sure enough, but the spell that bound Tsocathra was one of the mightiest sorceries ever worked by an entire race. There aren't many in the world today who can rival my mastery of the old secrets, and what you're askin' would be beyond all of us together.

"Which does not mean," he added, "that I can't teach you some invocations of use, Mr Raslo. There are spells, far more complex than anythin' you've yet seen, that might just do you good. The protections you've been usin', and your friend's talismans? They buy you time, but they don't improve your odds. With my instruction, you are far more likely to recover from your unfortunate affliction."

"I…" The temptation almost reduced him once more to tears. "That wouldn't help us with Tsocathra, though."

"No, it would not. You might best be served by simply getting' as far from here as you can before it all goes to hell. What do you think, son? You've got a mind for this."

Elliot was already shaking his head in refusal, though it tore at him. "I can't just abandon my home. My friends." *Nor do I want anything more to do with the occult, or ancient tomes, or spells and magic and "Ancient Ones." And even if I did, creepy and callous as you've seemed tonight, I couldn't even begin to trust you!*

"Well, that's a shame." A flick of the fingers, and Lafayette-Moses held a printed business card. He lifted the box, allowing his chauffeur to rise. With no apparent stiffness from the awkward position, the servant took the card, stepped over to Elliot, and slid it into the student's coat pocket. "In case you should change your mind," the old man said as the chauffeur returned to his side. "Before somethin' else changes it for you, I hope."

"You're all making this more complicated than it is." Billy, who had remained standing since they'd returned Ida to her seat, meaningfully reached under his coat and drew his snow knife. "This creature hasn't risen yet. We still face a collection of violent lunatics, or at worst, if the tales are true, an entity of flesh. And a thing of flesh can die."

"Can it?" Elliot asked. "We initially thought Chester was…" He didn't finish. It still hurt to say.

"We'll have to be more thorough." *As though it were that simple.* "But you heard Mr Lafayette-Moses. The… amalgamation… only happens if at least one of the corrupted knows the entire litany, directly from the stones. Without them, even if we cannot undo the damage already done, we limit how far the litany can spread, and we prevent something far worse from following. Right now, we know that means either Mr Hennessy or Mr Pembroke."

"You're talking about deliberately hunting down a man and killing him." Elliot began to pace, stopped himself, realized that instead he was all but vibrating in place. "Not in self-defense, but deliberate, cold-blooded murder!"

"Yes. I am. It's unpleasant, and if you've a better notion, by all means, now's the time."

He didn't, and a desperate casting about revealed only grim faces, told him no one else had, either.

The notion sickened him outright, let alone the fact that it might be Chester – or what remained of Chester – they were hunting. "What of the others?" he demanded. "The corrupted we'd have to fight through? We know now that some of them could potentially recover, given treatment and time. Are you so cavalier about slaughtering them as well?"

"I am 'cavalier' about none of this, Elliot, and you well know it. But willing? To prevent the alternative? Yes."

Again Elliot saw no disagreement in the remorseful but determined expressions surrounding him, and again, though he desperately racked his mind for some other option, he could provide none.

"How?" he asked, shoulders slumping. "My protective charm and your talismans were barely sufficient before."

"Ah-ha!" Lafayette-Moses stood, leaning on his cane, and now Elliot saw that he had not quite returned all the documents to the box which the silent chauffeur now held. In the old man's other hand were several of the papers he'd first removed before delving into the *Pnakotic Fragments*. "Now here, Mr Raslo, I might be of some further aid. Tell me, do you read Latin? The archaic alphabet, I mean."

"I'm afraid I only know a few words and phrases…"

"I don't believe you follow me, son. It doesn't much matter if you *understand* it, can you *read* it? Aloud?"

"Oh." Elliot pursed his lips, considering. "Most of my reading's been in the modern alphabet, but they're similar enough, and I've seen enough of the archaic that I guess I can puzzle it out."

"Good. 'Puzzle it out' in advance. You can't be hesitatin' or makin' mistakes when it counts." He handed over one of the documents.

Perusing the first few lines told Elliot that this was the ward the old man had used earlier, to protect all present from the recitation.

"You'll have to repeat it," Lafayette-Moses warned, "every few minutes, and keep your companions near when you do. But it should protect you from Tsocathra's refrain better than the incantation you've been usin', and your friends as well."

Elliot felt his stomach churn at the responsibility of warding the others in addition to himself, the realization that the consequences would not fall on him alone should he fail. Nevertheless, he was grateful, and said as much, even if he wondered still why the occultist seemed so eager to help.

For the good of others? That didn't seem like Hyrum Lafayette-Moses; it might be an unfair assessment, but Elliot could not shake his certainty that the man knew little of compassion. Perhaps he simply protected himself, hoping to avoid Tsocathra's rise – or protected Elliot himself, still hoping for an apprentice.

Well, he'd be waiting a long time for *that*, regardless of what the next few days might bring.

It seemed, whatever his motives, that Lafayette-Moses wasn't finished. After a brief hesitation he handed over a second document, also handwritten, but dustier and more yellowed than the first. It, too, was in the archaic Latin alphabet.

"If things grow desperate," he explained in reply to the student's unspoken question. "If you need help and all else has failed. But you heed me, Mr Raslo, I do mean *desperate*. Last resort. There's no tellin' what'll happen mixin' magics like that, openin' yourself to the Beyond in the presence of the litany. Could go poorly.

"But also, it is no friend of yours who'll come to your aid, and these magics are not near so tight a bindin' as you might wish. Once, and once only, you can probably risk it. Once, and you probably remain just another mortal in the teemin' millions. Any more than that, though, you will be *noticed*. And I do assure you, by whatever god you prefer, you do *not* want to be noticed!"

Unsure what to make of that, but frightened to his core, Elliot took the conjuration with greatest reluctance, holding it between two fingers as if he'd caught a scorpion by the tail.

That swiftly, Lafayette-Moses was all smiles, bobbing his head and taking a firmer grip on his cane. "Might be there are other dangers too, but you haven't time to go over every possible outcome. We'll all just have to… pray. Well, I do believe that's all I can offer. Best of luck with your endeavors, my friends. Mr Raslo, if both you and Arkham are still here when all's said and done, I hope you'll reconsider my offer. I look forward to hearin' from you."

Before any of his startled audience could utter a word, he was gone, his driver following behind with that plain, wooden box.

Nobody moved, it seemed almost that nobody breathed, until the outer office door shut with a solid *thump*. Elliot heard his friends shuffling around the table, but he could not tear his gaze from the papers – the *spells*– that had been left in his care.

And it was only then, too, that all the unasked questions came back to him.

What was Hyrum Lafayette-Moses's connection to the occult circles and witch cults of Arkham's idle rich? Who was he that they had, on his word – and Elliot was certain it had, indeed, been *his* word – elected to remain uninvolved in the search for Chester Hennessy?

Who was he to give that order, and *why* had he given it? How much of what was happening had he already known before Alice called him, before he set foot in Pembroke's office and demanded to hear their story?

What, in the end, was he after?

All questions Elliot had very much meant to ask, and all questions that had totally fled his mind at every opportunity to ask them. A convenient lapse for the mysterious old man – and one, after the compulsion he'd felt to answer Lafayette-Moses's own questions, Elliot wasn't prepared to chalk up to mundane distractions.

Thoughts racing and heart thudding, he turned his attention back to the others. They still had a great many labors ahead of them.

CHAPTER TWENTY-THREE

Silence reigned after the occultist's exit until, at long last, it was Ida who broke it.

"How're we even supposed to find Hennessy, or Pembroke, or whoever? The old man ain't said a thing about *that*."

More silence.

"That doesn't seem to be the sort of thing he'd overlook," Elliot said, thinking it through. "So either he couldn't help with that, or he didn't feel we *needed* his help with it."

Alice gave an unladylike snort. "If we don't, that'd be news to me."

Elliot couldn't help but agree. He hadn't the first notion, and all Lafayette-Moses's aid wouldn't count for much if they couldn't piece something together.

Billy stepped to the door, staring it as though he could see through the wood, through the outer walls, to the streets of Arkham. "You've already searched for your employer everywhere you could think of, Miss Bentley?"

She nodded – but then, "Well, almost," she corrected.

He turned back toward her and the others. "Almost?"

"Some of those properties of his I mentioned? A couple warehouses, a flophouse or two, are inside the influenza outbreak. Even if I wanted to risk looking there, it'd be tough to get past the police cordon without being caught – but there's no point in it, anyway. Mr Pembroke wouldn't dare stay there, no matter what he was hiding from. His momma died of the Spanish Flu back in '18…"

She trailed off, and though he'd known her for a matter of mere hours, Elliot swore he could hear the cogs turning in her head.

"Well, I'll be damned," she whispered. Then, more loudly, "Except it's not a flu."

Elliot's jaw nearly brushed the table. "No," he protested. "No, that's not… That doesn't…"

But it did. Hadn't she already told them Pembroke allowed Chester to use one of his flophouses as a place to hide the *Ujaraanni*, to study its secrets? Hadn't they theorized he'd sheltered there, in a period of relative lucidity, before making for his kin in Hockomock?

The authorities hadn't quarantined a sickness, in that handful of blocks in the slums beyond the Merchant Quarter. They'd quarantined an outbreak of contagious psychopathy.

They'd quarantined the litany.

He almost felt foolish for not considering the possibility earlier, except…

"What of the police? Wouldn't they have figured out what they were truly dealing with? Perhaps even become infected themselves?"

"Not if they were warned to keep their distance, maybe even shoot if anyone came too close." It would be an extreme response, certainly, but not one they would disobey, if convinced the epidemic was dangerous enough, though Elliot couldn't begin to guess by whom.

"No," he insisted. "No, they'd still be overrun by even a small crowd. It would only take one to get near enough for them to hear the chant."

In a rough, gravelly whisper, Ida said, "Only if they wanted out." Then, at their expressions, "None of my... None of 'em ever tried to leave. And they always gathered back at the Hennessy place. Maybe this bunch ain't going anywhere, either. Least not yet."

Somehow, Elliot didn't find that notion comforting.

"You suggested the police might have been warned," Billy said to Alice. "By whom? Who would know enough to do so?"

"Do you still not understand? Even after talking to Victoria McCutcheon, and learning the sorts of people she knows just from tiptoeing around the edges of cult circles? There's a good number of the rich and powerful in Arkham who know a *lot* about what's out there under the skin of civilization and science. Some who even dabble in it. And that includes government circles, Mr Raslo, Mr Shiwak.

"If something unnatural's sweeping across whole neighborhoods in this town, people educated enough to notice *will* notice. Even if they don't know near enough what in God's name to *do* about it."

Elliot's head swam; the chamber wobbled until he nearly grew sick.

So a few of Arkham's elite understood – not the true horror, the true danger, of what they faced, but that it was no mundane affliction. "Influenza" was a lie, a pretense for the citizenry, the press. And they'd set the police, albeit in ignorance, between the spreading horror and the rest of the city.

And still, for all that, it was down to *them* – a foreign hunter, an orphaned rustic, a criminal lieutenant they'd only just met, and a half-crazed university student – to stop it. Because while some of the Powers That Be might know something was amiss, none of them knew the *truth*.

It was hideously, grossly unfair. Unjust. Had he not been smack in the center of it, he would have laughed until he cried. But he *was* in the midst of it … and *someone* had to do something. He might wish it was someone else, anyone else, but he wouldn't walk away. Not now.

Billy seemed far less perturbed by their circumstances. "If this is so, it tells us much we needed to know. Not only where the center of the madness might be found, but also that we face only one source of it, not two."

That declaration snapped Elliot from his growing hysterics. "How do you figure?"

"Those afflicted," Billy explained, "cannot help but spread that affliction, and those in turn to spread it further. It is not a subtle thing, else your authorities would not have noticed, and we would not have dealt with … what we dealt with."

Nods, all around. They all followed so far.

"Your police have only cordoned off one area, not two. Your town whispers of one outbreak of sickness, not two. If both Chester and Pembroke were spreading their madness separately…"

Of course. "There would be two outbreaks," Elliot concluded.

"Precisely. As there is only the one, we know that either Chester never returned to Arkham, and the source is Pembroke… Or

Chester began the spread before he departed, and may have returned to it since, and Pembroke is either dead or just another of Chester's horde."

"Well, then." Alice pushed back from the table and stood. "I guess that means it's time to figure out how to get you all in there – and how to give you half a shot at surviving once we do."

Alas, though Elliot attempted to convince her otherwise, when Alice had said "you all," she meant it. She would provide supplies, would work to aid them in sneaking past the police, but accompanying them into the lion's den was where she drew the line.

Unhappy as it made him, Elliot couldn't blame her. Although she believed in what was happening, certainly took it seriously, for her it remained theoretical. Tales told by strangers and lore gleaned from old books. She hadn't experienced it, couldn't *feel* the threat posed to Arkham, and God knew how much of the world beyond, as the three of them did.

And she remained, after all, a smuggler and a fence. Not a career path that tended to attract those of an altruistic nature. They had, Elliot knew, good cause to be grateful Alice had proved even as solicitous as she had.

A bit more disturbing, to his mind, was how readily she went along, knowing it might well be her employer they would have to hunt down and kill. When he'd brought it up, however, she'd offered a shrug best described as philosophical.

"If he's become what you say he might, then he's already gone. And we both knew this wasn't the safest business; leaving aside monsters and curses, we deal every week with entitled rich folks who haven't got the slightest compunction about breaking the law. Always figured the day would come when he went out to meet someone and never came back. I can keep this place running. Probably even improve it. I've been handling most of the day-to-day business anyway. And if I've got any mourning to do for my boss and my friend, it's sure not going to happen in front of all of you."

And that was the end of that.

They gave brief consideration to waiting until the following day to act, and just as swiftly dismissed the idea. They had far worse to worry about now than the deadline Daisy had set before she went to the police, and no way to know whether the time remaining until the manifestation of the Thousandfold Dream was measured in weeks or days.

Or even less.

Thus were the following hours occupied by planning and preparation. Elliot found the process surprisingly inspirational. However dangerous and however horrid it was to contemplate, that he was finally *doing* something that might end all this, might spare others a terrible death – or worse – stiffened his resolve as never before.

The Chester he'd known and loved would be proud of him. He smiled at the thought.

He read over the invocations Lafayette-Moses had provided, ensuring he could pronounce them properly when the time came. Ida and Billy loaded weapons – not only the pistols they'd brought with them, but heavier firepower Alice lent them – and then twisted fabric into makeshift earplugs, as nobody wanted to rely entirely on Elliot's constant chanting.

They pored over a map of Arkham, focusing on the restricted blocks and Pembroke's properties. No guarantee the heart of the insanity remained in one of those structures, even if it had begun there, but it was at least a place to start.

They planned how to get past the cordon, what Alice could do to provide a diversion. Once they were inside, she would then use Pembroke's contacts among the rich and powerful to get word to those believers in the municipal government, explaining the greater nature of the threat; what the hazards were; that the afflicted must be fully isolated to have any chance of recovery and to avoid spreading their madness.

They might well not believe her, of course. Even practicing occultists might have trouble swallowing the tale she had to tell. Should they prove at all recalcitrant, it could well be too late by the time they *did* come around to acting.

"And of course," she warned, "if they *do* believe me, they might just send in the police to burn down the entire neighborhood and shoot anything that moves. So I suggest you don't dawdle."

Finally, nothing remained but to gird their loins, say what prayers they felt appropriate, and go.

"Officer. Officer, help!"

Bentley certainly sounded convincing as she dashed toward the police, gathered about their vehicles and the wooden barriers set up along the streets and sidewalks. If Billy Shiwak hadn't known better, he'd have thought she was genuinely frightened.

But then, the woman and her missing employer both had to be convincing liars, did they not?

Crouched in a darkened alleyway nearby, clutching a sawed-off shotgun under his coat and hyper-sensitive to the harsh breathing of his companions – did *none* of these folks know how to be stealthy? – he watched as the blue-clad officers, shaken from their boredom by Bentley's cries, moved to investigate the ruckus.

A research student beset by a curse and a woman choking on grief and guilt. These should have been the last two people he wanted at his side in battle. Yet Billy's nerves, howling over what was to come – though he'd never let it show – were calmed ever so slightly by their presence.

After what they'd shared in the past few days, he was glad to have them beside him – even if they did have all the stealth of a musk ox.

"What seems to be the problem, miss?" the nearest policeman asked from beneath a mustache so thick it mightn't look out of place on the rear end of a small pony.

Gasping for breath, she pointed back the way she'd come, struggling to speak.

Then again, she didn't have to. Taking only a few steps from their blockade, the police found themselves able to see down one particular side street. There, bathed in the light of a street lamp only faintly diffused by a thin fog, a trio of men tussled, two of them shoving the third. A few strained shouts drifted across the way, their words impossible to make out.

Equally unclear, at this distance, were the facial features of the three brawlers. Nevertheless, Billy realized that the "victim" of the other two was in fact the same man who'd been tailing him, on Bentley's behalf, outside the Hennessys' hotel.

Although they gathered a few paces from the wooden barricades to better observe, the police seemed in no rush to abandon their post. It was just a fistfight, after all. If it dragged on much longer, maybe a couple of them would wander over and break it up, but otherwise it was hardly worth–

As if deliberately planned for optimal dramatic effect – which, of course, it had been – only then did the third man, apparently frightened or angry at being outnumbered, pull a revolver from inside his coat and fire.

The round flew well over the heads of the other two, who retreated in sudden fear. The appearance of the gun, however, and the report of the shot, instantly shifted the nature of the cops' response.

Shouting for the suspect to drop his weapon and raise his hands, their own revolvers now drawn, the entire lot charged the intersection. The trio vanished down the side street, where Billy knew they'd already planned their escape routes after putting on their little pantomime. They'd be well and truly gone before the police caught up with them.

The cordon would remain abandoned for mere moments.

Billy hissed something, not really a word, and broke into a sprint of his own. He felt no need to look behind to see if Elliot and Ida kept up; their clumsy steps and, in the student's case, desperate gasps, were evidence enough.

From one alley to another, one side of the wooden barricades to the other. Simple. After all, the police were hardly alert for people trying to sneak *into* a pocket of raging influenza, were they?

And just like that, they found themselves once again within the radius of a madness too terrible to contemplate. Only this time, they had gone knowingly, willingly, with every intention of delving deeper still.

Perhaps, Billy thought to himself, though he would never say such a thing aloud, *we've all truly lost our minds already.* He briefly wished he'd departed Arkham back when he first acquired the *Ujaraanni*, then cast the thought away as unworthy of him.

They crept along, keeping to the shadows between the streetlights, making use of alleys and back ways where they could. Wherever the streets stood open, providing line of sight to other intersections at the edge of the slums, to other police at their cordons, they took greater care still. Often it took them minutes to cross a single roadway, so cautious were their steps.

They had expected, once more than a block or two in, to be able to walk normally, assuming they would appear to be more of the "sick" contained within the neighborhood. They discovered, however, that the streets here were utterly abandoned. Other than a few sporadic lights in windows here or there, they observed no signs of life. If anyone here had managed to avoid being corrupted, they kept themselves locked inside. That much didn't surprise Billy; it was the only sensible choice.

But where were the others? Where were the citizens already corrupted by that foul liturgy? Back at Ida's home, they had wandered the community aimlessly, searching for more ears into which they might spill their poison words, or else gathered about the Hennessy house, the beating heart of their unnatural obsessions.

Here, they found no wanderers. Here, the isolated area was small enough that, if the corrupted were all gathered in one spot, Billy and his companions ought to hear them.

Instead, all he heard was Elliot's constant murmur as he repeated Lafayette-Moses's protective spell, again and again. Billy knew nothing of Latin, of course, but the young man's occasional pauses or stammers as he stumbled over a word here, a pronunciation there, were unmistakable in any language.

"Elliot..." he growled, wincing at a particularly egregious stutter.

"I know. I'm trying!" Even in a hushed whisper, his voice nearly cracked with nerves. He sounded near breaking point, despite all they'd been through already.

Billy had neither the time nor patience to coddle him. "We're relying on you," was all he said, before deliberately turning his focus back to the next intersection.

"We're relying on you."

Yes, I damn well know that. Elliot wanted to scream, rant and rave, to shatter the grating silence until it was nothing but flecks like grains of sand. *That's precisely the problem!*

He couldn't do this. The fear for himself, for his life or his mind; the muttering, ever present, of the infectious litany winding through every thought he had; his awareness that he might be forced to kill innocent souls whose sanity might not be beyond saving; the terrible knowledge he had now of the Weaver of Flesh, of what awaited Arkham, and the world beyond, if they failed... Those were all bad enough, any one of them sufficient to crush the will of men Elliot thought of as far braver than he.

But it was this spell, this Latin chant, that he knew would be his undoing. He'd gone over it a dozen times in Alice's office. He knew how to read it, had readily figured out the differences between the archaic and modern alphabet. It should, by all rights, flow smoothly, close to effortlessly, from his lips.

If it had been like the French charm he'd used before, if he alone had counted on it, it would have.

It was the fact that he protected Billy and Ida too, now – that they were, as Billy said, relying on him – that petrified his tongue until he could scarce form the syllables. The responsibility was too heavy. His fear of failing them would be the reason he failed them.

He couldn't do this, and damn him to hell for not recognizing that until it was too late. They couldn't go back. They had no alternative.

He clenched his teeth, took a deep breath. If it *had* to be him, if he was the one to do this, then he damn well would not let his companions down.

Blinking hard, so unshed tears would not blur his view of the page and impede him further still, Elliot began again at the top.

For some time, he dared not even glance up from the paper. He counted on Billy and Ida to watch for danger, to keep them from discovery, and followed where he was led. He stumbled over the words, far more than once, but at least he made it through *occasional* repetitions without flaw. Without a solid idea of how long each successful recitation would last – he knew only, from what Lafayette-Moses had said, that its effectiveness was brief – he had no way of knowing how well or how consistently they were protected. He felt himself sweating, even in the late-night chill.

When he did look up, look around, his nerves imposed onto this old, ramshackle neighborhood a lowering malevolence. Buildings seemed to sag deliberately toward the narrow streets, as if to slowly engulf, absorb, digest whoever had the misfortune to pass by. The cracks and crevices shaped the stones beneath his feet into unclean teeth, while the sporadically lit windows were the glaring, angry eyes of great beasts only just rousing themselves from a deep yet restless slumber. Although the night's fog was not thick, still each island of illumination cast by the streetlamps was smaller and farther away than the last. Sounds from mere blocks away seemed unable pass through it, leaving them in a pall of unnatural silence.

Or was it his nerves at all? Elliot thought back, despite himself, to the fever-dreamlike trudge through the Hockomock, to the resting place of the *Ujaraanni*, to the swamp's vague corruption and the almost desperate efforts of nature itself to purge the intrusion.

He would never be certain how much of that had been real, but neither would he ever believe it had been entirely in his head. Who was to say, then, that this was?

A frantic study of his companions offered no enlightenment. Billy looked as stoic, as determined, as ever, but even if he were seeing the world as Elliot did, would he have let it show on his face? And Ida… So rarely did she appear more than half present in the moment, who could guess what Ida thought any more?

Then Billy's expression *did* change, but not due to any abnormality in the environment, real or imagined. He raised a hand and hissed at them to halt as the end of the narrow side street came into sight – along with the people beyond it.

Two of them, the first the trio had seen since their arrival, wandered aimlessly about the intersection, a T where this smaller byway intersected with a more major street. They appeared almost stuck; Elliot would have said they looked lost, if their movements weren't confined to so small an area. Over and over, one side of the street to the other and back, from this building to that and then back to this.

He couldn't see their faces, and if they were repeating that dreadful and by now all-too-familiar chant, they did so at a low mutter at best, else he'd have heard it. Nevertheless, the distracted, almost hollow way they moved was enough to convince him they were, indeed, corrupted.

And he wondered: this peculiar, repetitive shambling, constrained to the intersection and a few yards beyond…

Could this be their half-mindless, instinctive version of standing sentry? Were these two men a guard of some sort?

He bent close to Billy to whisper his hypothesis, and the other nodded. "Wait here." Billy didn't utter the words so much as mouth them, then crept ahead, darting through shadows, occasionally crouching behind a hedge or a raised stoop.

Minutes passed. The two corrupted continued their awkward cycle. A streetlight flickered, dimmed, brightened again. Elliot watched Ida's fists clench and unclench, over and over, around the grip of her own weapon, a pump-action Remington she'd gotten from Alice.

He worried about her, in those moments when he wasn't distracted by his own fears. She'd been so withdrawn since they'd reached Arkham, even more so since Lafayette-Moses's revelation… If they survived what was to come, she would need intense psychological treatment. He hoped he could help her find it.

When Billy moved, it was a burst of speed that took even Elliot by surprise. He dashed across the intersection, completely passed the nearer of the two sentries. The second had just drawn near the brick wall of a building across the street and begun to turn around when Billy shot toward him, leaping the last few paces, hand outstretched…

Palm met skull, driving it with brutal force into the bricks. It sounded to Elliot like a baseball bat striking an overripe melon; sickened, he turned away. When he looked back, seconds later,

Billy was standing above the body of the second man, his pana bloodied.

The hunter placed a finger to his lips for silence, then motioned his companions forward. Elliot advanced, struggling not to look at either corpse or the smear on the wall. Billy wiped his blade clean on the dead man's sleeve and returned it to its sheath.

"Was that necessary?" Elliot demanded.

"Yes." Billy pointed, first at the structure with the bloodstain, then the building next to it. "Those are both Pembroke's property. Warehouse, flophouse. Not a coincidence these two chose this intersection to guard."

Elliot took a deep, ragged breath, then nodded. "All right. So which do we–?"

It began in the flop joint.

"*... vshuru shelosht escruatha ...*"

So many voices, dozens or more. They gradually came into hearing already partway through the chant, a hushed sound becoming audible, so that it seemed they'd moved closer from somewhere distant. Whether their arrival was coincidence or somehow provoked by the death of the sentries, Elliot neither knew nor, in that instant of heart-stuttering terror, much cared.

"*Svist ch'shultva ulveshtha ikravis...*"

The front door flew open and they emerged, one by one, an endless stream. They were, the lot of them, filthy, unkempt, unshaven; some undressed or under-dressed, others clad for work, all rumpled and unwashed.

And some... Oh, dear Lord!

Some were no longer entirely human.

Here, Elliot saw a neck that had sagged until the chin melded with the sternum in a permanent, impossible maw. There, a hand and fingers had stretched like putty to dangle and trail against the street. It seemed, impossibly, as though some of these bodies, the flesh and skin, were little more than ill-fitting outfits carelessly donned by something else. Something *other*.

All of them, mangled or not, were a single chorus, orating in perfect unison.

Elliot felt the power of the litany wash over him, but it was muffled, remote – more so even than when he'd been protected only by the French charm and his borrowed Inuit amulet. Even in his mounting fear, he felt a knot of tension uncoil as he realized the incantation over which he'd been struggling was, for the moment, proving effective.

It would do them little good, though, if they were overwhelmed.

"We have to run!" He heard the hysteria in his voice, but couldn't bring himself to be ashamed. "We have to–!"

"*Isslaach ikravis vuloshku dlachvuul loshaa…*"

Not only from the encroaching mob, this time, but also from far nearer. From over his shoulder.

God, no…. Please…

As if dragged against their will, Elliot and Billy turned to look behind them.

"*Ulveshtha schlachtli vrulosht chevkuthaansa…*" chanted Ida Glick.

CHAPTER TWENTY-FOUR

Stunned, Elliot moved only when he felt something snag him by the collar and haul him backward. He flailed, shouting, until he realized it was Billy, and even then barely got himself under control.

Before him, the throng advanced from one direction, Ida from the other, and cresting like a wave before them, that *Goddamned chant*. Clouded as it was, held at bay by two different incantations and the protective talisman, still it pounded in his head, calling up his own psychic infection in response.

Billy dragged him through a doorway, seeking shelter in the only nearby building from which none of the corrupted were emerging: Pembroke's warehouse. He slammed the door and began piling boxes in front of it; a slapdash barricade, one they both knew wouldn't hold long, but the only readily available option.

"Help me with this!" he shouted, but Elliot couldn't move. The few sane thoughts he retained wouldn't stop racing around his skull, demanded answers.

How had Ida been exposed? It couldn't have happened just

now, outside. The ward Lafayette-Moses had given him was working, he *knew* it was working – and even had it not, the transformation should not have been so instantaneous. Elliot knew, from his own experience, from Chester's and from everything he'd seen in Ida's home, that it usually took minutes, hours, even days.

Days…

Elliot sagged, ignoring the increasingly urgent appeals from his friend, the pounding on the door and the muffled refrain from beyond.

So many times since their return, Ida had seemed to fade away, only half present, lost and distracted. He'd attributed it to her grief over all she'd lost, her horror over what she'd had to do. Perhaps some of it had been, but the rest? He should have recognized it. He'd seen it in Chester before his disappearance. He'd heard Alice describe it in Pembroke. He'd felt it himself, that lack of focus, that preoccupation with something only the corrupted could hear.

And he realized only now, when it was far, *far* too late, that in all the chaos, all the terror and exhaustion, and in his own near-maddened state… It had never occurred, either to him or to Billy, to ask Ida the precise details of what happened that night in the swamp, when she'd led her whole community on a lethal chase so the two of them might slip unnoticed into the Hennessy house.

Had she been too scared to tell them, to admit she'd been exposed? Or had her grief and despair been so overwhelming that she'd lost the ability to care about the consequences?

He'd never know, of course. Never know if he could have helped her, as he had himself.

Never fully rid himself of the guilt that now threatened to

suffocate him because it had never occurred to him to try.

I'm sorry, Ida.

"Damn it, Elliot!"

It wasn't Billy's admonition that finally dragged his mind back to the present, but the brief thunder that followed. A ragged hole appeared through the door and one of the stacked crates, sending shards and splinters flying. Billy recoiled with a curse, thin streaks of blood welling up on his cheek.

Ida's shotgun. Even in the grip of the litany, she retained the wherewithal to use the tools at hand. A quick nod to his companion to indicate he was with him once again, and then he studied the rude shelter in which they found themselves.

The warehouse was a small manmade cavern, a vast chamber of wooden walls and occasional metal catwalks above. It held little in the way of goods, compared to its capacity; most of it stood open and empty, with only a few sporadic hills of crates, islands in the barren space. A goodly number were covered in a thick frosting of dust, obvious even from a distance. Whatever they contained was clearly not in high demand.

Between the dim lighting and those occasional heaps of boxes, Elliot couldn't see all the way to the warehouse's far side – a realization that finally made him stop and wonder why he was able to see at all. High above, among the rafters, dull electric lights hung in flimsy fixtures. They must have been left on when the warehouse personnel were taken.

Well, he'd accept the tiny lick of good fortune for what it was. "There must be another door somewhere," he said, wincing at the sound of another shot.

"Go!" Billy crouched behind the feeble barricade, his own shotgun in his hands. "Find it."

Elliot ran. Somewhere in the shadows, a window shattered, and he pushed himself faster still.

It didn't take long to find the exit. A small side door, it was conveniently marked with an overhead sign.

It was also, rather less conveniently, blocked by one of those dusty stacks of crates.

Elliot stretched up and gave the top crate a perfunctory shove. As anticipated, it didn't budge. No way he and Billy were clearing the path on their own.

This had to be deliberate. Pembroke's people had blocked the back entrance quite some time ago, probably to ensure nobody snuck in to interfere with any illegal goods they were moving.

A series of shots sounded from across the warehouse. He tried to ignore it, tried to think.

Pembroke was a fence and a smuggler. Which meant...

Elliot dashed back across the massive room, moving in circles, searching frantically. And there it was.

In the back corner, opposite the door he'd tried and failed to reach, a large hatch sat recessed in the floor. Standing over it, he could smell even through the thick wood that it led into the musty, fetid depths of Arkham's sewers.

All right, that made sense. If one could tolerate the filth, the vapors, the rats and the insects and worse, the larger tunnels would make a viable smuggler's route, allowing travel from the Miskatonic River to all sorts of locations within the town.

And if Pembroke's other properties had similar trapdoors, it would explain why the arrival of the corrupted from the flophouse had sounded as though they approached from a distance, already chanting. They'd come from below.

"I've got a way out," Elliot called. "You won't like it, though."

Pounding feet, and Billy was at his side in a flash. "We'll like staying a lot less." As if to punctuate his assessment, a final crash announced the collapse of the partly shredded front door, as well as the broken crates that had blocked it.

Without a word, they reached down and hauled the hatch open.

They fully anticipated the waft of sewer air, and all its varied mélange of scents. It still nearly blew them back from the opening with a physical force. Mixed in with it, though, or somehow beyond it, was another odor, something that reeked of putrescence even more than the sewer's own liquifying waste.

Wincing against the stink, Billy climbed over the edge and began making his way down the rusty ladder beneath.

"Never in all the time we've worked together has anything remotely good come of cellars or underground," Elliot groused. As Billy either didn't hear or elected not to respond, he could do nothing but follow. He'd have preferred they close the trapdoor after them, perhaps hide their trail for a short while, but it had taken them both to open the thing. No way either alone could haul it shut, and the ladder forbade cooperation from this direction.

With a loud click, Billy's flashlight illuminated the passage below. The tunnel writhed in the beam, and Elliot realized with a horrified shiver that he was seeing literal sheets of roaches and other vermin coating the walls, scattering in the alien light. Beyond them was brick, old and worn and glistening with the residue of years, sloping upward in a gentle curve toward the ceiling.

If nothing else, Elliot could at least give thanks that the river of sludge flowing down the center of the corridor was shallow here, in the sewers' uppermost level. The walkways along either side, though filth-encrusted and treacherously slick, remained unsubmerged despite the abnormally rainy season. He and Billy shouldn't need to walk in the offal.

Still, between the scents, the thick, mucous sounds of the flow, and the skittering of a hundred thousand legs, he found himself unable to take that last step off the ladder. Even the driving fear of what followed behind proved momentarily insufficient to overcome his revulsion. His fists tightened despite his commands, threatening to shred skin against the scabrous rust.

"You should probably resume Lafayette-Moses's spell," Billy called softly over his shoulder. "No telling if we're still warded."

The reminder that his friends needed him – well, *friend*, he corrected – was enough to spur him onward. He dropped to the narrow walkway, flailed for balance, then removed both the paper and his own flashlight from his coat. He wondered, idly, if Billy had done that on purpose, had noted his paralysis and said what he must to break it.

Either way, it was a good point. Letting the hunter take the lead, shifting his light from Latin script to corridor floor and back, he once more read through the incantation. Then again. And again. When Billy called a halt, scarcely louder than a whisper, and gestured to a doorway ahead, Elliot felt confident he'd gotten the pronunciation correct more often than not.

"What's in there?" Elliot whispered back – but even as he asked, he heard it. Something, scarcely audible, a peculiar combination of voices and other, more disturbing sounds he could not begin to identify.

Billy looked at him, flashlight in one hand, shotgun in the other. Elliot carefully tucked the paper back into a pocket and drew a pistol: a Remington Model 51 automatic, yet another weapon provided by Alice Bentley. Not a very powerful weapon, but well suited to an inexperienced gunman.

He nodded, reached out and threw the door open. Billy darted past, double barrels raised and ready to fire.

They saw little, even with the flashlights, for the chamber was massive; nearly the size of the warehouse from which they'd come, in length and width if not height, though no such room should exist in the sewers. A few scattered bricks, visible at the edges of their light, suggested that it might have been several separate spaces until recently.

Even nearly blind, however, they knew something was horribly wrong.

The scent hit them again, that decaying, fleshy aroma, but now it was mixed with more familiar, if no less unpleasant, odors: the sweat of unwashed bodies, halitosis, human waste in smaller but far purer quantities than the sewage outside the door.

And dear God, the *sounds*. Elliot heard the shuffling of nervous limbs, a terrible grinding and a wet, slurping noise he could liken only to mud or soft clay being slapped together and squeezed, over and over.

Those, and the litany. Oh, it was different, murky, muddled, as if multiple voices tried to speak through mouths full of old porridge, but he felt the impact in his head all the same. Every nerve screamed at him to back out of the room, to face the horrid sewer or even the mob of corrupted that had doubtless followed them down here, rather than discover what abomination shared this chamber with them.

Then, from out in the corridor, he heard, too, the echoes of far too many footsteps, and a much clearer chorus – fully in sync with the recitation here in the massive hall – and he knew they would come pouring through the doorway any moment. That running was now physically, let alone rationally or ethically, no longer an option.

Billy, as usual, had more quickly assessed the situation and chosen a course of action. A sweep of his flashlight ended on a large handle on a metal bracket beside the door.

A knife switch, Elliot realized, even as Billy lunged for it. Probably for the lights. It made sense. The municipal workers would want it close to the entrance…

A moment of strain, a rain of rusty flecks, and Billy shoved the switch upright, completing the connection. Electricity sizzled, and a series of large, enclosed bulbs lit up along the ceiling, their high-pitched hum all but inaudible in the cacophony.

Together, Elliot and Billy saw what awaited them in that chamber, deep beneath the streets of Arkham, and together they screamed.

Dozens of the corrupted stood around the far edges of the room. In the shadows at the edges of the light, it seemed almost as if they *were* the far edges of the room, their outlines faintly blurred as though they'd begun to conform to the shapes of the corners, the walls, even one another. Elliot couldn't entirely make it out, his eyes somehow refusing to focus where things joined together that should have remained apart.

Lips and eyes fluttered and twitched in unison, still struggling to push the words of their unholy liturgy through malformed orifices. Slow tides flowed through the morass of former humanity, and with each wave and ripple, the wavering bodies moved a fraction of an inch along the wall, along the floor, toward the greater mass at the center of it all.

There, the beating heart of this nightmare in skin, was a column of what had once been a half dozen other bodies, now melded into a single shape. New limbs had formed, whole chains of bones now wrapped in flesh, and had Elliot not already screamed until his lungs ached and he choked on his own bile, he would have shrieked at their *familiarity*.

He had seen those in his dream: the hundred-jointed tendrils of Tsocathra. The Weaver of Flesh sat at his terrible loom, his rebirth already underway.

Only a single recognizable person remained as part of that grotesque amalgamation. Near its top, protruding at a canted angle as though drunk, were the head and a single shoulder of the man around whom all had gathered, the vile sun around which everything else orbited.

Chester Hennessy.

Though some of the wounds they'd inflicted upon him had closed up, his lips were half gone, and his eyes had sunken fully into his head to make way for another, multifaceted, that bulged from his cheek. But his face still retained some of its former shape, and his mustache remained horrifyingly perfect; enough so that Elliot had no doubt who he was.

Behind them, the mob from above filtered into the room, chanting, and Ida was among the first.

Elliot did the only thing he could think of, the only thing that made even an iota of sense. He raised his pistol and opened fire at the thing that had once been his dearest friend.

Beside him, Billy did the same, emptying both barrels of the shotgun and then drawing his pistol, squeezing the trigger again and again.

They accomplished nothing, nothing at all. The bullets and

pellets vanished into the hideous mass with barely a ripple, and the creature didn't so much as flinch. Chester's head turned its unblinking insectile eye their way, and the whole thing began to slouch toward them with the most unnatural motion, a combination of worm-ish humps and a sticky slide without obvious means of propulsion.

Face glistening with sweat even in the sickly yellow light, Billy dropped his empty pistol, broke open the shotgun and struggled to reload. Elliot retreated a step, only to hear a metallic *click* from behind.

Ida stood, mouth moving, her own shotgun aimed at Elliot's head. He felt his legs go watery as he realized her inability to keep track of her ammunition, in her tainted state, was the only reason he didn't lie dead on the floor.

Mechanically she turned the weapon around, wielding it by the barrel as a club, and the others began to fill the room around her. The sounds of the litany beat against his wards, and he knew they would not hold for long.

Billy's shotgun fired again, both barrels. And again, he might as well have been hurling invective and profanity at the constantly pulsing, growing mass, for all the good it did.

They had no options. No useful weapons, no room for retreat. So Elliot did what he'd somehow known, though he'd desperately hoped otherwise, he would always have to do.

"Keep them off me!" he shouted, as he drew Lafayette-Moses's other spell from his pocket.

In the corner of his vision, he saw Billy fly past him, calling out in Kalaallisut, pana in hand. He saw fists fly, saw members of the throng hurled to the floor by limbs and joints, saw blood arc as the snow knife struck. But he saw, too, the corrupted gathering, surrounding his friend, and he knew even Billy couldn't stand long against such odds.

Saw it all, and did his best to shut it out, to focus solely on the ancient script before him.

He'd looked over the invocation earlier, tried to master the pronunciation in his head. Unlike the protective ward, however, he'd never attempted reading it aloud; he wouldn't dare, for fear of getting it right at the wrong time. He feared getting it right even now, dreaded to see what it might conjure, yet following that fear came a strange sense of calm. As though he'd somehow known everything would come to this, and it was only a matter now of letting it happen.

He struggled with the text, trying to fit his tongue around the Latin, his brain around the handful of symbols that differed between the archaic and modern alphabets. It wasn't a lengthy text, this spell – in fact, it disturbed him greatly just how brief and simplistic it was – but still he stumbled over it, had to start over more than once.

More of the corrupted swarmed around Billy. Several others, Ida included, advanced on Elliot, and he found himself backpedaling before them, coming disturbingly close to the semi-viscous but still moving bodies plastered against the walls.

They were nearly within arm's reach when he finally shouted the last words of the conjuring, loud enough to be heard clearly over the constant inhuman chorus.

A chilling gust swept through the chamber, bringing everyone, even the corrupted, to a momentary halt. They felt it on the skin, it bit at the lungs, yet it never rustled one hair or scrap of clothing. From far away, Elliot heard... He couldn't quite describe *what* he heard. It was a low, all-but-inaudible roar, the loud silence at the edge of a vast chasm or other unfathomable void. A sound of absence, not of being.

From high above came a hint of motion. It was distant, so distant, unfathomably far beyond the ceiling itself, yet he could see it still, and he grew dizzy at the contradiction. Space itself seemed twisted in that spot, so that the stone he knew was mere feet overhead had instead receded an immeasurable ways.

And from that distance, something approached.

It writhed, twisted, coiled, shadow on shadow. Elliot would have called it serpentine, whatever it was, but it was accompanied by the methodical beat of flapping wings.

He looked away. He had no choice; between the spatial distortion and the winding darkness, it was more than his already battered sanity was worth to do otherwise.

The corrupted began to move again, driven by inhuman will, but the thing above was faster, oh, so much faster. Coils of shadow unwound, wrapping around the nearest figure to Elliot and yanking him into the impossible gulfs above, accompanied by a fearsome hiss, like a hundred vipers at once, and the flash of what might have been the shining of distant stars – or might have been fangs.

The briefest of pauses, as though it were some methodical, horrific hunter, carefully selecting its next prey, and then it lashed down again, a dusk- and scale-wrapped stroke of lightning. Another of the corrupted vanished, hauled away to be consumed or God knew what other fate. And another.

And Ida.

Elliot saw the shadow wrap about her, and he cried as she was lifted upwards. Even at the last, her mouth still moved and he saw no recognition – of him, her coming doom, or anything else – in her eyes.

Over and over, the half-seen thing struck from above, until the horde of dozens was scarce more than a handful. Only then did the distant roar of the gulfs fade, the freezing gusts cease, the ceiling settle once more in its proper place.

Elliot noticed little of it.

With the fourth or fifth stroke, the old occultist's first warning had proved prescient indeed. The combination of magics, the desperate conjuring with Tsocathra's litany, was disastrous.

No way for Elliot to know precisely what had happened, if the presence of the unnatural creature had somehow empowered the growing form of the Thousandfold Dream, if his own brief connection with the thing he summoned left his mind vulnerable, or if it were some other reaction entirely.

He knew only that the wards on which he counted, the discipline he'd built up over weeks of fighting his own burgeoning corruption, were suddenly, woefully insufficient. He had just long enough to observe what was happening to him, to scream inside, before he knew only those terrible words.

"*Isslaach thkulkris, isslaach cheoshash…*"

No, not only those. Elliot knew, too – to the extent he could be said to know anything, to the extent there was an Elliot at all – that Tsocathra called.

His fingers slackened, letting the document drift like an autumn leaf to the floor. Then Elliot strode readily to the pulsating mass of viscous flesh that had dragged itself to the center of the room, let himself fall into it and was gone.

CHAPTER TWENTY-FIVE

"Elliot!"

A hopeless cry, utterly futile. Billy could do nothing but watch the student slip beneath the undulating surface of the abomination as if its skin were nothing but the muddy waters of the Hockomock. And while he'd never have admitted it to anyone, while he was indeed racked with grief for Elliot, it was a cry mostly of fear.

Alone. Billy stood alone, the recitation pounding as a furious blizzard upon his wards, against this embryonic amalgam that would soon form itself into the Great Old One who had last walked the Earth a thousand centuries gone by.

It scarcely even paid him heed. The face that had once been Hennessy's turned away, the tendrils curled aimlessly rather than reach for him. He was no threat, nor was he fit for consumption.

Yet.

The corrupted fell back, chanting still, letting the profane liturgy do its work. Billy snarled at them, reloading his shotgun again. He would not be a part of this detestation, and he would not fall without a fight. He meant to *make* them kill him. He–

Something *cracked*, a single, sharp sound loud enough to hurt the ear. Billy winced, but what followed was far worse.

From every one of its unnatural mouths, the form that would eventually be Tsocathra howled. Much like those whom it had infected, its voices were many and one simultaneously; some high pitched, some deep, all bubbling and burbling with liquid corruption.

Elliot flew from the fleshy mass, purged as though he were some sort of poison, to land in a moist, slick heap upon the stone floor. He skidded several yards until he fetched up against one of the corpses cut down earlier by Billy's blade. Whether he was sane or whole, Billy couldn't tell, but at least he breathed.

The hunter stepped toward him, jaw agape, wondering why Elliot had been rejected after succumbing so thoroughly as to offer himself up. Wondering...

Until he saw the amulet. The protective talisman, one of the many Billy's angakkoq had provided, that he'd lent to the younger man so long ago. The ward that had, along with his own amateur spellcraft, saved him for so long.

The talisman, carved from ivory and etched with ancient symbols, that was now broken almost perfectly in half.

That's what he'd heard, that ferocious report: the amulet breaking. Breaking, as it exhausted its magics in preventing Elliot from merging with the terrible mass.

Billy didn't stop to think, to ponder whether such a gamble could possibly pay off. He acted, as he'd learned to do in long, treacherous hunts across the icy wilds of Greenland. He grabbed at the leather thongs about his neck, hauling all but one of the dangling charms over his head, and charged.

One of the tendrils struck at him, a fearsome whip that extended near the length of the room, but it was a casual stroke. Billy tumbled under it with ease. The creature that was Tsocathra-to-be still saw him as an irritation at worst, no true danger.

He came back to his feet and leapt with the momentum of his roll. Leapt – and slung the talismans around the protruding head of Chester Hennessy, the heart of the beast and the only man in its entire makeup who had known the *entirety* of the antediluvian litany.

No scream this time. It froze, all of it, then shuddered obscenely, ripples and twitches running through it. The corrupted along the walls, linked to it only by extended limbs that stretched like taffy, moaned and recoiled, their connection severed.

Other bodies fell away from Chester in lumps of meat, masses of tissue that boasted only a stunted arm here, a partial visage there, as a reminder they'd ever been human.

And through it all, the talismans shattered and tore – ivory cracking, leather tearing, wood splintering – in rapid succession.

In the end, Chester stood alone, and now he *did* shriek and burble and howl to the heavens. His face remained mangled, one of his legs split at the knee into multiple smaller limbs like a cephalopod, and his left arm had become one of the great tendrils that had protruded from the larger shape. He was still inhuman, still the core of what would become the Fetid Thought, but he was alone.

With a fearsome shout of his own, Billy fired…

To no more effect than before. Chester absorbed the shot

without so much as staggering. A man of less discipline than Billy would have sobbed.

He'd slowed the process, nothing more. He had no weapon that could harm the thing that had been Chester, no means of killing it.

For the moment, Chester merely stood, keening from a handful of separate mouths, the tendril mounted to his shoulder lashing out randomly like a dying eel – not from Billy's feeble attack, surely, but the shock of losing those with whom it had melded. Billy knew, however, that it wouldn't be long before the thing regained control, before it struck out and slaughtered him for daring to hurt it. Then it would simply start anew, with the people still waiting about the edges of the room, the corrupted wandering the buildings above, and whoever else it needed. It would move out from the sewers of Arkham, spreading madness before it, and taking who it needed.

Tsocathra would live.

Billy once more drew his pana and readied himself for one last, purely symbolic, act of defiance.

At the rapid-fire sounds of the amulets shattering, Elliot's eyelids fluttered open.

He watched from where he lay, unmoving, as the outer layers sloughed away, leaving Chester exposed. As Billy tried, and failed, to kill him and braced to go down fighting.

He saw, and he recognized everything that was happening for what it was, but he found it difficult to think. Not because of the litany, oh, no; that had receded once more to its usual persistent itch.

Because of what he'd been forced to *know*.

He had opened himself completely to Tsocathra's call. For endless seconds, what shreds remained of his mind had joined with the others; with the single gestalt built around what had been Chester. They were one.

And Elliot had known that this horror before him was the barest seed, the tiniest kernel around which the Great Old One would form. That Tsocathra would tread over whole civilizations, and never notice, save for the briefest alleviation of its endless hunger, its endless need to absorb the corrupted, to grow ever larger, ever stronger. That it would maim and madden and destroy, not for any cause, not even out of hatred for the lives it would take, but because it couldn't be bothered *not* to.

It was the shock of his ejection that snapped Elliot back to sanity, back to who he was, but it was a brief reprieve. Already he felt the tug of the call, the urge to slip back into the shared oblivion he'd tasted. He had moments, at best – but that was long enough to decide.

If the amalgamation grew beyond these walls, escaped from beneath Arkham, it would be unstoppable. The Weaver of Flesh would never be sated. The Thousandfold Dream would be the nightmare of all humanity.

So he couldn't allow it to escape, no matter the cost to himself. Whatever horrid fate he courted, surely it was better than becoming a permanent part of civilization's destroyer.

Elliot reached out, dragged himself across the floor to the lonely scrap of paper, lying near to where he'd dropped it. Ignoring Lafayette-Moses's sternest warning; forcing himself to be calm, not rush, despite the fear coursing through him... Ignoring the sight of Chester drawing nearer to Billy, step by terrible, limping step, still screaming and lashing out in random fits… He read the conjuration a second time.

Again the freezing wind, the muted drone of the infinite gulfs. Again the first signs of movement far above, so much higher than the ceiling should have allowed.

Yet Elliot sensed, even then, that something was different. Wrong.

The first time – God, was it only moments ago? – he'd had no communication with the nightmare he evoked. He'd given no commands, either aloud or in the silence of his thoughts. He'd simply known, without any idea how, that the entity would prey upon those he needed it to, hunting his foes while leaving him and his companion be.

Now? He felt no such certainty, only a sudden boneshaking shudder that had nothing to do with the cold.

Overhead, the shadows coiled, an expanding darkness that might or might not have been the spread of membranous wings, and the razor-edged glimmer of starlight fangs. They swiftly grew larger, larger…

Closer.

The admonition he'd ignored in his panic had come true. Elliot Raslo had been *noticed*.

It reached down for him in constant winding circles, so that it appeared almost as a sequence of concentric rings descending from above. All the strength drained from his body, and he fell hard to his knees. The painful shock of impact went all but unnoticed, as did the paper once more slipping through his fingers.

His mind began to give way once more, to the call and the litany. He wondered what fate awaited him, within the grasp of the vile predator he'd called, and hoped only that his death would be quick. Let him go with minimal pain, and before his sanity disintegrated once more, and he would call it... not good, but perhaps enough.

Under his breath, he began, brokenly, to pray. The first of the snaking coils surrounded him, started to constrict...

Something else lashed out from across the chamber, wrapping the serpentine body in its own unbreakable grip.

The conjured hunter spun, writhed, spitting its impossible, hissing shriek, and Elliot could only stare as the tendril of endless joints entangled the thing like a chain of flesh and bone, dragging it off him and toward the spindly mass that was the seed of Tsocathra.

It was almost certainly sheer chance that had saved him, Elliot knew. Between the mutated madman's random thrashing, and the sheer size of the other entity, accidental contact had always been possible, perhaps even probable.

But maybe, just maybe, there was more. In the days to come, Elliot would wonder: had his brief melding with the amalgamated creature, the blending of their minds into one, made a connection? There, at the very last, had something of Chester, some final lingering ember, recognized him for who he was?

However unlikely, however much he knew better, he liked to think that his salvation had come, not at the whims of fortune, but from one final act of the man he'd loved and who – in his own way, if not how Elliot might have wished – had loved him in return.

Of course, he would never really know.

He knew only, as the tendril compressed around the shadow

serpent, and its own coils wound tight in turn about the shape that had been Chester... As scale and bone and other things shattered with deafening cracks... As the two figures rose, twisting and rotating about one another, until they faded from all mortal sight, accompanied by the methodical beating of unseen wings, leaving only the unmarred and unbroken ceiling behind... As Chester Hennessy vanished one last time...

...That somehow, by some miracle he could scarce believe, they had won.

EPILOGUE

Elliot Raslo and Billy Shiwak emerged, cold and sopping, from the bank of the Miskatonic River.

It had been an easy, if unpleasant decision. Already in the sewers, with the river's muffled rush reverberating through distant halls, they'd chosen to make their exit from the quarantined neighborhood underground, rather than risk being spotted and shot by the police. They'd taken more than a few wrong turns, encountered several dead ends, but eventually the sound of the Miskatonic had guided them true.

Other than the foulness and circuitousness of their route, they had no trouble making their escape. The corrupted had ignored them, standing silent for the first time since they'd succumbed to the litany. Something within them had been shaken, stunned by the loss of their source, their core. It was only a temporary circumstance – they would, before long, resume their wandering, their chanting, their efforts to corrupt others, even if there was no longer any ultimate point to it – but for now, the fleeing pair had been more than happy to take advantage and slip away unhindered.

Elliot knew it was temporary because he still heard the refrain himself, back in its den at the base of his skull, where it had lurked since he'd first heard those cursed words so many weeks ago – and perhaps always would. He was, for the moment, too exhausted to ponder or even truly feel the horror of such a possibility, but he knew that time would come.

Even from the river, they could hear the edges of the commotion, and returned, curious, to the streets beyond the Merchant District. Elliot shivered the entire way, between the unseasonable temperatures and his soaked legs and feet. Billy, of course, gave no indication he even noticed, so accustomed was he to far harsher cold.

Although, once his trousers had begun to dry, Elliot noticed he felt more comfortable than he had earlier that night. Was Arkham growing ever so slightly warmer? Was the lingering winter finally breaking?

He wondered if he were imagining things. He wondered, too, about the timing of the belated spring, assuming he was *not* imagining things, and then firmly drove the question from his mind. Even after all he'd experienced, some questions, some connections, didn't bear scrutiny.

An enormous force of police officers, backed up by a hastily assembled throng of burly citizens – stevedores, brawlers, veterans of the Great War – gathered near the cordons. They wandered and mingled, bragging and questioning; all were armed with firearms or bludgeons, and carried earmuffs and other similar protections. Well-coiffed men in expensive suits worked at separating them into manageable groups, then giving them their instructions. Other Arkhamites watched the proceedings from open windows or nearby side streets, fascinated at the martial gathering. A few were curious or brave enough to call out, but their shouted questions went unanswered.

Alice Bentley had obviously reached someone of power in Arkham's municipal government, someone with a passing knowledge of things beyond the accepted bounds of science, who believed her story. From what Elliot overheard, the police and other volunteers had been told that the "fever" was actually a psychosis caused by a sub-audible frequency whose origins the city was still investigating.

Elliot supposed it sounded a believable enough story to anyone not well versed in the appropriate sciences. In a way, it wasn't even that far from the truth.

He would have to find Alice herself at some point. She deserved to know that Chester had, indeed, been the one and only epicenter of the spreading horror, and thus that Jebediah Pembroke was almost certainly dead or lost among the remaining corrupted. It wasn't much of an answer, but he owed her that.

Later, though. Not tonight.

Just as it began to rain – a warmer, more cleansing shower than any Arkham had seen in months – he witnessed several men and women in hospital whites gathered around a corner, waiting until they were needed. Around them were wheeled stretchers, all equipped with leather straps. They were led by an irritable older man whom Elliot recognized, from having his appendix out over a year ago, as Dr Regensteiner, Chief Physician at Saint Mary's. The doctor was in the midst of arguing with another nattily dressed municipal official.

"... ridiculous expenditure of resources," he was barking. "We'll hold them for testing for a few weeks, but anyone still suffering after that is off to the asylum." He shook his head, oblivious to the other man's efforts to shush him. "I've had it with this, you hear me? This is the last time I'll keep your damn secrets. I'm retiring come summer. Retiring, hell, I'm getting out of this cursed town. Let Dr Mortimore take over, see how *he* enjoys..." Regensteiner trailed off, glaring about him, as he finally realized how loudly he was ranting. Elliot dutifully looked the other way.

"Come on," Billy said, taking Elliot by the shoulder. "There's nothing more for us to do here. Leave them to their cleanup."

A part of him wanted to stay, just to be absolutely sure, to see for himself that it was over. He wondered, furthermore, how the authorities would ensure the silence of anyone who might see the malformed remnants in the underground chamber, assuming they found it. They certainly wouldn't be attributing *that* to any "unheard frequencies". Billy was right, though. It was time, and past time, to go.

They slipped away, just two more curious onlookers who'd decided they'd seen enough.

Elliot sat alone in the dormitory room he had once shared with Chester, and stared at nothing. The silence was broken only by the *flip-flip-flip* of the stiff rectangle of paper he turned over and over in his hands.

They had told the conclusion of their tale to Daisy Walker, or as much of it as they could expect her to believe. She'd shared their regret over Ida, done her best to comfort Elliot for what was now clearly the permanent loss of Chester, congratulated Billy on the completion of his quest. After a bit of discussion, she had also agreed to speak with Mr Combs at the museum, and try to have the Lindegaard Stele locked away where even staff and experts in the field could no longer view it. The odds against anyone else learning how to transliterate the symbols were astronomical, but then, they'd not been any higher when Chester had managed it. And while nobody could master the entire litany without the *Ujaraanni*, another bout of spreading madness would be bad enough even without the threat of a risen Tsocathra behind it.

Daisy made it clear that she was available to talk, should Elliot need anything at all, but thus far he'd not taken her up on that offer. There seemed precious little she could possibly say.

Billy was gone, having left Arkham on a train that was but the first of many stages on his journey home. The *Ujaraanni* went with him, of course, safely locked within several layers of boxes and trunks. Before he left, he had clasped Elliot's hand, called him brother, and then removed the last of his amulets to place it around Elliot's own neck.

"Perhaps it will help until you can finally rid yourself of those damned phrases," he'd said.

Elliot, of course, protested. Hadn't Billy told them that long exposure to the *Ujaraanni*, even by guardians who couldn't read a letter of it, eventually caused a madness of its own?

"Indeed, but that happens only after years. My journey home should take only weeks. Months, at worst, if the weather and the shipping schedules are against me."

"Yes, but you're not a… an angakkoq! What if it works faster for–"

"I don't believe it does. But if so? Then I will manage, and my family will care for me. You need the protection far more than I."

And Elliot hadn't been able to argue any further, because he knew it was true.

Nor was that his only lingering fear. The thing he'd summoned had seen him, turned on him, knew who he was. Did its disappearance make him safe? Was that danger passed? Or did it – or something akin – still lurk in unfathomable spaces, waiting until it was summoned back to the world once more, biding its time until it could hunt him down?

He would never know, until it happened.

So now he sat at home, alone; the talisman about his neck, the words of both French and Latin protection charms fresh off his tongue. Spread out on the bed beside him were copies of both spells, photographs of Chester, and a letter from the Miskatonic administration. The brief, excruciatingly formal missive ordered him to make an appointment with the dean at his earliest convenience.

An appointment to make a case as to why, after missing so many classes and the associated assignments, he should not be expelled from the university. So far, he hadn't thought of a single compelling argument, and he wasn't certain he cared.

Wasn't certain there was a point to caring.

"Maybe one out of five, one out of six," the old occultist had said. A twenty percent chance, at best, that Elliot would ever recover, could free himself of the litany before he lost himself for what, he knew, would be the final time. Lost himself, and began to infect others.

Twenty percent… without help.

Elliot Raslo flipped Lafayette-Moses's business card over and over in his hands, and stared at nothing.

In a very private room, well across Arkham, in a building that nobody knew he owned, Hyrum Lafayette-Moses also sat in thought.

He leaned back in his most comfortable chair, upholstered in rich leather of a sort not readily identified, and held in one hand a snifter of Kentucky bourbon. The drink was entirely illegal, of course – but not nearly as much so, had anyone proved able to identify that leather, as the chair.

To his left, by one of the room's two doors, the silent chauffeur cocked his head in mute query.

"No, Lemuel," Lafayette-Moses said, somehow aware of the gesture without looking. "I won't be needin' anythin' else from you tonight. You go and get yourself some rest, now."

Already rippling and losing its shape, the servant turned and was gone from the room with a terrible liquid sound, leaving only the driver's uniform in a rough trail through the doorway.

His master glanced over at it, and at the coat rack, and shook his head. The creature was so quick to pick up most of the quirks and behaviors of the human form on which Lafayette-Moses insisted, but it seemed utterly unable to grasp the concept of cleaning up after itself.

Well, he'd get it on his way out. For now, the clothes could wait.

Lafayette-Moses took a sip of his drink, swiftly losing himself once more in thought.

They'd done it. He could scarcely believe those fools, those children, had actually *done* it. Oh, he'd hoped, hoped with near desperation that they would, that he wouldn't need to involve himself any further, but he couldn't have dared to expect…

It hadn't gone perfectly, of course. He'd had to reveal himself, to them and to the local faithful, to Carl Sanford and his "Silver Twilight Lodge," who were so much more than the people of Arkham knew. Sanford had almost been a problem, had disliked being told by an outsider to keep his people away from Chester Hennessy or anything to do with unfolding events. Lafayette-Moses had been forced to pull rank, to remind the stubborn bastard that he had come to Arkham on behalf of a power that transcended any mortal cult. He'd worried he might have to prove himself with a show of power, but Sanford had wisely, if sullenly, backed down.

If he'd had to force the issue, or if the rank and file of worshipers – here or across the world – had learned what was happening, it could have sown chaos, and not the proper sort of chaos. Could have cast doubt that the leaders of the many sects and factions knew what they were doing. Could have thrown the entire order of the worshipers of the Ancient Ones into tumult.

And if Lafayette-Moses had been forced to act personally, the old gods alone knew what might have come of it. His own sorceries would probably have been enough to prevent the rise of the Thousandfold Dream, assuming he caught the process early enough – but Lafayette-Moses hadn't lived so long as he had, hadn't obtained his power and his office, by relying on "probably" and "assuming." Even he, for all his learning, had no certain idea how swiftly Tsocathra's power grew, or what the results might have been from mixing human magics with those of the antehuman sorcerers *and* powers far more ancient still. It might have been disastrous indeed!

Still, he'd have done it. Though it would have put him at terrible risk, might even have backfired and hastened the catastrophe he meant to avert, he'd have done it, for that was his duty. The time was not yet, the stars not right, the Others not yet prepared to rise.

If Tsocathra had awakened now, before the proper time, the repercussions would have proved unfathomable, throwing into disarray plans that had been laid down before mortal life had learned to walk upright.

No, it could never have been allowed! But while Lafayette-Moses knew he *wouldn't* have allowed it, the fact that, in the end, he hadn't needed to – that he'd accomplished his goals with a nudge here, a few answers there – was proof enough that something mighty and all-knowing watched over his efforts.

His mouth stretched in an ugly grin, nothing akin to the polite smile he'd offered his pawns. He'd wait here in Arkham a while, see if he might find a way to manipulate the black-market trade in relics through Alice Bentley, or if Elliot Raslo might yet come to him. He'd make a useful apprentice, that boy.

Either way, though, he had to depart before *too* long. He had other duties, in other parts of the world.

He had, too, a man who needed tending, who would require very special care for a very long time.

Because he had to live, this man, perhaps for many years. Had to survive until the stars *did* come right. So that, at the proper time, when the Ancient Ones must rise, the Weaver of Flesh would stand among them.

Hyrum Lafayette-Moses stared at the far wall, at the one-way glass window that allowed him an unobstructed view of the locked room beyond.

And he watched, in silence provided by the thick glass and the padded walls, as Jebediah Pembroke continuously repeated, in its loathsome and apocalyptic entirety, the unholy litany of Tsocathra.

ABOUT THE AUTHOR

ARI MARMELL is the author of the Mick Oberon urban fantasy series, the Widdershins YA fantasy series and many others, alongside novels in *Magic: the Gathering* and the video game, *Darksiders*, as well as writing for several roleplaying games.

mouseferatu.com
twitter.com/mouseferatu

RETURN TO THE DEPTHS OF MADNESS

An international thief of esoteric artifacts stumbles onto a nightmarish cult in 1920s New England in this chilling tale of cosmic dread.

A mad surrealist's art threatens to rip open the fabric of reality, in this twisted tale of eldritch horror and conspiracy.

When a movie director shoots his silent horror masterpiece in eerie Arkham, moving pictures become crawling nightmares.

Venture into a land of duty and warfare, with Legend of the Five Rings

The discovery of a mythical city amid blizzard-swept peaks offers heroes an opportunity to prove their honor, but risks exposing the empire to demonic invasion.

When a charming slacker aristocrat is dragged away from a life of decadence, he discovers a talent for detection, uncovering a murderous web of conspiracies.

In an isolated Dragon Clan settlement beset by monsters who run riot at full moon, two rival clans must join forces to investigate the lethal supernatural mystery.

WORLD EXPANDING FICTION

Courageous heroes save the realm from monsters and a new tide of darkness set in the epic fantasy game, DESCENT.

One faction will rise to conquer the galaxy, in the stunning epic space opera of TWILIGHT IMPERIUM.

Explore the Crucible's vast patchwork of countless worlds where anything is possible, from the hit game, KEYFORGE.